THE OTHER WOMAN

SANDIE JONES is a freelance journalist and
has contributed to the *Sunday Times*, *Daily Mail*,
Woman's Weekly and *Hello* magazine, amongst others.
If she wasn't a writer, she'd be an interior designer
as she has an unhealthy obsession with wallpaper
and cushions. She lives in London with her
husband and three children.

SANDIE JONES

THE OTHER WOMAN

PAN BOOKS

First published 2018 by Pan Books
an imprint of Pan Macmillan
20 New Wharf Road, London N1 9RR
Associated companies throughout the world
www.panmacmillan.com

ISBN 978-1-5098-8517-6

5 7 9 8 6

A CIP catalogue record for this book is available from the British Library.

Typeset by Palimpsest Book Production Limited, Falkirk, Stirlingshire
Printed and bound by CPI Group (UK) Ltd, Croydon, CR0 4YY

For Ivy Rolph

My nan – who always encouraged me
to be who I wanted to be

PROLOGUE

She looks beautiful in her wedding dress. It fits her perfectly and is exactly what I'd imagined she'd go for: elegant, understated and unique – just like her. My heart breaks that her day will never come, but she doesn't need to know that yet.

I think about the guests who won't attend, the picture frames with no photographs, the first dance that will be silent, the cake that won't get eaten, and I feel my resolve weakening. I pull myself up. This is not a time for doubt.

There is still so much work to do, so much more pain to inflict, but I will not be deterred. I failed once before, but this time, I'll get it right.

There's too much at stake to get it wrong.

1

There weren't many things that I didn't like about Adam when I first saw him across the crowded bar at the Grosvenor Hotel in London, aside from his lack of empathy. I'd just come out of an incredibly dull 'Future of Recruitment' conference and needed a drink far more than he or the barman realized.

I'd been standing at the bar for what felt like an eternity, theatrically waving a battered ten-pound note in the air, when, just along from me, a dark-haired man muscled his way to the front, holding a credit card. 'Yep. Over here, mate,' he said, in a booming voice.

'Er, excuse me,' I said, a little louder than I intended. 'I think you'll find I was here first.'

He shrugged and smiled. 'Sorry, but I've been waiting ages.'

I stood and watched open-mouthed as he and the barman shared a knowing tip of the head, and without him even saying a word, a bottle of Peroni was put in front of him.

'Unbelievable,' I mouthed, as he looked over at me. He smiled that smile again, and turned to the throng of men beside him to take their orders.

'You've got to be kidding me,' I groaned, before letting my head drop into my arms while I waited. I was sure that it would be an inordinate amount of time until my turn.

'What can I get you?' asked the man behind the bar. 'The guy over there reckons you're a rosé kind of girl, but I'm going to bet you're after a gin and tonic.'

I smiled, despite myself. 'As much as I'd like to prove him wrong, I'm afraid to say a glass of rosé would be perfect, please.'

I went to hand him the tenner as he placed the glass in front of me, but he shook his head. 'No need,' he said. 'Please accept it with the compliments of the gentleman who jumped the queue.'

I didn't know who I loved more: the bartender who, in my opinion, ought to be elevated to chief sommelier, or the really rather nice fellow smiling down the bar at me. Oh, the power of a chilled pink blush.

My face flushed the same colour, as I held the glass up to him and headed over to where my seminar colleagues were gathered in a corner, each nursing their own alcoholic preference. We'd been strangers up until seven hours ago, so it seemed that the general consensus was to get your own drink and not worry about everybody else.

Mr Peroni obviously doesn't have the same arrangement with his own acquaintances, I thought, smiling to myself as I looked up and saw that he had continued to order his round.

I took a sip of wine and could hear my taste buds thanking me as the cold liquid teased them before hitting the back of my throat. What is it with that first taste that can never be replicated? I sometimes find myself postponing that initial swig for fear of losing that sensation.

I'm making myself sound like a raging alcoholic, but I only ever drink at weekends, and on mind-numbingly tedious Wednesdays, after being holed up with two hundred HR personnel for the day. We'd been helpfully informed during a lecture entitled 'Nobody Likes Us. We Don't Care' that a recent survey had revealed that recruitment consultants were fast becoming the most disliked professionals, second only to estate agents. I wish I could defy the haters and prove that we're not all morally lacking, unethical dealmakers. But as I look around at the brash, loud, would-be City boys with their slicked-back hair and insincere expressions, I have to hold my hands up in defeat.

Despite having introduced myself in the 'forum' earlier in the day, I felt I had to do it again, as I approached the baying mob.

'Hi, I'm Emily,' I said awkwardly to the guy on the outermost circle. He wasn't someone I was particularly interested in talking to, but talk I had to, if I wanted to finish my glass of wine without looking like a complete

Norman no-mates. 'I'm a consultant at Faulkner's,' I went on.

I offered my hand and he took it, shaking it brusquely in a slightly territorial fashion. 'This is my manor and you're on my turf' was the message he conveyed, even though we'd spent the entire day learning how to do the exact opposite.

'Be open. Be approachable,' Speaker No. 2 had stated earlier. 'Employers and employees want to deal with a friendly face. They need to feel that they can trust you. That you are working for them, not the other way around. Deal with your clients on *their* terms, not on yours, even if it does put a dent in your pride. So, read each situation individually and react accordingly.'

I'd always prided myself on doing exactly that, hence why I'd been the top consultant at Faulkner's seven months in a row. In person, I was the antithesis of what people expected: honest, considerate, and blasé about target-chasing. As long as I had enough to pay my rent, eat and heat, I was happy. On paper, however, I was smashing it. Clients were requesting to deal exclusively with me, and I'd secured more new business than anyone else across the five-office network. Commission was flooding in. Perhaps *I* should have been the one standing on that podium, telling them how it's done.

The man, from an obscure agency in Leigh-on-Sea, made a half-hearted attempt at pulling me into the throng. No one introduced themselves, preferring instead to eye me up and down, as if seeing a woman for the first time. One of them even shook his head from side to side, and let out a slow whistle. I looked at him with disdain, before realizing it was Ivor, the bald, overweight director of a one-office concern in Balham, who I'd had the misfortune of partnering in the role-play exercise just before lunch. His breath had smelt of last night's curry that I'd imagined he'd scoffed impatiently from a silver-foil container on his lap.

'Sell me this pen,' he'd barked, during our 'How to Sell Snow to an Eskimo' task. A cloud of stale turmeric permeated the air and I wrinkled my nose in distaste. I'd taken a very normal-looking Bic biro from him and had begun to relay its redeeming qualities: the superior plastic case, the smooth nib, the flow of the ink. I'd wondered, not for the first time, what the point was in all this. My boss, Nathan, insisted that these conferences were good for us: that they kept us on our toes.

If he was hoping that I'd be motivated and captivated by new and exciting ways to do business, he'd booked the wrong day. And I'd certainly been paired with the wrong man.

I'd continued to enthuse about the pen's attributes, but as I'd looked up, Ivor's eyes hadn't even been attempting to look at the tool in my hand, preferring instead to fixate on the hint of cleavage beyond.

'Ahem,' I'd coughed, in an attempt to bring his attention back to the task in hand, but he'd merely smiled, as if relishing in his own fantasy. I'd instinctively pulled my blouse together, regretting the decision to wear anything other than a polo neck.

His beady little eyes were still on me now. 'It's Emma, isn't it?' he said, stepping forward. I looked down at the name badge secured to my left bosom, just to check for myself.

'Em-i-ly,' I said, as if speaking to a toddler. 'It's Em-i-ly.'

'Emma, Emily, it's all the same.'

'It's not really, no.'

'We were paired up this morning,' he said proudly to the other men in the group. 'We had a good time, didn't we, Em?'

I'm sure I felt my skin crawl.

'It's Em-i-ly, not Em,' I said, exasperated. 'And I didn't think we worked particularly well together at all.'

'Oh, come on,' he said, looking around, his face betraying the confidence in his voice. 'We were a good team. You must have felt it.' I stared emptily back at him. There were no words of recourse, and, even if there were, I wouldn't have wasted my breath. I shook my head as the rest of the group looked awkwardly to the floor. No doubt as soon as I turned on my heels, they'd be patting him on the back for a job well done.

I took myself and my half-drunk wine to the space at the end of the crowded bar. I'd only been there two minutes before I realized that the reason no one else was standing there was because, every few seconds, I was getting hit in the back by a bony elbow or shouldered out of the way by the waiting staff, as they busily collected drinks and returned glasses. 'This is *our* area,' barked a young girl, her face all pinched and pointed. 'Keep it clear.'

'Please,' I said, under my breath, but she was far too important to stand still long enough to hear it. Still, I edged up a little to remove myself from 'her area' and rummaged around in my bag for my phone. I only had three more sips, or one big gulp, of wine left. Four minutes max and I'd be on my way.

I surreptitiously ran through my emails, in the hope that a) I wouldn't be bothered by anybody and b) it'd look like I was waiting for someone. I wondered what we'd done before mobiles and their far-reaching information trails. Would I be standing here perusing the *Financial Times* or, better yet, feel inclined to strike up a conversation with someone who might prove to be interesting? Either way, I'd most definitely be better informed as a result, so why, then, do I log on to Twitter to see what Kim Kardashian's up to?

I groaned inwardly as I heard someone shout, 'Emily, fancy another drink?' *Really?* Did he not get the hint? I looked over at Ivor, but he was engrossed in conversation. I had a furtive glance around, embarrassed to know that the person who had said it would be watching my confusion. My eyes fleetingly settled on Mr Peroni, who was grinning broadly, revealing straight white teeth. I smiled to myself as I remembered Mum's erstwhile advice. 'It's all in the teeth, Emily,' she'd said after she met my last boyfriend, Tom. 'You can always trust a man with nice teeth.' Yeah – and look how that turned out.

I put more importance on whether someone's smile reaches their eyes, and this guy's, I noticed, definitely did. I mentally undressed him, without even realizing I was doing it, and registered that his dark suit, white shirt, and slightly loosened tie were hanging from a well-built body. I imagined his wide shoulders sitting either side of a strong back that descended into a narrower waist. Triangular shaped. Or maybe not. It's difficult to tell what a suit is disguising; it could be hiding a multitude of sins. But I hoped I was right.

Heat rose up my neck as he stared intently at me, his hand pushing his hair to one side. I offered a watery smile, before turning my head a full 360 degrees, looking for the voice.

'Is that a yes or no?' it said again, a little closer now. Mr Peroni had manoeuvred himself so that he was now my next-door neighbour but one. What an odd expression that is, I thought to myself, oblivious to the fact that he was now standing right beside me. Can you also have a next-door neighbour but two, and three, I wondered?

'How many have you had?' He laughed, as I continued to look at him blankly, though not without acknowledging that he was taller when he was close up.

'I'm sorry, I thought I heard someone call my name,' I replied.

'I'm Adam,' he offered.

'Oh. Emily,' I said, thrusting out my hand, which had instantly become clammy. 'I'm Emily.'

'I know, it's written in rather large letters across your chest.'

I looked down and felt myself flush. 'Aha, so much for playing hard to get, eh?'

He tilted his head to one side, a naughty twinkle in his eye. 'Who said we were playing?'

I had no idea whether we were or weren't. Flirting has never been my strong suit. I wouldn't know where to start, so if it was a game he was after, he was playing on his own.

'So, what's the deal with the name badge?' Mr Peroni, aka Adam, asked, as coquettishly as a man can.

'I'm a member of an elite conference,' I said, far more boldly than I felt.

'Is that so?' He smiled.

I nodded. 'I'll have you know I'm the cream of the crop in my industry. One of the highest-ranking performers in the field.'

'Wow.' He smirked. 'So, you're part of the Toilet Roll Sellers seminar? I saw the board for it when I walked in.'

I suppressed a smile. 'Actually, it's a secret meeting of MI5 agents,' I whispered, looking around conspiratorially.

'And that's why they wrote your name all over your chest, is it? To make sure nobody finds out who you are.'

I tried to keep a straight face, but the corners of my mouth were curling upwards. 'This is my undercover name,' I said, tapping the cheap plastic. 'My conference pseudonym.'

'I see, Agent Emily,' he said, rolling up his sleeve and talking into his watch. 'So, is the gentleman at three o'clock also an agent?' He waited for me to catch up, but I didn't even know which way to look. I was twisting myself in every direction, haplessly trying to find three o'clock on my internal compass. He laughed as he caught hold of my shoulders and turned me to face Ivor, who was gesticulating wildly to a male colleague, whilst looking longingly at a female dressed in tight leather trousers behind him. She was happily unaware that his eyes were drinking her in. I shuddered involuntarily.

'Negative,' I replied, one hand to my ear. 'He is neither an agent nor a gentleman.'

Adam laughed, as I warmed to the theme. 'Can we class him as the enemy?'

'Affirmative. Take him down if you wish.'

He squinted, in an effort to read the perpetrator's name badge. 'Ivor?' he questioned.

I nodded.

'Ivor Biggun?' He looked at me, waiting for a reaction. It took me a while, a long while in fact, to get it, but until I did, he just stood there, staring at me.

2

I wasn't looking for a boyfriend. I hadn't even known I'd wanted one until Adam showed up. Pippa, my flat-mate, and I were blissfully content, going to work, coming home, eating our tea on trays, then gorging ourselves on chocolate whilst watching back-to-back episodes of *Prison Break*. It's heaven on earth for those few short hours, but the next morning, I'd get on the scales and damn my nine pounds of winter weight gain. It's the same every year – and not helped by the fact that I never go to the gym that I pay seventy-two pounds a month for. I can no longer fit into the size-twelve jeans I wore last summer, but instead of buying myself a size fourteen, I'd rather scour the shops to find a more generous size-twelve pair that I can pour myself into. I'd spent the entire summer 'in denial', and was *still* kidding myself that the promised Indian summer would be sure to see my motivation return.

I'll go out every once in a while, particularly around payday, but nights out aren't what they used to be. Maybe it's because I'm getting older, or everyone else is getting younger, but I see little benefit in standing in a crowded pub and having to elbow your way to the bar every time you want a drink. Pippa's dragged me kicking and screaming to a few gigs, though not, unfortunately, at the O2. She favours underground caverns, where bands, most of whom she seems to have slept with, thrash about the stage and encourage their audience to do the same. I'm the one standing alone at the back, with hidden earphones blasting out *Musical Theatre's Greatest Hits*.

Thank God for Seb, my best friend and a male version of me. I'd have married him years ago if I thought there was a single hair on his body that I could have turned straight, but, alas, I must make do with evenings locked in a soundproof karaoke booth, each of us competing for the best lines in *Les Misérables*. We met during what he refers to as my 'hairdressing period'. Discontented with secretarial work, I'd booked myself on to a night course for hair and beauty. Obviously, I had visions of becoming a female Nicky Clarke, with a trendy salon in the middle of Mayfair, and celebrity clients having to book months in advance. Instead, I spent three months sweeping up other people's hair, and developing eczema on my hands from the caustic shampoo. I used to have these half-baked ideas, and rush off to start making them happen, but I was forever deluded by grandeur. Like the time I enrolled on a home-making course at my local college. It was never my intention to learn how to make a pretty cushion or spend hours rubbing five layers of eggshell off an old chest of drawers.

No, I was going to be the new Kelly Hoppen, and bypass all the graft and groundwork that learning a new skill entails. I was heading straight for New York, where I would be immediately commissioned to design a vast loft space for Chandler from *Friends*. Needless to say, the cushion never got finished and all the wallpaper samples and fabric swatches I'd acquired never saw the light of day again.

Seb has seen me through at least four career changes, and has been nothing short of overwhelmingly enthusiastic with each and every one, assuring me that I was 'made for it'. Yet, as each phase came and went, and I'd be lamenting on the sofa at how useless I was, he'd convince me that I was never really cut out for it in the first place. But now, I've finally found my calling. It came a little later in life than I'd planned, but selling people is my thing. I know what I'm doing, and I'm good at it.

'So, he's an IT analytical analyst?' Seb reiterated suspiciously, as we sat in Soho Square, sharing a sandwich and a salad bowl from M&S the following day. 'Whatever that may mean.'

I nodded enthusiastically, but inside, I was asking myself the same question. I placed real people in real jobs: retail assistants in shops, secretaries in offices, dental assistants in surgeries. The IT sector is a whole new ball game, a monster of an industry, and one that we at Faulkner's leave to the experts.

'Well, he sounds a right laugh-a-minute,' Seb said,

desperately trying to keep a straight face. 'What did he do? Enthral you with his megabytes?'

I laughed. 'He doesn't look like you'd expect.'

'So, he doesn't wear glasses and have a centre parting?'

I shook my head, smiling.

'And his name isn't Eugene?'

'No,' I mumbled, through a mouthful of bread and roast beef. 'He's tall and dark, with really good teeth.'

'Oh, your mum will be pleased.'

I swiped his shoulder with my hand. 'And he's got a really sexy voice. All deep and mysterious. Like Matthew McConaughey, but without the Texan bit.'

Seb raised his eyebrows quizzically. 'Which would make him nothing like McConaughey.'

I persisted. 'You know what I mean. And big hands . . . really big hands, and nicely manicured nails.'

'What the hell were you doing looking at his hands?' asked Seb, spluttering out his still lemonade. 'You were only with him for fifteen minutes, and you've already managed to check his cuticles out?'

I shrugged my shoulders petulantly. 'I'm just saying that he obviously takes care of himself, and I like that in a man. It's important.'

Seb tutted. 'This all sounds very well, but on a scale of one to ten, how likely is it that you're going to see him again?'

'Honestly? A one or two. Firstly, he looked like the

type to have a girlfriend, and secondly, I think he had his beer goggles on.'

'Was he drunk or just merry?'

'Hard to tell. It was someone's leaving do, and I think he said something about coming from a pub in the City, so they'd obviously been going for a while. Adam looked okay, a bit dishevelled maybe, but then I don't know what he normally looks like. One or two of his mates were definitely well on their way, though – they could barely stand up.'

'Oh, I bet the Grosvenor loved having *them* there,' Seb said, laughing.

'I think they were asked to leave at the same time as I came away,' I said, grimacing. 'The well-heeled guests were starting to arrive, and the bar looked more like something on the Magaluf strip than Park Lane.'

'It's not looking good, kid,' said Seb.

I wrinkled my nose. 'No. I think the likelihood of hearing from him again is pretty slim.'

'Did you give him the look?' he asked.

'What look?'

'You know the one. Your take-me-to-bed-or-lose-me-forever face?' He fluttered his eyelashes and licked his lips in the most unsexy way, like a dog after a chocolate-drop treat. He'd once been told by a potential suitor of mine that I had 'bedroom eyes' and 'engorged lips', and I'd not heard the last of it. 'Well, did you?'

'Oh, shut up!'

'What were you wearing?' he asked.

I screwed my face up. 'My black pencil skirt with a white blouse. Why?'

'He'll call you.' He smiled. 'If you'd been wearing that tent of a dress that you bought in the Whistles sale then I'd say you've got no chance, but in the pencil skirt? Moderate to high.'

I laughed and threw a limp lettuce leaf at him. Every woman should have a Seb. He gives brutally honest advice, which on some days can send me off kilter and have me reassessing my whole life, but today I'm able to take it, happy to have him evaluate the situation because he's always darn well right.

'So, how are you going to play it when he calls?' he asked, retrieving the stray leaf from his beard and tossing it onto the grass.

'*If* he calls,' I stressed, 'I'll play it like I always do. Coy and demure.'

Seb laughed and fell onto his back, tickling his ribs for added effect. 'You are to coy and demure, what I am to machismo.'

I was tempted to empty the rest of the salad bowl onto his head as he lay writhing on the ground, but I knew it was likely to end up in a full-on food fight. I had a packed diary that afternoon, and wanted to spare my silk shirt the onslaught of a balsamic-dressing attack. So I gave him a playful nudge with the tip of my patent court shoe instead.

'Call yourself a friend?' I said haughtily, as I stood up to leave.

'Call me when he calls,' Seb shouted out after me. He was still cackling as I walked away.

'I'll call you *if* he calls,' I shouted back, as I reached the gates to the square.

I was in the middle of an appointment later that afternoon, when my mobile rang. My client, a Chinese businessman who, with the help of a translator, was looking for staff for his expanding company, signalled to me to take it. I smiled politely and shook my head, but the 'No Caller ID' displayed across the screen had piqued my interest. When it rang three more times, he looked at me imploringly, almost begging me to answer it.

'Excuse me,' I said, before backing out of the room. It had better be important.

'Emily Havistock,' I stated, as I swiped my iPhone.

'Havistock?' a voice repeated.

'Yes, can I help you?'

'No wonder they didn't put your surname on your badge.' He laughed.

A redness crept up my neck, its fingers flickering at my cheeks. 'I'm afraid I'm in a meeting at the moment. May I call you back?'

'I don't remember you sounding this posh either. Or is this your phone voice?'

I remained silent, but smiled.

'Okay, call me back,' he said. 'It's Adam, by the way. Adam Banks.'

How many men did he think I gave my number to?

'I'll text you,' he said. 'Just in case my number doesn't come up.'

'Thank you, I'll revert to you shortly,' I said, terminating the call, but not before I heard him chuckle.

I couldn't concentrate for the rest of the appointment, and found myself trying to wrap it up prematurely. But then, I didn't want to appear over-keen by calling him back too quickly, so when the translator said my client would like to show me around the new office space, a few floors above, I gratefully accepted.

Over dinner, a week later, I had to explain to Adam why it had taken me three hours to call him back.

'You honestly expect me to believe that?' he asked incredulously.

'I swear to you. I'm not one for holding out just to appear cool. Making you sweat for an hour, perhaps. But three? That's just rude.' I laughed.

His eyes wrinkled up as he tried to suppress a smile. 'And you were seriously stuck in a lift for all that time?'

'Yes, for three *really* long hours, with a man who hardly spoke English, and two super-smart phones, neither of which were smart enough to be able to ring for help, it seems.'

He choked on his Sauvignon Blanc and spluttered, 'That's Chinese technology for you.'

By the time I introduced Adam to Seb, a month later, we'd seen each other eighteen times.

'Are you serious?' Seb had moaned, when I'd told him for the third consecutive night that I couldn't see him. 'When do you think you might be able to fit me in?'

'Ah, don't go getting all jealous,' I'd teased. 'Maybe tomorrow night?'

'If he doesn't ask to see you again then, I suppose?'

'I promise, tomorrow night is yours and yours alone.' Though, even as I was saying it, I felt a tad resentful.

'Okay, what do you want to do?' he asked, sulkily. 'That film's out – of the book that we both loved.'

'*The Fault in Our Stars*?' I said, without thinking. 'Adam and I are going to see that tonight.'

'Oh.' I could feel his disappointment, and I instantly wanted to slap myself.

'But that's okay,' I said cheerily. 'I'll go again tomorrow night. The book was amazing, so the film will be too, right? We've *got* to see it together.'

'If you're sure . . .' Seb said, his voice lifting. 'Try not to enjoy it too much with your boyfriend.'

Chance would have been a fine thing. I was too conscious of Adam fidgeting in his seat, looking at his phone. 'Well, that was a happy little tale,' he said, as we came out of the cinema a couple of hours later.

'It's all right for you,' I said, sniffing and surreptitiously wiping my nose on a tissue. 'I've got to go through it all again tomorrow.'

He stopped in the street and turned to look at me. 'Why?' he asked.

'Because I've promised Seb I'll go and see it with him.'

Adam raised his eyebrows questioningly.

'We both loved the book and always vowed that when they made the film, we'd see it together.'

'But you've seen it now,' he said. 'Job done.'

'I know, but it's something we both wanted to do.'

'I need to meet this Seb who's taking you away from me,' he said, pulling me in towards him and breathing in my hair.

'If he was straight, you'd have a problem on your hands,' I said, laughing. 'But you've got nothing to worry about.'

'All the same. Let's get together one night next week, so that we can all discuss the merits and flaws of the silly film we've just seen.'

I playfully punched him on the arm, and he kissed me on the head. It felt like we'd been together forever, yet the excitement of just being around him fizzed through me, setting every nerve alight. I didn't ever want that feeling to go away.

It was way too early to tell, but there was a growing part of me, the part that no one saw, that hoped this *was* something. I wasn't brave enough, or stupid enough perhaps, to be singing from the rooftops that Adam was 'the one', but I liked how it felt. It felt different, and I had all my fingers and toes crossed that my hunch was right.

We were comfortable with each other, not to the point where I'd leave the bathroom door open, but I wasn't obsessing about whether my nail colour matched my lip shade either, and not many guys had been around long enough to see them clashing.

'Are you sure it's not too early for the Seb-o-meter?' Seb asked, wiping his eyes as we walked out of the same cinema twenty-four hours later. 'I mean, it's not even been a month yet, has it?'

'Well, thanks for your vote of confidence,' I said. I was snivelling again too, but as I was with Seb, it didn't matter. I put my arm through his, uniting us in our sadness at how the film had ended.

'I don't mean to sound negative, but it's all a bit full-on to last, don't you think? You're seeing him almost every night. Are you sure it won't just fizzle out as quickly as it started? Don't forget, I know what you're like.'

I smiled, despite feeling a little hurt at the insinuation that what Adam and I had could be just a fling. 'I've never felt like this, Seb. I need you to meet him because I think this might be going somewhere. And it's important to me that you like him.'

'But you know you're going to get a very honest appraisal,' he went on. 'Are you ready for that?'

'I think you're going to like him,' I said. 'And if you don't, just pretend you do.'

He laughed. 'Is there any topic that's off-limits? Like the time you asked me to marry you, or when you threw your knickers at Take That?'

I laughed. 'No, it's all good. You can say whatever you want. There's nothing I wouldn't want him to know.'

'Hang on,' said Seb, as he bent forward and made a retching sound. 'There. That's better. Where were we?'

'D'you know that you're a right royal pain in the arse when you want to be?' I laughed.

'You wouldn't want me any other way.'

'Seriously, he's pretty laid-back, so I don't think you'll be able to faze him that easily.'

That was the only thing with Adam: if he was any more laid-back he'd be horizontal. In his world, everything is calm and under control, like a sea without waves. He doesn't get exasperated when we're stuck behind a painfully slow driver. He doesn't call South-eastern trains every name under the sun when leaves on the track cause delays, and he doesn't blame social media for everything that is wrong with the world. 'If you don't like what it represents, why do you go on it?' he'd asked, when I moaned about old school friends posting every burp, fart and word their child offered.

None of the trivial stuff that had me spitting tacks almost every minute of my day seemed to touch him. Maybe he was sitting back, carefully navigating his way around my own waves and currents before revealing his own, but I wanted him to give me more. I needed to know that blood coursed through his veins and that he'd bleed if he cut himself.

I'd tried to provoke a reaction from him several times, even if just to check he had a pulse, but I wasn't going to get a rise out of him. He seemed happy just ambling along, with no real need or desire to offer anything more. Maybe I'm being unfair, maybe that's just the way he is, but every now and again I like to be challenged, even if it's only a debate over an article in the *Daily Mail*. It wouldn't matter what it was, just anything that would give me an insight into his world. But no matter how hard I tried, we always ended up talking about me, even when I was the one asking the questions. There was no denying that, at times, it was a refreshing change, as the last guy I'd gone out with had prattled on about his video-game obsession all night. But Adam's constant deflection left me wondering: what did I *really* know about him?

That's why I needed Seb. He's the type of person who can get right in there, burrow his way through the complex layers of people's characters, and into their souls, which they are often baring within minutes of meeting him. He'd once asked my mother if my dad was the only man she'd ever been with. I'd immediately put my hands over my ears and la-la-la-ed, but she confessed to having had a wonderful affair with an American she met, just before her and Dad got together. 'Well, it wasn't the type of affair that you youngsters talk about nowadays,' she said. 'We didn't have clandestine meetings and illicit sex, and neither of us were married, so it wasn't an affair in the sense that *you* know. It was just a beautiful meeting of two people who were utterly in tune with each other.'

My mouth had dropped open. Aside from the shock that my mother had obviously had sex more than twice, from which she'd conceived me and my brother, it had been with someone *other* than my father? As a daughter, you so rarely get to discover these golden gems of times gone by, and before we know it, it's too late to ask. But when you're with someone like Seb, every little nugget is teased out, without you even realizing.

The following weekend, Adam, Seb and I arranged to meet in a bar in Covent Garden. I didn't like to suggest dinner, just in case it felt a little forced and awkward, but I was hoping that's how the evening would end up, organically. We'd not even finished our first drink before Seb asked Adam where he grew up.

'Just outside Reading,' he replied. 'We moved down to Sevenoaks when I was nine. What about you?'

There it is again.

But Seb wasn't going to be thwarted. 'I was born in Lewisham hospital, and have stayed there ever since. Not in the hospital, obviously, but literally just two roads down, off the High Street. I went to Sevenoaks a couple of years ago, a guy I was seeing had a design consultancy down there. Very pretty. What made you move there from Reading?'

Adam shifted uncomfortably. 'Erm, my dad died. Mum had friends in Sevenoaks and needed a bit of help with me and my younger brother. There was nothing to stay in Reading for. Dad had worked for Microsoft for years, but with him gone . . .' he trailed off.

'Yeah, I lost my dad too,' offered Seb. 'Crap, eh?'

Adam gave a sad nod.

'So, is your mum still on her own, or did she meet someone else?' asked Seb, before guiltily adding, 'Sorry, I assume your mum's still around?'

Adam nodded. 'Yes, thank God. She's still in Sevenoaks and still on her own.'

'It's difficult when they're on their own, isn't it?' asked Seb. 'You feel a lot more responsible for them, even when you're the child and they're supposed to be the grown-up.'

Adam raised his eyebrows and nodded in agreement. I couldn't add to this conversation as thankfully both my parents are still alive, so I offered to get a round in instead.

'No, I'll get them,' said Adam, no doubt relieved to extract himself from Seb's searching questions. 'Same again?'

Seb and I nodded.

'So . . . ?' I asked, as soon as Adam's back was turned.

'Very nice,' Seb said. 'Very nice.'

'But?' I sensed one coming.

'I'm not sure,' he said, as my heart sank. 'There's something, but I can't quite put my finger on it.'

That night, after we'd made love and were lying side by side, tracing our fingers over each other's torsos, I raised the subject of his parents again.

'Do you think your mother would like me?' I asked.

He rolled over and pushed himself up onto one elbow. The light was off, but the curtains were open and the moon was bright. I could see his silhouette close to me, feel his breath on my face. 'Of course she would. She'd think you're perfect.'

I couldn't help but notice the turn of phrase: 'she'd' instead of 'she'll'. There's a big difference between the two – one hypothetical, the other intentional. The sentence spoke volumes.

'So, you're not planning on introducing us anytime soon then?' I asked, as lightly as I could.

'We've only been together for a month.' He sighed, sensing the weight of the question. 'Let's just take our time, see how it goes.'

'So, I'm good enough to sleep with, but not to meet your mother?'

'You're good enough for both.' He laughed. 'Let's just take it slowly. No pressure. No promises.'

I fought the tightness at the back of my throat, and turned away from him. *No pressure. No promises?* What was this? And why did it matter so much? I could count on two hands how many lovers I'd had. Every one of them had meant something, apart from a shockingly uncharacteristic one-night stand I'd had at a friend's twenty-first birthday.

But despite having been in love and lust before, I couldn't ever remember feeling this safe. And that's how Adam made me feel. He made me feel all of the above. Every little box had a tick in it and, for the first time in my adult life, I felt whole, as if all the jigsaw pieces had been slotted into place.

'Okay,' I said, annoyed by my own neediness. I would have gladly shown him off to my mother's half-aunt's second cousin, twice removed. Clearly, he didn't feel the same and, despite myself, it hurt.

3

A horn blared.

Pippa, who was hanging out the window, sneaking a cigarette, shouted, 'Your boyfriend's here, in his posh car.'

'Ssh,' I retorted. 'He'll hear you.'

'He's three floors down. And half the bloody street can hear *him*, so I wouldn't worry about it.'

I squeezed through the same window and gave him a wave. He tooted back, and Bill, our next-door neighbour, looked up from washing his car. 'It's all right, Bill,' Pippa shouted down. 'It's Emily's fancy man.'

Bill shrugged and got back to the task in hand. He was the best type of neighbour you could have: keeping a lookout when he needed to, and turning a blind eye when he didn't.

Pippa and I weren't the typical demographic for the area; young married couples, with 2.5 children, were the norm. They claimed to love Lee, this diverse enclave between Lewisham and Blackheath, but we and they knew they were just biding their time until they were able to climb that very big step up to the latter. SE3 was where everyone wanted to be, with its quirky village feel and vast open spaces. They say that the plague victims of the seventeenth century were buried up on Black-heath, hence the name, but it doesn't bother people enough to stop them holding impromptu barbecues on a summer's evening. Many a time, Pippa and I have joined the masses pretending to live there, by lighting up a disposable foil tray that we've hastily bought at the petrol station. We always end up going up there too late to get the best spots by the pubs, and by the time we've trusted the British weather, it's gone 4 p.m. and Sains-bury's BBQ section has been stripped bare.

'Ooh, you look nice,' remarked Pippa.

I smoothed down the front of my body-con dress, even though there was nothing to smooth down. 'You think?'

I'd spent the best part of an hour choosing what to wear, agonizing between the casualness of a pretty blouse and white jeans, and the more formal look of a structured dress. I didn't want to look like I'd tried too hard, but not making enough effort was probably worse, so the navy dress won out. The crêpe cinched in at my waist, out again over my hips and fell just below the knee. There was just the tiniest amount of cleavage showing, and the fabric shaped my breasts perfectly. As my mother would say, 'That dress hangs in all the right places.'

'Nervous?' asked Pippa.

'I'm all right, actually,' I lied. She didn't need to know

that a further hour had been spent on blow-drying my hair, putting it up, then down, then up again. It was longer than it had been in quite a while, falling just below my shoulders, and I'd had a few highlights pulled through my natural auburn colour to give it a lift. I'd settled on pinning it up, and had coaxed a couple of loose curls to fall either side of my face to soften the look. The French manicure I'd had done a couple of days before was holding up well, and I'd kept my make-up light and natural. Effortlessly chic was the image I was going for – I was, after all, only meeting my boyfriend's mother – but, in reality, I'd done less preparation for a good friend's wedding.

'Good luck,' she called out as I reached the front door. 'She's going to love you.'

I wished that I shared her confidence.

I caught sight of Adam watching me as I walked down the path, with a bouquet in my hand, and emphasized my strut. 'Whoa, you look gorgeous,' he said, as I got in and reached over to give him a kiss. It went on a little longer than we'd expected and I lambasted him for ruining my lipstick.

'Yeah, you might need to reapply that,' he said, smiling as he wiped his lips. 'You got a spare pair of tights as well?' His hand travelled up between my legs. 'Just in case I rip these.'

I looked up at Bill, who was buffing his car bonnet, and playfully swiped Adam's hand away. 'Will you stop it? The poor man's already had one heart attack. I don't want to give him another.'

'It's probably the most action he's seen in years.' He laughed.

I tutted and carefully laid the flowers on the back seat. 'Trying to impress someone, are we?' he asked, smiling.

'Oh ha-bloody-ha,' I said.

'You feel okay about this?' He reached over and took my hand in his.

'A little bit sick,' I replied, honestly. 'I've only ever met one mum before.'

He laughed. 'Well that couldn't have gone too well, then, if you're here with me.'

I gave him a playful dig. 'It's a big deal. If she doesn't like me, I'm doomed. You probably won't even give me a lift back.'

'She'll love you,' he said, going to ruffle my hair.

I caught his hand in mid-air. 'Don't even think about it. Do you have any idea how long this up-do has taken?'

'Bloody hell, you don't even make this much effort when you're going out with *me*. Maybe I should introduce you to my mum more often.' He laughed.

'I don't need to impress you anymore,' I said. 'I've got you wrapped around my little finger, right where I want you. It's your mum I need to get under my spell now. If I can get her on side, I can rule the world.' I let out a sinister cackle.

'I've told her you're normal. You'd better start acting like it.'

'You've told her I'm normal?' I shrieked, in mock protest. 'Well that doesn't make me sound very exciting, does it? Couldn't you have sexed it up a bit?' I watched his face break into a grin. 'What else have you said about me?'

He thought for a moment. 'That you're funny, clever, and can make a mean English breakfast.'

'Adam!' I moaned. 'Is that it? Is that all I am to you? A purveyor of sausages?'

We both laughed. 'Do you think she'll like me? Honestly?'

'Honestly, I think she'll love you. There's nothing not to love.'

If that was his way of saying he loved me, I'd take it. It wasn't perfect, but it would do. He hadn't said it properly yet, but we'd not yet been together for two months, so I chose to see it in the things that he did, like showing up at my office at lunchtime, with a sandwich for me to have at my desk. Or when he turned up at the flat when I had a cold, and laid on the bed with me as I sneezed and sniffed all over him. Those things were surely worth more than three stupid little words? Anyone can say them and not mean them. Actions speak louder, was my philosophy, and I was sticking to it, until of course he said the immortal, 'I love you', and then actions wouldn't mean diddlysquat.

We headed out to the A21 listening to Smooth Radio; it was his mum's favourite station, he said. It would help get me in the right frame of mind. I could have done with something to think of other than meeting his mum, rather than channelling her favourite tunes into my head.

'So, what's she like?' I asked.

He considered it for a moment, and rubbed at the bristle on his chin. 'She's like any mother, I suppose. A homemaker, peacemaker, fiercely loyal and protective of her children. I hope I offer the same loyalty in return. I won't hear a bad word said about her. She's a good woman.'

If I wasn't already feeling the pressure of needing her to like me, his comment compounded it even further. And God forbid, if I didn't like *her*, I already knew I was on my own. I had to make this work for both our sakes.

I was thankful when Will Smith's 'Summertime' came on the radio, and we both sang it, word for word, until the line, 'the smell from a grill could spark off nostalgia'.

'It's not "grill".' He let out a laugh. 'It's "girl"!'

'Oh, don't be ridiculous.' I retorted. 'Girl? The smell from a girl sparks off nostalgia? They're at a barbecue, they're not going to have sausages sizzling on the rack and comment on a passing girl's aroma, are they?'

He looked over at me as if I was mad. 'What kind of grill smell would spark off nostalgia?'

'I can't believe we're even having this conversation. Everyone knows it's grill.'

'We'll google it when we get to Mum's.'

I liked the way he said 'Mum's', rather than '*my* mum's'. It made me feel more included. 'This Smooth Radio is a revelation,' I said. 'I didn't have your mother down as a fan of *Big Willie Style*. Who knew?'

His face changed and a chill filled the car. 'That's my mother you're talking about,' he said, an edge to his voice. 'I don't think that's very appropriate, do you?'

I laughed, assuming he was playing me along. Though as I watched his features change from soft to pinched, I should have sensed that it wasn't a joke.

'Ooh, don't go getting on your high horse.' I chuckled, waiting for his face to crack, but it remained taut.

'You're being disrespectful.'

I suppressed a giggle. 'Christ, I was just—'

'You were just what?' he snapped. He indicated over to the slow lane and my chest tightened as I played out the next few minutes in my head. I could see him turning around at the next exit. Me being left on the pavement outside the flat, whilst he sped off. How had we gone from joking around, to him rearing up like this? How had it all gone so horribly wrong in such a short space of time?

His knuckles were white as he gripped the steering wheel with both hands. I reached across and gently placed my hand on top of his. 'I'm sorry,' I offered, though I didn't really know what I was apologizing for.

'Do you want to do this or not?' he said, his voice

softening. ''Cause we can just cancel if you're not ready . . .'

He made it sound like I was the subject of some kind of test. Perhaps I was.

'I'm sorry,' I said softly. I didn't want my voice to sound so conciliatory, but I was so shocked I couldn't help it.

He flicked the radio over to Kiss FM and we drove the rest of the journey in silence.

4

'I always vowed I wouldn't be the kind of mum that would do this, but just let me show you this one.'

Adam groaned as his mother flicked through the large, maroon leather-bound photo album resting on her knee.

'Oh, stop moaning,' she chastised. 'You were the cutest baby.'

She patted the floral fabric of the seat beside her on the sofa, and I sat down.

'Look here.' She pointed. 'That's Adam and James in our garden, back in Reading. There's thirteen months between them, but you can't tell them apart, can you? They were such good babies. All the neighbours would say what bonny faces they had, and you'd never hear them cry. They were perfect.'

I looked up at Adam, who had tutted and wandered over, hands in his pockets, to the bookcase in the corner of the room. His head tilted to one side as he read the spines of the twenty or so albums gracing the shelves, each carefully documented by year.

'It's lovely to have so many photos,' I commented. 'Ones that you can really look at.'

'Oh, you're so right, dear. Nobody even prints them anymore, do they? They just take them on their phone things and probably never look at them again. Such a shame. This is the way photos should be displayed.' She stroked the plastic film that separated her from the photo of a beaming four-year-old Adam, proudly holding a fish, albeit a tiddler, aloft. A man grinned into the camera lens from behind.

'Is that Adam's father?' I asked, tentatively.

Adam had apologized for snapping at me earlier, but I still felt on edge. I'd never seen that side of him before. I wondered if I'd been 'inappropriate' by asking about his father, but he didn't turn around to face me. He stayed stock-still, shoulders set.

There was a momentary pause before his mother answered. 'Yes,' she choked. 'That's my Jim. He was such a good man, a real pillar of the community. "Here come Pammie and Jim", everyone would say, wherever we went. We were the perfect couple.'

Her chest began to heave and she quickly pulled out a hanky from her cardigan sleeve. 'I'm sorry, dear,' she said, as she blew her nose. 'It still gets to me now, all these years later. So silly of me, but I can't help it.'

I reached my hand across to hers and gave it a squeeze. 'Not at all. It must be terribly difficult for you. I can't even begin to imagine. Your husband was so young, too, wasn't he?'

'Come on Mum, you're okay,' said Adam softly, as he

came over and knelt down in front of her. She immediately dropped my hand and held his face between hers, her fingers stroking his two-week beard. Tears rolled down her cheeks, and he gently wiped them away. 'It's okay, Mum. It's okay.'

'I know, I know,' she said, pulling herself up straight, as if the gesture would give her more strength. 'I don't know why I still get like this.'

'I'm sure it's perfectly normal,' I offered, as I removed my hand from where she'd dropped it on her knee.

I tucked a loose curl behind my ear and, as I looked at Pammie, a wave of guilt washed over me. I'd spent the best part of three days planning this whole event in my head: what I was going to wear, how I wanted to be perceived, how I should act and what I should say. How selfish of me. This woman, no matter how well she looked after herself, could never hide the years of hurt and grief that quite literally made her shoulders stoop with the weight. The feathered hairstyle, cut close around her face and neck, with its *en vogue* streaks of grey, so evenly distributed that it could only have been done in a salon, could never disguise her pain. Nor could her porcelain-smooth skin that fell into deep creases around her sad, hollow, eyes as she looked at me, biting down on her bottom lip. The shock and grief of losing her beloved husband all those years before, so soon after becoming parents, was still etched on her face. Here was a couple who were embarking on a new and exciting chapter in their lives, but then she'd been widowed and left on her own to cope with two children. The importance of how I looked, and what I should wear, now seemed pathetically trivial. So too did Adam's sharp words earlier. There was a much bigger picture going on here, and if I wanted to be a part of it, I'd be wise to remind myself what was important and what wasn't.

'And I suppose we've got this lovely girl here to thank for this new addition?' she smiled half-heartedly, whilst still ruffling Adam's beard.

I held my hands up in mock remorse. 'Guilty as charged,' I offered. 'I love it. I think it really suits him.'

'Oh, it does, it does,' she crowed. 'Makes you even more handsome.' She pulled him to her and nestled against his shoulder. 'My handsome boy. You'll always be my handsome boy.'

Adam awkwardly extricated himself from her, and looked at me, his face flushed. 'Shall we get some lunch? Is there anything we can help you with?'

Pammie's sniffs were beginning to subside. She pulled at the arms of her cardigan and smoothed down her tartan skirt.

'Not at all,' she said, wagging a finger. 'It's ready, I prepared it all this morning. Perhaps, Adam, you could help me fetch it in from the kitchen?'

I went to get up from the sofa. 'No, no,' she insisted. 'You stay here.'

She carefully laid the photo album on the cushion

next to me, and followed Adam into the side room. 'We won't be a moment.'

I didn't want to carry on looking through the pictures without Pammie or Adam being there – it somehow felt intrusive – but I allowed my eye to fall on the open page that was laid bare in front of me. Top right was a photo of Adam with his arms wrapped tightly around a woman, his lips softly brushing her cheek. My heart lurched as I picked it up for a closer look. The couple exuded happiness as the camera captured the candid shot. It wasn't posed or set up, it was a spontaneous moment caught on film, the pair oblivious to the prying lens. I fought the tightness in my chest, and staved off the vice-like grip that was threatening to snake its way up my throat.

I knew he'd had girlfriends before me – of course he had – but that didn't stop the insecurities from creeping in. He looked so relaxed and at one with himself; I thought he was happy when he was with me, but this was a different expression, one I hadn't seen before. His hair was longer, and his face fuller, but most of all he seemed carefree, smiling at life. The girl was equally at ease, soft brown curls fell around her face, and her eyes laughed as Adam's strong arms engulfed her.

I found myself asking if that's what we would look like if a photo was taken of us. Would our faces show the same abandonment? Would our feelings for each other be clear for all to see?

I chastised myself for allowing doubt and petty jealousy to sneak in. If they'd been that happy they wouldn't have split up, would they? They'd still be together now, and our paths would never have crossed.

'That's life,' Adam had said when I'd asked him, three weeks into our relationship, why he and his last girlfriend had broken up. 'Sometimes things happen and you have no way of understanding them. You try to find a reason to justify it, but there isn't always an answer. It's just life.'

'You make it sound like you didn't want to break up,' I'd said. 'Did she call it off? Did she cheat on you?'

'No, it was nothing like that,' he'd said. 'Let's not talk about it. That was then, this is now.' He'd put his arms around me, pulling me into him. He'd held on as if he never wanted to let me go, inhaling my hair and kissing my head. I'd looked up at him, taking in his features: his hazel eyes, tinged with green specks, that glistened under the streetlamps of Borough High Street, and that strong jawline that I'd once called chiselled, to which he'd laughed and said, 'You make me sound like something in a tool box.' He'd held my face in his hands and kissed me, gently at first, but then more deeply, as if doing so would stop anything from coming between us. Ever.

That night, our lovemaking had felt different. He'd held my hand as we climbed the stairs to his apartment above the market. We'd rarely made it much past the hallway without losing at least two items of clothing, but that night we waited until we were in his bedroom, where he undressed me slowly. I'd reached out to turn off the lamp on his bedside table, keen to keep the parts of me I didn't like in the dark, but he'd caught my hand. 'Don't. Leave it on, I want to see you.'

Still, my hand lingered, my insecurities at odds with a desire to do what he asked.

'You are absolutely beautiful,' he'd whispered, as he ran his thumb across my lips. He'd kissed my neck as his fingers trailed down my bare back, feather-light touches that sent pulses through my body. His eyes didn't leave mine as we made love. They bored into me, searching for something hidden within. For the first time, he gave me something he'd never given before. What it was, I can't explain, but I'd felt a deep connection with him. An unspoken commitment that what we had was real.

Now, as I look at the photo in front of me again, I wonder if she was the woman he had been trying to get away from that night. Was he throwing away the manacles that had bound him to her? Had he chosen that time to sever all ties?

Pammie and Adam came back into the living room, Adam ducking his head to get through the beamed door.

'Here you go,' said Pammie, as she placed a tray on the table in front of the window. 'This will fatten you up.'

I closed the album as I stood up, but not before I caught a fleeting glimpse of the caption written underneath the photo: *Darling Rebecca – miss you every day*.

5

'You're fucking kidding me?' spluttered Pippa, as she shoved a pizza slice into her mouth.

I shook my head.

'And you're sure they were a couple? Like, a proper couple, not just good friends? Maybe they were mates, part of a bigger group.'

I shook my head again. 'I don't think so. They seemed very into each other. As you'd imagine a boyfriend and girlfriend to be.'

Pippa stopped chewing and a swathe of pink-tinged fringe fell over her left eye. 'She might not be dead.'

'She must be. What else would explain "miss you every day"? You'd never write that about someone who was happily living half a mile down the road.'

'Maybe his mum . . . Pammie, is it?'

I nodded.

'Maybe she just really liked her and, when they split up, she was upset and really missed her?' She knew she was clutching at straws.

I shrugged my shoulders. If the truth be known, a little part of me selfishly hoped that the woman *was* dead, rather than be that 'missed' by Pammie, to the point where she felt the need to write it under a photograph. That was a lot to live up to.

'Why didn't you ask Adam when you were driving back?' asked Pippa.

'I didn't want to upset the apple cart,' I replied. 'We'd had an odd exchange on the way down there and he's clearly very protective of his mum, so I have to tread carefully.'

'But you're not asking about his mum, you're asking about the possibility of him having had a girlfriend who's now dead. It's a pretty big deal, Em. And if that is the case, you'd have thought that would have come up in conversation before now . . . wouldn't you?' She added the last two words gently, as if to soften the blow of the sentence before.

I had no idea what to think. Every time I tried to answer the question, I had to remind myself that we'd only been together for a little over two months. It felt longer because it had been so intense, but how can you possibly expect to tell somebody about the decades of your life in eight weeks? We'd touched on exes, of course, but we were still skirting around things to a certain extent, not wishing to get too heavy, too soon. Anytime we'd spoken about our pasts, we'd both been careful to keep things light-hearted. A dead girlfriend wouldn't have fitted comfortably into any conversation we'd had up until now. Nor would the subject of my ex, Tom. But I'd been happy to share the small misdemeanour of my solitary one-night stand with Graham or Giles – or whatever his name was.

'That's shocking!' Adam had laughed as we sat opposite each other, sharing a Rocky Road Sundae at TGI Friday's in Covent Garden, a couple of weeks before. 'You had sex with a man and you didn't even know his name?'

'Oh, like that's never happened to you?' I'd chided.

'I'll hold my hands up to a one-night stand, but I definitely asked her name first and I still remember her name now.'

'Go on then, holier than thou, what was it?'

He'd thought for a moment. 'Sophia,' he'd exclaimed, proudly.

I'd scoffed at his smugness.

'And then there was Louisa, Isabelle, Natalie, Phoebe . . .'

I'd sucked a mini marshmallow up with a straw and launched it at him.

'So, what are you going to do?' asked Pippa, bringing me back into the present. 'Is it something you need to know, or are you prepared to leave it where it is?'

'I really like him, Pip. And, this aside, everything is going really well. I've never felt like this before, and I don't want to do anything to jeopardise it. It's just a little blip on the landscape. I'm sure it'll work its way out eventually.'

She nodded in agreement, and reached out to touch my hand, for added reassurance.

'So, what was his mum like? Do you think she liked you?'

'Oh, she was just the sweetest thing. She went out of her way to make me feel welcome. I had a horrible thought, especially after the incident in the car going down there, that I was the latest in a long line of girls that he'd taken to meet her. But she actually took me aside as we were leaving and said, 'You're the first girlfriend he's brought home in a long, long while . . .'

'Okay, well that's a big plus point right there,' Pippa said matter-of-factly, trying to pull me back from the ex-thing that was nagging at my brain. 'His mother loves you. They say the way to a man's heart is through his mother.'

'I thought it was through his stomach?' I laughed.

'Ah, that too, but we all know that it's really via his dick!'

I choked on my wine, and she fell off the sofa.

There's never a dull moment when Pippa's around. Her ability to stick two fingers up at life when it isn't quite working out is what drew me to her when we first met working at a shoe shop. Our old boss there, Eileen, didn't quite appreciate Pippa's feistiness, and it was only a matter of time before things came to a head.

'I'm afraid I don't have that boot in a size 40,' she'd

heard Pippa say to a customer, 'but I do have this baller-ina pump in a size 34, if that's any good?'

Tears had rolled down my face, and I'd had to excuse myself from my customer to run to the stockroom. Pippa had quickly followed, with Eileen in hot pursuit.

'A certain level of professionalism needs to be adhered to when dealing with clients,' she'd said, wagging a finger. 'You have both crossed the line today and I will be taking it up with my superior.'

'Oh, Come On Eileen,' Pippa had said, in a sing-song voice. 'I think what you mean . . .'

My breath had caught in my throat, my face had turned red, and my bladder had threatened to collapse as Eileen, who happened to have dark curly hair, had glared at her. 'If you think you're being funny . . .' she'd said.

'Have you ever thought about dungarees . . . ?' Pippa asked politely, before walking out. I had only survived a week longer before following suit, though I sensibly worked my notice. I'd have loved to have Pippa's chutzpah, but I wasn't quite as brave or bolshie as she was. I happened to believe that I needed a reference for where I was going, but Pippa didn't give a stuff, and, to her credit, she was right. She'd got every bar job she'd applied for, and was in the middle of an Open University degree in healthcare.

We were so different, yet so alike. I couldn't think of

anything worse than going out to work at night, and I'd rather stick pins in my eyes than go back to school, but it made for the perfect set-up. I worked all day Monday to Saturday, with Wednesdays off, and she worked every evening at All Bar One in Covent Garden and studied during the day. We were never under each other's feet, so it was always good to get together on a Sunday to catch up on what the week had thrown at us. It was invariably me that needed guidance and grounding, as most of life's tribulations seemed to be water off a duck's back for Pippa. She was much more happy-go-lucky than me, batting men into left field on a whim, and not one for kowtowing to the rules of the establishment. I'd have liked a little more of her abandonment, instead of being laden down with a crippling need to over-analyse every situation. But on the odd occasion I'd thrown caution to the wind, I'd invariably come unstuck, so maybe it wasn't all that it was cracked up to be. It was wanting to be more like Pippa that had led me to act so out of character with Grant or Gerry – it had definitely started with a 'G' – at Beth's twenty-first.

'Why didn't you stop me?' I'd moaned the next day, as we lay on my bed watching Netflix, remembering him picking me up, my legs wrapped around his waist as he carried me outside. 'It must have been so obvious. Everyone would have seen.'

'That's what's so awesome,' she'd said. 'For once in

your life, you didn't care. You just did what you wanted to do, and didn't give a fig about anyone else.'

That was the problem.

'I'm never going out again,' I'd groaned, burying my face in my hands, and right there and then, I'd meant it.

6

As much as I tried, I couldn't keep Rebecca from nagging at my brain. I wanted to know who she was, and what had happened between them, but I was wary of opening a can of worms that I wasn't entirely sure I wanted open. Adam also hadn't seemed himself in the two weeks since we'd been to his mum's, so I found myself still skirting around the whole 'miss you every day' conundrum, hoping that somehow, we'd stumble upon a way to talk about it.

My first chance came as Adam and I dressed the Christmas tree in my flat. He was worried that he was taking the job away from Pippa, but she didn't have the patience for such a fiddly chore. I'd done it by myself three years running, mostly whilst she sat watching, throwing Maltesers up in the air and catching them in her mouth. She was always grateful though, and repaid me for my efforts with a bottle of Advocaat. It had become something of a tradition, though why she did it, neither of us was quite sure.

'There must be a very good reason why we don't drink this stuff all year round,' I'd said to her last Christmas.

We were three snowballs in, neither of us bothering with the cocktail cherry anymore.

'I know,' she'd agreed. 'But it sits there, ever hopeful on its Christmas shelf in the supermarket, all optimistic, pleading with passing shoppers, "Please buy me, I'm only here for a short time. You know you'll regret it if you don't."'

I'd laughed and chimed in. '"What if someone pops round, unannounced over the festive season, asking for an eggnog? How will you cope if you haven't got me?"'

It was such a time-honoured tradition, yet we'd not once had a visitor requesting an Advocaat and lemonade. Not even when neighbours popped round to my parents' house throughout my childhood. Not in nearly thirty years. Not ever.

Still, there was nothing like it to get me in the Christmas mood, and I fetched it from the back of the kitchen cupboard and swilled the congealed yellow concoction around in the bottle.

'Can I tempt you?' I asked Adam – well, his bum, seemingly the only part of him that wasn't under the tree – as he fiddled with the extension lead.

'I'm assuming that's last year's offering?' he said, extricating himself from the branches and looking up.

I nodded apologetically. 'But it never goes off.'

'I'm all right, thanks.' He grimaced. 'Here, what do you think?'

We stood back, admiring our workmanship. 'Now to

see if we should have tested the lights before we put them on,' he said.

Miraculously, for the first time in years, they worked straight away, and we slumped back onto the sofa, relieved and proud.

I brought my leg up underneath me, and turned to look at him. He was grinning from ear to ear, such a difference from the serious face of the last couple of weeks. 'I'm fine,' was all he'd ever said whenever I'd asked why he was so quiet.

'How's work?' I asked now, as I watched the dubious-looking mixture curdle in my glass.

'Better.' He sighed. 'I've finally got my head above water this week.'

So, it was work that had been playing on his mind. All the 'what-ifs' that had been whirring in my brain were silenced. *What if* he didn't want to be with me anymore? *What if* he'd met someone else? *What if* he was trying to find a way to tell me? I exhaled slowly, content now I knew that his job was the problem. We could work with that.

'How come? What was holding you under?' I asked.

He blew out his cheeks. 'The account I'm working on has become bigger than any of us had anticipated. I thought I had it covered and was managing to get on top of it, but then we stumbled upon a problem.'

'What was that?' I asked, my brow furrowed.

'Just an IT glitch; something that I can deal with. But it was going to take a lot longer than we'd allowed for.'

'So, what's changed?'

'The powers that be have finally seen sense and brought someone else in on the desk. It's made a real difference, thank God.'

'Great,' I said. 'Do you get on with him?'

'It's a woman, actually,' there was the slightest of pauses, 'and yeah, she's actually okay.'

Two 'actually's in the same sentence? He was normally so eloquent. I willed my smile to remain unchanged, to not even flicker against the muscles pulling it tight.

'Cool,' I said, as casually as I could. 'What's her name?'

'Rebecca,' he said matter-of-factly. I waited for him to offer more, but what more of an answer could he give? Yet why did I think his reticence spoke volumes?

'That's funny.' I didn't know what else to say.

'What is?' he asked warily, as if already sensing what I was about to say, even when I wasn't quite sure myself.

'That her name's Rebecca.'

He turned to look at me.

'I assume it's not *your* Rebecca?' I gave a little laugh, to lighten the weight of the question.

He looked at me for a moment, his brow knitted, then shook his head slowly and looked away.

I didn't know whether I wanted to know more about the Rebecca at work, or 'his' Rebecca. It was difficult to know which was more problematic.

'That would have been weird, though, right?' I went on. 'Imagine an ex turning up at work. How would you feel?'

He rubbed at his eyes with his thumb and forefinger. 'That's unlikely to happen.'

'What's she like then? This Rebecca?' I decided I'd deal with the immediate threat first. 'She's obviously been a help to you.'

'She's good, yeah. She seems to know her stuff, so that saves me the bother of having to go through everything with her. She's been in the company a while apparently, though I've no idea where they've been hiding her.'

Did that mean he'd have noticed her if she hadn't been hidden away? I didn't want to know how good she was at her job, I just wanted to know her vital statistics and the colour of her hair. I was aware that the questions bouncing around in my head would make me sound like an obsessive, paranoid girlfriend if they were to make themselves heard. But wasn't that what I was? Wasn't that what Tom had turned me into? I couldn't help myself.

'Is she hot then?' I asked. His brow crinkled as if working out the most diplomatic answer. If he said 'No' too quickly, I'd know he was lying. If he said 'Yes', he'd be mad. We both knew he couldn't win.

'She's all right, I suppose,' was all he could muster, which, given the options, was his best shot.

'Does your ex, Rebecca, work in the City?' I asked.

He sat up straight. 'No,' he said hesitantly.

Was that all I was going to get?

'So, she doesn't work in your industry? That wasn't how you met?'

'I wasn't aware that I'd mentioned Rebecca,' he said tightly.

A rush of heat spread up from my toes as it slowly dawned on me that he hadn't. I'd put his reluctant 'let's not talk about it', together with a picture of him and a woman who I guessed was called Rebecca, and let my mind run riot. I wanted to suck all my stupid, insecure words back in.

'What's all this about?' he said, turning towards me, his face serious.

I moved closer to him and lifted his arm over me, as I laid my head in his lap. A diversion tactic to give my cheeks time to cool down.

'I guess I just feel that there's large chunks of your life that I don't know about yet,' I said, 'and I just want to know everything that there is to know.' I gave a little laugh and picked up his hand from where it rested on my stomach, and held it to my lips.

My heart was thumping as I waited for a response. Had I pushed it too far? Was he just going to get up and walk out?

The seconds ticked by like hours and I tried to gauge which way he was going to go as the pulse in his thigh beat against my cheek.

'What do you want to know?' he said, finally.

I let out the breath I'd been holding in. 'Everything!'

He laughed. 'By that, I assume you mean my love life. Isn't that the only thing that girls really want to know about?'

I lifted my shoulders and wrinkled my nose. 'That obvious, eh?'

He looked down at me, and I could see the fairy lights in the tree reflected in his eyes. My stomach flipped as he smiled. 'Okay, you go first . . .' he said. 'Where's the most unusual place you've ever made love?'

I almost choked, and sat up. 'That's easy . . . I had a one-night stand on a cricket pitch, but you already know about that.'

'Tell me again . . . slowly,' he teased.

I went to hit him round the head with a cushion but he caught it mid-flight.

'Okay, so have you ever been in love?' he asked.

'It's not your turn,' I said.

He tilted his head to one side and raised his eyebrows. 'Yes or no?'

The moment had suddenly become laden with anticipation. Funny, isn't it, how the very real physical act of sex, even with unnamed strangers, can be spoken about with humour and joviality, yet talking about an unseen emotion called love is fraught with tension.

'Once,' I said, determined to keep my voice calm and steady.

'Who with?'

'A guy called Tom. I met him at work, when I was going through my retail period.'

He looked at me questioningly.

'You know. Between my hairdressing and interior design phases.' I'm sure I'd given him a quick run through my haphazard CV at some point.

'Ah.' He sighed. 'The enlightenment years.'

I smiled, grateful to him for relieving the intensity of the conversation.

'So, what happened?' he asked.

I cleared my throat. 'We met when I was twenty, went out for close to three years, and I began to think we had a future.'

'But?'

'But, despite how I felt about him and how he claimed to feel for me, he still managed to sleep with someone else.'

'Oh,' he mustered. 'How did you find out?'

'It was with a very good friend of mine, dear Charlotte, who decided that she was actually more in love with him, than she was a friend to me.'

'Christ. I assume you're not friends anymore.'

I laughed wryly. 'Funnily enough, no. I haven't spoken to her since, and have no intention of speaking to her ever again.'

'So, was he your last boyfriend . . . before we met?' he went on.

'Seriously, you've had five hundred questions and I haven't even had one,' I said, laughing. 'He was my only serious boyfriend. I've had other relationships over the three years since, but nobody of any significance, until I met you.'

He smiled.

'Now, it really *is* my turn,' I said.

He sat back and stared straight ahead, avoiding my gaze.

'So, what about you? Have you ever been in love?'

His foot nudged the edge of the cobalt-blue rug that lay under the coffee table. I didn't want to force anything, if it was still too raw. I waited a moment longer. 'It's not important,' I said, far more brightly than I felt. 'If it's . . .'

'Yes,' he said quietly.

I chanced it. 'With Rebecca?'

He nodded. 'She was the one I thought I was going to spend the rest of my life with . . . but it wasn't to be.'

His answer made me wish I'd never asked.

'But anyway, enough of all that,' he said, as if shaking himself out of the place he was in. 'I wanted to ask how you'd feel about spending some time together over Christmas. If it's difficult, I understand . . . you know, if it's . . . I just thought . . .'

I reached across and put a finger on his lips. Smiling, he said, 'Is that a yes, then?'

He pulled me towards him and kissed me. 'So, you'll come for Christmas dinner?' he asked excitedly.

I wrinkled my nose up. 'I can't come on Christmas Day.' His shoulders dropped. 'But you could come down to my parents. They'd love to meet you,' I added.

'And you know that I can't,' he said, sadness in his voice. 'Mum's on her own as James is having lunch with his girlfriend Chloe, so she needs me there. It's a tough time of year for her.'

I nodded. He'd already told me that his father had died two days before Christmas.

'Why don't you come down on Boxing Day?' he said.

'But my brother and his wife are coming for lunch, and they're bringing the baby.' Though even as I was saying it, I knew it was an easier ask of me to go to him, rather than him come to me. My parents had each other and Stuart, Laura and the baby. Pammie would be lucky to see a neighbour.

'I guess I could drive down late afternoon . . .' I offered.

'And stay over? We could go for a drive the next day, find a nice pub or something.'

We sounded like two over-excited children hatching a plan.

The next day, I called Pammie to check that she was okay with it. It seemed the courteous thing to do.

'Well, this is a turn-up for the books,' she said, which immediately put me on the back foot.

'I'm so sorry, Pammie. I thought Adam had already spoken to you. He said he'd call you first thing this morning.'

'No, dear,' she said. 'But no matter. It'd be lovely to see you. Will you be staying down here?'

'Yes,' I said. 'Though I probably won't be there until early evening.'

'So, will you be wanting tea with us?' she asked.

'My mum's doing a turkey for lunch, so just a little something in the evening would be lovely,' I said, not wishing to come across as rude or ungrateful.

'But we won't wait for you . . .'

'Goodness no, you just carry on and I'll be there when I can.'

'Well, it's just that Adam gets so hungry and he'll be starving by then,' she went on.

'Yes, of course. I understand. You go ahead and I'll just have tea with you all later.'

'So, we'll all eat together then?' she went on, as if she wasn't hearing me.

'Perfect,' I said, though I didn't really know what I was agreeing to anymore.

7

It had sounded a great idea at the time but, in reality, once I was at Mum and Dad's, I'd have been happy to stay there. It was warm and cosy and reminded me of Christmases past when, as an excited seven-year-old, I'd shake my little brother awake in the middle of the night. We'd creep down the stairs, so terrified of seeing Santa Claus, yet not wanting to miss him either.

'He'll know we're not asleep,' Stuart would whisper. 'And if we're not asleep, he'll not leave any presents.'

'Ssh,' I'd reply, my heart in my mouth. 'Cover your eyes with your hand and just look through the tiniest crack in your fingers.'

We'd feel our way along the banisters and shuffle slowly towards the tree in the corner of the front room, passing the fireplace where we'd left a glass of milk and a mince pie. I'd peer out between my fingers, the light of the moon illuminating the room just enough to see the remainder of a mince pie on the plate. I'd gasp.

'What is it? Has he been?' Stuart would cry eagerly.

I would be able to make out the shapes of wrapped presents under the tree and my heart would leap for joy.

'He's been,' I'd say, barely able to contain my excitement. 'He's been.'

Twenty years on, and not much has changed. Despite it being Boxing Day, we're still treating it as if it was Christmas Day itself. We're still gathered around the same old tree. 'If it's not broken, don't fix it,' Dad has repeated for the past decade, even though there's clearly a withering branch or two needing assistance. Mum is still insistent that the presents underneath it have nothing to do with her, and Stuart and I exchange a look, as if willing ourselves to believe it.

'So, how's the new romance going?' my sister-in-law, Laura, asked in between mouthfuls of Mum's famous roasties.

I nodded, my own mouth full of crispy Yorkshire pudding. 'It's going well,' I said, smiling.

'Ah, she's got that twinkle in her eye,' said Dad. 'Didn't I tell you, Valerie? I told your mother you had that twinkle in your eye again a couple of weeks back.'

'*Again?*' I asked.

'Didn't I, Val?' he called out to the kitchen, where Mum was filling a second boat with gravy. 'Didn't I say she had that twinkle in her eye again?'

'What do you mean, *again*?' I asked, laughing. Stuart and I rolled our eyes at each other. It wouldn't be Christmas if Dad didn't have too many sherries.

'He means since Tom,' tutted Mum, as she bustled into the dining room, her obligatory apron still on, though why she only wore it at Christmas when she cooked every other day, I'll never know. 'Honestly, Gerald, you've got the tact of a . . .'

I looked at her expectantly.

'Go on, Mum,' said Stuart. 'The tact of a what?'

'The tact of a . . .' she repeated, though where she was going with it was anybody's guess.

I snorted.

'We've got three different conversations going on here,' moaned Mum in mock protest. She gives off a good impression of it all being too much, but I know for a fact that she loves nothing more than having her family around her. And now we have little Sophie she's even happier.

'So, whose eyes were twinkling?' asked Dad, almost to himself.

'You said Emily's were,' Mum said, rolling her eyes. 'Because she's got a new boyfriend.'

'When am I going to get to meet him, then?' asked Dad loudly. 'I hope he's not a bastard like that other fella.'

'Gerald!' Mum shouted. 'Watch your language.'

'How long have you been together?' asked Laura, genuinely interested.

'Oh, only three months, not that long,' I said flippantly, but instantly regretted making what Adam and I had sound like a casual fling. 'But I'd like you to meet him.'

'Well, you just make sure he treats you right this time. Don't take any of his . . .'

'Gerald!'

We all laughed, and I wished that Adam was there. I wanted him to meet my nutty lot just so he knew what he was letting himself in for.

I left reluctantly, knowing I'd miss the drunken charades and Mum's inability to remember how many syllables were in *Dances with Wolves*. Stuart gave it to her every Christmas, just so we could see her attempt to mime it, yet, every year, she treated it as if it was the first time she'd ever heard of it.

'Take care of yourself, sweetheart,' Mum said, as she hugged me at the door.

If it wasn't Adam I was going to, I'd have stayed right there, in her warm embrace. She smelled of mulled wine and oranges.

'Thanks Mum. I'll call you when I get there.'

'Do you fancy an eggnog before you go?' asked Dad, as he came to the door, his paper hat askew. 'I bought a bottle specially.'

'She can't, Gerald,' chastised Mum, 'she's got to drive. And who drinks that stuff anyways?'

I smiled to myself and kissed them all goodbye, and gave baby Sophie an extra squeeze, before dragging myself out into the cold air. Unsurprisingly, the roads were clear – I imagine because most sane people were settled in for the night, unwilling to leave the warmth of their fires and unable to resist the lure of one more sherry.

It was dark by the time I pulled up outside Pammie's cottage, one of five in a row, their flintstones cheek to jowl. The white wooden door swung open before I'd even turned my lights off, and Adam's bulk filled the porch, his cold breath billowing, at odds with the warmth of the light that spilled out from the hall behind him.

'Come on.' He beckoned, like an excited little boy. 'You're late. Hurry up.'

I looked at my watch. 5.06 p.m. I was six minutes later than expected. We kissed on the porch. It felt like forever since I'd seen him. It had only been three days, but when Christmas is in between, it makes you feel like you've lost whole weeks sitting indoors, watching telly and eating until you're sick.

'Hmm, I've missed you,' he whispered. 'Come in. We've waited for you. Dinner's about to be served.'

'Dinner?' I faltered. 'But . . .'

He kissed me again as I took off my coat. 'We're all starving, but Mum insisted we wait for you.'

'All? But—' I began again. Too late.

'There she is,' exclaimed Pammie, scurrying forward to hold my face in her hands. 'Oh, you poor mite, you're freezing. Come on, let's get you fed. That'll warm you up.'

I looked at her questioningly. 'Don't worry about me,

I've just eaten . . .' I started, but she had already turned and was heading towards the kitchen.

'I hope you're hungry,' she called out. 'I could feed an army with this lot.'

Adam handed me a glass of fizz and, nerves frayed, I was grateful for the cold tingle on my tongue.

'What have we got for tea?' I asked, careful to keep the word 'tea' light, as if I could actually *will* it to be.

I kept a fixed smile on my face as Adam said, 'It'll be easier if I tell you what we *haven't* got.'

'Adam, I can't . . .' I tried again, as we walked into the dining room, but when I saw the table, beautifully laid out for four, with sparkly placemats, crisp white napkins carefully rolled into silver rings, and a red-berry and pine-cone centrepiece, I didn't have the heart.

'Here you go,' said Pammie, in a sing-song voice, as she carried in two plates, laden down with a full Christmas dinner and all the trimmings. 'This one's for you. I've given you extra as I knew you'd be hungry by the time you got here.' My heart sank. 'I do hope you like it. I've been in the kitchen most of the day.'

I smiled through gritted teeth. 'Looks lovely, Pammie.'

'You sit here,' she said. 'And Adam, that's you there. Sit, and I'll go and get the other two.'

I looked at him as she left the room, and tilted my head towards the empty seat, its place setting laid out just as beautifully as the other three.

'Oh, that's for James, my brother,' he replied, in

answer to my silent question. 'He showed up unexpectedly on Christmas Eve and he's been here ever since. Thought I told you that on the phone?'

I shook my head.

'James,' Pammie called out. 'Dinner's ready.'

I looked at the plate in front of me. Even if I hadn't eaten for a week, I still wouldn't be able to get through this mountain of vegetables. I could just about see the corners of the thick turkey slices poking out from beneath two Yorkshire puddings. The colour of the crockery was unknown.

My bloated stomach groaned and I discreetly undid the top two buttons of my skin-tight trousers as I sat down. Thank God for my long blouse, as I was straight back up again as James walked into the room.

'Don't get up on my account.' He smiled, holding out his hand. 'Nice to meet you, finally.'

Finally? I liked that. It implied that we'd been together longer than we really had. And Adam had clearly spoken about me.

I smiled tightly, suddenly aware of how awkward it felt to be sat with a complete, yet very relevant, stranger.

Adam hadn't spoken much about James, aside from to say that they were polar opposites: Adam worked in a high-pressured job in the city, whereas James had started up a small landscaping business on the Kent–Sussex borders. Adam was the first to admit that he was motivated by money, yet James was quite happy to live from one day to the next, as long as he was outside doing what he loved.

I watched him as he sat down, then reached across for the salt and pepper, his mannerisms the same as Adam's. They looked very much alike too, except James had longer hair and sharper features, his face unlined and without the telling strain of working in the city.

Maybe we'd all look like that if we weren't out there, slaving away, fighting for the next deal and, no doubt, working ourselves into an early grave. Meanwhile, he just ambles along, doing what he loves, and hey, if he gets paid for it too, that's just a bonus.

'James here has had a bit of girl trouble,' whispered Pammie conspiratorially.

'Mum,' he moaned. 'I'm sure Emily doesn't want to know about that.'

'Of course she does,' she said indignantly. 'There isn't a woman in this world who doesn't love a gossip.'

I smiled and nodded, still summoning the strength to pick up my knife and fork.

'Mind you, we're not quite sure she was right for him in the first place, are we?' she went on, clasping her hand around his as it rested on the table between mouthfuls.

'Mum, please.'

'I'm just saying, that's all. Just saying what everyone is thinking. She had a lot of, what shall we call them? Issues. And if you ask me, he's better off out of it.'

I managed a small bite of everything, bar the Brussels

sprouts, eight of which were lolling about in a swathe of gravy.

'Oh, goodness,' Pammie cried, as she caught me putting my cutlery down. 'Do you not like it? Have I done something wrong?'

'Not at all,' I replied, embarrassed by the boys' concerned looks. 'I'm just—'

'You said you'd be hungry, though, didn't you?' she went on. 'You said you'd be wanting tea when you got here?'

I nodded mutely. This isn't *tea* from where I come from.

'You feeling okay, Em?' Adam asked.

'Ah, young love,' chirped Pammie. 'I remember when my Jim used to fuss over me.'

'Mum's gone to a lot of trouble,' said Adam quietly.

'I'm fine, and it's lovely, honestly – I'm just taking a break,' I said, head down.

'But Em, you've hardly touched it,' she went on. The 'Em' seemed to sound sarcastic, like a taunting child in a playground.

I looked at her then, square in the eyes, careful to keep my features soft. She returned my stare, but I could have sworn there was almost a glint of smug satisfaction.

'So, how's things in the recruitment business?' James asked me brightly.

Another tick. Adam's certainly made himself busy.

'I'm sure Emily doesn't want to talk about work.' Pammie laughed.

'Sorry, I . . .' he faltered.

'I don't mind,' I said honestly. Anything to distract me from what was on my plate. 'It's still pretty strong in the sectors I work in, though the ever-present threat of online recruiting is snapping at our heels.'

He nodded. 'And I guess the IT industry is hotter than ever?' he said, patting Adam on the shoulder. 'If anything this fella says is to go by.'

'Ah, has he been bigging himself up again?' I said, laughing. 'The hot-shot IT executive.'

'Something like that,' James said, smiling.

'I keep telling him that it's old hat,' I joked. 'This tech thing will never last.'

I looked at Adam and he offered a smile, but it didn't reach his eyes.

James laughed and I felt I should look at him, but I could feel his eyes on me and didn't know where to direct my gaze.

'Maybe I should get my welly boots on and start shovelling manure with you, bro,' said Adam, returning what I now saw as a patronizing pat of James's shoulder. Funny, it hadn't looked like that when James did it to Adam. I chastised myself for encouraging sibling rivalry; having a brother myself, I should know better.

James toyed with an errant sprout with his fork.

'So, do you live locally?' I asked, desperate to dispel the atmosphere that had flooded the room.

He nodded. 'I've got a casual agreement with a guy a few villages away. He lets me a lodge on his estate in return for keeping the gardens neat and tidy.'

'Trouble is, it's this lass's father,' added Pammie.

I pulled a face and looked at him. 'Ah, I see.'

'It's complicated,' he said, as if to justify himself. 'Another fine mess I've got myself into.'

I smiled. 'So, how's the horticultural business? Keeping you busy?' I didn't think it was my place to make conversation, but both Pammie and Adam were on mute, preferring instead to devour their dinner.

'I love what I do,' he said, with real conviction. 'And, as people who love what they do often say, it's a vocation, not a job.'

'Ah, I used to say that when I was working in a shoe shop,' I said. 'All those poor feet needing help and assistance. I would have done it for nothing, such was my passion.'

His face broke into a wide grin, his gentle eyes not leaving mine. 'You're one of life's true warriors. I thank you from the bottom of my heart.' He held a hand to his chest and, for a moment, it felt like we were the only people there. The sound of Pammie and Adam's knives and forks scraping their plates clean brought me back into the room.

'Excuse me for a second,' I said, rising from the table and pushing my chair back.

I'd eaten all I could manage, and my body was beginning to fight back, my intestines gripping and twisting. I didn't know whether I was more panicked by that or the unsettled feeling that James had created in me. I was sure no one else had noticed, so did that mean I'd imagined it? I sincerely hoped so.

Once we'd cleared the table and tidied away in the kitchen, I waited until Pammie and James were out of earshot before leaning into Adam.

'Do you fancy a walk?' I asked him quietly.

'Sure,' he said. 'I'll get my coat.'

'Where are you off to?' Pammie asked Adam in the hall. 'You're not heading off, are you?' There was panic in her voice. 'I thought you were staying.'

'We are, Mum. We're just going for a stroll, to work off that delicious dinner.'

'We?' she asked. 'What, you mean Emily's staying as well?'

'Of course. We'll stay for the night and go home tomorrow after breakfast.'

'Well, where is she going to sleep?' her voice was quieter now.

'With me,' he declared.

'Oh, I don't think so, son. Young James is here as well. There's not enough room.'

'Well then, James can sleep on the sofa, and Emily and I will take the spare bedroom.'

'You can't be sleeping together in this house,' she said, her voice wobbling. 'That's not right. It's disrespectful.'

Adam laughed nervously. 'Mum, I'm twenty-nine years old. It's not like we're teenagers.'

'I don't care how old you are. You're not sleeping together under my roof. It wouldn't be right. Anyways, Emily said she was staying in a hotel tonight.'

What? It was a good job I was still in the kitchen as it took all my resolve not to shove the tea towel in my mouth and bite down on it. At what point did I say I was staying in a hotel?

'Emily was never going to go to a hotel, Mum,' Adam said. 'That wouldn't make sense.'

'Well, that's what she told me on the phone,' she said indignantly. 'If she's going to stay here, she can sleep on the sofa. You and James can sleep in the spare room.'

'But Mum . . .' started Adam. I walked into the hall to see her hand in the air, her palm just a few centimetres away from his face.

'There are no buts. That's the way it's going to be, whether you like it or not. If you loved me and respected me, you wouldn't have even asked.' The tears began to flow then, slowly and quietly at first, but when Adam didn't go to her, the sobs became louder. I stood there dumbfounded, silently willing him to stand strong. When her shoulders started to heave, Adam took hold of her and held her to him. 'Ssh, it's okay, Mum. Sorry, I didn't mean to upset you. That's fine. Of course it is.'

'I never said—' I started, before Adam's eyes told me to stop.

'Whatever you'd like us to do,' he said soothingly, rocking her back and forth like a baby.

He looked at me and shrugged his shoulders apologetically, as if to say, 'what more can I do?' I turned away from him as he went up the stairs.

There was the tiniest frisson of anger bubbling up inside me and, if I hadn't had too much to drink, I most probably would have left and driven home. Had I known that James would be here, and that I'd be expected to sleep on an old sofa, I would have stayed with my parents. I wanted to be with Adam, and I thought he wanted to be with me, but here I was, having to pander to his Mum's needy behaviour and defend myself.

'You don't mind, do you?' Pammie asked, a little brighter now, as she fetched a duvet and pillow down from upstairs.

I fixed a smile on my face and shook my head nonchalantly.

'It's just that there have to be boundaries. In our day, we wouldn't think about getting into bed with anyone before getting married. I know it's different now, but that doesn't mean I have to agree with it. I don't know how you young people do it, just sleeping with anyone that takes your fancy. It's such a worry for me and my boys. Next thing we know, we'll have some tart turning up claiming to be pregnant with their child.'

Was she talking about me? I took a couple of deep breaths and exhaled just a little too loudly. It wasn't quite a sigh, but there was enough for her to pick up on.

'Oh goodness,' she went on. 'I'm not saying you'd do something like that, but we can't take our chances, can we? And if it's not pregnancy we have to worry about, it's catching a disease.'

Why was she using the term 'we' instead of 'he'?

'Here, let me get that,' said James, coming in and taking the two corners of the duvet cover that I was reluctantly holding up for his mother. He shook the cover down.

'I'm sorry, and it's lovely to have you here, but had I known you were staying . . .' Pammie was still going on.

'Mum, why don't you go and get a sheet from the airing cupboard?' said James. 'We can lay it on the sofa.'

I watched her as she left the room, and then turned to look at James. It was taking all my willpower not to blow my cheeks out in exasperation.

'Sorry,' he said. I obviously wasn't hiding my feelings very well. 'She's just old-fashioned.'

I smiled, grateful for his acknowledgement.

'You can sleep in my bed if you like.'

It was an innocent comment, but it made my cheeks colour all the same. I plumped up a pillow that didn't need plumping.

'I'll bed down here with Adam,' he continued. 'It's not the most romantic Boxing night for you two, I know, but I'm afraid it's the best I can offer.'

'I appreciate it,' I said genuinely, 'but it's fine, really it is.' I looked at the lumpy, uneven cushions on the sofa. 'I've slept in worse places.'

James raised his eyebrows and smiled, displaying a dimple I hadn't noticed before. 'I'll take your word for that.'

I suddenly realized how my comment could be mis-construed. 'I mean, when I used to go camping with my family,' I said. 'We used to go to this place in Cornwall, which to an eight-year-old was like something out of an Enid Blyton novel. The babbling brook, the cows that used to sit down if it was going to rain, the boulders we had to find to hold the tent down, the gnats that were friends with the fairies . . .'

He was looking at me as if I was mad. 'I used to read a lot of books and write a lot of stories as a child,' I said apologetically.

'That's nothing,' he said, as if in competition. 'When I was younger, I battled monster pterodactyls and woolly mammoths . . .'

'Ah, you were a reader too,' I said.

'I was nine, what can I say?' he said defensively.

We both laughed. 'It sounds like we both had over-active imaginations,' I said. 'I sometimes wish I was that age again – life was a lot simpler. Now, you'd have to pay me to sleep in a field with a noisy stream, dirty cows, uncomfortable rocks, and biting flies!'

'So now this old sofa is looking strangely appealing, eh?' he said. I smiled.

'Where are you two lovebirds going to head to then?' asked Pammie, as she came back into the room, busily unfolding a sheet.

'Emily's very nice,' said James, 'but she's my brother's girlfriend, so I'm not sure what you're implying and what that says about me.' He laughed heartily.

'Oh, my goodness,' Pammie shrieked. 'I thought you were Adam!' She turned to me. 'They look so alike – they always have done. Like peas in a pod.'

I kept my smile painted on.

'There's a lovely pub about a mile or so down the road,' she said. 'If I remember rightly, they've got a few rooms there too. They'll probably be all booked up, what with it being Boxing night and all, but it might be worth asking, seeing as you said—'

'You ready?' called out Adam as he came down the stairs, hat and gloves in his hand.

I was too dumbfounded to respond immediately, so Pammie did it on my behalf. It seemed she was good at that.

'Yes, she's here. You two go and have a lovely walk. I'll make a fresh brew for when you're back.'

I wrapped my scarf tightly around me, covering my

mouth just in case the words I was thinking came tumbling out.

'Sorry about that,' Adam said, grabbing my hand as we made our way down the dimly lit lane.

Relief flooded through me. So I wasn't going mad. He'd noticed it too.

'I know it's not ideal, but it *is* her house,' he went on.

I stopped stock-still in the middle of the road and turned to face him. 'That's all you're apologizing for?' I asked.

'What? I know it's a pain, but it's only for one night, and we'll get up and go early tomorrow. I want to get you back to my place.' He came towards me, and his lips brushed mine, but I stiffened and turned my head away.

'What's wrong with you?' he said, his tone changing.

'You don't get it, do you?' I said, louder than I'd intended. 'You're completely blind to it.'

'What are you talking about? Blind to what?'

I tutted and almost laughed. 'You go around in your cosy little world, not letting anything bother you, but guess what? Life's not like that. And all the time you've got your head stuck in a little hole, shutting all the sound out, I'm out here taking all the shit.'

'Is this for real?' he asked, about to turn back to the house.

'Can you not see what's going on here?' I cried. 'What she's trying to do?'

'Who? What?'

'I told your mother that I'd have a little tea and she's forced a full Christmas dinner on me, and I also told her that I'd be staying over, and she assured me that was all right. I would never have come had I known . . .'

'Had you known what?' he asked, his nostrils flaring ever so slightly. 'In our house, tea means dinner. And are you absolutely sure she agreed to letting you stay with me? Because she's only allowed one girl to do that, and we'd been together for two years. We've only been together, what? Two months?'

His words felt like a physical blow to my chest. 'It's three, actually,' I snapped.

He flung his arms in the air and, exasperated, turned around to walk back up the lane.

Had she asked me if I was staying? *Had* I told her I was? I know I definitely didn't tell her I would be staying in a hotel, but could she have assumed that was what I meant? I couldn't think straight anymore.

Adam was still walking away, and I rolled fast-forward in my mind to see him crashing back into Pammie's house with little me trailing behind him twenty seconds later. I couldn't let that happen.

I cried then, real tears of frustration. God, listen to me. What was I doing? Making a defenceless old woman out to be some kind of maternal monster. It was crazy. *I* was crazy.

'I'm sorry,' I said, and he stopped, turned around and

walked back towards where I stood, a snivelling mess in the middle of the road.

'What's wrong, Em?' He put his arms around me, pulling me towards him. I could feel the warmth of his breath on the top of my head as my chest heaved up and down.

'It's fine. I'm fine,' I said half-heartedly. 'I don't know where that came from.'

'You worried about going back to work?' he asked gently.

I nodded. 'Yeah, I think the stress must be getting to me,' I lied.

I wanted to tell him what had really upset me. I didn't want there to be any secrets between us, but what was I supposed to say? 'I think there's a chance your mother could be a vindictive witch?' It sounded ridiculous, and what proof did I have to back the theory up? Her selective memory and a penchant for over-feeding people? No, any opinion I had on his mother, that she was deranged or otherwise, would have to remain unsaid for the time being.

8

I'd intended to stay out of Pammie's way for a while, just to give me time to calm down and re-evaluate her odd behaviour. After all, I was sure that was all it was, just a mother looking out for her son. If I stayed on that line of thought, I could begin to understand it. But three weeks after Christmas, two days before my birthday, she called Adam to ask if she could take us both out to celebrate.

I tried everything to get out of it, but I was beginning to run out of excuses. 'I've got to arrange something with Pippa and Seb,' I told Adam. 'And the office said they wanted to take me out.'

'You can go out with them anytime,' Adam said sternly. 'Mum wants to treat us.'

'Treating us' meant going to a restaurant of her choice, in her home town – Sevenoaks. So even though it was *my* birthday, we were still having to do things on *her* terms.

'Oh, Emily, it's so lovely to see you,' she gushed as she reached the table where we'd been waiting for her for over twenty minutes. Her eyes travelled up and down, as if sizing me up. 'You look . . . well.'

She was sweetness and light whilst we ate our starter, and I was beginning to relax, but then she asked what Adam had got me for my birthday. I looked across the table at him, and he nodded, as if giving me permission to tell her.

'Well, he's taking me to Scotland,' I said excitedly. I watched her face flicker between confusion and displeasure. Her mouth formed an 'O', but no sound came out.

'I've not been up there for years,' said Adam.

'And I've never been,' I said, chipping in.

'W-well . . . when will you be going?' she stuttered.

'Tomorrow!' we both exclaimed.

She looked like somebody had pushed her, as she slumped back into the chair, the air sucked out of her.

'Are you all right, Mum?' Adam asked. 'You look like you've seen a ghost.'

Pammie shook herself, and it took her a few seconds to find her voice. 'So, where will you stay?' she asked eventually.

'I've booked a really nice hotel for a couple of nights,' said Adam. 'Auntie Linda said we could stay with her, but I didn't want to impose.'

I felt ridiculously triumphant. 'Auntie Linda said we could stay with *her*,' I repeated in a sing-song voice in my head. 'So there.' I lambasted myself for being so immature.

'Oh, well, I'm shocked,' she said. 'I had no idea.'

I wondered why she thought she should.

'Linda said she'll have us up for lunch,' said Adam. 'She'll get Fraser and Ewan over. I'd like Emily to meet them all.'

'Goodness, this *is* a surprise,' said Pammie, patting Adam's hand. 'Well, that's lovely, just lovely.'

The conversation was stilted whilst we waited for our main course. I greeted my seabass like an old friend, thankful to have something to focus my attention on. When Adam excused himself to go to the toilet, I wanted to run in there with him.

'So, things are moving along pretty quickly, then?' said Pammie, without waiting for the gents' door to close.

'Mmm,' I smiled tightly.

'How long have you been together now?' she asked, pursing her lips to take a sip of her white wine spritzer.

'Four months.'

'Goodness, that's no time at all,' she said, a fixed grin on her face.

'It's not always about time, though, is it?' I questioned, careful to keep my voice light. 'It's about how you feel.'

'Indeed, it is,' she said, nodding slowly. 'And you feel that Adam is the one?'

'I hope so.' I didn't want to give her any more than necessary.

'And you think he feels the same?' she asked, with a withering look on her face, as if she was dealing with a naive child.

'I would hope so. We're practically living together, so yeah . . .' I deliberately left it hanging, as if I was almost willing her to say something else, yet knowing that I wouldn't want to hear it.

'You'd be wise to back off a bit,' she said. 'He likes his own space, and if you crowd him, you'll have him running for the hills.'

'Has he said something?' I couldn't help myself. Her mouth had spread into a smug grin, and I instantly wished I could tie a knot in my tongue.

'Just this and that,' she said dismissively, knowing full well I wouldn't be able to leave it there.

'Like what?' I asked. 'This and that what?'

'Oh, you know, the usual. How he feels hemmed in. How he has to answer to you every time he wants to step outside the front door.'

A rush of heat spread across my chest. Was that how I made him feel? *Don't be ridiculous*, I remonstrated with myself. *We're an equal partnership. That's not who we are. What we're about.* But then I caught sight, in my mind's eye, of me having a go at him for coming in late last Thursday. And on Sunday, I'd asked how long he'd be at the gym for. Was I that person? Was he tired of being questioned, to the point he'd tell his mother?

I looked at her as my brain frantically whirred away and wondered, not for the first time, whether she knew what she was doing. Or had I got it all wrong? Again?

Sensing Adam walking back towards us, she grinned and put her hand over mine.

'I'm sure it's nothing to worry about,' she said cheerily, her voice saccharin sweet, like butter wouldn't melt.

'So, is she just some batty old woman who's lonely and bored?' asked Pippa, when Adam dropped me back after the meal. He'd wanted me to stay at his, but Pammie had left me mentally exhausted and I wanted to go home.

I shook my head and shrugged my shoulders.

'Or is it more spiteful than that?' Pippa went on in her most sinister voice. 'Is she playing some kind of game here?'

'I really don't know,' I offered honestly. 'Sometimes, I think it's just silly pettiness, but then something gnaws away at me, chipping and chipping until I'm convinced she's a bitter, jealous psychopath.'

'Whoa, wait up a minute, let's calm down a bit here,' Pippa said, hands aloft. 'She's sixty-three, isn't she?'

'Yeah, so?'

'So, I can't think of too many psychotic sexagenarians, that's all.'

I had to laugh. The whole thing sounded ridiculous when it was said aloud, and I made a mental note to remind myself of that the next time I let it get to me.

9

The text read: Of course. Would be lovely to see you son. What time do you think you'll be here? I do hope she isn't off cavorting. It happens so often these days. Mum x

What? I read it again. What the hell was Pammie talking about? I scrolled through my message history. The last text I'd sent her was a reluctant 'Thank you' for my birthday dinner the week before.

I read her text again. *I do hope she isn't off cavorting.* It clearly wasn't meant for me. She must have meant to send it to James. He was back with the girlfriend she didn't think much of. That would go some way to explaining it. Poor girl. Sounded like she was getting an even rougher ride than I was.

I listened for the running water of the shower, before reaching across the bed to retrieve Adam's phone from his bedside. I quickly flicked through his texts. One, from twenty minutes earlier read: Hi mum, Emily's off to a work conference this weekend so I was thinking about popping down to see you. Does Saturday work for you? x

A hotness filled my head. She *was* talking about me. She'd sent her reply to me instead of him. I held down a frustrated scream and clenched my fists, resisting the temptation to throw myself on the bed and pummel the pillows. The door handle to the bathroom turned, and I practically threw Adam's phone onto his bedside.

'Hey, what's up?' he said, wearing nothing but a towel around his waist. I didn't know if he could see the guilt in my eyes, or the anger brewing within me.

'Nothing,' I said tightly, turning to open the wardrobe. Most of my clothes were at his place now because that's invariably where I spent most of my time. I was still paying rent on the flat with Pippa, but I was spending less than two nights a week there, so Adam and I had been talking through our options.

'Do you not want to move in here permanently and give yours up?' he'd asked just the night before, as we were lying in bed.

I'd tried not to let the squeak of excitement escape when I spoke. 'It doesn't seem to make sense doing what we're doing at the moment, does it?' I'd said, as nonchalantly as possible, though I was sure he could hear the slightly hysterical lilt in my voice.

He'd shaken his head.

'But I don't think this is where I want to live permanently.' I'd wrinkled my nose and he'd sat up, propping himself on an elbow.

'What? You don't like the 5 a.m. wake-up call from the stall vendors?' he'd smiled. 'All that shouting and hollering at some ungodly hour on a Saturday morning? What's wrong with you?'

I gave him a playful slap on his arm.

'So, do you want to ditch both flats and look at getting something together?'

I smiled and we sealed the deal by making love.

This morning, we'd woken up full of excitement and were getting ready to go and trawl the agents in Blackheath, albeit lettings, but who'd have thought little old me would wind up in SE3? I'd been buzzing, until his mother's text had pinged up on my phone, and now I had an uncomfortable tightness around my chest, as if she'd got her hand in there, pulling me down.

Of course, I could tell Adam exactly what the problem was and read him her message, to show him how hurtful she could be. But then I had to rely on him being honest too. He needed to acknowledge that the message was meant for him and about me. I didn't know if he would. He'd no doubt just bat it away and say, 'Oh you know Mum, she doesn't mean anything by it.' But whether she meant anything by it or not is irrelevant. If I'm upset by it, then I'd expect him to stand by me and support me, not side with his mother.

Though if I was honest with myself, I was already doubting who Adam's priority was, after one or two comments he'd made earlier in the week, whilst we'd been in Scotland.

'So, will we be hearing wedding bells anytime soon?' Lovely Linda had teased, in her soft Scottish lilt. I'd affectionately nicknamed her as such because she was so, well . . . lovely. I tried to see past the family resemblance, the small pointy nose and the thin lips. Linda won out because she had warmth in her eyes, whereas her sister Pammie had none.

'Whoa, steady on now,' said Adam, laughing. 'We've only just met.'

I'd smiled along with him, but I couldn't stop myself from feeling a little hurt at how flippantly he described our relationship.

'Yes, but when you know, you know, don't you?' she said, with a wink.

'We'll see,' said Adam, taking my hand.

'What would you do?' she pressed on. 'Would you have a big traditional wedding?'

'*If* I was ever going to get married,' I'd giggled, emphasizing the 'if', 'I'd like to go off somewhere hot, with just our nearest and dearest, and do it on a beach somewhere.'

'Ooh, imagine that,' cried Linda. 'What a fabulous idea.'

'We couldn't do that,' exclaimed Adam, looking at me as if I were mad. 'Our families would go ballistic.'

'Mine would be okay,' I said.

'And don't you be minding us,' pitched in Linda. 'You do what *you* want to do.'

'Mum wouldn't be happy,' said Adam. 'I'm sure she'd like a big do up here, so all the family could be there.'

'It's *your* day,' said Linda. 'It hasn't got anything to do with anyone else.'

'You could always pop down to Gretna Green,' piped up Adam's cousin, Ewan. 'It's only up the road and you don't even need a witness.'

We'd all laughed, but in amongst the titters I heard Adam saying, 'I'd never get away with that!'

So, I knew where I stood, and all the while I was second best, I'd pick my fights carefully. I wanted to enjoy today for what it was, for what it could be. I wanted to wander through Blackheath Village like other couples that I used to see. Look excitedly into agents' windows before going in and reeling off our requirements. Yes, we'd decided that a second bedroom would be beneficial. Yes, if we didn't have to compromise on location, a small garden would be a huge plus point. No, we didn't have any pets. We'd run through our wish list like little kids, the night before, until it had got silly. No, we wouldn't consider a subterranean basement with no windows. Yes, we would like to overlook the heath if there's a remote chance that it'll cost less than our combined take-home pay.

It could be a great day, so should I tell him what she'd done and how it made me feel? Or should I stay schtum? Was there really any choice?

Adam came up behind me, wrapped his arms around my waist, and let his towel fall to the floor. I'd lost focus on what I was looking for. I couldn't even see the shirts and blouses I was pulling along the rail. There were just blocks of colour, no item seemed to register, the anger building with every hanger.

'You sure nothing's wrong?' he said as he nuzzled my neck.

Say something. Don't ruin it. Say something. Don't ruin it. This could so easily go one of two ways.

'No, honestly,' I said, turning around and returning his kiss. 'I'm just thinking about work. There's a lot going on.'

'I've got something that will relax you,' he murmured. 'That will clear those cobwebs.' I watched as his head dropped and he peeled back the flimsy lace of my bra, circling my nipple with his tongue.

I could feel the rage within me dissipate as his fingers travelled down, pushing my knickers to one side.

I made a half-hearted attempt to push him away. 'We can't. We've got things to do.'

'There's plenty of time for all that. First, just let me see if I can free you of all those worries and stresses.'

There was no point in stopping him. We both knew I wouldn't even try. I needed him as much as he needed me, sometimes even more. I'd always thought sex was over-rated before I met Adam. Of course, I liked it, but I was flummoxed by the constant stream of articles in women's magazines telling us that if we weren't having it five times a week, and swinging from the chandeliers on at least two of those occasions, then there must be something wrong with us.

Even with Tom, who I had been the most adventurous with, I didn't really get it. We made love twice a week, with him on top, until he came, and then he'd satisfy me in other ways. Sex was sex and I was fine with that. But with Adam, it was entirely different. I'd finally been able to see what everyone else was raving about. He knew me, and I knew him. We were the perfect fit. Not many days would pass before one of us needed the other. Our moods could swing and change on the strength of it. Sex had gone from being the least important part of a relationship to high on the priority list.

I moaned as his head moved further down, my breath catching in my throat.

A picture of a horrified Pammie flashed across my mind and I forced the image away. *I'll get to you later*, I thought to myself, as I felt Adam's tongue. *But first your son is going to make love to me.* A warped wave of satisfaction flooded over me that not even Adam himself could transcend.

We were still entwined, our breathing deep and heavy, when a text pinged through on his phone. He extracted himself and rolled over, reaching across to the bedside.

'Who's after you?' I asked casually, wondering whether Pammie had now sent the text to him.

'Pete from work, and my mum.'

'Oh, is your mum okay?' I feigned casual interest.

'Yeah, all good. I was just checking that she's around next weekend. I'm thinking of popping down there whilst you're at the conference.'

'Good idea. Is she okay with that?' I pushed.

He tapped out a reply while I waited. 'Yep, all sorted.'

I willed him to relay the message, so that we could laugh about it and call her a silly old cow, but he didn't.

'I'll go and see her on Saturday,' he said. Damn you, Adam. Why couldn't you have been honest?

10

I was at work when the text pinged through on my mobile.

Are you mad?

I didn't recognize the number, so threw the phone into my bag, out of reach and out of temptation. But I was only able to leave it for a couple of minutes. How can you ignore a text like that?

Sorry? I typed back.

Are you a glutton for punishment? came the reply.

I was getting a bit freaked out. I either knew this person well, or this was a dodgy offer from an S&M dungeon.

I don't think I'm either, so you must have the wrong person, I wrote.

You've got to be a fruit bat if you think going to see my nutty family is worth taking time off work for.

I leant back in my chair and thought for a moment, before a smile spread across my face. There was only one person this could be.

James?

Er yeah . . . who else would it be?

Me: Hey, how are you?

J: I'm good. How were your few days with the hillbillies?

I laughed out loud, and Tess, my colleague on the desk opposite mine, smiled and raised her eyebrows.

Me: Lovely! I wouldn't knock it, you're surprisingly alike.

J: Eh? How come?

Me: Fraser and Ewan are the very same as you and Adam. The apples don't fall very far from that particular tree.

J: Oh, well that's a bit awkward as they're both adopted.

Me: Oh my God – I'm so sorry, I had no idea.

J: You didn't comment on a resemblance, did you? They're super-sensitive.

I ransacked my brain, desperately trying to remember whether I had or not. It would have been a typical comment for me to make, a way to make idle conversation.

Me: I hope not. I feel really bad now.

J: You'd know if you had, cos Fraser would have gone for you. He's got a real short fuse that one.

I had to assume that I hadn't said anything, but that didn't make me feel any better.

J: You still there? James asked, after I'd been quiet for a few minutes.

Me: Yep

J: And you didn't say anything about Auntie Linda being married to her brother, did you?

What? The little sod.

Me: Oh very funny!

J: Had you there though didn't I?

Me: No! Not sure how that side of your family are so nice?!? You should go see them more often. You could learn a lot!

J: I can't. I get a nosebleed whenever I go north of the River Thames.

I covered my mouth to stifle a laugh.

J: You ready for Adam's party? Got your dress?

Me: Yes. Have you got yours?

J: Ha ha . . . mine's red, just so you know. I don't want us clashing.

Me: You wearing your hair up or down?

J: Oh definitely up. Do-ups are all the rage these days.

Me: It's not a do-up, it's an up-do!

J: It's the same difference.

Me: Will Chloe be coming? I had no idea why I'd asked that, and instantly wanted to retrieve the message, but it was too late.

J: Yep, she'll be there. I think she's wearing blue so we should be OK.

The tone of the conversation had changed, and I suddenly felt like a petulant child wanting to go back to how it was.

Great, I typed. I'll be sure to say hello.

The mention of his girlfriend seemed to throw us both off kilter as he came back with a winking emoji and a kiss.

I didn't respond.

11

'Happy Birthday dear Adam, happy birthday to you.'
The chorus turned to applause and calls of 'speech,
speech' rang out around the rugby club.

Adam put his hands up and walked across the dance
floor to the mic. 'Okay, okay. Ssh, settle down. Thank
you. Thank you.'

'Get on with it,' cried out Adam's best mate and
fellow prop, Mike. 'Bloody hell, he speaks with the same
speed he uses on the pitch . . . Slowwwwly.'

All the rugby boys cheered and slapped each other's
backs, like Neanderthals around a cave fire.

I smiled along with the rest of them, but shared the
same resignation as the other girlfriends there, all of us
knowing that, at some point in proceedings, all our boy-
friends, bar none, would have their underpants round
their ankles, swigging beer and singing 'Swing Low,
Sweet Chariot'. I'd only been down to the club three
times, but Adam had exposed himself on every occasion.
I looked towards Amy, Mike's girlfriend, and we both
rolled our eyes. I'd met her once or twice before, but I'd
never seen her all dressed up. She made a great show of
flicking her long brown hair back over her shoulders,

revealing a pair of breasts that strained against the confines of the barely-there triangles of her black dress. I eyed the thin spaghetti straps that were having to work hard to keep the garment in place, and couldn't decide whether I wanted them to snap to expose her assets, or stay steadfast so that every male in the room didn't have a heart attack.

'Your mum's having a bit of a hot flush,' Pippa whispered into my ear, interrupting my jealous thoughts. 'Am I all right to open one of the windows?'

I looked across to the table my lot had commandeered, in the darkest corner of the room. They were happy there, hunkered down, away from the bawling masses. Dad was nursing a pint of bitter, his second and last one, Mum had reminded him, whilst she was sitting protectively beside a silver ice bucket with a bottle of prosecco in.

'To celebrate us finally meeting,' Adam had announced as he'd presented her with it, its poshness at odds with the spit and sawdust of its surroundings.

I'd watched him, so at ease, and wondered why it had taken so long to introduce them. On the three previous occasions we'd set something up, Adam had been called into work on two of them and had had to placate his mother on the third.

'Em, it's me,' he'd said breathlessly, when he'd called as I sat waiting in Côte Brasserie in Blackheath. Mum and Dad had been on their way.

'Hi,' I'd smiled. 'Where are you?'

'I'm sorry babe, I don't think I'm going to make it.'

I'd thought he was joking around. He knew how much I'd wanted him to meet my parents. I'd been sure he was playing, but my stomach had lurched all the same.

'It's just that Mum has got herself all in a state.'

'I'm sorry,' I'd said, trying desperately hard to keep the anger from my voice, all the while smiling through gritted teeth.

'Yeah, sorry.'

'What do you mean, your mum's in a state?' My indignation startled the couple at the table next to me, who both looked at me, and then at each other, with raised eyebrows.

'She's got herself worked up about a letter she's received from the council.'

The conversation of the previous night resounded in my head. The one where I overheard Adam telling Pammie on the phone of our plans.

'You've got to be kidding me?' I'd hissed.

'Er, no. And you would do yourself a favour by dropping the attitude,' he'd said.

I'd lowered my voice. 'You can deal with her sodding letter from the council tomorrow. I need you here tonight.'

'I'm pulling into Sevenoaks now,' he'd said. 'I'll come by there if I get back early enough.'

I'd cut him off. He was already there? How could he have gone to her, when I was waiting for him? *We* were waiting for him?

Looking at him now, a month later, with an arm around my mum, he was charm personified.

'Oh, I *do* like him,' Mum had enthused, her cheeks flushed. 'What an absolute gentleman.'

'Isn't he?' I'd gushed. 'Do you really think so?'

'Oh, he's a keeper, for sure.'

Mum's relatively easy to please; it's Dad any potential suitor has to win over.

'So, what do you think?' I'd asked him, as soon as Adam was out of earshot.

'He'll have to go a long way to prove his worth,' he'd said gruffly.

'He *loved* him,' Seb had said sarcastically, from his seat beside him.

I looked back at Pippa, now standing in front of me. 'Is Mum all right?' I asked. I could see that the windows behind their table were steamed up and running with condensation.

'Yeah.' She nodded. 'It's one of her usual ones, but she's worried about opening a window because it's so cold outside.'

It wasn't yet March, and there was a bitter chill in the air. 'Someone's bound to complain,' I said. 'But they'll just have to get on with it.'

Pippa nodded. 'No problem. And by the way, who is

the guy over my right shoulder? The one in the pink shirt?'

I glanced over and my heart did a little leap, though I had no idea why. 'Oh, that's Adam's brother, James,' I said, far more casually than I felt.

'Oh my God. He is dish delish,' she said.

I smiled. 'He's taken, I'm afraid.'

'Aw, no way. Who by?'

I made a convincing show of looking around for a girl in a blue dress, but I was already pretty sure she wasn't there. I'd tried to find her before. So, either she hadn't come, or she was wearing a different colour.

The boys were getting rowdy again, and it was only a matter of time before one of them exposed their manhood to a bunch of like-minded exhibitionists.

The only saving grace was that Princess Pammie was in attendance, which went some way to sorting out the boys from the men. Though, if I had the choice, I'd rather see sixteen flaccid penises being paraded by their far-prouder-than-they-should-be owners, than Adam's mum. I should be saddened by that admission but, with half a bottle of prosecco inside me, I found it quite amusing. The very thought of it made me smile. I wasn't going to let her get to me, no matter how hard she tried.

'Wait a minute,' cried Pammie, as she scurried towards Adam across the wooden floor. Her long, tight-fitting skirt restricted her leg movements, making her top half look as if it were going faster than the rest of her. She pasted on a smile and gave a nod to the guests she hadn't yet acknowledged, as if it were her own party. 'Oh, Gemma, how lovely to see you,' she said, blowing a kiss.

I reminded myself of my mantra, as I watched her fawning and pontificating. *I won't let her get to me, no matter how hard she tries.*

'When you're ready, Mum,' Adam said over the loud-speaker.

'Yes, yes,' she huffed. 'I just want to get a photo.'

'What, *now*?' asked Adam.

'Yes, now,' tutted Pammie theatrically. Her audience tittered. She was at her best in front of a crowd, yet she pretended she hated it. 'Just a quick one, whilst we've got the chance, and before you all get pie-eyed. Now, where is everybody? Where's the family? I want one of all the family.'

Adam rolled his eyes, but watched patiently as the queen bee buzzed around, ushering her relatives into three rows of eight. James came from behind me and placed a hand in the small of my back as he passed.

'So, Lucy and Brad, you little ones kneel down here,' Pammie said. 'Your mum and dad can go behind, and Albert, you stand at the back. We won't be able to get you up again if you kneel down.'

Canned laughter from the gallery.

'Okay, have we got everybody? Emily? Where's Emily?' she called out.

I walked over, glass of prosecco in hand, conscious of the bystanders not invited to be a part of the Banks' family album.

'Adam, give me your phone,' demanded Pammie. 'Mine's no good. We'll take it on yours.'

Adam made a show of handing her his phone with mock reluctance.

'That's it. Now Emily, give me your glass.'

I did as I was told, and stood waiting to be directed into place, embarrassed by the quiet that was now descending over the drawn-out proceedings.

She stood back to check that everybody was in place. 'Okay Toby, you move a little bit across so I can squeeze in the middle. There you go.'

She turned and handed me the phone with a quick, 'Thanks, Emily,' before running into the frame, pasting on her best smile. 'Say cheese!'

A heat that started at the very tips of my toes worked its way up my body, like a rush of lava erupting from a volcano. Every inch of me tingled and my stomach lurched. The tell-tale pull at the back of my throat told me that tears were imminent, but I fought them back down, blinking furiously to stem the flow. I quickly turned my back on the other guests so that they couldn't see the humiliating redness creeping up my neck. I tried to smile, to pretend that I would never have expected to be in the 'family' photo. After all, I reasoned, I'm not family, so it's no big deal. Except it was, and it really hurt.

I looked at Adam on the back row, all smiles as I took the photo, with not a care in the world, and I felt my heart break in two.

'Okay, so where was I?' asked Adam, resuming his place behind the microphone.

I quickly lost myself in the watching crowd.

'Yes, yes,' persisted Adam over the din. 'Quieten down. I've got something important to say.'

The crowd hushed.

'So, now I'm thirty, I've got to be all grown up and mature.'

'That'll never happen,' shouted Deano, another team-mate, from the back.

'A-ha, you'd be surprised, my friend. So, first, I'd like to thank you all for coming. It means the world to me to have you all here. I'm especially chuffed that my cousin Frank flew over from Canada just to be here tonight.'

The crowd cheered, and more backslapping ensued.

'I'd also like to thank my beautiful girlfriend, Emily, for putting up with me and just being amazing. Em, where are you?'

I felt a hand on my back pushing me forward, but I kept my gaze down and feebly stuck a hand in the air to show where I was.

'Come on Em, come out here.'

I shook my head, but the pressure on my back was mounting, propelling me forward, when all I wanted to do was to go further back, into the shadows, where Pammie obviously believed I belonged.

I thought the very cheeks of me would explode with the heat trapped beneath them as I walked towards him. I could see James standing on the far side of the semi-circle that had been naturally created by bodies. Pippa was standing beside him. There was still no sign of a girl in a blue dress.

Every pore on my torso felt blocked, as if I was cooking from the inside, with no extractor fan to cool me down. I looked back to Pippa's concerned face, as she slowly mouthed, 'Arrre yooou oookkkaaay?' I gave her a small nod as I took Adam's hand, and fixed a smile onto my face.

'This woman here is my reason for living. She makes the good days even better and the bad days go away.'

A mist descended over my eyes, making everything blurry, but I could just make out Mum staring out from the circle, wide-eyed.

Adam turned to look at me. 'Honestly, I adore you. I couldn't live without you. You are the best thing that's ever happened to me.'

Embarrassed, I ruffled his hair in an attempt to lighten the situation and get the spotlight away from me. But then he dropped down onto one knee.

The *ahh*s turned to short, clipped gasps as I struggled to keep my vision steady. What the hell? Is he doing what I think he's doing, or is this a big joke? I looked around at all the pensive faces peering their heads into the bubble I'd created around me. Everything seemed to be going in slow motion, as if I was watching myself from outside my body. Adam's voice sounded as if he was under water and, all the time, the inane grins and wide eyes kept getting closer and closer. All except one, whose face, crumpled with grief, seemed to get further and further away.

'Will you please do me the honour of being my wife?' Adam said, one knee still on the ground.

I can't remember exactly when the whoops of joy turned to screams of horror. But I know I had a square-cut solitaire diamond on my finger by the time I was stroking Pammie's hair as she lay on the beer-sodden floor.

Adam was kneeling beside us, holding his mother's hand, and James was pacing the floor, telling the ambulance where to find us.

'Please hurry,' I heard him shout. 'She's out cold.'

It had all happened so fast that my brain couldn't process it. I'd lost the ability to put things in the order that they were occurring, no longer able to determine what was real and what I'd imagined in my head. Had Adam just asked me to marry him? Did Pammie really collapse? The edges between reality and make-believe were becoming more and more blurred with every passing second.

'Mum, Mum,' Adam was saying over and over again.

His voice becoming more animalistic with each frantic call.

Her head moved ever so slightly and she murmured her confusion.

'Mum,' Adam called out again. 'Oh, thank God. Mum, can you hear me?'

She didn't answer, her eyes just flickered open before closing again.

'Mum, it's James. Can you hear me?'

She murmured something inaudible.

A shaft of light pierced through as the crowd around us parted to let the paramedics in. They laid the stretcher down beside Pammie.

'It's okay, Mum,' said James, kneeling down beside me. 'You're going to be okay.'

He looked at me, panic-stricken, as if he expected me to say something that would take his pain away. I wished I could give him what he needed but, as I stared down at Pammie, I had nothing to offer him.

'Oh, Jesus Christ, please save her,' cried Adam, his shoulders beginning to rise and fall.

Mike put a steady hand on his back. 'It's going to be okay, mate. She's going to be okay.'

I watched numbly as they called her name, got no response, and lifted her onto the stretcher.

It wasn't my place to go in the ambulance. Adam and James went with her, whilst I was left in the surreal void they left behind: a celebration that had so abruptly been halted. The music had stopped, the lights were on, and the heart-shaped balloon that had carried my ring lay shredded on the floor, its shrivelled rubber now unrecognizable.

Shocked guests filed past me with sympathetic smiles, bidding premature farewells and their best wishes to pass on to Pammie and her boys. I vaguely remember one or two awkwardly wishing me luck for our engagement, their congratulations at odds with the commiserations that quickly followed.

'I'm so sorry, Em,' said Seb, reaching out to embrace me. 'I'm sure she'll be okay. What do you want to do? Shall I take you home, or do you want to stay here?'

I looked around the hall that, just fifteen minutes earlier, had been bursting with friends and family. The place where Adam had celebrated his thirtieth birthday and the place where he had asked me to marry him. Neither seemed to matter anymore.

'I guess I should see everyone off?' I asked, unsure of the right answer myself.

'We can get rid of everyone pretty quickly,' he said reassuringly. 'You get your stuff together and I'll chivvy the stragglers up. Okay?'

No. Nothing was okay. I'd just been proposed to, but could barely remember it now, the memory blurred and the occasion forever marred.

'Darling, I don't know what to say,' said my mum, arms outstretched, pulling me into her. 'Come here.'

The first tear fell then, and once the floodgate was open, I couldn't stop. Big wretched sobs racked my chest as my mother attempted to soothe me.

'Ssh, it's okay, everything's going to be okay.' There's something about your mother's voice that nobody else can replicate. That takes you back to school, when you were little and waiting in the nurse's office for her to come and pick you up. I remember being pushed over in the playground by a bully called Fiona, and hitting my forehead as I fell onto the black tar floor. A bump, of *Tom and Jerry* proportions, had throbbed just above my eye and the nurse had hurried me away to her office, which was actually just a little bed and desk behind a curtain in a side corridor.

I'm sure I would have been as right as ninepence if I'd just sat quietly for a few minutes before rejoining my class for our music lesson. But, by the time I was on that tiny chair behind the screen, all I wanted was my mum: to take away both my physical and emotional pain. My bump would no doubt disappear within hours, but the mental scar would remain. What if Fiona was mad with me for going to the nurse? Would she do it again tomorrow? Would she bully me forever? They were conundrums that only my mother could answer, well, at least in my nine-year-old's head. I felt guilty for making her leave work, but not guilty enough to say no when the nurse asked if I'd like to go home. I fretted over whether she would be cross with me. Whether my injury would be sufficient to warrant calling her. But I so needed to feel safe, it was a risk I was prepared to take. It felt like hours before she arrived, though I knew she was there even before I saw her. I just sensed her, and when she peered round that curtain I felt as if my heart was about to burst. That feeling, when only your mother will do, never really goes away, and as she whispers in my ear that everything will be all right, my heart breaks for Adam, who no doubt has the same memories, but is now in danger of losing the only person who can make everything better.

12

It was six o'clock in the morning when Adam called. Mum and Dad had come back with me, but had figured that I needed to sleep and had left me, with strict instructions to call them as soon as I heard anything. I couldn't have slept if you'd paid me. My mind was full of whirring thoughts, and I paced the kitchen floor with a large glass of red. Back and forth, until the shrill ring of my phone made me jump.

'Em?' He sounded tired.

'Yes, how is she?' I asked. 'What's happening?'

'She's okay,' his voice broke.

'She's going to be okay?'

I could hear soft sobs at the other end of the line.

'Adam . . . Adam.'

'I'm just so relieved.' He sniffed. 'I couldn't bear it if anything happened to her, Em. Honestly, I don't know what I'd do.'

'But she's going to be okay?' I asked again, desperate for confirmation.

'Yes. Yes. She's sitting up in bed, drinking a cup of tea, looking like she doesn't have a care in the world.' He let out a tight laugh.

My voice caught in my throat. 'So, what happened, then? What have the doctors said?'

'They've carried out all sorts of tests – blood pressure, heart, urine – and she's as good as new.'

I stayed silent.

'Em?'

'So, what could have caused it?' I asked, trying to keep the edge in my voice from creeping in.

If he noticed the intonation, he didn't say. 'They think it must have been a case of dehydration. She's admitted to not looking after herself these past few days, being all stressed about the party and forgetting to eat and drink. She's then gone and chucked back a couple of glasses of wine and it was goodnight-vienna.'

'Wow, so that's all it was?' I managed.

'Well, not exactly, dehydration is pretty serious in itself, but they've got her wired up to a saline drip and say she can leave as soon as the bag's finished. I'm going to bring her back to ours for a few days, just so she can rest and I can keep an eye on her.'

I could feel the sting of tears at the back of my throat. 'Why can't James look after her?' I blurted out, before I could stop myself.

'James?' he questioned, his tone a little tighter. 'Because he's busy and he's got enough to deal with. That girlfriend of his is still giving him the run-around and I don't think work is going too well. Anyway, we've got a spare bedroom now, thank God, so let's put it to use.'

'I assume she's going to let us sleep together at ours?' I asked curtly, trying to keep my selfish misery from creeping in.

He laughed, but it sounded empty. 'I think she's going to have to, don't you? Now that you're about to become Mrs Banks.'

I smiled through my tears, desperately trying to remember the moment he'd proposed; the moment that I'd spent years dreaming about. As a child, I'd imagined my prince going down on one knee and asking me to be his wife in front of thousands of people gathered in a town square. I'd had romantic notions of a cathedral wedding, with me dressed in vintage lace with a train the length of Princess Diana's – Mum had been a huge fan of hers, and I remember the Sunday morning that she had woken me up, with tears streaming down her face, to tell me that the Princess had died. We sat in front of the TV all day, along with millions of others, praying that someone had got it wrong. I was too young to understand who she was and how big a deal it was, but I remember being mesmerized by the clips of her wedding to Prince Charles – by how beautiful she was, and how magical her day had been. I'd spent weeks walking up and down the landing in a white Disney gown retrieved from the bottom of my dressing-up box, with a sheet pegged to the back of it. Whilst I was in cloud cuckoo land, my dad was complaining to anyone who would listen that I was a fire risk, and Stuart was trying

to relieve himself of his obligatory role as chief bridesmaid just as soon as he could.

I'd always assumed that when my moment came, it
would be ingrained in my memory forever, be something I could tell my children and grandchildren about.
I'd recount how I'd proudly shown off the promise of
betrothal as it sparkled on my finger. How I'd looked
deep into my fiancé's eyes before whispering yes. The
excitement of family and friends as they rushed to con-
gratulate us and ask when the impending nuptials were
likely to be.

Yet here I am, just a few hours later, barely able to
recall if it had ever happened. I must have said yes;
I had the ring to prove it. But as Pammie's collapse had
happened at precisely the same time, I couldn't picture
anything but the shock and horror etched on people's
faces, and the ensuing panic thereafter. It was as if our
moment had never happened at all.

'Might you stay up? Wait for us to get home?' Adam
asked.

I absently looked at my watch and acknowledged that
it was three minutes later than the last time I checked.
It didn't matter. Even though it was now Saturday, and
usually a work day for me, I'd already booked it off as
holiday. Though I'd presumed I'd be sleeping off a monster hangover, rather than staying up on my own, into
the early hours, wondering whether my future mother
in-law was going to last the night.

'I'll try,' I managed, 'but I can't promise anything.'

'It's been a hell of a night.' He sighed heavily. 'I was hoping we might be able to consummate our engagement.'

It was a statement rather than a question. I wondered how he could even think about sex at a time like this. But I guess in any other circumstances, it would have been a given. No doubt we would have spent the night and the entire following day in bed, alternating between making love and looking at wedding venues on our iPads. I couldn't imagine doing either of those now. I guess that must be one of the fundamental differences between how the male and female minds work.

'We'll see,' I said.

I put the phone down, poured myself another glass of wine, and sobbed hot selfish tears. Pity wasn't an emotion I often applied to myself, but it was the only one that I could relate to. I didn't feel happy or sad, I just felt incredibly sorry for myself, numb from the resounding questions spinning in my head. What had I done to deserve this? Was I really the best thing that had ever happened to Adam? Why did Pammie hate me so much?

But the question that banged on the door the loudest, the one I refused to let in, was: did she do it on purpose?

13

True to form, from the moment she'd arrived, Pammie had dominated our very existence, from moaning about the flat's temperature, to pulling a sulky face when Adam told her I'd made up the spare bedroom for her.

'But it's a single bed,' she whined. 'A put-you-up, no less. I won't get a wink of sleep in that.'

I knew what was coming before Adam even opened his mouth.

'Okay, why don't you go in our bed and Em can sleep in here?' I could feel him looking at me to gauge my reaction.

'Oh no, I can't put you out like that. Why don't you just take me home? I'll be fine there.'

I plumped up the pillows, willing myself to turn the conversation off in my head. I needed space. I needed to get out of there.

'Don't be silly,' said Adam. 'That's not a problem, is it, Em?'

I shook my head, still not looking at him. I didn't want to watch him as he pathetically grovelled to her.

'But where will *you* go?' she asked.

'I can bed down on the sofa for a few nights. It's honestly not a problem.'

'Well, if you're sure,' she went on. 'I really don't want to put anybody out.' How ironic, given that it seemed that that was precisely what she was put on earth to do.

Three days later, when she cleared the top of my dressing table into a box and replaced my lotions and potions with her own toiletries, I turned up on Seb's doorstep. 'I can't cope anymore. Can I stay at yours for a couple of nights, just till she goes home?'

'Of course you can,' he said, 'but are you sure it's the right thing to do? You're a proper couple now, not just playing at it. You're getting married, for God's sake, so you need to work through this together.'

'There is no "together" when it comes to his mum,' I complained. 'It's me against them. They come as a pair. He just doesn't see what she does and how she behaves.'

Seb let out a heavy sigh. 'Maybe he knows exactly what she's like and chooses to ignore it.'

I slumped back into his sofa, laying my head on its orange upholstery, remembering the night before. 'I do hope that's organic mince you're using?' she'd sniffed haughtily as she watched me stirring bolognese. 'It's what Adam prefers, and is so much better for him.'

'It's also three times the price,' I'd reminded her, wondering if 'organic' had even been invented when Adam was still living at home.

'I've spoken to Adam twice today but I forgot to ask

him what time he'll be home.' She'd then laughed, underlining how close they were. It wasn't lost on me that when I'd called him at lunchtime, he was too busy to speak, but not, it seemed, to her. Twice.

'He's working late,' I'd said abruptly. 'He'll be home around ten.'

'Do you not worry about him working such long hours?' she'd said.

I know I shouldn't rise to it, and I'm all too aware that I give her what she wants, but I almost want to test how much she knows. To see if she really does know more about Adam than I do.

'Why would I worry?' I'd said.

'Well, just that he's doing what he says he's doing.' She'd smirked. 'You never know what these young men get up to, especially someone as handsome as my Adam.'

I silently mimicked 'my Adam' as I continued to stir the bolognese, more furiously than before.

What was I supposed to say to that? What did she want me to say? That, up until now, it hadn't even occurred to me? But, hey, now you come to mention it, you could be right. Maybe he *is* screwing his twenty-two-year-old blonde colleague.

Instead, I'd said, 'He's got a lot on at the moment, but normally he's home by now.' Feeling as if I somehow needed to validate him, his work, and our relationship. To offer an excuse for something he so often did, which, until now, I'd not questioned. Largely.

'That may be so,' she'd said. 'But you need to be careful if he's feeling stressed. He only needs someone at work to turn his head and he'll be gone. It happens so easily these days.'

I sank further into Seb's sofa, brought my hands over my face, and let out a frustrated scream.

'She's undermining me in front of him all the time. But does he pick up on it? Does he say anything to her? Of course not.'

'He just wants an easy life, Em,' said Seb. 'It's probably his way of placating her. He's known her a long time, so we've got to assume that he knows what works and what doesn't.'

'But it's not about placating *her*. It's about standing up for *me*, the woman he supposedly wants to marry. Honestly, Seb, I'm really not sure I can go ahead if it stays the way it is.'

'Well, then, you've got to talk to him. Tell him exactly how you feel and how you need his support and backup on this issue.'

I nodded sagely.

'It's important, Em. This should be one of the happiest times of your life. You've got a great new flat together, he's gone and put a ring on it, and you're supposed to be planning your wedding. This is your happy time.'

'I know.' I sighed. 'I will talk to him. I have to. But can I stay here? Just for tonight?'

He nodded and went off to fetch another bottle of wine from the kitchen while I called Adam.

'What do you mean you're staying there?' he barked down the phone.

'I don't want to argue,' I said wearily. 'We're busy chatting and it's getting late. I'll pop back in the morning to get ready for work.'

'That's ridiculous,' he said. 'There's no need for you to stay there.'

'Adam, I'm tired, and to be honest, I need a break, just for tonight. It's gone ten already so it's not as if you're going to miss me.'

'Get yourself home now,' he said, before putting the phone down.

A burning sensation raged in my throat and hot tears sprang to my eyes. I battled to hold them back, but as soon as Seb walked back in the room, they sprang onto my cheeks.

'Hey, what on earth's the matter?' he said, pulling me towards him, the bottle still in his hand. 'What's happened?'

'He just . . . doesn't understand,' I said, between sobs.

'Come on now,' soothed Seb. 'Stay here tonight and everything will feel better in the morning. I promise.'

'I can't . . . I've got to go home . . .' I stuttered. I would have given anything to stay in Seb's embrace – it felt safe – but I had to go home. Adam was right.

Two days have since passed, and I still haven't had

the guts to say anything. Not because I'm worried I'm wrong, or I'm scared of Pammie finding out, but I just can't call which way Adam is going to go on this. How crazy is that? That I honestly don't know how the man I love, more than life itself, is going to react. And therein lies the problem: however long I've known him and however much I love him, I'll never be able to compete with his own mother. They have a bond like no other, one that simply cannot be broken or even tampered with.

'Emily, Emily.' I could hear her calling but needed to take one more deep breath before I answered.

'Yes, Pammie?'

'Be a love and pop the kettle on. I'm parched.'

I'd literally just walked through the front door. I was still in my coat, drenched from the sudden downpour that had started the minute I got off the train. She must have heard me as I struggled with the lock. I'd have to get the landlord to take a look at it before it seized up altogether.

I counted to ten and walked into the kitchen. All I wanted to do was pull out every sodding piece of crockery and smash it all over the floor. But, instead, I carefully placed her favourite cup onto the granite worktop and silently wondered how easy it would be to administer cyanide.

'Oh, you are a dear,' she said, shuffling in, much slower than I'm sure she was capable of.

'How's your day been?' she asked, but I didn't have time to answer. 'You'll see I did the washing up that was left from last night,' she went on, picking up a cloth and wiping down the spotless surfaces. 'If you leave that sort of thing lying around for too long, you'll end up with all kinds of pests, and I doubt your landlord would be too happy with that. He's probably got enough on his plate with that Italian restaurant downstairs. The mess and rubbish they leave out back is shocking. They'll have rats running amok all over the place.'

I gave her a fixed grin. It had been a long day, and all I wanted to do was have a bath, get my pyjamas on, and chill out on the sofa with a box set. Sex with my fiancé, for the first time in almost a week – in fact, since he'd proposed – would have been high on my to-do list as well, but seeing as he was out on a work do, and we had the devil incarnate sleeping in our bed, the chance of any intimacy was highly unlikely.

'Oh, you've got your hair different,' she said, as if seeing me for the first time. 'What have you done to it? Ooh no, I don't like that. I prefer it the other way. The way you usually have it.'

'I just got caught in the rain,' I said wearily. 'It goes a lot curlier when it's wet.'

She gave a little snigger. 'Don't be letting Adam see you like that. He'll wonder what on earth he's let himself in for.'

My coat still on, I poured myself a glass of wine from the fridge and headed to the bathroom.

'It's a bit early for that, isn't it?' was the last thing I heard before I slammed the door shut.

14

I waited up for Adam. His mother and I had spent the entire evening in a power struggle of the pettiest nature. From what we were having for tea, to who was in charge of the remote – anything that required a decision had us both vying for control. It was pathetic, and took me back to when I was a girl on the cusp of puberty, battling against the iron will of my ten-year-old brother.

'But you promised,' Stuart would whine, as I flicked over to *Blue Peter*. 'You said I could watch *Byker Grove* tonight. You pinkie-promised.'

'Did no such thing,' I'd snarl.

'Yes, you did. You watched *Blue Peter* yesterday. It's my turn today.'

I'd glare back at him. I glared a lot during those years. A sullen look seemed to garner a far better response than the confused vocabulary that often spilled out of my mouth. The thoughts I had in my head rarely had any correlation to how they were voiced.

I find myself sulking again tonight, with Pammie, who I've now decided to refer to as Pamela, as it suits her better; it's not nearly as friendly or affectionate-sounding. I also happen to know she hates it.

'There's a programme I wanted to watch tonight,' she said.

'Oh, me too,' I replied, surreptitiously reaching for the remote on the sofa between us. 'What's it called?'

'*Britain's Biggest Scams*, or something like that.'

'Ah, mine's a drama.' I feverishly flicked through the channels searching for anything that sounded or looked vaguely dramatic. I reluctantly settled on a repeat of *Pride and Prejudice*, something so far off my wish list that, if Adam had been there, he would have referred to it as 'my worst nightmare'. But such was the underlying battle of wills between us, that I would have gladly watched anything rather than let her get her own way.

'Why don't you go to bed?' she said, half an hour later, as my eyes began to close and I loosened my grip on the remote, feeling it sliding towards the chasm between us.

Her voice coursed through me, bringing me back into the room.

'What? Why?'

She laughed. 'You're obviously tired out. Go to bed, I'll stay up for Adam.'

'He's thirty years old, Pamela' – I saw her wince – 'neither of us needs to stay up for him, least of all his mother.'

'I always used to wait up for my Jim,' she said.

'He was your husband.'

'And soon, Adam will be yours. It's what a wife's

supposed to do. Not a single night went by when I'd go to bed without him.'

'I suppose you put a ribbon in your hair as well, did you?' I mumbled.

'What?'

'I think you'll find times have changed since you were married.'

'I'll have you know I'm still married, young lady. And if you plan on your marriage surviving much past a year, you'd do well to take a leaf out of my book. You should be subservient. You shouldn't even be out there working all the hours that you do. A woman's place is in the home.'

I let out a loud guffaw. 'Talking of home, when do you plan on returning to yours? You'll have been here a week tomorrow.'

She made a grab for the remote control resting on my knee. I got there first. This was ridiculous.

'When Adam is happy for me to,' she snapped.

'Adam? It's not his decision.'

'We spoke a couple of days ago.' Her tone was conspiratorial, intended to let me know that they'd had a conversation which I had no part in. 'And he said he feels more comfortable knowing I'm here, where he can look after me.'

But he's not looking after you, I am, I thought bitterly.

'So, when Adam and I feel I'm well enough, I'll go back home.' She yawned and looked at her watch.

'Of course, Pamela. You should only go when you feel ready. I'd hate to think of anything happening to you whilst you're on your own. I mean, you could go again at any time, so we need to be careful.' I put the 'go' in speech marks with my fingers. I don't know whether her jaw clenched at *that*, or being called 'Pamela' again.

'It's late. You go to bed. I'll wait up for Adam,' I went on. 'You're right. I should stay up for him. You never know what he might need or want.'

Her face didn't show it, but we both knew it was one point to me.

'Good girl,' she said, pushing herself up off the sofa.

I watched as she stood and stretched her arms high above her head. Something she never would have done in front of Adam, for fear of showing how agile she really was. She'd become a master of deception, subtly changing her demeanour, prowess, and even her voice, I'd noticed, when he was around.

'So, you'll make sure he gets in safely?'

I nodded.

'And if he's been drinking, don't start with your nagging. He's allowed off the leash every once in a while.'

I looked at her, and shook my head in disbelief. I wondered if she'd really had the kind of marriage she purported to have had with Jim. I couldn't see her as a downtrodden wife, waiting on her husband's every whim and fancy. She was too strong a character. But then, perhaps it was losing him that had given her such strength. She'd had to step up to care for her two boys. I couldn't ever imagine being able to do that. I wondered if that had created this abnormal bond. One that she now felt was threatened by her sons being in normal relationships. There was a tiny part of me that could begin to feel sorry for her, that wanted to sit her down and tell her that I wasn't taking her son away. That she could still be a part of his life, *our* life. It didn't have to be this virtual tug of war, with both of us seemingly trying to prove who Adam loved the most. But then I remembered all the things she'd done and said, the unnecessary hurt she'd caused me. We could have been friends. Christ, she might even have gained a daughter, something she'd once told me she felt she'd missed out on. But that chance had been and gone – all of her own doing – and if that's how she wanted it to be, then so be it, but I wasn't going to allow her to break me down, especially in my own home. She had to go.

The DVD player had illuminated 12:24 the last time I looked, but God knows what time it was when Adam fell on my head in a clumsy attempt to get his shoes off.

'Jesus Christ,' he said, in answer to my yelp. 'What are you doing there?'

I sat up, bleary-eyed, on the sofa, my neck knotted and tight. 'Waiting for you, like a good wifey,' I whispered, still trying to get my bearings.

He was shoeless and standing in front of me, swaying

ever so slightly. 'Ah, that's so sweet,' he managed. 'What have I done to deserve this?'

'It's not so much about what you deserve, as about what I need,' I said, half laughing, pulling him towards me by his belt. 'It's been such a long time.' His trouser zip was in line with my face, and I reached for it.

'We can't,' he mumbled, half-heartedly. 'She might come in.'

I shrugged my shoulders and carried on.

'Ssh, no, Em. Seriously, we can't.' He was giggling now and I knew I was going to get my own way because I knew he wanted me to.

'It's been almost a week,' I whispered, my hands still busy. 'How much longer are we expected to wait?'

He suddenly held my fumbling hands still. 'Just a little longer. Till she's back on her feet properly.'

'*How* much longer?' I went on, brushing his hand aside. 'I need a date, something I can work towards, to know when we'll finally get our flat back.'

'I know it's hard, Em, but just give it a few more days.'

'So, by Sunday?' I pushed.

He hesitated.

'Promise me Sunday, or I'm going to carry on.'

'That puts me in a lose–lose situation.' He laughed.

I took him in my hand and felt his whole body tense.

'Christ,' he breathed.

'What's it going to be?' I teased. 'Say Sunday and I'll stop.'

I picked up the pace.

'Jesus, Em.'

'Sunday and stop, or Sunday and keep going?' He was right – he couldn't win.

He moaned, and I knew there was no way he was going to ask me to stop now. 'Just keep going,' he whispered. 'Don't stop.'

That's what I thought. The dynamics in this three-way relationship needed to shift, and darling Pammie needed to know that it was me and Adam against the world, together as equals, as the couple we were, not the two separate entities that she'd confused us for, in her warped, twisted mind.

I could never have imagined that seeing her angelic son in my mouth would do the trick.

15

We didn't hear anything from Adam's mum for three weeks after she'd walked in on us. The shock of seeing us in such a compromising position had, apparently, left her shell-shocked and emotionally scarred.

'No mother should ever have to see that,' she'd dramatically confessed to James, who told us when he popped by to talk about the arrangements for our impending wedding. There'd been a sudden flux of activity as Adam had found a beautiful hotel in Tunbridge Wells that had a chapel attached, and with only one Saturday free this side of summer, we'd gone ahead and booked it. Now, faced with only a couple of months to organize everything, the panic was setting in and things were having to get sorted on the tout de suite, though I imagined the stag arrangements would get more airtime between James and Adam.

'I don't want to discuss this,' Adam had snapped, as the three of us stood in the kitchen, listening to James recount his mother's overwrought outburst. I made to go to him, but he turned away and huffed off towards the bedroom, leaving James and me in his wake.

We both pulled faces and stifled a giggle. A dimple

dented his left cheek. 'I feel bad for laughing, but if I don't, I'm going to cry,' I said.

James peered at me over the top of his coffee mug, his eyes smiling. 'It could have been worse.'

I looked at him as if he was mad. 'Er, how exactly?'

'Well, I don't know,' he mumbled. 'But I'm sure there's someone out there who's been in a worse predicament.'

'Oh, and that's supposed to make me feel better, is it?' I laughed.

He put a finger to his lips. 'Ssh, don't let him hear us laughing. He'll only get mad.'

'He's mad enough already,' I said quietly. 'He's been foul ever since it happened. He blames me for doing it in the first place.'

'You've got to be kidding me?'

I shook my head.

'Well, maybe he needs to be reminded that it takes two to tango?' He raised his eyebrows.

I was aware that we were talking in hushed voices, and didn't want Adam to think we were talking about him, even though we were.

'So . . .' I said loudly. 'Another coffee?' I couldn't think of anything else to say. He held up his half-full mug and shook his head. I made myself another, banging about in the kitchen as I did so.

'Any ideas on what we can do about your mother?' I asked, aware that I might be crossing a line. I screwed up my face as I waited for his response.

'She'll get over it,' he said softly.

I smiled. 'I don't think it'll be anytime soon. You know what your mum's like. She'll drag it out for as long as she can.' I wasn't sure whether I'd meant to say that out loud.

'Her bark's worse than her bite,' he said, after a long pause. 'She'll come round.'

The breath that I'd been holding in escaped through my lips, and the tension in my shoulders ebbed away. If Adam hadn't been in the next room, I would have told James everything. It was all there, waiting on the tip of my tongue, desperate to get out. I wished that Adam could be more like James, it would be easier to talk to him about his mother. James would understand how I felt, how *she* made me feel. He'd support me and back me up when she had me in a corner. I knew he would.

He smiled that smile again, as if he was reading my mind. 'She just needs a bit of time, that's all.'

I didn't mind that. She could have all the time in the world. Take as long as she needed. It wasn't as if I was missing her. If the truth be known, I was secretly thrilled that it had put some distance between her and us. But I ought to be careful what I wished for, as, since it all happened, Adam's sex drive had fallen through the floor. It was nigh on impossible to get him in the mood for anything other than a chaste kiss when he left for work. I tried to convince myself that it was just a coincidence, that he was under pressure at work and was tired. But every time I pictured Pammie seeing us, and feeling the shock run through Adam's body, I knew it had had a bigger effect on him than I could even begin to imagine.

'I'm sorry, I just don't feel like it,' he said, later that night, as I sauntered into the bedroom in a new lacy underwear set from Victoria's Secret.

'When do you think you might feel like it?' I said sulkily. 'Anytime soon?'

'Just not tonight.'

'But I can make all your troubles slip away,' I teased, as I got into bed and reached for him.

'Just give it a break,' he snapped, before turning his back on me and switching off the light.

My mood wasn't helped any the next morning, when two of my trainees called in sick. I knew one of them was flaky, but I was surprised and disappointed with Ryan. His diary was chock-a-block with appointments, which left me having to juggle both our schedules and somehow work a miracle by being in two places at once.

By midday, I felt like I had steam coming out of my ears. My boss, Nathan, wanted me to step into a new business pitch, and a client I'd been working on for weeks was about to award the contract to a rival agency. I had allowed for neither.

My mobile had rung at least thirty times, and my stress level was increasing with every call.

'Yep, Emily Havistock,' I barked, a tad more aggressively than I'd intended.

'That bad, eh?' said the male voice.

'Sorry? Who's calling?' I hadn't recognized the number, and already regretted answering it. I didn't have time for a cold caller.

'It's James,' he replied.

I waited for something to click. 'Sorry, James . . . ?'

'Adam's brother,' he offered hesitantly.

'Oh,' I said, 'sorry, I was trying to place a James at work. Hi, how are you? I'm not with Adam, if that's why you're calling. Is it Pammie? Is she okay?' I was rambling as my mind raced through a million different scenarios.

'Yeah, she's fine. It's all good.'

I was rather hoping for more than that, but he was making me work for it. 'So, what's up?' I asked. 'Are you okay?'

It felt odd to be talking to James on the phone. Texting was somehow different. Our once-easy friendship felt like it was crossing a line.

'Yes, I'm all good.' He drew it out slowly. I waited, unsure what to say next.

'It's just that . . . erm . . . I'm in your area, and wondered if you were free for a quick coffee?'

'What?' I don't know if I said it out loud.

'Hello?'

'Erm, yeah, hi.'

'I didn't catch that. Was that yes or no?'

'Ah . . . I'm sorry, I'm in Canary Wharf right now.

That would have been great, but I'm up to my neck in it today. I've got back-to-back appointments. They drive us hard in this industry.' I heard myself give a fake laugh to lighten the mood. I doubted he knew me well enough to tell.

I thought of the man at the other end of the line. I'd always pictured him up to his ankles in soil, raking over a flowerbed and wiping his hands down a grubby grey t-shirt that used to be white. His features, so much like Adam's, but younger, sharper, more chiselled. His fingernails caked in dirt as he pushed back his hair from his face.

Now he was here, in what I'd heard him refer to as the concrete metropolis. I'd assumed he wasn't a fan of the city, so what was he doing here? And would he now be in a suit, walking through the maze of high-rise buildings, becoming more and more desperate to return to the green pastures that he adored?

The realization that I'd imagined him, and clearly not for the first time, made me blush.

I stuttered into the gaping silence, 'Erm – maybe another time?'

'Yeah, sure, no biggie,' he said quickly, sounding embarrassed and desperate to get off the phone.

I said goodbye into the silence he left behind, and stood stock-still on the corner of Cabot Square, the bitter wind whistling around me, perplexed and staring at my phone.

I tried to concentrate on work, but there was a niggle at the back of my mind that I just couldn't shake off. *I'm in your area . . . ?* Was he really, or was it more contrived than that? And if it was, why?

16

I don't know why I didn't tell Adam that James had called. I felt I should mention it, but was there really anything to tell? As James said, it was 'no biggie'. Yet, had Adam called James's girlfriend, on the off chance, just because he was passing, I'd have thought it spoke volumes. I was well aware there were double standards at work here.

I'd spent the three weeks since the 'incident' trying to apply the same grown-up attitude to the stalemate that remained between me and Pammie. What had happened was regrettable, but once I really thought about it, it occurred to me that the issue was far greater for Adam and his mum than it was for me. Yes, I was embarrassed, but I was merely a pawn caught in the middle. If, God forbid, it had happened the other way around, and it had been *my* mum that had seen what Pammie saw, I'd have been absolutely devastated. So, although I doubted that she'd ever be my favourite person in the world, I decided I'd try my utmost to make it up to her, when the time was right. Though I hadn't expected to put my new-found philosophy to the test so soon.

We arranged to meet for lunch, the following Sunday,

in a fish restaurant in Sevenoaks. 'I think it would be better if we met on neutral territory,' Pammie said. She made it sound like two heads of state were meeting in an attempt to stave off World War III. So, doing what we were told, as we always do, we met in Loch Fyne, just off the High Street. We parked up in a bay round the back of Marks & Spencer and Adam threw his arm around me as we cut through the passageway. It was a simple enough gesture, and one that he'd done a hundred times before, but when we'd not slept together for almost a month, his touch sent shivers through me. *I'll try again when we get home*, I thought to myself. But there are only so many times you can keep putting yourself out there, knowing that you are going to be rejected. I keep a thin smile pasted onto my face and pretend it doesn't matter, pulling him towards me for a cuddle, on the odd occasion he'll let me. But it does matter. It really hurts, and once again, it's all her fault.

A chilly breeze took me by surprise as we rounded the corner and I pulled my coat tightly around me, thankful for both it and the chunky-knit jumper I had on underneath. It wasn't my most glamorous look, but I wasn't feeling in the least bit glamorous. I hadn't even bothered to wash my hair this morning. It was almost a waste of shampoo and conditioner, as she was going to make a derisory comment regardless, whether my hair was in a greasy ponytail or cascading over my shoulders in shiny, bouncy curls.

Even though we were five minutes late, I knew she wouldn't be there. She never is. She likes to give it a good fifteen minutes before making her entrance, both to ensure she has everyone's attention, and to save her feeling embarrassed whilst she waits on her own. There's many a trick up Pammie's sleeve, and I've learnt a few, but I imagine even I would be shocked if I knew them all.

'So, are we going to talk about what happened?' I asked Adam, as the maître d' took his coat. I opted to keep mine on until I'd thawed out a little.

'No,' was all I got in response.

'But don't you think it needs to—'

'Jesus, Em. Just leave it alone. She's been through enough. I'm sure she doesn't need it to be raked up again. I know I sure as hell don't.'

Oh, what a joy this was going to be. Two, possibly three, hours stuck between a woman who couldn't stand the sight of me and a fiancé who couldn't bear to be near me. It only occurred to me then, as we were sitting down at a booth-like table, that James might come along as well, to support his poor aggrieved mother. Great, could this get any worse?

Right on cue, a quarter of an hour after we'd arranged to meet, in came Pammie, her face a complicated mixture of love and hatred. She gave Adam a big hug as she greeted him.

'Oh, darling, it's so good to see you, I was beginning

to wonder . . .' She left it hanging there, and looked down to the floor with sad eyes for maximum effect.

'And Emily?' she said, turning to me, almost feigning surprise that I was there. 'It's been a while.' Her tone was cold and she'd already turned away from me when she said, 'But you're looking well. You've put some weight on, which was much needed.'

I signalled to Adam, in the hope that he'd see my plight, but he just discreetly shook his head and looked back to her.

'I haven't, actually, it must just be this big coat and jumper.' I said, pulling at the rib of it as if to prove its volume, but they were both already chatting about something else.

Three glasses of Pinot Grigio in, and it was just getting worse. It felt like they had their own private club, one which I didn't have a membership to.

'Oh, do you remember when you and James found those crabs on the beach in Whitstable?' She laughed.

Adam grinned widely. 'And we wrote our names on their backs and raced them.'

'That's right,' she said, through an over-exaggerated fit of the giggles.

'Mine never won,' he said.

'Wasn't there an almighty rumpus over something?' asked Pammie. 'I remember James crying all the way home.'

Adam rolled his eyes. 'Don't you remember? He got

all stressed because we went to fill our buckets up from the sea, only to come back and find his crab all smashed up.'

Pammie nodded slowly. 'I remember. I still don't know how that could have happened.'

Adam laughed. 'A rock must have come in with the tide and given it a proper bashing. Or else it was the perfect murder . . .'

He looked at me. 'And I've never eaten crab since.'

I forced a smile.

I tried to reassure myself that he was just putting on a show, to get their relationship back on track, but what about *our* relationship? Isn't that the one that needed saving? We had barely spoken since she'd walked in on us, let alone been intimate, and it was all beginning to gnaw away at me . . . nibbling, nibbling. Everything between us would be perfect if she just behaved normally, like a mother is supposed to.

By glass four, just around the time she was asking Adam what they could buy Linda's son Ewan for his twenty-first, I could feel an unpleasant sensation rising up within me.

'So, you think a nice wallet would be well received?' She was asking Adam, not me. She'd not looked at me since her comment about my weight, and even then, I don't think she actually saw me. If she had, she might have noticed that I'd actually lost weight, but what would be the fun in that?

'I think he'd be chuffed with that. If we all chip in fifty quid I reckon we can get him something decent, perhaps a Paul Smith,' said Adam.

'Okay,' Pammie wheezed, all excited. 'I'll put in fifty pounds, you put in fifty pounds and James we'll have to see about, as you know he doesn't earn as much as you.'

She was speaking directly to Adam.

'I'll obviously put in twenty-five,' I butted in. 'Half of Adam's share, just so, you know, it's from the both of us.'

She looked at me with real disdain. 'Thank you, dear, but that really won't be necessary. It's a present from the family.' She gave a light laugh and turned back to Adam.

'But I am family,' I hissed. I knew I'd had too much to drink because my mouth didn't feel like it was a part of me. My lips were moving, but I couldn't control what was coming out of them.

'That's all right, Em. I'll put in for us,' said Adam.

'I don't want you to put in for me,' I said, emphasizing 'put in'. 'If my name's going to be on the gift tag, then I'd like to contribute.'

Pammie tutted and looked at me patronizingly. Her rimless glasses were perched on the end of her nose, making her look like a headmistress.

'Okay.' Adam sighed. 'Do what you want to do.'

'Well, it seems ridiculous to me,' laughed Pammie. 'You hardly know him, so you shouldn't have to dig into your pocket when it's not even your family.'

'But Adam's family *is* my family.' I didn't seem to have any control over the volume of my voice. 'We're getting married in two months, and I will become Mrs Banks.' I saw her visibly flinch. 'And as such, we'll all be family.'

'If that's what she wants to do Mum, then that's fine,' said Adam.

Yes! Thank you, Adam.

'Well, I just think . . .' started Pammie, but I held my hand up, signalling for her to stop.

'And whilst we're at it,' I said, 'are none of us going to be brave enough to address the elephant in the room?'

'That's enough, Emily,' said Adam, a hardness to his voice.

'That's enough of what, Adam?' I'd wanted to stay so composed, be in control, but it felt as if weeks of pent-up frustration were bursting to get out. 'Does your mother have any idea what our relationship has been like these past few weeks? Since she "discovered" us, doing what most normal couples do?' I used to hate people who put words in speech marks with their hands, but with her I couldn't help myself.

Pammie tutted in disgust, and Adam took hold of my elbow. 'Sorry, Mum,' he said, as he guided me up and out of my chair. 'I don't know what's come over her. I'm really sorry.'

'It's what couples in love do,' I sneered, shrugging off Adam's grip. 'You must remember that—'

'Emily!' shouted Adam. 'Enough.'

He tightened his grip on my arm. 'I'm so sorry, Mum,' I heard him gush, forever trying to placate her. 'Will you be okay getting home?'

'Of course,' she replied, shooing us away from the table. 'I'll be fine, you've got enough on your plate. Don't worry about me, just see that you get her home safely.'

Adam offered her a tight smile as he pushed me towards the door. 'I'll call you once we're home,' he said. I pulled a face, as if mimicking him, and turned my head back to where she was sitting, expecting to see her pitiful face, the one she reserved for Adam, to let him know how hurt and vulnerable she was. Except *he* wasn't looking, *I* was. So instead, she smiled slowly and raised a half-full glass of red wine.

I can't recall another word being said until we got home, when he put his key in the front door and said, 'You're drunk. Go upstairs and sort yourself out.'

Yes, I was tipsy, I'd had one or two more than I should have, but I didn't say anything I didn't want to say. Had I been more sober, I would have perhaps approached it in a slightly different way, but it was what it was, and I didn't regret it. The only part of it that stung was that, once again, I'd been made to look like the bad guy, whilst she remained firmly on her throne.

17

It took three days for Adam to talk to me, bar saying, 'Excuse me', as we met each other coming in and out of the bathroom. And when the ice was finally broken, there was no big sit-down heart-to-heart, which is what we so desperately needed, it was, 'What do you want to do for dinner tonight?'

'I don't mind. Fancy a takeaway?'

'Okay, then. Indian or Chinese?'

And so, we were at least back on speaking terms. I wasn't intending to apologize to him, and it seemed he wasn't prepared to apologize to me, so we were right back where we started.

We exchanged pleasantries as we ate, but it felt awkward, like two strangers meeting on a blind date. His eyes never left his chicken chow mein for fear of them meeting mine.

'So, how's Jason doing at work?' I asked. I was more interested in how the new girl, Rebecca, was getting on, but it felt too risky a subject to bring up, so I settled for the safe option.

'Yeah, he's okay,' he said. 'He seems to have upped his game, so we'll see. And Ryan? How's he doing?'

'Better, thankfully. He's a good kid, and I think he's got real potential, but he's young and can't quite see it yet. It's a shame because I think they might get rid of him before we see what he's capable of.'

A silence stretched out between us as we both contemplated what to say next.

'So, what's going to happen with Mum, then?' he asked.

The question blindsided me. I wasn't expecting him to go there and, despite my best efforts, I felt my mouth drop open.

'Because clearly something has got to shift. I can't go on with things the way they are between you. You've obviously got an issue with her – or is it an issue with yourself? Is it that she just brings out the worst in you?'

I sighed heavily.

'You can't deny that something's going on,' he continued. 'You seem so tense whenever she's around, or even when she comes up in conversation. I feel like I'm walking on eggshells whenever her name's mentioned. You make me feel bad for wanting to see her, or even talk to her.'

'You don't see how she is,' I offered meekly.

'But I've never seen or heard her be anything other than perfectly civil to you. Why wouldn't she be? She thinks you're great. She always has.'

'You just don't get it.'

He pushed his plate away and folded his arms on the

table. 'Well, explain it to me, then. She's always looked out for you, hasn't she? Made you feel part of the family?'

I let out a small laugh. It wasn't meant to sound sarcastic, but that's how it came out.

He groaned. 'See, there you go again. What exactly is the problem?'

I didn't know how to explain it to myself, let alone to him, without it coming across as petty.

'Okay, so I'll give you an example.' I racked my brain for an easy one, but nothing was forthcoming. 'Erm . . .'

He politely stayed quiet while I thought, but I was beginning to feel like a fraud.

'Okay, so how about last Sunday, at lunch in the fish restaurant?'

'Christ, how can I forget that? You completely showed us up.'

I took a deep breath. I needed to keep my cool. I needed to explain myself eloquently and succinctly to have any hope of him understanding where I was coming from.

'So, she made an unpleasant comment about my weight as soon as she got there.' I cringed as I said it. I sounded like a schoolgirl.

'Oh, for God's sake, Em. Are you serious? Isn't that what most mothers do? Is that the extent of what we're talking about here?'

I smiled as I thought of my mum, who berated me

for asking for seconds, yet pushed me when I didn't. But then I pulled myself up. Pammie was not *my* mother.

'At your party, she lined everybody up for the family photo, and asked me to take it.' I really wanted to tell him that I thought she'd faked her fainting fit, but if I was wrong he'd never talk to me again, and there was no way of ever proving me right.

He looked at me blankly. 'And?'

'Well, I wasn't in it.'

'It was a photo.' He looked at me incredulously. 'There was lots going on, loads of people there . . . I'm sure there were other family members that were left out, but it wouldn't have been intentional.'

'But she asked me to take it,' I said, already feeling defeated.

'You're bigger than this, surely?' he questioned. 'Even if Mum has her little foibles – and believe me, I know she has them – are you not better to rise above it? So that we can get on with our lives, rather than you making a meal out of everything she says or does? And I'm not being funny, Em, but you make it sound as if she's got some kind of vendetta against you. She's over sixty years old, for Christ's sake. What do you think she's going to do? Run after you and batter you to death with her umbrella?'

I had to laugh. He was right, it did make me sound pathetically insecure and immature, and I am not that person. I am someone who can hold my own in any situation, fight my own battles, give as good as I get. Aren't I?

'So, do you promise you'll give her a chance?' he asked. 'For me?'

I looked up at him and nodded.

'Adam?' I said softly. He looked at me then, really looked at me. I could feel the intensity of his eyes as they bored into me. My stomach flipped and I felt a rush of heat, reminding me of our first time, when my senses were so overwhelmed it felt like a massive bundle of nerves had pooled in the pit of my tummy. A million and one scenarios had whirred around my brain then, each contradicting the one before.

I thought all those things again as he stared at me, except now it felt like there was a lot more to lose if I got it wrong. These weren't the heady days when one love affair merged into another, without risk. This was my future, our future, and it needed to be handled carefully.

The corners of his mouth turned up, ever so slightly, giving me all the indication I needed.

I stood up, leant across the table to kiss him on the lips and, without saying a word, walked out of the room.

He mumbled something but I didn't want to hear his excuses. I wanted him to make love to me. I *needed* him to make love to me.

By the time he came into the bedroom, I was un-dressed, bar the black-lace lingerie set he'd bought me from Agent Provocateur the previous Christmas. He either grinned or grimaced, I'm not sure which, as I walked towards him, the light from the solitary bedside lamp casting a warm glow across the room.

My heart raced and was thumping out of my chest, like an inexperienced young girl being intimate for the first time. I felt like I was moving in slow motion, as if my body was preparing itself for fight or flight, ready to take the knock-back as it came hurtling towards me. But would we be able to come back from this if he rebuffed me again? I almost didn't want to take the chance, yet, at the same time, my brain was screaming at me to keep going, to find out if we were going to be able to move forward, to become the couple we once were.

He came towards me, slowly, and, as we stood facing each other, I took his face in my hands, his soft stubble tickling my palms as I stared at him intently.

'Are we okay?' I whispered.

He nodded. 'I hope so. I just don't know if—'

I put my finger to his lips. I kissed him, softly at first, but then more deeply as I responded to his urgency. We fell onto the bed, and I could feel him as I pulled at his trousers, desperately trying to undo the buttons. So many thoughts cluttered my head, making it a much bigger deal than it should have been – I was desperate to close the gaping chasm that had appeared in our once perfect relationship. Sex wasn't everything, I knew that, but having lost that closeness, it highlighted so many other insecurities. I'd questioned my own attractiveness, my ability to turn him on, whether he was seeing someone else. I needed this for me, and I needed it for him, so that we both knew that it was going to be okay.

He knew before me that it wasn't going to happen.

'Leave it,' he said, pushing me away with his hand.

'Just relax,' I offered, determined to continue.

'I said, leave it.' His frustration was shared by us both.

I wanted to ask what I was doing wrong, but that seemed like something an actress would say in some B-rated coming-of-age movie. I needed to appear confident, even if I didn't feel it.

I moved towards him again. 'Do you want me to try—'

'For fuck's sake, Em,' he snapped. 'How clear do I have to make it? It's not going to happen.'

Inside, I crumbled, all thoughts of myself as an attractive, sexual woman broken into a million tiny pieces. I'd failed. It had always been so easy before, we were so in tune with each other and both knew what to do and when to do it. Nobody had ever made me feel like Adam did, and he said the same of me, so how had it all gone so wrong? I had to make this okay.

In one last attempt, I straddled him.

'Jesus Christ,' he yelled, pushing me off and jumping

up from the bed before hastily pulling on his boxer shorts. 'What bit are you not understanding?'

I sat up, stock-still.

'Just relax . . . Do you want me to try . . .' he mimicked. He was pacing up and down across the room.

'But we just need to—'

'*We* don't need to do anything,' he spat. 'It's not your problem. It's mine. So, quit telling me what *we* need to do and what *we* ought to try.'

His spit was hitting my face and I pulled back. I'd never seen him like this before.

I shook my head numbly. 'I'm only trying to help,' I said, my voice barely audible.

'Well, I don't need your help. I need a fucking miracle.' He walked out of the room and slammed the door so violently that the architrave broke away from its fixings.

I sat there, dumbstruck. My eyes stung and I chastised myself for being so selfish. This wasn't about me. This was about him.

I thought back to the last time we'd attempted to be intimate, albeit briefly, when his mother had been staying over. I remembered him recoiling away from me in horror as she called out his name, like a teacher telling off a naughty schoolboy. 'Adam! What on earth do you think you're doing?' she'd cried.

It was as if her walking in on us, seeing what she had seen, had caused him physical pain. Maybe it had, but even now that that pain has surely gone, the mental block remained, and that was so much harder to recover from.

18

I hadn't expected to hear from James again but, a week after his first call, he claimed to be 'just passing', and, as I had a free half hour and was beyond curious as to what he actually wanted, I found myself agreeing to meet him for a coffee.

We were nestled in the corner of a tiny Turkish cafe on Villiers Street, the windows steamed with condensation as the heat of the interior fought against the bitter chill outside. It was unsettling that the man behind the counter was barking out orders. Who eats kebabs at 11 a.m. on a Wednesday morning anyway? But at least it created a diversion from the odd feeling of intimacy that being with James created. I kept telling myself that he'd soon be my brother-in-law, which made this perfectly normal, yet it still felt wrong. Was that just me, or did he feel it as well?

'So . . .' he began, before I had the chance to say the same. It seemed the only opener to a conversation, the direction of which was entirely in his hands. Though now it appeared that even he didn't know where it was heading.

'How's things?' he asked.

'All good, yeah, all really good,' I said too quickly. 'How about you? Still with Chloe? All going good?' I had no idea why I'd mentioned his girlfriend, a woman I'd never met, before asking about his business. Or indeed why I'd used so many 'goods' in one sentence. The sense of ease I'd always felt around James had been replaced by an unnerving tension, our usual banter now stilted conversation.

'It's up and down,' he said, 'but it's still early days.'

'How long's it been?' I enquired, as casually as I could.

'Oh, only four or five months, so anything could happen.' He raised his eyebrows and laughed. 'You know what I'm like. I haven't exactly got a great track record.'

I smiled awkwardly. I didn't know what he was like, not really, so his comment made it sound as if we were closer than we were.

He edged his arms out of his navy wool overcoat, his elbow banging on the peeling dado rail that ran around the tight corner we were sitting in. He mouthed 'Ow', and I laughed, as he untied a tan scarf from his neck to reveal a smart blue shirt with the distinguishable polo player on a horse emblem on its top pocket. Adam favoured a certain Mr Lauren's brand as well, but whereas his shirts were bursting at the seams, due to his broad shoulders and gym-honed upper arms, James looked comfortable in his, and the collar sat just as it should.

'And work? Are you busy?' I asked.

He nodded as he took a sip of his cappuccino, leaving a white foam moustache above his top lip. I laughed and gestured to my own. His cheeks flushed a little.

'Yeah, it's going great. I've had to take two guys on to help me out, and I'm here in town for another meeting to hopefully secure some corporate work.'

'Oh, great,' I offered, already thinking of another question to ask.

'A developer is looking for a local business to take care of some communal gardens, for a new residential site up by Knole Park.'

I nodded. I'd heard Pammie talking about Knole Park, but I couldn't recall ever going or its exact whereabouts.

'I've got to go and pitch to them at the company headquarters in Euston but I was a tad early, so I thought I'd see if you were about. You don't mind, do you?'

'Not at all. It's worked out well, as I have an appointment in Aldgate. I'm just sorry that I wasn't able to catch up last time you called. I'm often here, there and everywhere.'

'No worries, it was just on the off chance. I know how busy you are. Still, you're here now.'

I looked at him and smiled.

'And how's your mum?' I really didn't care, but it felt rude not to ask.

'She's okay. She said you had a nice time at Loch Fyne.'

I felt like I'd been punched in the chest. 'Did she?' I asked incredulously. 'Really?'

'Yes.' He laughed. 'Why, didn't you?'

'Well, it was a little fraught . . .'

'In what way?' he asked, clearly confused.

'We . . . had a bit of a disagreement.'

He waited for me to go on.

'I'd had too much to drink, your mum said one or two things that I didn't like, and I'm ashamed to say, I retaliated.'

'Oops!' He laughed.

I smiled. 'Exactly!'

'So how did it end? Are you friends again?' He made it sound like we were two toddlers who had fallen out over a toy.

I wrinkled my nose. 'I hope so, though I don't know how *she* feels. In hindsight, she was probably only trying to be helpful, but I gave her pretty short shrift.'

'Well she certainly didn't mention anything to me,' he said. 'Sometimes Mum can say the wrong thing at the wrong time, but once you get to know her better you'll just learn to take it with a pinch of salt.'

I felt oddly insulted that he thought I didn't know her well enough by now, but had to remind myself that it had only been six months. How well can you know anyone in such a short space of time?

'I hope so,' I said honestly.

'Trust me,' he said, putting his hand over mine and looking at me intently.

It felt like I'd been given an electric shock as his skin touched mine, but, although my instinct was to pull away, I didn't want to make him feel awkward.

'Excuse me, I ought to check my phone,' I said, my voice slightly more high-pitched than normal. I hoped he couldn't tell how nervous I was.

I reached for my phone in my bag.

'And how's things going with Adam?' he said, stopping me in my tracks.

I looked at him, and his deep-blue eyes were staring back. I suddenly had an overwhelming urge to cry. Embarrassed, I reached for a serviette from the holder on the table and dabbed at my eyes.

'You okay, Em?' he asked, concern written all over his face.

Hearing him call me that, like an old friend, made it even harder to hold back the deluge. I swallowed the lump in my throat.

He reached across the table and pulled my hand away from my face, holding it still.

'Do you want to tell me what's going on?'

I could. I so wanted to. But how would that be fair? I shook my head.

'I need to go,' I said, suddenly desperate to get out of there. I pushed my chair back from the table, but he still had hold of my hand, his gaze unwavering.

'I'm always here for you, Em,' he said. And, as I looked into his eyes, I believed him.

I could hear my own heartbeat pounding in my ears, thumping like a drum. A sudden whoosh made me feel as if I was underwater, drowning in my own thoughts.

I grabbed my bag off the back of the chair and pulled away from him. 'I have to go,' I said, before turning in a daze and weaving though the confines of the eight-table cafe that should only have four. I banged into shoulders and knocked cups as I went, spilling tea into saucers, warranting the 'oi, watch yourself!' that I heard as I reached the door.

My head filled with James's words as I rushed up the incline towards the Strand. *I'm always here for you.* I wanted to run. I had to get as far away as possible. Otherwise I was in very real danger of going straight back to him.

19

'What the hell . . . ?' said Seb.

I had to tell somebody – somebody who wouldn't judge me – and although I knew I could tell Pippa in confidence, we hadn't seen so much of each other since I'd moved out, so Seb's was the first pair of ears I could trust.

'So, you just walked out of there?'

'Please, you've got to help me,' I implored. 'You've got to make me see sense in all this.'

I'd calmed down in the twenty-four hours since I'd met James, but my head was foggier than ever. What had happened there? And why was it affecting me so much? He hadn't meant anything by what he said, I was sure of it, but I still couldn't shake the feeling of unrest. It wasn't what was said, it was more about the unsaid.

'I mean, do you think he was coming on to you? Like, seriously?' asked Seb.

'Yes! No . . . I don't know.' I groaned, dropping my head back onto his sofa. 'It was just, in that moment, I honestly felt like I was capable of anything. I wanted to talk to him, kiss him, run away with him . . .'

'Well, the latter wouldn't have been very wise, but you probably could have got away with a kiss!'

'You're not helping,' I said, slapping him on the arm. 'This is serious. What am I going to do?'

'Okay,' he said, his face suddenly stern. 'What do you want to do? Let's explore your options. The way I see it is this: you love Adam more than anything?'

I nodded.

'But you think his brother is hot?'

'Seb!'

'Sorry, okay, right back with you. You *don't* think his brother is hot?'

I remained expressionless.

'Ooh, okay, so you do? Just a little bit? Am I getting warm?'

'No, I don't know. He's just so different to Adam. He listens to me, offers advice, doesn't think I'm being paranoid about Pammie. He really seems to understand where I'm coming from, and we have a genuine respect for each other.'

'And he's as hot as hell?'

I threw a cushion at him. 'Yes, he's also as hot as hell!'

'I knew it!' said Seb.

'But it's more than that. He makes me feel valued in every respect. Honestly, Seb, you know what I'm like, I can't see a ten-tonne truck until it's on top of me, but I could see it in his eyes. He would have done anything to help me, and knowing that makes me feel wanted. And right now, that's a dangerous place for me to be.'

'So, have things not improved any with Adam?' asked Seb, serious now.

I shook my head. 'No.' I could feel a stinging at the back of my throat. 'James has just caught me at a low ebb, and I'm pathetically flattered by the attention. If it had happened at any other time, I would just bat it away and think nothing more of it.' I didn't know who I was trying to convince: Seb or myself.

'Okay, so that leaves us with a man you love, who you're not having sex with, and a man you don't love, but who you'd kill to have sex with?'

'Well, thanks, Sherlock, that seems to wrap things up pretty nicely. But it's not just about sex, it's more than that.'

'So, you haven't imagined, for one second, being in bed with James?' asked Seb, his gaze unwavering.

I shook my head vehemently, whilst feeling my cheeks going red.

'You're so shit at lying!' He laughed.

'But that's really wrong, isn't it? I mean, there's seriously something badly wrong with that.'

'It is if you do anything about it, but for now, it's locked up in a lovely little fantasy room that we're all allowed to have and like to look into, but never actually enter. That's the difference.'

'So, what do I say to Adam? Do I tell him I've seen James?'

'You've already got a whole world of hurt going on with that family, so I strongly recommend you don't make it any harder on yourself. I think you should have told Adam that you'd met, but if you were going to do that, you would have done it last night. And you didn't?'

I shook my head. I'd thought about it, all night. I was like a cat on a hot tin roof, running it over in my mind again and again, reaching a different outcome every time. I thought about telling him that James had needed some recruitment advice, but that would lead on to another lie, and I could see it all quickly unravelling.

Hot tears sprang to my eyes. 'What a bloody mess.'

Seb shuffled up the sofa and put an arm round me. 'Hey, come on, don't get upset. You should think yourself lucky, having two men fighting over you. I can't even get *one* to have a fight with himself!'

I laughed tightly.

'So, you think I'm doing the right thing? I'm playing it right?'

'As I said, there should be no guilt associated with fantasizing, just be sure not to act on it.'

I sniffed. 'I never would, not in a million years.'

So why, then, did I agree to meet James for a drink after work when he called again a week later?

I don't know, is all I can offer. It's not a good enough answer, but it's the only one I've got.

I'd not stopped thinking about how he'd made me feel, and I naively believed that if I saw him again, I'd be able to rationalize it in my head and put it to bed. How stupid I am. I should know that life doesn't work like that, so why am I prepared to put myself in an untenable situation, as if to prove to myself that I'm in control, that I've got this, when, deep within, I know that, all around me, the sky is falling down.

I could blame Adam. I could say that I no longer felt attractive, or wanted; that my husband-to-be made me feel unloved. I could say that he didn't understand me or support me. And perhaps that was all true, but none of those justified me being unfaithful.

'I'm not going to sleep with him,' I assured Seb, when I called to tell him I needed to see James one last time, 'for closure.'

'Who are you trying to convince? Me or you?' He laughed wryly. 'Because I have to say, I'm not on the same page as you on this one. Go have your ego stroked if that's what you need, but you're playing a dangerous game here and you need to wake up to the consequences. If Adam finds out about this, even if nothing happens between you, you're going to be in a whole heap of trouble.'

'I know what I'm doing.' I sighed heavily.

'Do what you want, but don't come running to me when the shit hits the fan.'

I felt a bolt across my chest at that. Seb was open-minded about anything and everything, so to be told in no uncertain terms where I stood, compounded the gravity of the situation.

'Call me when you've got your sensible head back on,' he said, before putting the phone down.

There was a tiny part of me that wanted James to cancel. It would have made things easier, drawn a line under whatever this was. But he didn't, so, with butterflies dancing in my stomach, I walked into the American Bar at the Savoy, and his eyes met mine as I walked towards him.

'Good to see you,' he said, holding my shoulders and kissing both cheeks. 'You look incredible.' The word resounded in my head. *Incredible*. That isn't how your future brother-in-law should describe you. *Lovely*, yes. *Well*, yes. Even *great*, yes. But *incredible*? Absolutely not. My heart raced at the thought that I'd not imagined the look he'd given me in the cafe, nor the sentiment behind his words.

'What can I get you?' he said, whilst raising a hand to the barman.

'A glass of prosecco, please.'

'Two glasses of champagne, please,' he said to the white-jacketed man behind the bar.

'What are we celebrating?' I asked.

'You are looking at the official gardener for Lansdowne Place at Knole Park.'

'Oh, fantastic,' I cried, instinctively pulling him towards me for a congratulatory hug. 'You got the job.'

There was the briefest moment when our faces collided, unsure of whether this was just a hug, a kiss, or both. We awkwardly extricated ourselves, but the touchpaper had been lit.

'So, does Adam know you're here?' James asked, his eyes not meeting mine.

'No,' I said honestly. 'I haven't told him.'

He tilted his head to one side, his hair flopping with it. 'Why not?'

'I don't know.'

'I didn't mean to make things difficult for you,' he said softly.

If he could just stop staring at me like that. Stop brushing my leg every time he moved.

'You haven't. It's worked out perfectly, actually. I was just around the corner at a meeting and with the Tube strike, it makes sense to wait a while before attempting to get home.' That was all true. It was a normal day, just like any other. The part he didn't need to know was how I'd spent it trying to convince myself that my French Connection miniskirt and silk blouse were my normal work attire, even though I'd worn nothing but trousers for over a month.

'Are you bloody mad?' Adam had asked, as he watched me dress that morning, tying his tie into a thick knot. 'It's going to be freezing today.'

I mumbled acknowledgement.

'*And* there's a Tube strike, so none of us know where

we might end up. You'd be better off in boots today rather than those heels.'

'I'm all right,' I'd said, 'stop fussing.' But the shards of guilt cut through my chest.

The barman placed a glass of champagne in front of me, its tall stem resting on the double-layered coaster beneath it.

'Cheers,' chimed James, raising his glass. 'It's really good to see you.'

We locked eyes as we took our first sips. I looked away first.

'So, how have you been?' he asked, setting his glass back down on the bar.

'Mmm, fine,' I said casually. 'Really good.'

'Strange . . . Your eyes are telling a different story.'

I blinked and looked away.

'Do you want to talk about it?' he asked.

'It's complicated,' I said. 'We'll work it out.'

'Are you happy?'

What a loaded question. Was I? I honestly didn't know.

'I'm not *unhappy*,' was all I could offer.

'Don't you think you deserve more than that? Don't you think that someone else might be out there who could truly make you happy?'

The air in my body felt like it had been sucked out of me. Tiny pinpricks of heat emitted from every pore, and my mouth felt like it was full of polystyrene, rendering me speechless.

He looked at me, his eyes desperately searching mine for a response.

'James, I . . .' was all I could manage.

He reached for my hand and held it. A frisson of electricity travelled along my arm, literally standing the hairs on end.

Images flashed behind my eyes like an old-fashioned cinematic film, shuttering madly. I could picture us, making our way to a room on one of the floors above. I imagined us kissing in the lift, unable to contain ourselves for a second longer than it took for the doors to close. The urgency as we'd make our way along the carpeted corridor, my shoes being kicked off as we'd hang the *Do Not Disturb* sign on the door.

We'd ignore the chilled bottle of champagne standing on the dressing table, and I'd picture the anonymous faces scurrying along the bustling street below, none the wiser to the deceit and betrayal that was unfolding just a few metres away.

I'd wrap my legs around him as he pushes me up against the wall, our kisses intensifying as the heat in our bodies rises. We'd be clawing at each other, pulling our clothes off as he carries me over to the bed. We'd sink into the luxurious white sheets and his eyes would never leave mine as—

Enough!

I stopped my mind from racing on, knowing that it would only end with us lying there, lamenting what we'd done, and wishing we could undo it.

'I'm sorry, I shouldn't have . . .' he said, releasing my hand.

I willed him to touch me again, so I could feel that bolt rush through me one more time.

'I love Adam,' I said. 'We're getting married. We've got our problems, but we'll work them out.'

'You deserve better,' he said. 'Adam—'

'Don't,' I said, cutting across him. 'This isn't right.'

I lifted myself off the stool. 'I'm sorry, James. I just can't do this. This is all wrong.'

I thought of how carefully I'd selected my underwear that morning. What the hell had I been thinking? Had I really intended to go that far?

'I need to go,' I said, grabbing my coat and throwing it over my arm. 'I'm really sorry.'

The cold air hit me as I pushed through the revolving doors onto the street, the wind whipping up from the Thames making a buffeting sound as I exited.

'Have a good evening,' said the doorman, smiling and tipping his hat to me.

I didn't know which way to go. I thought of calling Seb to see if he was still in town, but just as I tapped his name on my phone, I was hit by a sudden urge to get home to see Adam. I needed to know that he didn't suspect. Selfish on my part, but I couldn't stop my stomach turning over at the thought of him knowing. What would he make of this? Of knowing that I'd come here to meet his brother, with the merest hint of intention. Wasn't the intention almost as bad as going through with it?

I tried to pretend to myself that the tears streaming down my face were caused by the wind I was battling against, and not the shame of what I might have done. But the brain's not stupid, and by the time I'd reached Charing Cross, I was having trouble convincing myself that I hadn't gone through with it. My head felt as if it had been screwed, even though my body knew it hadn't.

I squeezed onto the 19.42. The Tube strike had clearly held commuters up as they made their way across town, as it was more like the 18.02, and everyone was packed in like sardines. I was held upright by the overweight bald man behind me, his breath so close to my ear that he could have licked it, and the young twenty-something woman in front of me who had had the foresight to get her phone out and in texting position before she got on the train. Now, stuck as I was, my upper limbs pinned to my sides, I had no chance of letting Adam know I was on my way.

Pinpricks of sweat jumped to the surface of my back, the rush to get the train catching up with me. I imagined a thin streak of dampness, the length of my spine, seeping through the silk of my emerald-green blouse, compounded by the heat of other bodies pressed up against me. Those nearest to the windows, the people who had had the luxury of sitting in their seats for the past ten minutes, waiting for the train to depart, were reaching up to close them as we crossed the river. They sank their faces further into their woollen scarves whilst I battled the oppressive heat that was engulfing me.

I shifted a little, angling my body away from the man behind me, his rotund stomach filling the concave of my back, and he grunted. I wondered if he could smell the deceit on me.

Adam was in the kitchen. A waft of frying onions and garlic hit me as I let myself in and hung my coat on the hook behind the door.

'Hey, is that you?'

I could tell from the tone of his voice that all was well, and the heaviness in my chest began to lift. I didn't know if I was going to be honest with him, but I wanted to be.

'Who else were you expecting?' I laughed.

'You made good time,' he said, kissing me, wooden spoon in hand. 'It was murder a couple of hours ago.'

'Thought it might be. That's why I decided to wait a bit. Get some work done.' So once again, without even thinking about it, I'd made the decision to lie.

'Grab some cutlery and pour us some wine. It'll be ready in ten minutes.'

'Will do,' I replied, 'let me just get out of these clothes.'

I walked into the bathroom, unbuttoning my blouse and wriggling out of my skirt. I needed a shower, to wash the dirt, both real and imaginary, from my body. The water ran hotter than felt comfortable, but it numbed the nerve endings, stopped them from jangling. Eyes still closed, I reached for the towel on the hook, but a hand caught mine, making me jump.

'Jesus Christ!' I yelped, my heart thumping.

Adam laughed. 'Sorry, didn't mean to scare you. Thought you might like this whilst you're in here.' He handed me a towel with one hand and a glass of red with the other. I smiled and sipped it gratefully, feeling its warmth as it ran into my chest.

He sat on the side of the bath as he watched me dry myself, his eyes roaming my naked body.

Suddenly self-conscious, I wrapped myself in a towel. 'You really are quite something,' he said, standing up and walking towards me. 'Take it off. Let me look at you.'

I smiled and slowly held the towel open.

He took a sip of my wine before dipping his finger in the glass and offering it up to my mouth. He traced my lips and my taste buds sprang into life as I sucked the wine from his finger. I could feel a pulsing in my groin as he watched me, his eyes never leaving mine.

We shared the remains of the glass, and, as Adam passed it between us, some of it spilled, dripping down my chin and onto my breasts. He bent his head down to slowly lick them. My back arched as he came up to meet my mouth, his fingers running down my spine, sending goose bumps to my skin. I shivered involuntarily.

He picked me up, and I wrapped my legs tightly around him as he carried me into the bedroom and laid me down on the bed.

'God, I love you,' he said.

I cried as he entered me, hot tears of relief and wanting, but most of all guilt. How could I have risked losing this?

20

'Tell me about Rebecca,' I asked afterwards, buoyed by our renewed closeness.

'What do you want to know?'

'I want to know who she was, how you felt about her, and what happened between you.'

He pulled himself up against the headboard, his brow furrowed and eyes narrow.

'It was a long time ago, Em.'

'I know, but she was important to you – like Tom was to me.'

He raised his eyebrows and looked at me questioningly.

'Oh, come on, we're grown-ups here.' I laughed. 'Don't go getting all jealous.'

'Do you still think about him?' he asked.

'Occasionally, yes, but not because I wish I was still with him. Just in a "I wonder what he's up to" way. Is he still with Charlotte? Was their deceit worth it? Do either of them ever think of me?'

He nodded, but his face was solemn. 'I met Rebecca when I was twenty. We knew friends of friends and were introduced at a party.'

'Down in Sevenoaks?' I asked.

'Yes, but she was from a little village just outside called Brasted. Anyway, we just clicked. Neither of us had been in a serious relationship before, so it was special. We were young, thought we were in love, and everything and everyone else just took a back seat.'

'So, where did it go wrong?' I asked, failing to understand how such an intense relationship could wither away and die.

He sighed. 'We were properly into each other. Rightly or wrongly, we dropped our mates, and even our families when they said we were spending too much time together. We wouldn't hear of it. We honestly thought we were going to be together forever, and everyone else would just have to take us as we were or not at all. There was no alternative as far as we were concerned.'

'I don't understand then. What changed?'

'We'd been together for five years. I was doing well at the bank, and she'd finished her teaching degree and had got a job in an infant school, close to where she lived. We'd found a place to rent in Westerham, our first home together, and were about to move in.' His voice cracked.

'Tell me,' I coaxed gently. 'What happened?'

'She was so excited, and had taken a couple of days off from school to get the place set up. I was on my way there after work, when Mum called to say something had happened.'

'What? What had happened?' I pressed.

'It didn't make sense, because I'd called just before I left the office to tell her I was on my way, and she sounded so happy. She said she'd made a chilli and to hurry on up.'

His eyes filled up. I'd not seen Adam cry before and I didn't know whether to feel sad or resentful that someone other than me had caused it.

'I ran all the way from the station, but by the time I got there, it was too late. The ambulance was already there, but there was nothing the paramedics could do to bring her back.'

I gasped as my hand flew to my mouth.

'She was gone.' He was sobbing now, hard, gut-wrenching sobs from the pit of his stomach, and I moved up to hold him.

I didn't know whether to push him any further, but it would have felt odd not to know how or why.

'What happened?' I asked.

'She'd always been asthmatic since she was a little girl, but she had it under control. She was able to lead a normal life, partying, going to the gym – as long as she had her inhaler, she was able to manage it. It was something we had to think about, but it didn't stop us from doing anything. She was fit and happy.'

'So why didn't she use her inhaler?'

He laughed sarcastically, but I knew it wasn't aimed at me. 'That was the million-dollar question. She never went anywhere without it, but in all the excitement of moving, we think she just forgot.'

'We?'

'Me and her parents. She'd left one at theirs, but she always had a few dotted around, just so there was one at hand if she needed it. I found one in the kitchen drawer but it had run out. So she must have just forgotten, or lost sight of where they were, and which ones needed refilling.'

'I am so, so sorry,' I whispered. 'Why haven't you told me this before? I could have been helping you all this time. So that you didn't feel alone.'

'I'm okay.' He sniffed. 'Mum has always been there for me. She found her and called 999. It was hard for her because she adored Becky as much as I did.'

I felt a small stab in my chest at that. Suddenly it was 'Becky', and between her, Adam and Pammie, they had a bond that I could never be a part of, and which could never be broken. It felt like a competition that I just couldn't begin to take part in. I berated myself for being so selfish.

I should be looking at it as a way forward, to help find answers in the complicated dichotomy that is the Banks family. It certainly went a long way to explaining why Pammie behaved the way she did towards me, and I softened at the thought that it was more to do with grief for Rebecca than a hatred towards me. I could begin to understand that: it gave me something to work with, something to use in her defence.

Adam shifted from beneath me, and pulled himself up to sit on the side of the bed. He sniffed and wiped his eyes with the back of his hand.

It wasn't important, but I couldn't resist. 'Would you still be with her now, if that hadn't happened?'

He snorted, shook his head, and stood up. 'You're unbelievable,' he said, before picking up a t-shirt and shorts from the end of the bed.

'I'm just asking.'

'What do you want me to say to that?' he said, his voice rising. 'That yes, if she hadn't died so tragically, we'd still be together? Would that make you feel better? Would it make you feel good to know that?'

I shook my head, suddenly embarrassed.

'Well then, don't ask stupid questions if you don't want to know the answers.'

I hadn't meant anything by it, but I could understand how it might have come across. I thought that now we'd finally been able to make love, Adam would feel happier and less stressed, but it still felt as if he had an anger just bubbling under the surface. All the time – directed at me.

'I'll go and finish dinner,' he said.

21

I don't know how Mum had become involved in the organization of my hen do. I'd officially handed the baton to my chief and only bridesmaid, Pippa, but then Seb had put his ha'penny in, and Mum a ha'penny more, and suddenly we all found ourselves tiptoeing through a minefield.

Pippa was bitching about Seb's need for control, Mum was moaning that Pippa was keeping things from her, and I was just a pawn in the middle, not knowing whether I was coming or going.

The only stipulations I'd given them were no strippers, no matching hen t-shirts, and definitely no blow-up dolls. 'Less is more,' I'd gently encouraged, hoping for a slightly classier occasion than my brother's wife Laura had had. She was taken to Blackpool for the weekend, had all of the above, but thankfully had no recollection of it. Still, there were at least six of us at the wedding who'd not consumed quite enough alcohol to erase the memory of her sliding up and down a pole and being given a lap dance.

Of course, the four-day bender that Stuart and twelve of his mates had had in Magaluf went by without incident, it seemed. For them, it was, apparently, rounds of golf, early dinners and quiet nights in. That's the fundamental difference between them and us: men do what they do, not a word is whispered, and they carry on as if nothing happened. 'What goes on tour, stays on tour,' is the mantra we're all supposed to live by, and us women could, if we didn't come over all nostalgic two bottles of prosecco in and decide to video it all, for posterity, and to show our kids how wild we used to be.

'I really don't mind,' I said to Mum when she called up to ask if I'd like it to be abroad or somewhere in the UK. 'I think you'll find Pippa's already on it.'

'Well, she is,' she said, 'but she's not making it very easy for people who don't have the money to be swanning about all over the world. She's suggesting a yoga thingy in Iceland, or Las Vegas even. Some people just don't have that kind of money, Emily.' And nor would Pippa, usually; her dad was treating her.

'I know, Mum. I don't want anything too extravagant either, and besides, Adam and his mates are going to Vegas, so that rules that one out.' I laughed, but she just tutted. 'Look, Pippa knows what she's doing and I'm sure she'll take everyone into account.'

'Well, Pammie wants to go to the Lake District,' said Mum indignantly. A bolt shot across my chest.

'Pammie? What's she got to do with anything?' I asked. I'd hoped that by giving the job to Pippa, I'd be exonerated of all responsibility as to who was invited and who wasn't. That way, if Tess, my rather dreary work colleague, didn't make the cut, it wouldn't be my fault – and I couldn't imagine Pammie being on the list.

'She called yesterday to ask what the plans were,' said Mum. 'She wanted to arrange a little something for you, if nothing else was being organized.'

So, Pippa *hadn't* invited her, it was my mother who had put her foot in it. I groaned inwardly.

'What did you say to her?' I said, keeping my voice chirpy. I hadn't told Mum about my run-ins with Pammie because I didn't want to worry her. I also didn't want to create any unnecessary tension between them. I'd be stressed enough for everybody on our wedding day. I just wanted my family, especially Mum, to enjoy herself, without having to worry about what was going on behind the scenes. Pammie was *my* problem, and I'd deal with it.

'Well, I told her that your friend was making enquiries,' she answered defensively. 'Was I not supposed to say that? See, I don't know what I'm allowed to say to whom. It's all getting a bit much.'

'No, that's fine, Mum. You can say whatever you like. Probably the only person you shouldn't say too much to is me, because it's meant to be a surprise.'

'Yes, I know that dear. I'll just keep it between me, Pippa, Seb and Pammie.'

I put the phone down and thought about calling Pippa or Seb, just to check how things were going, but

I fought the control-freak in me down and left them to it.

There were still whisperings of discord right up until the day I embarked on my mystery tour. I'd tried to ignore them, but the pettiness was beginning to get to me. 'Your mum says I shouldn't invite someone I want to invite,' moaned Pippa. 'I think your cousin Shelley should be coming, but Seb says Pippa doesn't think you'd want her there,' said Mum, sounding exasperated. By the time I went to bed the night before the 6 a.m. start, I was ruing the day I ever agreed to a bloody hen do.

'Wakey, wakey, sleepy head,' whispered Adam as he kissed me. 'The day for us to make our last mistakes before we get married is here.'

I gave him a sleepy punch. 'You'd better not,' I threatened, before turning over and pulling the duvet up around my ears.

'Come on.' He laughed. 'You're being picked up in an hour.'

'Can't we just spend the next four days in bed?' I asked.

'You'll be fine once you get going. I, for one, am actually looking forward to my last hurrah,' he teased.

'That's because you're flying to Las Vegas!' I exclaimed. 'I, no doubt, am headed to Bognor. But don't you worry about me. You go have the time of your life, gambling, haggling and shagging your way around Nevada.'

'Hey, less of the gambling and haggling,' he called out from the bathroom. 'I won't be doing any of that there.'

We both laughed, but there was a part of me that felt unsettled, not just about Adam and what he might get up to, but at the thought of where I might be heading and with whom.

Fifty minutes later, after saying goodbye to Adam – who looked smartly casual as he walked across the road in his chinos and polo shirt, with a weathered, brown leather weekend bag in his hand – I found myself being propelled into the back of a car, blindfolded.

'Is this really necessary, Seb?' I laughed. 'Are you sure you don't want to handcuff me as well?'

'That's not really my thing,' he said.

'Is there anyone else here? Hello? Hello?' I called.

'We're on our own, you bloody fool.' He laughed. 'Any idea where we might be going?'

'I'm hoping for a hedonistic paradise in Ibiza, but knowing you lot, I'll probably end up on a pottery course in the Shetland Islands.'

He untied the blindfold once we were on the M25 and, as soon as I worked out we were heading west, I knew that Gatwick airport was a possible destination. And by the time we veered left onto the M23 slip road, it was either that or Brighton.

I envisaged the inside of my suitcase, its contents look-ing like I was heading to a festival in an unpredictable British summer. Boots, sarong, a mac, and denim shorts were the last thing I threw in as I panic-packed, not knowing whether I was going skiing, sunbathing or somewhere in between.

'What if I haven't brought the right stuff?' I implored Seb, turning to him.

'Don't worry, it's all been taken care of,' he said mysteriously. It had all been taken care of by whom? If it were left to Pippa, she'd have ferreted in the depths of my wardrobe and found the items that I vowed to get back into some day, those jeans from when I was nineteen, which I refused to believe had seen their last wear. The fact that they were two sizes too small and hideously old-fashioned, with their boot-cut bottoms and fly buttons, seemed lost on my ever-optimistic pride. If, God forbid, Mum had had a secret root through, she'd have picked the floral playsuit and the wrap-over cardigan, which had been bought in a fit of pique in the end-of-summer sales. Both had the tags still on, because both made me look like a twelve-year-old.

I groaned. 'Please tell me you asked Adam for inspiration, at least. If anyone has any idea of what I like or what suits me, he'd be the first person to go to.' I looked pleadingly at Seb, but he just smiled and turned to look out of the window as the distinctive orange flash of an EasyJet tailgate flew low over the field beside us.

I was blindfolded again as the car pulled into the drop-off area outside the south terminal. 'I can't imagine security is going to let you get away with this,' I mused, as Seb pulled it tight. 'This takes people smuggling to a whole other level.'

He laughed as he guided me through the entrance tunnel and into the departures concourse, my hearing heightened to the buzz of excited travellers all around me. We veered left, and then off to the right, before we came to a halt when it was suddenly deafeningly quiet.

'One, two . . . three!' shouted Seb, as he pulled the blindfold off. I stumbled as the cheers and catcalls propelled me backwards. My eyes couldn't quite focus on all the faces that were milling in front of me, their wide grins looming, like caricatures of themselves.

The bundle of people was upon me, ruffling my hair and offering air kisses. I couldn't begin to ascertain how many were there, let alone who they were.

'Hey, here she is,' called Pippa.

'Oh bless, she looks like she's going to cry,' said Tess, my work colleague.

I spun round, disorientated, desperately trying to match all the faces to the voices, the thousands of pixels floating in front of my eyes slowly beginning to form real features.

'Oh, darling, you look shell-shocked,' said Mum, laughing. 'Are you surprised?'

'I can't believe how many of you there are,' I said.

'There's nine of us,' said Pippa. 'Well, there was, but now there's ten.'

I raised my eyebrows questioningly.

'I'm so sorry,' she mouthed.

I looked around the bustle, my eyes settling on Pammie. It was no big deal. After talking to Mum, I'd resigned myself to her being there. There was no real way around it.

'It's okay,' I whispered to Pippa, but she looked away, her face fraught with tension.

And then I saw her. Just standing there. Her blonde curls bouncing around her shoulders, a simpering, almost pitying smile playing across her full lips.

Charlotte.

My heart felt like it had come to a standstill. Like a hand had reached inside my chest and squeezed the last beat out of it.

Everything around me seemed to stop: the noise, the light, the air, all I could see was her, as she came slowly towards me with outstretched arms. She could only have been three or four steps away, but my brain was computing everything in slow motion and it seemed to take an eternity for her to reach me.

'Hello, Em,' she whispered in my ear as she embraced me, a waft of fresh citrus encircling us. Jo Malone's Grapefruit was obviously still her signature scent.

'It's been such a long time. Too long. Thank you so much for including me in your celebrations.'

The last time I had seen Charlotte, she was naked and straddling my boyfriend, Tom. I'd never got that image out of my head, yet my mind had gone some way to protecting me, by only recalling the shock on their faces and the stereotypical covering up with a sheet. I'd eventually found it laughably ironic that I'd seen both of them naked more times than I'd had hot dinners, yet they'd deemed it necessary to mask their upper bodies rather than extricate their genitals from one another. Which, let's be honest, were the two parts that were the deal-breaker. He was still inside her, no doubt not quite so firmly, when I walked out again.

I'd thought I was going to marry Tom. We were practically living together, yet that night, he'd called me from work to say he wasn't feeling well and that he thought it better, and kinder, if he spent the night at his place.

'Believe you me,' he'd said, sniffing. 'You don't want to get this.'

I remember thinking how considerate he was being.

'But it's probably just a common cold,' I'd implored, in the hope of changing his mind. 'It may feel like full-blown man-flu to you, but if I, as a woman, was to get it, I'm sure it'd amount to no more than a little snuffle.'

'Oh, piss off.' He'd laughed. 'Here's me trying to be thoughtful, and all you can do is take the mickey.'

'If you come over to mine, I'll rub some Vicks on your chest.'

'Tempting, but I really don't think it's fair on you. Honestly, I feel like shit,' he'd said.

Not quite shit enough, it seemed, to stop my best friend writhing up and down on him when I paid a visit with some medication and a batch of Sainsbury's oven-ready lasagne. All I thought of as I let myself in was whether or not I could pass the pasta off as my own. *Surely that would make me a much more considerate girlfriend*, I'd thought to myself, quietly laying my keys on the window ledge, and tiptoeing up the stairs.

I think I heard the noises as I was about halfway up, but my naive brain translated his groans into coughs, and her panting into a shortness of breath. *Maybe I ought to get him a glass of water*, I remember thinking, as I hesitated on the top step, still unsuspecting. I sometimes pretend that I *had* gone back downstairs to get him a drink, and, by doing so, had alerted them to my presence. I imagine her being stuffed unceremoniously into his wardrobe whilst we embarked on a caper of *Carry On* proportions.

Maybe, then, I'd be blissfully ignorant to this day, about to go off with my fellow hens to celebrate my final moments of freedom before our impending marriage. Charlotte would have been my chief bridesmaid, and I'd be none the wiser.

She was still clinging onto me when Pippa yanked my hand and pulled me away.

'Come on, we need to check in,' she said.

I'd lost the ability to function, and stood there, dumbstruck.

'Just keep smiling,' Seb said. 'I have no idea what the hell is going on.'

'But her . . .' I faltered. 'How did this even happen?'

'I really haven't got a clue,' he said. 'It's always been nine of us. Pippa says she just appeared out of nowhere.'

'What do you want to do?' she asked, ushering me towards the waiting clerk at the Monarch desk, whose thin lips were pressed together in impatience. I was vaguely aware of the Faro sign behind her, but nothing was sinking in. All I knew was that I wanted to get as far away from there as possible. Alone.

'What are my choices?' I asked sarcastically. 'Right now, I can't see that I have any.'

'We can tell her to leave,' said Pippa. 'I don't have a problem doing that, if that's what you want.'

I couldn't think straight.

I wanted to cry, but I'd be darned if I was going to give Charlotte the satisfaction. Her face was a smiling blur over Pippa's shoulder.

'I can't believe this is happening,' I said.

'So, what do you want to do, Em?'

I looked around at all the excited faces, knowing that, for Trudy, Nina and Sam, my old workmates, this would be the only break they had all year. They'd paid good money for their flights and accommodation. It wasn't fair of me to ruin it before we'd even got off the ground.

'Do you want me to tell her?' asked Pippa.

I stopped my brain from racing ahead and tried to remember who I'd told about Charlotte and Tom. Right now, it felt like they all knew, and were laughing about it whenever my back was turned. But once I thought about it rationally, I realized that it was only Mum, Seb and Pippa. I had felt ashamed and embarrassed at the time – I hadn't shouted it from the rooftops. If I caused a scene now, everyone would find out, and it'd be the talk of not only the hen weekend, but the wedding as well.

'Let her come,' I said sharply. 'I'll deal with it.'

I'd spent so long imagining this moment, wondering what it would be like to bump into her again. What would happen? Would I launch myself at her and want to tear her hair out? Or would I ignore her? It turns out, it was neither. I just felt numb.

'Where are we even going?' I asked glumly.

'Portugal!' said Pippa, over-enthusiastically.

I could tell she was trying to buoy me, to keep my spirits up, but my mood was going to be hard to lift.

I tried to concentrate on what people were saying to me as we sat in the departure lounge, a couple of bottles of prosecco already drained. They were all so happy, so keen to make it special, even competing, it seemed, for my attention. I turned my head this way and that, smiling, offering over-exaggerated gestures. But it all felt false, as if I was trying too hard, for fear of the elephant in the room making itself known.

Carrier bags clinked as everybody went to get up as our flight was announced, our duty-free purchases bumping into each other. 'I think we've got enough booze here to sink a battleship,' said Pippa. 'Cliff Richard needn't be worried about us drinking his vineyard dry.'

'Are we seeing Cliff Richard?' piped up Mum.

'No,' I said. 'He makes wine out there, doesn't he?'

'I can't be drinking too much,' said Tess, as we all started walking. 'I've got a big presentation next week.'

We all groaned. 'I see what you mean about her,' Pippa said, laughing loudly as she slapped my back, her edges already blurred by alcohol.

'What a surprise to see Charlotte,' said Mum quietly, hanging back to catch me on my own. 'Everything okay now?'

I smiled tightly.

'I'm so pleased you sorted everything out. You should have told me.'

I didn't know what to say. I was too dumbfounded to even begin to piece together what was going on here.

I managed to avoid Charlotte for the entire journey, side-stepping every time I sensed her sidling up to me. Pippa and Seb were my buffers, although the constant supply of in-flight drinks was doing nothing to help their judgement.

'I promise I'll be more reliable tomorrow,' Seb slurred, as he gave up on the fight for my case as Charlotte eagerly made a grab for it on the conveyor belt.

I took it without saying a word. I couldn't even look

at her, because I knew that if I did, the vision of what she'd done would come back and hit me like a tonne of bricks.

I made sure I was the last one onto the minibus, so I didn't run the risk of her sitting next to me. I couldn't go on avoiding her like this for four days – this was supposed to be my happy time. Something had to give. I could almost hear myself laughing wryly at the thought of Pammie being my biggest problem this weekend.

22

I could see Charlotte's reflection behind me, as we both looked out of the window into the dark, curious as to where we were going. I wondered if, like me, she remembered the last time we'd done a journey like this, as a pair of innocent eighteen-year-olds, about to enter the lion's den of Ayia Napa. We'd cruelly laughed as our fellow holidaymakers had been dropped off at their hotels by the coach, each place looking less salubrious than the one before. 'I'm glad we're not staying there,' she'd shrieked. 'I'd never get in that pool.'

Our naivety wasn't lost on the coach driver, who kept looking at us in his mirror, smiling and shaking his head. Clearly he knew something we didn't, because when he dropped us off, in the middle of nowhere, he'd laughed at our confused faces.

'No, this can't be right,' insisted Charlotte as we stepped off the coach and straight into squelching mud. 'The brochure said it was in the heart of things.'

Our driver, who we now saw from his name badge was called Deniz, shook his head and smiled.

The harsh spotlight glaring above the porch guided

us down the narrow path, sending geckos scurrying out of our way, as we forlornly dragged our cases.

'Ciao,' shouted Deniz cheerily, before pulling away, and all I wanted to do was run after him. Even with his twirled moustache and beady eyes, he seemed a safer option than the matronly-looking woman who was sitting behind the reception desk, sweating and swishing away flies with a swatter. It had taken three or four rakis to see the funny side of things, and I'm still not quite sure how many more before we passed out, waking up on a mouldy sunbed the next morning, with the heat of the Cypriot sun burning down on us.

We'd referred to it ever since – well, at least until we stopped talking – as our 'coming of age' journey: a mystical escapade of raki, riot and rampage. I smiled, despite myself.

Pippa's excited voice invaded my thoughts, bringing me back to the present. 'This looks like it,' she said. 'We're here!'

The villa, with its peach-coloured walls gently illuminated by uplighters, was beautiful. But I wanted to be here with the people I loved, not a psychotic future mother-in-law and a woman who had slept with my last boyfriend.

'Wow!' cried everyone in unison.

'Not too shabby, eh?' said Pippa.

They excitedly crowded round the front door as she fumbled with the lock. I held back, desperately fighting the urge to get on the departing minibus, though to where, I didn't know. I batted away stinging tears and then felt a hand in the small of my back.

'You okay?' Mum asked gently.

I managed a nod and swallowed down the lump in my throat. My mum was here. Everything would be okay.

Pippa had booked a table at BJ's, a restaurant on the beach, for dinner. 'Appropriate name,' called out quiet Tess, as we navigated the steep steps from the dusty car park. 'Going down!'

'Bloody hell, how many has she had?' Pippa laughed.

I felt a tug on my hand, pulling me back, and, on turning round, I realized it was Charlotte. 'You haven't said a word to me, not even hello,' she said.

'Not now,' I replied. 'I'm not in the mood.'

'So why did you invite me, then?'

I stopped in my tracks and turned to face her.

'Invite you? You think *I* invited you?' She looked like she'd been slapped in the face.

'Well, yes, that's what Pammie said . . .' she faltered. 'Didn't you?'

A heat rushed to my ears. Charlotte's mouth was moving but her words became muffled. *Pammie?* I couldn't even begin to comprehend how this could have happened. I searched for a connection, some way of putting them together. My brain whirred with images of Pammie, Adam, James, even Tom. They were all laughing, their features contorted like *Spitting Image* puppets, rocking back and forth. I felt like they were trampling me underfoot, but I couldn't see who was pulling the strings.

Do they know each other? How did they meet? When? My mind was racing as it struggled to make sense of it all.

A moving image of Charlotte sitting astride Tom played out in front of me, and it took all my resolve not to push her over the edge and into the sea below.

'Pammie?' I asked, praying that I'd heard wrong. Every fibre in my body was preparing for fight or flight. I hated myself for being so weak. I needed to stay in control.

'Yes, she said that she was inviting me on your behalf.'

'What? How?' I asked, shaking my head.

'I don't know,' she said. 'I just know that Pammie called me and said you'd like me to come to your hen weekend. I asked if she was sure she'd got it right. She said yes, and I was over the moon. I couldn't believe it.'

'But how can you think that I'd ever want to see you again, after what you did to me?' My eyes filled with tears as I looked at her properly for the first time. I felt a jolt as my confused emotions poisoned my brain with an overwhelming desire to hug her. I fought the urge back down, but it wasn't easy. I hadn't realized how much I'd missed her until she was in front of me.

Her eyes fell to the floor. 'I'm truly sorry,' she said in barely more than a whisper. 'I still can't believe I did it.'

'But you did,' I said tightly, before turning and walking down the stairs.

I needed a drink and, thankfully, our glasses had already been filled with wine by the time I reached the table. I took a large slug before I'd even sat down.

'Okay, so who's up for Fuzzy Duck?' called out Tess. 'Line your glasses up, ladies.'

'And gentleman,' Seb said, correcting her.

I could only smile and look straight ahead because, if I looked left, I'd see Charlotte, and if I looked right, I'd see Pammie, and I couldn't look at her face right now as I was frightened of what I might do.

'What about truth or dare?' chipped in Seb.

'Yesss!' shouted Tess.

I kept my smile fixed firmly on my face, only parting my lips to take another mouthful of wine. It was already going some way to numbing my nerve endings.

The terracotta bottle that had so recently been filled with Lancers Rosé rocked and rolled as it spun, before slowing down and settling on Seb.

'Truth or dare?' asked Pippa.

'Dare!'

'Okay,' she said. 'When the waiter asks what you'd like to eat, you have to do your best to order in Portuguese.'

He smiled and called the waiter over.

'So . . . I'd like ze, how you say, spaghetti bolognesia con pan du garlic as un aperitif.'

We couldn't contain our giggles. 'There must be three different languages in there, but I'd bet my life that none of them is Portuguese,' sniggered Tess.

'Would you like parmesan cheese as well, mate?' asked the smiling waiter, in a cockney accent.

Everyone laughed, though all I could hear was the loud silence coming from the end of the table. I refilled my glass, drank it, and looked at Pammie. She glared back at me, with a look of defiance, as if calling the fight on.

No one else would have noticed, but then no one else knows her like I do. They don't know that the sweet old woman, ambling along, playing the martyr, is actually a calculating, scheming bitch. But if she wants to play that game, to systematically chip away at me until she hopes there's nothing left, then I'm ready.

The bottle spun and landed on Charlotte.

'Truth or dare?' Seb declared.

Her eyes darted to me. 'Truth.'

'I've got a question,' Pippa called out. 'What's your biggest regret?'

She seemed to know what was coming. 'I stupidly thought I was in love,' she said. 'Only problem was, he wasn't mine to love, he was my best friend's.'

I could feel Pippa and Seb bristling beside me.

Tess gasped loudly.

Charlotte went on, 'I naively believed that everything would work out for the best, but of course it didn't. It never does.'

'So, what happened?' asked Tess. 'Did your friend find out?'

Charlotte stared straight at me. 'Yes, in the worst possible way, and I'll never forget the look on her face. She was broken into a thousand pieces.'

My chest tightened.

'Was it worth it?' Tess pushed. 'Did you stay together?'

'No,' she said quietly. 'We both loved her more than each other, and once we'd realized the hurt we'd caused, it was over. A silly mistake with so much consequence.' A tear fell down her cheek and she quickly wiped it away. 'I wouldn't advise it,' she laughed tightly, in an attempt to lighten the mood.

I swallowed back my own hot tears, only realizing fully at that moment the pain I'd been holding in for all those years. I'd never really stopped to take stock of the enormity of losing my boyfriend and best friend, seemingly to each other. I'd just stuck my head in the sand and soldiered on, in complete denial of the damage it had done. Maybe I thought that by not acknowledging it, it would somehow make it go away, make it seem as if it'd never happened. I'd almost convinced myself that it was the best thing that had ever happened to me; it had certainly sorted out the wheat from the chaff and I was better off without them. Except I wasn't. Until then,

Tom had been the love of my life, the man who I was going to have babies with. And Charlotte? Well, she'd been by my side since we met in Year Three of primary school.

'Joined at the hip, those two are,' my mum had commented to her mum at the school gate. 'They'll be together forever.' Her mum had nodded, smiling, and from then on, not a day passed without us speaking to each other. We'd gone to the same secondary school, been on holidays together, and even got our first jobs just a few streets away from each other behind Oxford Circus. I'd call her mum every few days for a catch-up, as she did mine. It felt like we'd come from the same mould, had the same stamp running through us. But she'd proved we were nothing like each other at all.

Looking at her now, as she wiped the tears from her eyes, I grieved for the times we'd lost. The love and laughter we could have had, instead of the pain and hatred.

'Okay, so who's gonna be next?' cried Seb, as he spun the bottle again.

A chorus of 'whooaaah' grew louder as the bottle began to slow down.

'Emily!' They all called out, clapping. 'Totally deserved,' shouted somebody. 'The mother hen needs to repent of her sins.'

I smiled unconvincingly. 'I have no skeletons in my closet.'

'We'll see about that,' Pippa said, laughing.

'Can I ask?' pleaded Tess.

I drained my glass and turned to her expectantly. 'Truth or dare?' she asked.

'Truth.'

'Okay, have you ever been unfaithful?' she asked.

I didn't even need time to think. 'Never.'

There was a collective groan. 'What, never? Not even when you were younger?' Tess asked.

'Nope, never.' I looked to Charlotte, my oldest friend, to vouch for me.

She shook her head.

'Well, it all depends on what constitutes being unfaithful,' said Tess, rather forthrightly. 'I mean, are we talking snogging, sexual relations, or full-on sex?'

They laughed and feigned shock at normally quiet Tess's outburst.

'What are sexual relations even about?' asked Pippa. 'They talk about that all the time on *Jeremy Kyle*, you know, when they do the big lie-detector reveal. "Have you, since going out with Charmaine, had sexual relations with anyone else?"'

'Well, it's more than a kiss, but not as much as proper sex.' Tess giggled. 'So, it's got to be anything in between.'

'Oh, well, that makes it a whole lot clearer, Tess. Thanks for enlightening us,' Seb said.

'Maybe it's about even more than that,' cut in

Pammie. 'Maybe even having the intention is enough to be deemed as being disloyal?'

'Crikey, Pammie,' called Pippa. 'If just the idea of it means you're being unfaithful, I'd be the biggest floozy ever known to man.'

I laughed as Pammie crinkled her nose in distaste. 'I'm not talking about the thought of it in your head. I'm talking about the very real intention of doing something wrong, such as agreeing to meet someone when you know that's the way it's going to go.'

'I don't know that that constitutes being unfaithful, Pammie,' stated Pippa.

'It is if you keep the meeting a secret from your partner . . . regardless of whether you go through with it or not. The mere fact that you went there, fully in the knowledge of what might happen . . . that's being unfaithful in my book.'

There was much tutting and disagreeing amongst the girls and Seb. 'That means I've been unfaithful to my Dan several times,' pitched in Trudy, suddenly downcast at the suggestion.

'So, you've met someone, specifically with the intention of going to bed with them?' asked Pammie.

'Well, no, but I've met guys on nights out that I've found attractive.'

'And have you ever arranged to meet any of them again, on the basis that both of you know why you're there? Because, let's be honest, that would be the only real expectation,' continued Pammie.

'Well, no . . .' said Trudy.

'So, you're fine then,' she went on. 'I'm just saying that if you were to meet someone with the sole intention of cheating, even if you don't go through with it, are you not being unfaithful?'

There were a few more muted nods than when she'd last posed the question.

'So perhaps you should ask Emily the same question again,' she went on.

My ears were starting to burn as I looked at her through narrowed eyes. Images of me and James flashed behind them: us looking cosy in the corner of a backstreet cafe; the pair of us perched on stools in an exclusive hotel bar, his hand on mine, the body language that must have screamed, 'will they, won't they'. I knew what it looked like in my head, and I could only imagine what it would have looked like to someone else. Had someone seen us? Is that what she was implying?

Tess looked at me. 'Okay, so I'll put it to you again, Miss Emily Havistock, have you or have you not ever been unfaithful, by intention?'

Pammie crossed her arms in front of her and raised her eyebrows, seemingly waiting for my response. She couldn't possibly know, could she? There would be no reason for James to tell her. Why would he? And the chances of someone seeing us and putting two and two together were a million to one. I was just being paranoid.

I looked straight at her. 'No, never.'

She bristled in her chair, and the others turned their attention to the next player, but she mumbled something under her breath and I was sure she said, 'James.'

23

'What a fun night,' said Mum, as we stood in front of the bathroom mirror, taking our make-up off. We were both swaying. Well, I was anyway. Maybe me swaying made it look like she was swaying too.

'I haven't laughed like that in years,' she said, as she lifted one leg up to unbuckle her shoe.

I smiled. 'I think that waiter had the hots for you.'

'Oh, stop it!' She laughed, before leaning precariously towards me, one leg still in the air. 'Ooh, Em, help!'

I caught her as she leant into me. 'What are you trying to do?' I giggled.

'Well, if I could just . . .' she said, before dissolving into hysterics. I caught hold of both her elbows before she fell to the floor. I'd never seen her like this before.

'And how good is it to see Charlotte again?' she said. 'I really am pleased that you sorted things out with her. No friendship is ever worth losing over a boy, especially not one like yours and Charlotte's. I said the very same thing to Pammie.'

Just hearing her name sobered me up. 'What did you say to her?' I said, careful to keep my tone light.

'Just that,' she said unhelpfully, still sitting on the

bathroom floor. 'When I told her what had gone on, I said how sad it was because you were so close, you and her, weren't you?'

There was a heat bubbling away under my skin. I sat down on the floor beside her. 'Why were you talking about it, Mum?'

'Pammie asked if there might be anybody that we'd left off the invite list. She was just double-checking that everybody that was supposed to be coming to the wedding was coming. I told her that I thought we had it covered, but when she started asking about friends from your younger years, it got me thinking.'

'Ah, that makes sense,' I said, although inside I was screaming, *what the hell's it got to do with her?* We were paying for our own wedding, and Mum and Dad had paid for our honeymoon. Pammie had no right to ask questions.

'So, I said that the only person that wasn't invited, who under any other circumstance would have been, was Charlotte.'

I nodded my head, feigning patience and trying desperately to sober up.

'And then you told her everything that had happened?'

'Well, to some extent, yes. I didn't think it appropriate to go into *how* you found out. I just said that Tom and Charlotte were seeing each other behind your back.'

There was a vice-like grip squeezing my chest.

'Right, let's get you up,' I said, holding her under her arms.

She giggled all the way into bed, and I quietly left the room and closed the door.

I went across the landing and down the corridor to the bedroom at the back of the house, my stride getting faster and heavier with each step.

I flung the door open without knocking.

'Who the hell do you think you are?' I hissed.

Pammie didn't even look up from the book she was reading. 'I wondered how long it would take you,' she said.

'How dare you?' I spat. 'How dare you invite yourself to my hen weekend and bring *her* with you?'

'I thought you'd be pleased,' she said. 'I thought it would be a wonderful opportunity to bring you back together again.'

She put the book down on the bed beside her and took her glasses off, rubbing at the bridge of her nose.

'It's such a shame,' she went on, 'to have a good friend and lose contact with them. Was it over anything in particular?'

So, she wanted to play? Okay, let's play.

'No, not really,' I said matter-of-factly. 'We just grew apart.'

'Well, when I heard that you'd met at school and used to be so close, I couldn't stand the thought of someone so special not being there on your big day,' she said, a glint in her eye. 'I ran a search on that computer thing, what do they call it? Book Face, or something?'

God, she was good. But she seemed to have forgotten that Adam wasn't here now. He couldn't hear the piteous tone in her voice or see the simpering look on her face. No doubt he'd glow with pride at her ingenious detective work. 'Ah, bless her,' he would have cooed. 'How thoughtful is that? Isn't she incredible?'

I smiled. 'Facebook, Pamela. It's called Facebook.'

She flinched and pulled up sharply, the childlike act gone in an instant. 'I don't have to be civil to you,' she hissed. 'But, for better or worse, you're going to be my daughter-in-law.'

I grinned. 'Indeed I am, and I, for one, can't wait.'

'You'd do well to lose the sarcasm,' she said. 'It doesn't become you.'

'And you'd do well to stop being such a bitch.'

Her eyes flashed dark as she drew in her thin lips, revealing the gum line above her two front teeth, like a snarling dog. 'Have you really no manners? Do you honestly think my son is going to stay with someone like you for the rest of his life?'

I sensed there was more to come, so I stood with my arms folded in front of me, waiting for the onslaught to continue.

'He could have anyone he wanted,' she went on. 'So why on earth he's settling for you, I don't know. But he'll see sense eventually, you mark my words. I just hope that it comes sooner rather than later.'

I smiled, as if her vicious words were rolling over me, like water off a duck's back, but every syllable was like a sword cutting through the very strings that held my heart in place. I felt as if I had gone back in time, been transported back to primary school, to when nasty Fiona had loomed over me in the corner of the playground, and had laughed as I lay sprawled on the ground, my blue gingham dress caught up around my waist.

'Why are your knickers dirty?' she'd sneered. 'Look, everyone. Emily's pooed herself.'

Other children came over to point and laugh, while I hastily pulled my dress back down and went to get up. Fiona offered me her hand, but as I reached up to take it, she pulled it away and I fell back again. 'Oh, silly, dirty Emily.' She laughed, and everyone around her joined in, if only for fear of being picked on themselves. 'You might want to go and change, 'cause no one is going to want to sit next to someone who smells of shit.'

I could still feel that shame and embarrassment. The heat that had scorched my cheeks, even though I'd battled feverishly to stop it. I'd run towards the toilet block, where the usual gaggle of kids blocked the way. I pushed through them just as the bell sounded for the end of playtime.

'Emily Havistock, the bell has gone,' shouted Mrs Calder from the other side of the playground, seemingly with eyes in the back of her head. I chose to ignore her, preferring to incur her wrath over Fiona's. I banged the cubicle door shut and locked it before pulling my knickers down to check for marks. There was nothing but a scuff of dirt where I'd fallen onto the dusty tarmac. I don't know why I'd believed it would be anything else. I burst into tears then, the type that you try so hard to hold in, for fear of knowing that, once they start, they may never stop.

The type that was threatening to fall now, some twenty years later, as I stood in front of another bully. I swallowed them back down and fixed Pammie with a steely stare.

'When are you going to realize that Adam and I are going to be together forever?' I said, my voice wobbling ever so slightly.

She tutted and rolled her eyes. 'I don't think so.' She sighed. 'You don't stand a chance.'

I moved closer to her. 'I'm marrying your son, and no matter what you say or what you do, you will never stop that. It *is* going to happen, whether you like it or not, so I suggest you start getting used to it.'

She leant in even more, so that our noses were almost touching. 'Over my dead body,' she spat.

24

'You seem to have quite a fan,' Adam mused, as he snuggled up to me. It was 2 a.m. and he'd been home for an hour, most of which had been spent making love. I was never going to turn that down, especially after we'd been apart for four days, and he'd no doubt had every imaginable temptation put in his way in between times. But now I was tired and needed to get some sleep before the alarm went off at six.

'Mmm,' I murmured. 'Who?'

'Mum,' he said jubilantly. 'She said she had a great time, and you made her feel really welcome.'

I drew in a deep breath, waiting for the sarcasm to pass before he told me what she'd really said. God, had she really got to him that quickly? Spoken to him even before I had? He'd only been on English soil for a couple of hours.

'So. Thank. You,' he whispered, in between planting kisses on my cheek.

I turned to face him.

'What?' He laughed.

I thought back to the vow I'd made – to never see her

again, after the wedding – when she'd questioned my relationship with Seb.

Her comment had come out of nowhere, whilst I was sunbathing by the pool, the morning after our fight. 'You do realize that you won't be able to see so much of Seb once the wedding's been and done with, don't you?' she'd said.

I hadn't even realized she was up, let alone lying next to me by the pool. I didn't move a muscle, just opened my eyes under my sunglasses to see Tess and Pippa snorkelling in the shallow end.

There was no one else around.

'Is that so?' I'd replied.

'Yes, it is so,' she'd sniped. 'It's not right, you having such a closeness to another man. Adam is prepared to put up with it until the wedding, but once you're married, Seb is going to have to go.'

I still didn't move, though my muscles were twitching beneath my skin and all I really wanted to do was jump up and tear her eyes out.

I kept my voice steady. 'Adam said that, did he?'

'Yes, he's always had concerns. He told me at the very beginning how unhappy he was about it.'

'I don't know if it's slipped your attention, Pamela, but Seb's gay.' As soon as it came out, I wanted to suck it back in again. It felt like I was justifying our relationship to her by saying that him being gay made it okay.

'I fully appreciate that,' she'd sniffed. 'But it's not

right. He shouldn't be here. Adam was horrified when he realized you were inviting him.'

Adam had not so much as breathed a word of it to me. He wouldn't dare. But now, thinking about it, we'd never had that conversation, ever. Mine and Seb's relationship was just what it was, had always been, long before Adam had come along, and I'd thought, assumed, that he'd accepted it, but perhaps he hadn't.

'What did he say, then?' I'd asked confidently.

'He just couldn't believe it,' she'd said. 'Gay or not, he's still a man, and he's cavorting with his girlfriend, going on her hen weekend. It's embarrassing for him.'

I took my glasses off then and sat up, but if Pammie noticed, she didn't let on. She stayed horizontal with a floppy hat covering the top half of her face.

'Adam actually told you I was embarrassing him?' I'd questioned. I hated myself for falling into her trap.

She'd smiled then, warming to her theme. 'Yes, but who wouldn't be? It's not Adam's fault, it's just a man's natural reaction. I don't know a man alive who'd be happy for you to spend as much time with another man as you do with Seb. It's not how a woman, betrothed to be married, is expected to behave.'

'We're not living in the eighteenth century,' I'd said, biting my tongue to stop the words I really wanted to say from spilling out. 'Times are different to your day. Women are different.' I was still trying to justify our relationship to her.

'That may be so,' she'd said calmly, the smile still toying on her lips. 'But all I'm saying, as a favour really, to save you getting into an argument with Adam, is that it's going to have to stop. He won't put up with it after the wedding.'

'It won't be Seb I stop seeing,' I hissed. 'It'll be you.'

Her hat fell onto the floor as she struggled to raise herself on the sunbed. 'What?'

'You heard. And if I refuse to see you, you know what that means?'

She looked at me, her face contorted with hatred.

'It'll make it so much harder for Adam to see you.'

'Good luck with that,' she said calmly, her voice masking any fear she may have felt. 'Do you honestly think he's going to choose you over me?'

'Who does he live with? Who does he share his bed with? Who does he make love to? I'd say your chances are pretty slim.'

'I wouldn't count on it,' she'd said, before getting up and walking slowly towards the house, her paisley kaftan billowing in the breeze. 'You kids having a good time?' she asked Tess and Pippa as she passed the pool, seemingly without a care in the world. Psychopath.

Now she's telling Adam that she had a great time and that I made her feel welcome? I immediately feel wrong-footed, as if she's playing a cat-and-mouse game. No prizes for guessing who the mouse is.

Adam pulled the duvet over our heads and I could

feel him hard again as he pulled me tighter towards him. 'It's been four days.' He laughed, as I tutted. 'I can't help it.'

'Go to sleep,' I said wearily. 'We've got to get up in a few hours.'

'I will, I promise. I'll bash myself with a hammer and won't bother you again, but only if you do me a favour.'

'For God's sake, what?' I laughed.

'Mum's asked if she can come with you to your final fitting.'

'What?' I gasped, sitting up abruptly and turning to face him. 'Seriously?'

'She said that you both got on so well while you were away that she wondered if it would be all right to come along to see your dress.' He screwed his face up, as if expecting a retort.

My mouth dropped open.

'Please, Em. It'd mean the world to her. As she said, she doesn't have a daughter so will never be able to share that special time with her. You're the closest she's got. She'd be so chuffed.'

'But . . .' I started.

'Your mum's already seen it, so it's not as if she'd be stepping on anybody else's toes as such.'

'But Pippa hasn't seen it yet, nor has Seb. The four of us were going to make a day of it on Saturday, go for lunch and that.'

Adam propped himself up on an elbow. 'Seb?'

I stopped breathing.

'Seb's going with you?'

I slid back under the duvet with my heart hammering through my chest. Had I imagined the change in the atmosphere? I must have, because Seb was a problem that Pammie had created in *her* head, not Adam's. So why did it feel like I'd just stepped on a landmine and was waiting for a delayed explosion?

'Of course,' I said nonchalantly. 'Why wouldn't he?'

'Because it's a girls' thing,' he said curtly.

I turned to face him and snuggled into his warm chest, sliding an arm around his back. 'You're being sexist,' I said, laughing.

I felt him pull away, both literally and mentally. 'So Seb's going to sit in a bridal shop with a gaggle of women?' he asked incredulously. 'He's going to see your dress before I do?'

'Oh, don't be ridiculous,' I remonstrated. 'It's *Seb*, for goodness' sake.' Had she got to him? Had she planted this absurd seed in his head?

'It just seems a bit much, to be honest,' he said sharply. 'Still, if *he's* going, I really can't see a problem with my mum going, can you?'

There was no answer to that, and I felt myself sink into the mattress, beaten and dejected. What did I have to do to get this vile woman out of my life?

25

Even Mum had struggled to keep the surprised tone out of her voice when I told her that Pammie was accompanying us on our special day out. 'Oh, okay then, dear, whatever you want to do. It's your day,' she'd said democratically.

'You are fucking joking?' screeched Pippa, who had no such trouble with her freedom of speech.

I'd ashamedly called Seb the day before to tell him that I'd had second thoughts about him seeing my dress.

'But I want to see you before anybody else does,' he'd said. I could tell he was disappointed.

'You still will,' I'd said. 'When you do my hair on the day.'

'Okay then,' he'd said abruptly, before putting the phone down.

I don't know why I kowtowed to pressure, but it just felt the easier thing to do. It took away another problem, which gave me one less to have to deal with or worry about. I had enough going on, and I just wanted a peaceful life.

We'd been waiting at Blackheath station for twenty-five minutes when Pammie decided to show up, making us late for our appointment at the bridal boutique. I hate being late, ask anyone I know what I'm least likely to do and they'll say, 'be late'. It's a real bugbear of mine, how people have so little respect for your time that they can happily waste it. I don't accept it at work and I don't expect it in my private life, unless of course there's a very valid reason. Fire, earthquake, and death are permissible, however Pammie could only offer, 'Sorry, I missed my train, haven't made us late, have I?'

I turned my head away from her insincere air kiss and strode on ahead, up the hill towards the heath, leaving both Mum and Pammie flailing behind, and Pippa puffing to keep up.

The door to the shop chimed as we walked in, and I was immediately hit by the heat from the sun blazing through the windows. An oversized arrangement of white lilies sat on a small round table in the middle of the boutique.

'Good morning, Emily,' cooed Francesca, my dress designer, as she sashayed towards us. 'Only two weeks to go till your big day! Are you ready?'

My face was red and blotchy, and I could feel the sweat as it began to collect at the base of my spine. 'Almost.' I smiled.

'I'm really sorry, but as you're half an hour late, we're under a slight time restraint as I have my next bride in thirty minutes.'

On what was supposed to be a special day, relaxed

and easy, my chest was already tight, a coiled spring of anxiety.

'But don't worry,' she went on, in an attempt to counteract her previous sentence. 'I'm sure we'll get everything done.'

I wanted to sit down, have a glass of water, and be calm, before going into the heat of the changing room, but it seemed that time didn't allow. It hadn't been a good idea to wear thick tights, as black woolly particles littered the plush cream carpet and stuck firmly between my sweaty toes. This was not going how I wanted it to go, and it took all my strength not to cry. I remonstrated with myself as to how that would make me look, like a pampered princess throwing a hissy fit over trivial details.

Francesca slowly pulled the dress down over my head, as I held my arms aloft, and then she shimmied it past my shoulders and onto my torso. 'Now for the moment of truth,' I said, holding my breath, as if that would make it fit better. 'Let's see if we need to let it out.' I offered a half-smile, confident that I'd maintained my goal weight, but doubting my willpower at the same time.

I caught sight of myself in the mirror and almost didn't recognize the woman staring back. Adorned with chiffon folds softly draping around my chest, my waist cinched in by invisible seams, the ivory silk falling in perfect rivulets to the floor.

How could I be getting married? I still felt like a child inside, playing at a make-believe wedding, yet here I was, supposedly all grown up, ready to take on the responsibilities of being someone's wife. Adam's wife. I pictured him standing at the top of the aisle, his face beaming but rigid with nerves as I approach him. My family are smiling, proud of the woman I've become, Mum in a navy netted hat and Dad in his smart new suit ('it's got a waistcoat, you know'). My brother and his own little family, baby Sophie attempting to escape the confines of her mother's clutches to the playground of the pews below. Then I turn my head to the right, past Adam, to his brother and best man, James, standing beside him, and guilt wrenches at my heart, squeezing the very life out of it. His mother, her face twisted with hate that only I can see, is clinging onto his arm.

'Are you ready?' Francesca asked, popping her head round the curtain.

I nodded nervously. I could hear the chatter on the other side, Pammie's shrill voice cutting through me like barbed wire.

'Well, come on then,' coaxed Francesca, 'let your public see you.'

I pushed the heavy velvet to one side and stepped out.

'Oh, Em,' cried Mum.

'You look so beautiful,' said Pippa, her eyes wide, and a hand to her mouth.

'You think?' I asked. 'Is it what you expected?' I directed the question at Pippa, but it was Pammie who answered it.

'No,' she said hesitantly. 'I thought it was going to be . . . I don't know . . . bigger, I suppose.'

I looked down at the sleek lines which clung to my curves, went in and out at my waist, and skimmed the shape of my thighs, before pooling on the floor.

'I think it's just perfect, Em,' gushed Pippa. 'It's so you.'

'It looks lovely, dear, it really does,' added Pammie. 'You'll get some wear out of it, that's for sure. It'll make a lovely outfit if you've got somewhere special to go.'

Her words stung, but Pippa and Mum didn't pick up on it. That's the thing with Pammie: she gives you a compliment that everybody hears, only to follow it with a barbed snipe that's barely noticeable, except of course by me, its intended victim.

'Will you be doing anything with your hair?' she asked. 'To dress it up a bit.'

Francesca stepped in with a simple diamanté tiara, attached to a one-tier veil.

'Are you wearing your hair up or down?' asked Pippa excitedly.

'I'm thinking up,' I said, wrinkling my nose, still undecided. Francesca scooped up my loose hair, pulling tendrils out around my face, and secured it with a few haphazard pins before gently placing the headpiece on.

'It gives you an idea,' she said.

'Well, it won't be exactly like *that*, will it?' Pammie scoffed. 'I assume you're having professionals in on the day.'

It was a rhetorical question that I didn't feel warranted a response.

'So, you love it?' I asked. 'What do you think Adam will think of it?'

A resounding chorus of 'amazing', 'he'll love it', 'stunning' reverberated around the shop, yet it was the word 'interesting' that seemed the loudest.

My head was pounding by the time we got out of there, exactly thirty-three minutes later. A low, bright sun sliced its way across my vision as we made our way back down through the village.

'I've booked your favourite, Due Amici, for lunch,' exclaimed Pippa. 'We're a wee bit early, but I'm sure they'll be able to seat us, or we can have a drink at the bar.'

'Actually, do you mind if we take a rain check?' I asked.

Pippa spun round to face me, her eyebrows raised, waiting for me to continue.

'I've got a killer headache, and I could just do with a sit-down and a cup of tea, to be honest.'

She took my arm, steering me away from the gossiping mums, who were too caught up in their conversation to notice. 'Am I getting this right?' said Pippa, 'Is this a cockamamie?'

I smiled. We hadn't used that expression in ages. Not since I'd been with Adam, at least. It was our secret code name for 'get me out of here', and I last remembered using it when I had been drunkenly persuaded to go back to some guy's house after meeting him at a karaoke night in the Dog & Duck in Brewer Street. Pippa was snogging his mate in the corner, and it all sounded like a great idea when we were doing shots whilst murdering 'Nutbush City Limits'. But once we were all in the cab, with Pippa sitting astride her new friend, I'd been suddenly and mercifully hit with the sensible stick. It was not what I wanted to do, and not where I wanted to be. 'Cockamamie!' I'd shouted, and Pippa had sat bolt upright as if she'd heard a jungle call from Tarzan.

'Seriously?' she'd cried.

'Yep. Cock-a-mam-ie.' I slowed it down, more for my benefit than hers. If it had come out wrong, God knows what a good time the boys would have thought they were in for.

'She's getting to you, isn't she?' Pippa asked now, tilting her head towards Pammie.

I nodded and felt tears prickle at the back of my eyes.

'Okay, do you want to come back to mine?'

I thought of Adam, waiting at home, all expectant, eager to hear the news of how my special day had gone, and I just didn't want to deal with it. I couldn't put on my happy face and lie through my teeth about how perfect it had all been, yet I didn't want to tell him how it had really played out: how his mother had yet again ruined it all. He was somehow under the misapprehension that we'd been getting along so much better recently, and it seemed that, all the time he thought that, me and him had been closer. There were no silly arguments about what he deemed to be my unjustified paranoia, whenever she came up in conversation. I'd learnt that it was a lot easier to listen, whenever he spoke about her, smile, and get on with it, because I was suddenly coming to the realization that she might be right: if the chips *were* down, and I did make him choose, I honestly didn't know which way he'd go.

'Ladies,' said Pippa, as she turned to the mums. 'Emily's not feeling too well, so I'm going to take her home.'

'Oh, what's up love?' Mum cried, as she rubbed my back. 'Do you want me to come with you?'

I shook my head. 'No thanks, Mum. I'll be fine, just come over a bit queasy, that's all.'

'She's probably not looking after herself,' interjected Pammie, as if I wasn't there. 'No doubt trying to lose weight on some crazy diet, to get into that dress.'

Pippa must have seen the look on my face, as she quickly steered me away, stopping me from punching the interfering bitch square between the eyes.

'Is it me?' I asked, once we were safely ensconced on

her sofa, cup-a-soup firmly in hand. 'Everyone says how thoughtful and kind she is, yet all I can see is a red-faced devil with horns coming out of her head.'

'But that's how she is with everyone else. She's seen as Little Miss Innocent, who kindly surprised you by bringing an old friend along to your hen do, begged to come along to your dress fitting because she'll never have her own daughter to share that special experience with . . . blah, blah, blah. And to be honest, Em, everyone's buying it. Even her own son can't see through her, and see the hurt she's causing you.'

'So, it *is* me, then?' I could feel tears welling up, and swallowed hard.

'Of course it isn't,' she said, moving up the sofa to put her arm around me. '*I* can see what she's doing, but I'm no use to you, apart from at times like this.' She pulled me towards her. 'You need your husband-to-be on side, to make him see what she's doing and how miserable she's making you. You can't begin a marriage with this much resentment hanging over you, because it will ultimately destroy it, if not you. You've got to talk to him, tell him everything.'

'I've tried that,' I cried. 'But when I say it out loud, it just sounds so pathetic, like I'm a spoilt child. Even *I* think that, so God knows what Adam makes of it all.'

'What did he say about Charlotte being on your hen do? That's not pathetic. That's a very real line she crossed, one that many wouldn't even think of, let alone do.'

'I haven't told him . . .'

'What?' exclaimed Pippa. 'You're getting married in two weeks, and you haven't told him something as important as that?'

I shook my head. 'We've only been back a few days, and the odd times we have been together we've either spoken about Las Vegas, or the wedding itself.'

'You're burying your head in the sand,' she said stiffly. 'It's going to make you ill.'

I nodded weakly, already aware that the situation was having an adverse effect on me. 'I'll talk to him tonight.'

When I got home, Adam was in the middle of watching a rugby game on TV.

'Can we talk?' I asked quietly, almost not wanting him to hear me, hoping I could push the inevitable under the carpet for another week.

'Yep, sure,' he said absently. 'But can it wait until the game's finished?'

I nodded and walked into the kitchen. I took some peppers out of the fridge and started hacking at them aggressively. He hadn't even asked how the day had gone.

'Actually, no, it can't,' I said, sweeping back into the living room, knife still in hand.

He sat up a bit straighter, but only to see past me to

229

the telly. I grabbed the remote control from the coffee table and switched it off.

'What the hell?' he called out. 'It's the semi-final.'

'We need to talk.'

'What about?' he moaned, sounding like a petulant child.

I sat down on the coffee table, directly in front of him, so that he couldn't shirk or fidget. He looked warily at the knife in my hand.

'We need to talk about your mother,' I said, placing it gently down on the wooden top beside me.

He groaned. 'Really? Again? I thought we'd got over all this?'

'You need to talk to her,' I went on. 'Her behaviour is just not acceptable, and I will not allow it to cause problems between us.'

'It doesn't,' he said naively. 'I thought you were getting on better. That was certainly the impression I got from her after your hen weekend.'

I rested my head in my hands, rubbing at my eyes, to give me time to think how best to approach it. 'She did something utterly unforgivable in Portugal,' I started. 'And it has caused me so much anxiety and pain that I can't move on until I tell you about it and you realize what she's done and how it's made me feel.'

He leant forward, but I could see he was in two minds as to whether to touch me reassuringly, or hold back for fear of being seen to go against his mother. He chose the latter. 'Well, what did she do that was so bad?'

I cleared my throat. 'She invited Charlotte.'

I waited for him to leap up and say, 'What the hell?' but he stayed where he was. 'Who's Charlotte?' he said, unfazed.

This wasn't going how I wanted it to go. 'Charlotte. Tom's Charlotte!'

He shook his head, nonplussed.

'Are you doing this on purpose?' I cried. 'My best friend, the one who slept with Tom.'

He looked confused. 'How did that happen?'

'Exactly! That's my point. Your mum thought it would be a good idea to reacquaint us, so she tracked her down and brought her to Portugal.'

'But that doesn't even make sense,' he said. At last we were getting somewhere, but he wasn't making it easy.

'She did it to spite me,' I went on. 'She went out of her way to find her.'

'But she wasn't to know,' he said defensively. 'How was she to know what went on between you?'

'Because my mum told her!'

'Oh, don't be ridiculous,' he said, rising up from the sofa. 'If Mum had had any idea of what had happened between you, she'd never have done it. She obviously thought she was doing a good thing, a nice thing, by surprising you.'

'Adam, what part of this are you not getting?' I cried,

tears springing to my eyes. 'She did it on purpose. She knew why we'd fallen out and got her there to upset me.'

'But she wouldn't dream of doing that,' he said. 'I think you're just being paranoid.'

'You need to speak to her, to find out what the hell her problem is because, if you don't, she'll destroy us.'

He let out a short laugh. 'A little melodramatic, wouldn't you say?'

'I mean it, Adam. You need to have it out with her. This personal vendetta against me has got to stop.'

'She's never said anything about you, against you, or to belittle you.' He was standing now.

'You can believe what you want to believe, but I'm telling you, you're living in cloud cuckoo land. You're completely in denial.'

'She's *my* mother, for Christ's sake. I think I know her better than you do.'

I looked at him and kept my voice calm and steady. 'Whatever her problem is, you need to sort it out. I will not put up with it any longer.'

He smiled and shook his head condescendingly.

'Do you hear me?' I shouted, as if to labour the point.

I walked into the bedroom and slammed the door shut. If he wasn't prepared to do something about Pammie, then I would.

26

I slid under the water as the doorbell rang, the sound suddenly deafened by the crackle of bubble bath quietly popping above me.

Go *away*, I silently pleaded.

And I thought my prayers had been answered, but just as I pushed myself up, the rudimentary chime echoed around the flat again.

'Oh, leave me alone!' I said out loud.

It buzzed and buzzed again.

'Okay, I'm coming,' I muttered, annoyed that my pampering session had come to a premature end. I scooped my hair up into a towel and grabbed my dressing gown from the hook on the wall.

'This had better be important,' I said, as I opened the door, expecting to see Pippa or Seb standing there.

'James!' I instinctively pulled my gown tighter around me, in the vain hope that it might somehow make me feel less vulnerable. 'Adam's not in,' I said, without opening the door another inch. 'He's having a drink with the boys from work.'

'I haven't come to see Adam,' he said, his speech a little slurred. He gently pushed on the door.

'Now's not a good time,' I said, my heart beating fast, my bare foot trying to hold the door firm.

'I need to talk to you,' he said. 'I've not come here to cause trouble.'

I looked at him, his kind eyes and soft features, his full lips upturned ever so slightly at the corners. He'd been drinking, but he seemed friendly, approachable. I eased the pressure off the door and moved out of the way, letting him come in. He smiled and pushed his hair back, away from his eyes. It felt like I was watching Adam from ten years ago, back when he was with Rebecca. I wondered if the peppered spots of grey at Adam's temples and the vexed frown he now wore daily were a result of Rebecca's untimely death. It couldn't have been easy, being such a young man, with his life planned out ahead of him, intending to share it with the one he loved, only to lose her so suddenly and so unnecessarily. I didn't give Adam enough credit for having pulled himself out of the hole he must have been in, and fighting back.

'Help yourself to a drink,' I said, signalling towards the kitchen.

He smiled and raised his eyebrows suggestively.

'A tea or coffee, I mean. I'll just go and get changed.'

I heard a cork being sucked out of a bottle, as I combed my wet hair in the bathroom mirror, the glass still steamed up from my hot bath. The water lay stagnant, the foam bubbles dissipated, and I reached in to remove the plug, then folded my discarded towel and hung it on the heated rail.

It didn't matter what I looked like – why would it? – but I wanted to check my reflection anyway. I rubbed a circle in the misted mirror, and pulled back as I saw James standing behind me, a glass of red wine in his hand.

Time seemed to stand still, the only sound the bath water gently gurgling as it ran away.

'James, I . . .' I spun round to face him, my wraparound gown falling open at the chest.

'I'm sorry . . . I . . .' he stuttered. 'I'll leave you to it.'

I quickly dressed in black leggings and one of Adam's shirts, rolling up the sleeves as I walked into the living room. It occurred to me then that perhaps I'd subconsciously made a symbolic choice to show I was Adam's girl.

'So, what brings you here?' I asked, as casually as I could.

'I just thought I'd pop by,' he said.

I walked over to the window. 'You've not driven, have you?' I couldn't see his car in the street below.

'No, I got a cab,' he said.

'All the way from Sevenoaks?' I exclaimed.

He nodded.

'Well, as I said, Adam's not here, so I'm afraid it's been a wasted journey.'

'I've not come to see Adam.'

I poured myself a glass of red from the bottle on the kitchen countertop to calm myself.

'So . . .' I said, choosing to stay standing rather than sit on the sofa next to him.

'I wanted to talk to you. Needed to talk to you.'

'James, don't,' I said, walking around the kitchen island. It somehow felt safer with a metre of granite between us.

'You need to know,' he said, going to stand up.

I could feel my defences weakening. There was a part of me that wanted to hear what he had to say, but I wanted to close my ears off to it at the same time. I didn't need any more confusion in my life. Adam and I had taken a huge step forward since I'd last seen James. If he told me how he felt, I feared I'd be taking two steps back again.

'I think you ought to go,' I said. I felt myself physically moving backwards.

'Can you please listen to me for a minute?' he said, reaching for my hand. 'If you give me a chance, just for a few weeks, I will prove to you how happy I can make you.' His piercing eyes stared at me intently.

'You're not being fair, James. I'm about to marry your brother. Does that not mean anything to you?'

'But he won't look after you the way I would.'

If I was honest with myself, he was probably right. James was the antithesis of everything that his brother stood for. Adam exuded confidence in any situation; he'd always be the first to introduce himself, take command in a restaurant, or pull his pants down during a rugby sing-song. That's who Adam was, and I was well aware that if he wasn't so forthright, we'd never have got together in the first place. James was reserved, more refined, and always seemed to consider what he was saying and doing before he did it. He'd still be listening to me, long past the point when Adam would have switched off. And he'd hold me up when, all around me, everything would be falling down.

His head was just inches away, his lips so close to mine that I could almost taste them. All I needed to do was close my eyes, and be transported to another place.

'You deserve better,' he murmured. 'I promise I will never hurt you.'

I pulled back. For all his faults, I knew that Adam would never intentionally hurt me. Was James suggesting he would?

'Adam's good to me . . .'

I was startled by a noise on the landing, and turned to see Adam standing there, clearly the worse for wear. We both jumped back, as if we'd had an electric shock. I hadn't even heard him come in.

'Hey, hey, what's going on here?' he slurred, as he

leant against the living-room door frame, loosening what looked to be an already loose tie.

'I . . . we . . .' I started, keeping my head down, trying to disguise the guilt I was sure would be written all over my face.

'I'm about to win a bet,' said James, reaching around my neck and pulling on my collar. 'I'm reckoning this is my shirt. You must have nicked it when we were both staying at Mum's over Christmas.'

'It's bloody not,' said Adam, attempting to walk towards us in a straight line. 'I'll have you know that's my Gant shirt.'

James leant in to take a peek, his breath hot on my neck. 'Ha, Eton! Told you. That's mine, you bloody thief.'

So, I was now wearing James's shirt? The irony wasn't lost on me.

'Hey, babe,' slurred Adam, giving me a wet kiss. I instinctively pulled back. His breath smelt of alcohol and kebabs, and he reeked of smoke.

'What's up, darling? Aren't you pleased to see me?'

'Of course I am,' I laughed nervously, 'but you stink. Have you been smoking?' I'd be surprised if he had, as he knew it was one of my pet hates.

'What? No, of course not.' He smelt the sleeve of his suit jacket and looked at me nonplussed, as if that proved I'd imagined it.

He slung an arm carelessly around me and leant his bulk against my shoulder.

'So, what are you doing here, J-boy?' Adam asked, his voice getting louder.

I looked at James wide-eyed, willing him to have a plausible excuse, ready to offer.

'I need to pick up the receipt for the rings from you,' he said calmly.

Adam clumsily patted himself down with his free hand. The other was still hanging over my shoulder, weighing me down.

'I haven't got it, you took it,' he said, looking confused. 'I dishtinct—' He pulled himself off me and crouched down on the floor, laughing. 'Ahem,' he said, clearing his throat. 'I distinctly remember you taking it.'

'Maybe you're right,' said James. 'I've checked my wallet, but maybe it's in my trouser pocket.'

'*That's* where it will be,' said Adam, shouting the first word, then mumbling, almost inaudibly, the rest of the sentence.

James and I looked at each other and smiled resignedly. 'And you thought *you* were drunk?' I said.

'Come on, big fella,' he said to Adam, reaching down to him. 'Let's get you into bed.'

'Only if you come with me.' Adam laughed. Neither of us knew who he was talking to.

James pulled Adam up, and put his body weight underneath him.

I rushed to the bathroom and quickly unbuttoned the shirt I was wearing. I don't know if I was surprised or not that the label clearly said 'Gant'.

27

Five days before the wedding, Pammie called to ask if six more guests could be invited to the service. Four days before the wedding, she asked if she could stay at the hotel with me the night before. Three days before the wedding, she wanted the seating plan emailed over to her.

I said a resounding 'no' to everything.

'She's only trying to help,' commented Adam, when I complained about her interference. 'The poor woman can't win.'

I looked witheringly at him, disappointed yet not remotely surprised. He'd made his position very clear. If I was honest with myself, I don't think I expected any different.

True to form, Pammie had turned on the waterworks and played the innocent, when Adam had, apparently, taken her to task over lunch a couple of days ago. She claimed to have no idea why Charlotte and I fell out, and swore blind that any misgivings I had about her and her motives were widely misplaced. 'All she wants, more than anything in the world, is to be your friend,' Adam had said when he got home.

'So, that's it?' I'd asked incredulously. 'She says that, and you believe her? End of story?'

He'd shrugged. 'What else am I supposed to do?'

'Believe *me*,' I'd said, before walking out.

The 'family dinner' was the start of our celebrations, a small, intimate affair, a time to be with our nearest and dearest before the craziness of the big day descended on us. If I had my way, it would just be *my* family, but I'm not selfish enough to deem my wishes any more important than Adam's.

'Do I look okay?' I asked him, smoothing down the crêpe of my black dress, and then picking up a silk scarf.

'Gorgeous,' he said, before planting a kiss on my cheek.

'You didn't even look,' I teased.

'I don't need to,' he replied.

'That was corny, even for you.'

I put two lipsticks in my clutch bag, one pillar-box red, reserved for nights I was going 'out, out', the other a nude, for when the evening was winding down. Still, I figured, tonight might end with me in red. It was, after all, the penultimate night before our wedding, and I wasn't ever intending to do this again.

Mum, Dad, Stuart and Laura were already in the bar of The Ivy when we arrived. Mum, cheeks flushed, happily raised a champagne saucer to us as our coats were taken.

'Eh up, your mum's on the sauce already.' Adam laughed.

'It'll likely be prosecco, rather than the real stuff,' I said. 'At least until she knows we're paying.'

The evening would have been perfect, had it just been the six of us, but the dark cloud of Pammie's impending arrival hung low over me. I could feel my body stooping as each minute passed, the weight on my shoulders bearing down heavily.

Half an hour after our agreed meeting time, Pammie made her entrance, with James at her side.

Seeing him ravaged my brain with confusion, but I refused to give in to it. Tonight, I was going to be the epitome of self-control.

'Good to see you,' I said to James. His lips seemed to settle on my cheek for just a second too long.

'Good to see you, too,' he said quietly. 'How are you?'

'Everything's just great,' I said, conscious of relaying the same sentiment with my eyes. 'Chloe not joining us?' I asked, looking around him.

'No, afraid not. Thought Mum had let you know?'

I shook my head and raised my eyebrows.

'We've gone our separate ways,' he said.

'Oh, sorry to hear that,' I mustered.

'It's for the best,' he said. 'It wasn't right, she wasn't the one.'

'You never know,' I said, almost cheerily. 'She might have been.'

'Don't think so. You know when it's right, don't you?' His eyes bored into mine.

I ignored him and turned to greet Pammie. Her mouth was held firm in a thin, tight line.

'Pamela, how lovely,' I enthused. 'Isn't this exciting?'

We both knew my words were dripping with sarcasm, but nobody else would have noticed.

'Emily.' She scowled. I waited for the comment I was sure would follow: about how much weight I'd put on, or lost, depending on her mood; about the colour of my hair, which was a little lighter than normal; or about the dress I was wearing. For the first time I actually felt ready for it, but nothing came.

'Darling,' she said, turning to Adam and hugging him, but her mouth remained pinched, as if she was keeping it clamped shut for fear of what might come out of it if she didn't.

'Mum, how are you?' he said, embracing her warmly.

Her eyes shot down to the floor. 'Could be better,' she said glumly. I silently pleaded with Adam not to ask, not to give her the satisfaction. Mum spilling the contents of her glass as she lifted herself off her bar stool seemed to be the answer to my prayers.

'Oops, sorry,' she said, regaining her balance. 'I hadn't realized I was so high up.'

Adam laughed as he took the glass from her and guided her by the elbow to our table. Pammie's joyless face could only follow. You had to hand it to her. She'd already created an atmosphere without barely saying a word.

'So, you all ready?' Mum asked eagerly, even though the answer remained the same as the three other times she'd asked me that day. But she was excited, and it was infectious. I'd rather that than be bearing the heavy load that Pammie had walked in with. Adam could carry that burden.

'Yes, we're all ready,' I said. 'There were a few niggles at the beginning of the week, but we straightened them out, and I can't see what can go wrong between now and Saturday.' I touched the wooden underside of the table. 'There's only one day left.'

'I wouldn't be too confident,' interjected Pammie dourly. 'The day I married my Jim, the band didn't turn up. We'd booked an Abba tribute act, only to find out after dinner that they weren't coming.'

Adam laughed, no doubt trying to lighten her mood. 'So, what happened, Mum?'

'They sent a replacement along,' she went on, her voice level, without its usual lifts and lilts. 'But they were something akin to Black Sabbath.'

The table fell about laughing, but Pammie's face didn't crack. Her abject misery was a formidable feat, even for her.

She looked down into her lap, wringing her hands. *Here we go*, I thought to myself, though there was every chance I said it out loud, as Adam turned to look at me.

Pammie doing what Pammie does best.

I wasn't going to validate her attention-seeking by asking what was wrong, but Mum, naive to her ways, asked the question instead.

'Oh, Pammie, what on earth's the matter?'

She shook her head and wiped away an errant tear, the only one she could manage to squeeze out.

'It's nothing,' she bleated, in her unique 'don't worry about me' way, that I was now adept at translating into '*everybody* worry about me'. I was beyond bored of it.

I drained my champagne saucer, and the attentive waiter was refilling it before I'd even put it back on the table. 'Oh well, chin up, P,' I said, raising my glass, 'it could be worse.'

'Emily,' chastised Mum.

'I don't think so,' murmured Pammie, her voice barely audible.

I laughed theatrically, like a pantomime dame. 'Why's that then?' I asked, putting the spotlight directly on her, right where she liked it. Let's give it to her, I thought, get it over and done with, and move on with the evening. Maybe then we can make it about Adam and me, like it's supposed to be.

'Em,' said Adam quietly. 'Knock it off.'

'No, come on, Pamela,' I went on, ignoring him. 'What's up?'

She looked down again, supposedly embarrassed by the scene she was causing.

'I wasn't going to bring it up tonight,' she said. 'It didn't seem right.'

'Well, we're all ears now, so you may as well,' I said.

She fiddled nervously with her necklace, her eyes not meeting any of ours, darting instead over the busy restaurant beyond.

'I'm afraid I have some rather bad news,' she croaked, working extra hard to push another tear out.

Adam let go of my hand to hold hers.

'What is it, Mum? You're scaring me.'

'I've got cancer, son,' she said. 'I'm sorry. I really didn't want to tell you tonight. I didn't want to ruin your special evening.'

The table fell into stunned silence. Mum sat there open-mouthed, and the rest of my family looked away awkwardly. James bowed his head, as if he was already privy to this information. I didn't know whether to laugh or cry.

'Oh my God.' I couldn't tell who the words had come from. My world had become hazy, everything moving in slow motion.

'What? How?' It was Adam.

'It's breast cancer,' she said quietly. 'It's stage three, so there's still a sliver of hope.'

'How long have you known? Who – where have you been?' asked Adam, his questions all merging into one.

'I'm being well looked after, son. I've got a wonderful consultant at the Princess Royal Hospital.'

'What are they doing?'

'They're doing all they can. They've done lots of tests, and I've had a biopsy.' She grimaced and put a hand to her chest for added effect. 'They're still not sure how far it's spread. I really didn't want to mention it tonight. Come on, let's not ruin this special evening.'

I couldn't even form the words I wanted to say in my head, let alone attempt to say them out loud, but that was probably for the best.

'So, when will they know more?' said Adam. 'When will we know what we're dealing with?'

'I'm going to have treatment, for sure,' she said, 'but they don't yet know how long for.' She gave a hollow laugh. 'Or if, indeed, it's even worth having at all. But you've got to take everything they throw at you, haven't you? Who's to say what little miracles might happen.'

Adam's head dropped into his hands.

'But come on,' she said, suddenly upbeat. 'Let's forget about all that now. This is Adam and Emily's time. We won't know any more until you're back from your honeymoon.'

'We won't be going anywhere until you're through this,' said Adam.

'What?' I heard myself ask.

Adam turned to look at me, an exasperated expression on his face.

'Don't be silly.' She smiled and squeezed his hand.

'There's nothing you can do. The pair of you must go on your honeymoon. Everything must carry on as planned.'

'But what about treatment?' he asked.

'I'm having chemotherapy, starting on Monday. I put it off until after the wedding, in case my hair fell out.' She gave a half-hearted laugh. 'I need to be looking my best.'

She looked at me and smiled pitifully. I locked eyes with her, daring her to show me a glimmer of guilt, a snatch of remorse for what she'd just done. But there was nothing but a self-satisfied glow, emanating from deep within her.

28

Unsurprisingly, after Pammie's earth-shattering news, dinner had come to a premature end, and both Adam and James had insisted on taking her home and making sure she was settled.

Mum had come home with me, whilst Dad went back with Stuart and Laura.

'I'll make us a cup of tea,' said Mum, busying herself in the kitchen as I sat numbly on the sofa. 'It'll make us feel better.'

Will it? I don't know why us Brits always think it will.

She was still in shock at Pammie's announcement; so was I, but for an entirely different reason.

She brought two steaming mugs into the living room, and set them on the coffee table. 'Well,' she said. 'I can't quite get my head around it, can you?'

I shook my head. 'It does seem rather unbelievable, doesn't it?'

If she noticed the intonation in my voice, she didn't mention it. She pulled out a tissue from the sleeve of her navy jacket, which she'd bought especially for this evening, and blew her nose. 'It's just so difficult to comprehend. One minute you think you're fine, and the next, you're being given news like that. It just doesn't bear thinking about, what's going through Pammie's head right now.' She bowed her head. 'Poor Pammie.'

I looked at my mum, my proud mum, who had only ever had mine and Stuart's best interests at heart, who had looked after my dad, who had put her own career as a nurse on hold to care for us all, and who had excitedly got her hair blow-dried for tonight. And then I thought of Pammie, who was so consumed by jealousy that she had set out to destroy me for her own warped amusement.

This wasn't right. Pammie could do her worst to me, but to do this to my mum? I wasn't prepared to let that happen.

I moved up the sofa to sit next to her and took hold of her trembling hands in mine.

'Mum, I've got something to tell you. Something that I really need you to listen to.'

Tears were rolling down her cheeks as she looked up at me, the worry and fear of what I might be going to say etched on her face. 'What? What is it?' she said.

'Pammie doesn't have cancer.'

'What? What do you mean?' she asked, shaking her head in confusion. 'She's just told us she has.'

'I know what she said, but she's lying.'

'Oh, Emily,' she gasped, as a hand flew up to her mouth. 'How could you say such a thing?'

'Mum, please listen. I don't want you to say a word until I've finished, and then you can say whatever you want. Okay?'

I told her everything. I started at the very beginning, from Boxing Day, right through to what she did with Charlotte at my hen weekend. Mum sat there open-mouthed, unable to articulate whatever it was she wanted to say. She kept trying, but the words wouldn't form.

By the time I'd finished, I was sobbing, and she held me to her, rocking me back and forth. 'I had no idea,' she cried. 'Why didn't you tell me?'

'Because I knew you'd worry about it,' I said. 'I'm only telling you now because I can't bear to see you like this.'

'So *Pammie* brought Charlotte to the hen party?' she asked incredulously. 'Even after everything I told her?'

I nodded. 'Yep.'

'If I'd have had any idea what was going on, I would never— What about those poor boys? Who would do that to their own children?'

'I'll look after Adam,' I said.

'Will you tell him?' she asked. 'Will you tell him what you know? Are you sure you've got this right, Em? It's one hell of an accusation to be throwing around, and if you're wrong . . .'

'I'll handle Adam in my own time,' I said. 'Let's get the wedding over and done with and then I'll work something out. I've tried to tell him, but he just can't see it. She can do no wrong in his eyes. Something will happen, though. If I give her enough rope, she'll hang herself.'

'Are you sure you should be going ahead with the wedding, if you're not sure . . . ?' she said.

'I love Adam with all my heart, and I can't wait to be his wife. I'm not marrying his mother, she's just something I'm going to have to find a way to deal with.'

'I'm so sorry, Em . . .'

'I'll work it out,' I assured her. 'And besides, Charlotte and I are talking again, so it's not all bad.'

We offered each other weak smiles and hugged. I felt a million times better already.

29

By the time Adam appeared, Mum had reluctantly gone home. 'Promise me you'll be all right,' she said on the doorstep. 'I'll stay if you want me to.'

'I'll be fine.' I said. 'I just need to make sure Adam is okay, and I'll see you at the hotel tomorrow afternoon. You know what you need to bring, don't you?'

She smiled. We'd been through it a hundred times. 'I've got my list,' she said, waving as she got into Dad's car.

Adam looked broken, like a man who had been crushed into a thousand pieces. I so wanted to take his pain away, but I had to wait. I had to be patient. I couldn't just steamroll in and say everything I'd told my mum. He was different. This was his mother we were talking about, and I had to be very careful how I played it.

'I can't believe this is happening,' he said, as he sat at the dining table with his head in his hands.

I went and held him from behind, but he was rigid in my arms. 'We'll get through this,' I said soothingly. 'Once the wedding and honeymoon are over with, we can work out a plan.'

'How can I go to Mauritius and lie on a beach, when Mum's back here fighting for her life? It's not right.'

'But we don't know what we're dealing with yet,' I said. 'By the time we get home, we'll have more information.' I didn't anticipate her being able to keep this cruel farce up for much longer than that.

'Maybe so, but if it's her first round of chemo on Monday, I want to be here for it,' he said.

I could feel my chest tightening and willed myself to stay calm.

'We're getting married . . . tomorrow,' I said, checking my watch. 'Let's deal with this one day at a time.'

'Right now, I don't even think the wedding can go ahead,' he snapped. 'It just doesn't feel right to be celebrating, when Mum could be dying.'

I didn't say a word. I just calmly walked away, leaving him to see the sense in what I was saying. When I got into the bedroom, I silently pummelled a pillow in frustration.

By the time he came in, I was dozing, but I came to as he slid into bed.

'How are you feeling?' I asked. 'Better?'

He let out a heavy sigh. 'I think we should postpone the wedding.'

I sat bolt upright, my head spinning. 'What?'

He cleared his throat. 'I don't think we, I, can go ahead under the current circumstances. It's such a huge shock, and I need time to think this through.'

'Are you being serious?'

He nodded.

'Honestly, for real?' My voice was getting louder and going up an octave with every syllable.

'It just doesn't feel right, Em. Admit it. This is not an ideal situation to be getting married in. We don't want our wedding to be a blur, do we?'

If he was looking for validation from me, he'd come to the wrong place.

'Your mum has cancer.' I put the c-word in inverted commas with my fingers.

'What the fuck does that mean?' He leapt up, naked except for his boxer shorts, and raked a hand through his hair. 'She's got *cancer*, Em. God!'

I looked at him, pacing the floor, and could literally feel the helplessness and rage emanating from him. He looked like a battery hen, cooped up with nowhere to go, nowhere to let off the steam that was building up within him. I could go some way to easing his troubles, at least, by lifting the lid on the pressure cooker he'd put himself in. I could tell him that I thought she was lying, *knew* she was lying. I could share my belief that she'd made it all up to stop the wedding. But that sounded so ridiculous. Who would do that? No normal, sane person could even imagine telling such a vile and wicked lie. I could tell him everything she'd done and said to me since we'd been together, how she'd moved mountains to split us up, undermined me at every turn, and had now resorted to this, her all-time low, in eight months of bitching and bullying. Would he believe me? Unlikely. Would he hate me? Most definitely. Would she have won? Undoubtedly.

No. There was nothing to be gained by telling him the truth, but I'd be darned if I was going to let her get her own way with her vicious lies. We were getting married, whether she liked it or not.

'Calm down,' I said, lifting myself off the bed and going to him.

'Calm down? Calm *down*? I'm supposed to be getting married tomorrow, and my mother has cancer. How the hell do you expect me to calm down?'

'*We're* getting married tomorrow,' I said, correcting him. 'We're in this together.'

I went to hold him, to put my arms around him, but his hand flew up, blocking me.

'We're not in this together at all,' he snapped. 'You've made no attempt to disguise your feelings for my mother, and, if the truth be known, you wouldn't piss on her if she was on fire, so let's not pretend you actually care and that you're feeling my pain.'

I stepped back. 'You're not being fair. Don't make this about me. Your mother has gone out of her way to make me feel unwelcome from the day I met you, and I have tried so hard to get along with her, but do you know what, Adam? She's made it impossible!'

His hand flew up and, for a split second, I thought it

was going to bear down on me, but he turned and smashed his furled fist into the wardrobe. The hat boxes that I kept my mementoes in slid off the top and emptied themselves as they hit the floor.

I stood, frozen. I went to open my mouth, but the words wouldn't form.

'I'm sorry, Em,' he cried, falling to his knees on the floor. 'I don't know . . . I just don't know.'

The part of me that loved him wanted to kneel down beside him and rock him in my arms, but another part felt strangely detached, as if I was witnessing a desolate stranger scrambling around, trying to pick up the broken pieces of his life. To discover this side of the man I loved, a side I'd never seen before, on the day before our wedding, unnerved and terrified me in equal measure.

I sat back down on the bed and waited. I needed to take my time to process what was going on, to ensure that I stayed in complete control, because the desire to unload everything that was in my head was overpowering. But so was the panic that was caught in my chest, as the realization that he might well call the wedding off began to sink in.

'I'm so sorry, Em,' he began again, half crawling towards me and resting his head on my knees. 'I just don't know what to do.'

I stroked the back of his head. 'Everything will be fine. I promise.'

'How can you? How can you promise? She might die.'

I wanted to scream at him. *She won't die, because she's not even ill.* Instead I said, 'We'll look after her. She'll be okay.'

He looked up at me, his eyes bloodshot. 'Do you think?'

I nodded. 'I think she'd want us to carry on with the wedding. In fact, I know she would. She wouldn't want us to create a fuss and call everything off.' I could almost hear myself laughing.

'You're probably right.'

'People are diagnosed with cancer every minute of every day.' Even as I said the words, I hated myself for putting Pammie in the same vein as the millions who were truly fighting the hideous disease. 'And their chances are good now.'

He nodded miserably.

'So much better than they used to be. They've made real advances.'

I could tell by the glazed look in his eyes that I wasn't getting through.

'People survive this, millions already have.' I reached for his hands and squeezed them. 'There's every chance that she's going to be okay. Let's see what we're dealing with, and support her through it.'

'I know. I know all that.' He sniffed. 'But I just can't deal with this on top of everything else right now.'

'I appreciate that, so let's carry on as normal. There'll be more to deal with if we cancel the wedding.' I gave an exaggerated sigh.

'But I'd rather do that than stagger through the day. I can't concentrate on anything other than Mum right now. She needs me to be there for her.'

He wasn't hearing me. My mind raced ahead, mentally scanning all the people that I'd need to contact if the wedding didn't go ahead. It didn't bear thinking about. This was not happening. I wouldn't allow it.

I got hold of his wrists and gripped them tightly, staring straight into his eyes. 'Listen to me,' I said firmly. 'We are getting married tomorrow and your mum is going to be fine. She'll enjoy the day, everyone will be there fussing over her, and we'll go on honeymoon. James will look after her while we're gone, he's more than capable, and then, once we're back, we'll both go along to the hospital with her, find out what's going on, and take it from there. Okay?'

He nodded, but I still wasn't convinced I was getting through to him.

He pulled himself up off the floor and started to get dressed.

'What are you doing now?' I asked, the panic rising in my throat. 'Where are you going?'

'I'm going to Mum's,' he said.

'What? You can't, it's five o'clock in the morning.'

'I need to see her.'

'For God's sake, Adam, you're overreacting.'

'How can you ever overreact when your mum's got cancer?' he hissed, his face close to mine.

I was scared. He was always so in control, the man that everyone looked up to. He was the go-to man. The one who headed up a team of analysts, the family member who everybody went to for advice, the man who had brought reason and structure to my life. He was all of those things, yet now he was a rabbit caught in headlights, not knowing whether to run towards them or away. It was pitiful to watch, and I hated Pammie even more for what she'd done to him. To us.

Tears sprang to my eyes. 'You can't leave me here, like this,' I said. 'I need you here.'

'No, you don't,' he said. 'What have you got to worry about, apart from cancelling a bloody bouquet and a cake?'

I looked at him, open-mouthed.

'My mother is dying, and you're fretting about a sponge cake? Get some perspective.'

'If you walk out of here, I swear—'

The door slammed shut just as I got to my feet, and, in that moment, I knew I had no choice but to show the world who Pammie really was.

30

I hadn't thought that sleep would be possible, but I must have dropped off, as it was light when I next opened my eyes. I looked at the clock on the bedside: 8.02 a.m. My head throbbed as I lifted it off the bed, the tension like a coiled spring, ready to ping. There was a hard lump at the back of my throat that I couldn't swallow away. I stumbled to the mirror and saw puffy eyes and a blotchy face staring back at me. My pillow had left tracks running down my cheek.

This was not how I was supposed to spend the eve of my wedding, if, in fact, I was even getting married.

I felt around the bed for my phone, and adjusted my vision as I looked at the screensaver, expecting to see a list of missed calls and messages pasted across the photo of me and Adam.

There were no messages and no missed calls. I had no idea where Adam was, or what the hell was going on. I called him, but it went straight to answerphone. I tried again and got the same.

I wasn't going to give Pammie the satisfaction of calling her, so I opted for second best – James.

He picked up on the second ring. 'Hi, Em?'

'Yes,' I managed. 'Do you know where Adam is? He went out early this morning and I can't get hold of him.'

'You sound shaky, you okay?'

No. Your family's seriously fucked up.

Instead, I said, 'Yes, I'm fine. Any idea where he might be?'

'He's with Mum. He took over from me a few hours ago, so I could come home and get some sleep.'

'Did he say anything to you?' I asked optimistically, trying to stop the desperation from creeping into my voice. 'We had a fight, and he's talking about calling the whole thing off, James. I don't know what to do.'

'Jesus.'

'He seems adamant it's the right thing to do.'

'Do you want me to come over?'

No. Yes. No. I don't know.

'Em? Do you want me to come over?' His voice was rising with concern.

'No, just get him to ring me. He's not picking up his phone.'

'This might be for the best,' he said, almost inaudibly.

What? Had I heard him right?

'To give you both time to make sure it's definitely what you want.'

'How can this be for the best?' I cried. 'But then, why would I expect anything different from you? You've been set on sabotaging this relationship since the very beginning. I bet you're loving this, aren't you?'

'I've only ever had your best interests at heart.'

'The only thing you've ever wanted was to get one up on your brother.'

'That's not true,' he said quietly.

'Right now, I don't really care. I just need to find out what the hell's going on.'

'I'll go over to Mum's now and call you from there,' he said solemnly.

I couldn't think straight until I'd spoken to Adam. There was so much to discuss. He couldn't back out now. What would people think? The plans and sacrifices they'd made to be there, to share our special day. Time off work, babysitters, train tickets – and that was just our guests. What would I say to the hotel, the registrar, the florist, the entertainment?

I called Pippa. She only had to hear me say her name and she was on her way. 'Don't move. I'll be there in ten minutes,' she said.

She took one look at me in the doorway and said, 'I swear to God, if he's laid a finger on you . . .'

I shook my head numbly. 'Pammie's got cancer, and Adam's gone AWOL.'

She raised her eyebrows questioningly.

'Exactly,' I said.

There was nothing she or anyone else could do, apart from make me tea and wait. The waiting, the not know-ing, was excruciating.

It was gone 10 a.m. when my mobile rang. Adam's name flashed up on the screen.

In that split second, Pippa swooped in, swiped the phone from my hand, and put it on loudspeaker.

'Now, listen to me, you motherf—' she said.

'Em?' said the male voice.

'If you don't get your arse back home within the next half an hour . . .' Pippa went on.

'Em, it's James.'

Pippa handed me the phone. 'Is he with you?' I asked breathlessly.

'Yes, but he's not great. His mind seems pretty made up.'

My heart broke into a million pieces. 'Put him on.'

'He doesn't want to talk to you right now,' he said apologetically.

'Put him on the phone now!' I almost screamed.

Pippa rubbed my leg, and caught hold of the hand that was flailing in the air, searching desperately for something tangible to hold onto, to keep me steady, even though I was already sitting down.

I heard a mumbling and then Adam's voice. 'I've made the decision,' he said matter-of-factly. How could he sound so cold? 'We're postponing the wedding until Mum's recovered.'

'But—'

'It's done, Em. I've already started ringing round, the people that I have numbers for, anyway. And I've spoken to the travel agent and she's looking into where we stand with moving the honeymoon or recuperating any costs.'

If it was possible for my blood to run cold, I felt it then. An icy coolness started in my neck and coursed downwards through my chest and into my intestines, whirring around and around, up and down. As it reached the hot acidity of my stomach, I threw the phone at Pippa and ran to the bathroom, retching.

It sounded as if she was talking underwater, and I couldn't make out any words, as I hung my head over the toilet, its very appearance prompting a contraction in my gut, propelling hot bile to sear up my throat.

Within seconds, Pippa was kneeling down beside me, holding my hair and rubbing my back.

'It's going to be okay,' she whispered. 'I'll sort everything.'

I went to shake my head, but threw up again.

Pippa forced me to have a shower and wash my hair, promising that it would make the world a slightly less intimidating place.

I gave her my contacts book and, by the time I came back into the living room, there was only the hotel and registrar left to talk to.

'I think that's something you need to do, I'm afraid,' she said. 'I could be anyone.'

I nodded in sad agreement.

'I'll make us a cup of tea,' she said, taking herself into

the kitchen and busying herself with much banging and slamming of cups and cupboards.

'Oh, my goodness, that's unusual,' said the insensitive wedding co-ordinator at the hotel. 'We've never had anyone cancel this late in the day before.'

'It's not out of choice,' I said dourly, barely aware of what she was even saying. I'd switched onto autopilot, unable to feel, or deal with real people and emotions. I felt like a robot, going through its pre-programmed manoeuvres, fearful of short-circuiting.

I was vaguely aware of the phone being taken out of my hand. 'Hi, it's Pippa Hawkins here, maid of honour, I'll be assisting you with anything else you need . . .'

My head dropped into my folded arms on the table, and my body began to shake as the sobs took hold.

31

Adam finally showed his face an hour before we were meant to be getting married. Our flat had seen a constant stream of visitors during the day and night that he'd been gone, all checking up on me, making sure I hadn't thrown myself off a bridge. But only Pippa remained, when he eventually returned home looking dishevelled, his face ruddy.

I'd imagined this moment a thousand times, but now, as he stood before me as I sat at the dining table, he looked like someone I'd once known. Not the man that I'd loved and lived with for the past eight months. It felt like we'd shared a fleeting encounter at some point in our past lives, and I could barely recollect the details. I didn't know if that was my brain's way of protecting me against the reality. Of cushioning the blow of what was really happening.

I could see Pippa picking up her coat in the corner of my eye, but I stared straight at him, daring him to come back at me. He avoided my gaze.

'I'm going to go,' said Pippa. 'Okay?'

I nodded, my eyes never leaving Adam.

The sadness and sense of embarrassment I felt had

been replaced by a very real anger now, so close to the surface that I felt like a feral animal being pulled back on its lead. He only needed to say one word, any word, and the chain would be off.

'I need you to understand,' he said.

I was up and out of my chair so violently that it fell backwards onto the floor.

'You don't get to tell me to do anything,' I spat. 'I have been through every possible emotion, and you dare to come in here and patronize me, telling me I need to understand?'

For a minute, I thought he was going to raise a hand to me – his shoulders were pulled back and his chest was puffed out, but then he deflated, like a popped balloon, and the air literally rushed out of him. I didn't know which I preferred. At least if he retaliated, I had something to work with, something to spar with. But this hollowed-out version of his former self was pathetic to watch, a crumbling ruin that was difficult to garner respect for. I wanted him to stand up and be counted, not collapse in a childlike heap at my feet.

'We need to talk,' he said quietly.

'You're damn right we do,' I said.

'Like adults.' He pulled out a chair from the other side of the table, the only thing that was stopping me from launching myself at him, and sat down wearily. He looked how I felt. Exhausted.

There was a fleeting moment when I thought she

might have told him the truth. Had the guts to tell him what she'd really done, but as I tried to imagine the scene in my head, it just wouldn't come.

'So?' I asked.

'You need to calm down,' he said.

'And you're patronizing me again, so if we're going to get anywhere, you'd do well to stop that.'

He bowed his head. 'I'm sorry.'

'So, seeing as I've done absolutely nothing wrong, why don't you start by trying to explain where the hell you've been and why you've been unreachable for the best part of thirty-six hours?' I was biting the inside of my lip and could feel the metal tang of blood on my tongue.

'I can only try to explain how I felt, how *it* felt,' he said.

I crossed my arms and waited.

'I was fully committed to getting married today. You need to know that.'

My expression didn't change.

'But when Mum told us her news, it just felt as if my whole world had imploded. It felt like everything had crashed down around me. I thought of the wedding, the honeymoon, Mum's diagnosis, and none of it felt real.'

'You lost perspective,' I offered.

'Yes, maybe I did. But it just didn't feel like I could function. I couldn't have walked into that chapel and held it all together.'

'No one was asking you to,' I said. 'You were getting married, and had been told that your mother has cancer. No one would have expected you to be anything other than emotional.'

'But it was like a full-on panic attack, Em. I had this crushing feeling in my chest, and my brain just seemed paralysed. I couldn't have got myself together in time for the wedding.'

'Yet here you are, seemingly out the other side, with forty-five minutes still to go,' I commented bitterly.

'Are we going to be able to get past this?' he asked, his head down.

'I need to be on my own for a bit, to work this out.'

He looked up at me, his face desolate.

'I don't care where you go, but I don't want you here, not until I've decided what I want.'

'Are you serious?' he asked.

His words didn't warrant a reply.

'Mum and Dad are staying here tonight, as they *thought* they were going to their daughter's wedding, and have now got nothing better to do. And Pippa and Seb will be here too, so . . .'

He lifted himself out of the chair. 'I'll go and pack some things.'

'You do that,' I said, turning my back on him to walk into the kitchen, where I poured myself a generous glass of Sauvignon Blanc.

I heard the front door gently shut a little while later

and fell down onto the sofa, crying. I didn't know whether it was because today should have been my wedding day, or because Pammie had finally won. I'd literally laughed in her face when she said Adam would marry me over her dead body. Now who was laughing?

32

I didn't take Adam's calls for ten days. Not because I was playing mind games, or seeking attention, but because I genuinely needed to be on my own, without his influence, to work out what I wanted. I forced myself to go back to work, even though I had the time booked off, naively believing that having a purpose would make me feel better, but when I found Adam loitering outside my office, I could no longer ignore him. I'd spent all that time not knowing how I was going to feel when I next saw him, or *if* I was going to feel anything, so when my breath was literally taken away just at the sight of him, I thought it must mean something. I felt winded, as if the air had been sucked out of me.

'This isn't fair. You can't cut me off like this,' he begged.

'Don't tell me what's fair,' I said, without breaking my stride as I headed towards Tottenham Court Road tube station. 'I need time and I need space.'

'I need to talk to you.'

'I'm not ready to have this conversation here and now,' I said, increasing my speed.

'Can you just stop for a minute?'

I turned to face him. He'd lost weight. His well-made suit hung off him and his belt didn't have enough holes to pull it tight around his waistband, leaving a gap big enough to fit my hand. His face looked gaunt, and it seemed as if he hadn't shaved since I'd last seen him.

'What for?' I barked, already knowing that it was worse than my bite. I didn't have the energy anymore, it had all been spent.

'Can't we please just sit down, talk things through?'

I looked across at Golden Square, its daffodils standing proud, yet, with the sun going down, it wasn't quite warm enough to take up one of the benches. There was a cafe on the corner and I signalled to it. 'Five minutes,' I said. 'We can go over there for a coffee.' Though I could have killed for something stronger.

'Thank you,' he said gratefully.

Ironically, those coveted five minutes were spent talking about everything other than the reason we were there. I told him that baby Sophie was walking, and he told me his gym membership needed renewing. It felt unbearably awkward making small talk with the man I had lived with. He may as well have been a stranger, I felt that detached from him. A hot tear threatened to fall at the realization, but I stopped myself from blinking and held it in.

Another five minutes was going slowly by, with both of us, at one point, looking out of the window, lost for words to say.

'We've been here ten minutes and you haven't even asked about Mum,' he said.

It hadn't occurred to me. Why would it? Because I knew that she was perfectly fine: free of cancer, free of conscience, and free of morality.

'So sorry,' I said, unable to keep the vitriol out of my voice. 'How is Pammie?'

'We're not going to be able to move on if you can't accept her, and accept what's happened,' he said. 'This is nobody's fault, Em. It's just how life pans out sometimes.'

'Am I supposed to forgive her because she says she's ill?' I asked.

'She doesn't *say* she's ill, she *is* ill,' he said sternly. 'How are you going to feel if, God forbid, something happens?'

I shrugged my shoulders. I couldn't care less.

He looked at me through narrowed eyes. 'You need to look at the bigger picture here. We can get married anytime. Mum might not be here for much longer.'

'Exactly, that's why you made the wrong call,' I said. 'We should have got married so your mum could be there.'

'Maybe so, but what's happened has happened, and we need to get through it, together.'

'So, how is Pammie doing?' I said, ignoring his veiled plea.

'She's doing okay, thanks,' he said, a hint of sarcasm

in his voice. 'We went to her first chemo last week and she's got another one coming up.'

I felt like I'd been hit by a ten-tonne truck. 'We?'

He nodded. 'Yeah, I took her to hospital last Monday. I just wanted to make sure she was okay. You'd do the same for your mum, Em, you know you would.'

I was struggling to get my head round this. He'd gone with her? To a fictitious appointment? How the hell had she pulled that off?

'It's so harrowing what they have to go through,' he went on. 'Mum's after-effects aren't too bad at the moment, she feels a bit sick and she's really tired, but she's been told to expect it to get worse as time goes on.' He rubbed his eyes. 'Honestly, you wouldn't wish it on your worst enemy.'

I was so shocked that I didn't even have the wherewithal to reach forward and give him a reassuring hand. For the first time since her 'announcement' I began to wonder if it could actually be true. The heat of the realization crept up from my toes to my neck, sending a flush across my cheeks. I surreptitiously shrugged my coat off in an effort to cool down.

It hadn't occurred to me for a second that she'd been telling the truth. I thought about how that would make me look. How my recent behaviour would be perceived by those around me. I was banking on her lies being uncovered. For her to be revealed as the cruel fraud she was. But what if it was all true?

'What's it like in there?' I managed. 'The hospital, I mean.' I had to be sure he was saying what I thought he was saying.

'They make it as comfortable as they can for the patients,' he said, my heart sinking with every syllable. 'There are a few other women in the room, you know, all having the same thing, which helps Mum, 'cause you know what she's like, not one to keep herself to herself.' He smiled. 'So it's good for her to be able to chat, to find out what might be around the corner, to prepare herself for whatever it may be. It also helps her to realize that she's not on her own, which I think is the most important thing.'

He bowed his head. 'It's not looking too good though, Em,' he said, before his shoulders caved in and shuddered with the rise and fall of his chest.

I moved round to his side of the table and slid along the bench to reach him. He sobbed as I put my arm around him, then grabbed my hand tightly and brought it up to his mouth. 'I love you,' he whispered. 'I'm so sorry.'

'Ssh, it's okay.' I was at a loss as to what else to say. I'd spent such a long time with the thoughts in my own head, going over the unfairness of it all, and the conspiracy I felt Pammie had been orchestrating since the day she met me, that I'd not thought about how Adam was feeling. I'd just written him off as a fool, a lesser man for allowing himself to be duped. But that wasn't how *he* was feeling; he was bereft. He'd cancelled his wedding to the woman he loved, and he believed, for he had no reason not to, that his mother was dying.

'It's probably not the best place to have had this conversation,' I said, half laughing, as we watched commuters rushing by the window.

'No, probably not,' he agreed, before turning to me and placing a wet kiss on my forehead. 'Will you come and see Mum? She really wants to see you, believe it or not, to say how sorry she is.'

Despite myself, I pulled back a little. 'I'm not sure,' I said, no longer in control of my thoughts, or how they played out on my lips.

'Please, it would mean the world to her – to us both.'

I nodded. 'Okay. Maybe.'

'She's got chemo again next Wednesday, your day off. Maybe you could drive down and meet us afterwards? Unless, of course, I can come back home and we can drive down together?'

I wasn't sure of anything anymore. Instead of easing the swarm of thoughts in my head, Adam's revelation that he was going to the hospital with Pammie only served to feed them, making them buzz and whirr away until they throbbed at my temples.

33

It wasn't Adam being back home that had given me this excruciating headache. It was the pressure of going to see Pammie that was stressing me out. I could literally feel the tightness working its way across my shoulders and creeping up into my neck.

I instinctively opened the fridge to get a bottle of wine, but stopped short. Alcohol had gone a long way to numbing my nerve endings, but I couldn't rely on it as a crutch forever. I needed to stand on my own and be in tune with my brain and body, to really feel what it was feeling, rather than exist in the misty cloud of depression and detachment that had enveloped me for a fortnight.

I looked longingly at the bottle of Sauvignon Blanc, chilled to perfection. Pippa must have brought it with her when she came round for dinner on Sunday night, though to think that it had lived long enough to tell the tale was a miracle. I hadn't intended to drink then, either, but when I told her I'd seen Adam, she demanded to come over to get all the details.

She'd sat open-mouthed on the sofa, as I paced up and down in front of her, no doubt boring her with every minutia of mine and Adam's conversation. Aside from the obvious stress I'd been under, it had been great having Pippa around again. I'd missed us living together, and the chats we used to have. She was the closest entity I had to a second brain; when mine was spouting drivel, hers was the voice of sanity that I so often needed.

'Are you sure you're doing the right thing?' she'd asked. 'Letting him come back?'

I nodded painfully slowly, whilst wringing my hands, unsure even of my own decisions anymore.

'But you're still going to have *her* to deal with,' Pippa had said. She hadn't even been able to bring herself to say the name 'Pammie'. 'She's always going to be there. Is Adam really worth it?'

'I love him, Pip. What am I supposed to do? And let's just give her the benefit of the doubt for a moment. She may well be telling the truth.'

'Nah, I'm not buying it,' she said, shaking her head. 'Remember when I joked about there not being too many psychotic sexagenarians in the world?'

I nodded.

'I was wrong.' We both laughed.

My mobile rang, and made us jump.

'Hello?' I'd still been laughing as I answered the phone.

'How are you, stranger? Nice to hear you sounding happy,' said Seb.

I instantly felt guilty, that I should put myself back in

my sad box, but then I realized that it was the first time I'd laughed in two weeks, and I'd done nothing wrong, though I reasoned that Seb was about to tell me differently.

'I'm sorry,' I'd said. 'I've been in a really weird place.'

'One that you couldn't trust your friend to help you out of?'

I'd sighed. I was painfully aware that I'd not returned a few of his calls, promising myself each time that tomorrow would be the day, but I'd still not got around to it and it had been nagging at me. Our relationship never used to be hard work. I could only think of one reason why it had become such, but I only had myself to blame for allowing outside influences to infiltrate the special bond that we shared.

'I really am sorry,' I offered.

'Are you at home? Can I come over?' he asked.

I hesitated. 'Er . . .'

'Don't worry, you're obviously busy,' he said dejectedly.

What the hell was I doing? 'Of course you can. Pippa's here. It'd be great to see you.'

He gave me a chaste kiss on the cheek as he came through the door, nothing like the hug I would have expected, given the circumstances. We chatted awkwardly through the first bottle of wine, skirting around the issue that seemed to be wedged between us, though what it was, I didn't know. He was reticent and unusually unanimated, which put me on guard as I constantly waited for him to drop the bomb. I knew I'd avoided him ever since the wedding had been called off, but then I'd avoided everyone aside from Pippa and my mum. But I knew, in my heart of hearts, that Seb would normally have been my stalwart in times of need, and he knew it too.

He was just opening the second bottle of Pinot Grigio when he said, 'So what was the real reason you didn't want me to come to your dress fitting?'

Of all the possible scenarios that had been bouncing around in my head over the past hour, that wasn't one of them. I instantly felt my cheeks redden.

'As I said to you,' I said, in a clipped tone. 'I wanted to save it for the big day.' Wasn't that the truth? I'd certainly gone some way to convincing myself that it was.

'So, it was nothing to do with what Pammie said to you, then?' He looked up from the bottle resting between his knees.

'What? When?' I said, though I was already being hit with a sickening realization.

'When you were by the pool in Portugal.'

I turned to Pippa for validation of what I thought he was saying, but she just shrugged her shoulders.

'I'm sorry, I'm not quite with you,' I said, hoping to call his bluff.

'I was sitting on the bench on the other side of the

hedge,' he said. My heart lurched as I frantically tried to recall every word I'd said to Pammie.

'I was rather hoping, banking on it actually, that when you said you'd choose me over her, you meant it.'

I stared at him, open-mouthed. 'But . . . I did. I mean, I have.'

He raised his eyebrows questioningly. 'Yet, as soon as we got home, you told me you didn't want me at your dress fitting, and I haven't heard a peep from you since the wedding was cancelled. I don't want to be a burden to you, Em, so if having me in your life makes things difficult, then I'd rather you just say . . .'

I shook my head vehemently as his words struck a chord, as if I was trying to shake the very truth of them out of my brain. 'That's not how it is,' I said.

'So, does Adam have a problem with me?' he asked.

I thought back to how he'd been at the cinema that time, before he'd even met Seb, and his cutting remarks when he found out he was going to see my dress. I pushed the doubt to the back of my mind.

'Don't be silly,' I said. 'Adam would never feel threatened by you. It's just Pammie being Pammie . . . you know what she's like.' I went over to him and put my arm around him. 'I'm sorry if you thought I was being offhand for any other reason than, I suppose, embarrassment and shame about the wedding.'

He pulled me into a warm embrace, the one I'd expected and wanted when I first saw him. 'But it's me,' he said. 'Since when have we let anything like embarrassment and shame come between us?'

I smiled.

'I'm always here for you,' he said. 'For better or worse.'

'Bloody hell,' interrupted Pippa. 'Maybe *you* two ought to get married.'

We had all laughed then, which, just a few days previously, had seemed impossible.

But now, as I sat in Adam's car, heading to Sevenoaks, life didn't seem quite so carefree, and I wished that I'd had that drink after all, just to take the edge off. My brain was so fuddled that I was having trouble seeing the wood for the trees.

'You okay?' Adam smiled, sensing my trepidation.

I smiled back, and he reached over to take my hand. 'It'll be okay,' he said reassuringly. I doubted that, but then I remembered that, actually, this wasn't about me anymore. This was about Pammie, who might or might not have cancer (my mind had swung this way and that, but it was tending to settle on the latter, nine times out of ten). Still, until I was absolutely sure that was the case, I promised myself that I would assume the worst. Ironically, I felt the load lighten a little when I allowed myself to believe that she was telling the truth. At least then we had something tangible to work with, and we could all get on with helping her beat it. But if she wasn't?

'Oh, Emily darling, it's so good to see you,' she said, embracing me at the front door. 'I cannot begin to tell you how sorry I am. Really. I am so, so sorry. I would never have said anything if I thought for just one moment that . . .'

I smiled tightly. Regardless of whether she was ill or not, I still didn't have to like her.

'Darling,' she exclaimed as Adam reached her. 'Goodness, how I've missed you.'

'I've only been gone for two days.' He laughed, rolling his eyes.

'Yes, yes I know. You should be home with Emily, that's where you belong.' I didn't know if she was trying to convince us or herself.

'How are you?' I asked, as sincerely as I could. 'How are you feeling?'

She looked down. 'Oh, you know, I've been better, but I can't complain. I've not been sick too much and I've still got all my hair.' She patted the top of her head.

'Ladies, shall we go inside, before the whole street hears?' said Adam, ushering us through to the low-ceilinged hall.

'Oh, of course, it's just that I'm so pleased you're here. The both of you.' She took my hand and led me through to the back sitting room.

'How have you been?' she asked me, almost genuinely. 'I've been thinking about you so much.'

I looked to Adam, and he smiled warmly back, like a proud dad. He bought every word she said. She had him wrapped around her little finger. I felt a very real pang of disappointment. Nothing had changed.

'I'm fine, actually,' I lied.

There was an awkward silence, but Adam seemed oblivious as we stood there, sizing each other up. 'We've not got much time,' he said. 'And the traffic's pretty lousy.'

'Oh, we should get going then,' said Pammie, gathering up her cardigan and handbag from a chair. 'Let's save the chat for later.'

I forced a grin.

'Now, I've made a few little sandwiches, just in case you get peckish. Just take the cling film off whenever you're ready, and there's cake in the tin in the pantry. Lemon drizzle, I made it myself,' she said proudly.

'That's lovely,' I said, aware of the falseness of our conversation. I couldn't remember the last time we'd exchanged such pleasantries. 'You shouldn't have gone to so much trouble.'

'Don't be silly, it's the least I can do for you coming down all this way. And we shouldn't be too long, anyway, they just need to get me attached and then we're off and away.' She pulled up the sleeve of her blouse to reveal a padded gauze stuck to the inside of her arm. 'Perhaps we can have a proper chat when I get back?'

I nodded, but looked to Adam.

'Do you not want Emily to come with us?' he asked, sensing my confusion. I'd not even contemplated them going without me.

'Goodness, no,' she said. 'There's no point in that. We'll have a cup of tea and some cake when I get back, okay?' She looked to me, then Adam, and we both nodded mutely.

'Sorry, I didn't know she was expecting you to stay here,' whispered Adam, as he leant in to kiss me goodbye. 'I'll be as quick as I can.'

'No worries,' I said tightly. 'See you when you get back.'

'Make yourself at home,' called Pammie as they headed out the door.

I watched her shuffle up the path and then tell Adam what she wanted him to do with her bag before he helped her in, placing a protective hand over her head as she slowly lowered herself into the passenger seat.

I made myself a cup of tea and sat on the sofa, wondering what I was going to do with the hours that stretched out ahead of me. I've always felt uncomfortable being in someone else's home when they're not there. There's something rather unnerving about being surrounded by someone else's possessions that you know you shouldn't touch. I picked up *The Lady* magazine from the coffee table and had a flick through, but it was full of features and ads aimed at a life other than mine. Alas, I had no need for a butler, bodyguard, or yacht staff at the moment.

I thought about putting the TV on, just for a bit of background noise to break through the silence, but then

I eyed the hi-fi in the corner, an old-fashioned stacking system, with a three-disc CD changer. I'd had one of those in my bedroom when I was a teenager, and I remembered the long afternoon it had taken me and Dad to read through the hi-tech instructions. As much as times have changed and moved forward, it still took me longer than it should have to find the 'on' button and press eject. Simon and Garfunkel's *Greatest Hits*, one of my mum's favourites, was already lying in the groove, so I clicked it closed again and pressed play. The opening guitar strum to 'Mrs Robinson' filled the room, taking me back to those Saturday mornings when Mum hoovered around our feet as Stuart and I sat on the sofa. 'Up!' she'd say as we both giggled.

The photo albums that Pammie had proudly flicked through on my very first visit here were lined up on the shelf above, sandwiched between two midi speakers. I looked along the spines, at the years written boldly in black pen. I could only remember that the album she'd shown me was maroon leather, but now, as I touched them, I saw that they were a cheap plastic, trying their best to imitate leather. I pulled the first of three maroon books from its place, its tacky cover sticking to its neighbours. The pages were overflowing with a young Pammie and Jim, clearly in the first throes of love, gazing adoringly at each other, whilst others around them could only look on. Adam was the spitting image of Jim, as a twenty-something young man – and James bore even more of a resemblance. Jim had his arm proudly around Pammie's shoulders, his presence a warning sign to any aspiring suitors. Another photo showed Pammie draped over the bonnet of a Hillman Imp, in a geometric shift dress, whilst her girlfriends, with their pinched faces, were duly ensconced inside. I could just imagine the envy-induced conversation going on, as the gorgeous Jim stood behind the camera, admiring his girlfriend. Another page on and Pammie, Jim and friends are lying on a picnic blanket, which, despite being sheltered between sand dunes, was still being lifted off the ground by a blustering wind. England in summer, no doubt – perhaps Camber Sands or Leysdown on the south coast. I imagined the freedom that being a young person living in the late sixties must have brought, and felt a pang of jealousy. To live with such abandon, with nothing to tie them down, must have been empowering. I wondered if we would feel the same about today, when we look back in the future.

The four couples, the men with their sideburns, and the girls with Coke-can curls in their hair, were all smiling, but it still felt like the Pammie and Jim Show. They were clearly the Elvis and Priscilla of their gang, always holding court and playing for laughs.

So, it seemed Pammie had been getting attention all her life. It was where she was comfortable, naively believing that it validated her somehow, that, without the drama, she'd be insignificant. I thought how exhausting that must be, to be constantly looking for the spotlight.

Towards the end of the album, the black-and-white photos were intermittently interspersed with a flash of colour, as the monochrome was gradually replaced by the real-life glow of a Polaroid. You could see the genuine astonishment on the faces of its subjects as they marvelled at the craziness of this modern-day invention. Would my grandchildren, or even children, look back through an antiquated iPhone and see the same look of wonderment on our faces?

I remembered seeing the first picture on the opening page of the next album, a photo of Jim and Adam, standing at the side of a pond, feeding ducks. Adam with half a slice of bread in his hand, looking up at his dad in awe. I wondered then whether, had they known they had so little time together, they'd have done anything differently. They say we wouldn't want to know when we are going to die, even if we could, but when I look at pictures like this, I wonder if it wouldn't be better. So we could use our time more wisely, spend it with people we loved.

I settled back down on the sofa, with the album on my lap, and flicked to the back, where I remembered seeing the picture of Adam and Rebecca, so helpfully left open by Pammie. When I thought about it, every little thing that Pammie had done, from the very beginning, had been contrived, meticulously planned to create upset and turmoil for me. No one else would notice, of course

– that's where she's clever. 'What a sweetie,' they all cried, after she so considerately cooked a huge Christmas dinner, when she knew I'd already had one, and when she secretly arranged for a long-lost friend to turn up at my hen party, fully aware that she'd slept with my last boyfriend. Yep, 'good old Pammie'.

I thumbed backwards and forwards, then backwards again, looking for the photo of Rebecca. This was definitely the right album; I recollected all the pictures in here. I went through it again, page by page, but there was no photo and no caption that read, 'Darling Rebecca – miss you every day.'

Where the hell was it? And why had she taken it out? I looked around the room and saw the drawers that sat under the hi-fi. Looking at the photo albums seemed intrusive enough, but I felt compelled to go further, despite the nervous butterflies in my stomach. I inched a drawer open, and could see piles of chequebooks, all used and held together with a rubber band. Statements and invoices were askew, slipping out of plastic folders. I lifted them up, careful not to disturb them too much, and eased the top chequebook out from its tight restraint. I thumb-flicked through the stubs, all neatly written with the date, payee, and amount payable. My eyes scanned at speed: British Gas, Southern Electric, Adam, Homebase, Virgin Media, Adam, Waterstones, Thames Water, Adam. I looked closer to see that Pammie had been paying Adam £200 a month for years, but when I tried to find a similar payment to James – after all, that would only be fair – there was no record of one. Confused, I carefully put the folder back in the drawer and tried to convince myself to stop there, but it felt like I'd picked at a scab and wouldn't be satisfied until I'd scratched it off. I justified it by telling myself I was on the hunt for the missing photograph, but this woman had so much to hide that I felt a frisson of excitement at what else I might find.

The other drawer of the dresser was awkward to slide, and I had to jemmy it this way and that to get it open. There were two stacks of garish cards, each bundled together with a ribbon. I slid the top card out, a birthday greeting to her from Adam. The one furthest back was a sympathy card, with a note inside, written in Adam's writing,

Dearest Mum,

Only you can understand how it feels to lose someone so suddenly, so needlessly. I keep asking myself, 'What if . . . ?' as I'm sure you must have done a million times. What if I'd been there? Would it have been different? Could I have saved her? Do these questions ever stop, Mum? Can you ever sleep soundly at night knowing that if things had been different . . .

My heart broke for him as I read his poignant words, and a tiny part felt for Pammie too. I couldn't begin to imagine how it must feel to lose somebody so close. The other pile, much bigger in comparison, was to her with love from James, for every possible occasion: birthdays, Christmas, Mother's Day, and even those that I didn't know there were cards for – Easter, St David's Day. She was lucky to have two sons who thought of her as often as Adam and James did. What a shame she didn't want to share that side of them, choosing instead to see every advancing female as a threat to the amount of time and love they had for her. By now, she could probably have had two equally doting daughters-in-law as well, both happy and willing to see her through what might or might not be her toughest battle yet.

There were no other nooks or crannies that held any mystery in the sitting room, so I did a quick sweep of the kitchen, but aside from the obligatory 'man drawer', which housed old batteries, takeaway menus and keys that no longer had locks for them, there was nothing but cutlery and utensils.

I'd pictured myself going back into the sitting room, picking up my tea, and listening to 'Homeward Bound', the track now playing on the CD. So how come my foot was now on the bottom step of the staircase? I looked up at the narrow treads, the carpet wearing thin, and I wondered what happened once the staircase turned right and disappeared. The chintzy lemon wallpaper, with its flamboyant trails of rhododendron, was beginning to fade where the sun ate away at it at various times of the day. But at the top of the staircase, where there was a constant shadow, the green of the leaves was still vibrant and bright.

I convinced myself that I was going up to have a closer look, to really appreciate the depth of colour, but I didn't even stop. My feet just seemed to lift themselves up onto those last three steps, the ones you couldn't see from the hall, and into the room with the open door.

The double bed and small wardrobe were enough to fill the room, but opposite, in the alcoves either side of the chimney breast, were tall chests of drawers. I swear I could still smell the pine scent emanating from the furniture, each piece its own shade of orangey-brown.

The sunlight filtered through a gap in the thin curtains, casting a sliver of light across the room. I moved around the bed, the floorboards creaking as I went, and sat on the floor in front of the chest furthest from the window.

The bottom drawer felt heavy, so I lifted the weight up and off its support as I slid it out. It was full of ornamental boxes and decorated trinkets. The nerve fibres in my hands tingled as my clumsy fingers struggled with the clasp on the wooden jewellery box that was just begging to be opened. There were little milk teeth laid carefully on a red velvet cushion, the white enamel having yellowed over the years, and two name-tag bracelets bearing Adam and James's names. Guilt washed over me as I caught sight of a pair of tarnished, silver men's cufflinks, presumably Jim's, and I slammed the top shut. I leant my head back on the mattress, my folded limbs trapped between the chest and the bed. What the hell was I doing? This wasn't me. This wasn't what I did. I'd allowed this woman to turn me into someone no better than her. Of all the terrible things she'd done, I would not allow her to change the very foundation of me: to distort the values and morals my parents had worked so hard to instil. I placed the box back inside the drawer, tilting it to make it fit. I jumped as it dropped heavily onto its back, its underside staring outwards, revealing a hidden compartment underneath.

I looked at it for a while, remembering the mantra I'd just recited, and willed myself to ignore it. 'Close the drawer,' I repeated out loud, in the hope that hearing myself actually say it would stop me from doing what I already knew I was going to do. I carefully lifted it back out again and slid the bottom section backwards. I don't know what I was expecting to see, some old bones or something, so it was an anti-climax to find nothing more than an old inhaler, the type I'd seen a girl at school with. Molly, I think her name was. I would never forget watching her collapse in PE, just after we'd been told to run around the field twice to warm up for netball. We thought it was a joke at first, but then she'd started wheezing and clutching at her chest. I hardly knew the girl, but I couldn't sleep that night, and almost cried when they told us in assembly the next morning that she was going to be okay.

I didn't know Pammie suffered from asthma, but perhaps it was Jim's, I reasoned. People find the oddest mementoes comforting. There was something beneath it, a cutting or a picture, and I carefully lifted the inhaler out to get a clearer view. My eyes snapped shut, as if desperately trying to stop themselves from sending the message they'd already received to my brain. I tried to retract it, battling furiously with myself to eradicate the image before it reached the part of me that recognized it. But I'd seen it and there was no way it could be undone. Rebecca. Smiling out at me, with the man she loved by her side. The missing photo from the album.

'Hey, I'm back,' Adam called out from downstairs.

What the hell was he doing here? He'd only been gone half an hour. I dropped the box, the inhaler falling out into the drawer, and I scrambled furiously to pick it up and put it all back. Adrenaline coursed through my veins, pumping extra energy through my hands, making it almost impossible to do even the simplest thing without shaking.

'You here?' he said. I could hear the creak of the floorboards as he walked through the hall to the kitchen. 'Em?'

If I could just stop my hands from trembling I could get it all back in position. I could make out his footsteps coming into the hall, and there was only one place for him to go from there. A burning acid tore through my chest and my throat constricted violently as it struggled to hold it down.

'Hey, what you doing up here?' he asked, reaching me just as I sat on the edge of the bed, my foot slowly closing the open drawer he couldn't yet see.

'I . . . I just . . .' I faltered.

'Jesus, Em, you're deathly pale. What's up?'

'I . . . I came over a bit funny downstairs, a migraine or something, so I brought myself up here to lie down.' I patted the pillows under the embroidered bedspread, still untouched and perfect.

'Oh,' he said, not noticing. 'How do you feel now?'

'A little better, but I think I just sat up too quickly when I heard you calling. You were quick. Is Pammie okay? I hope she's not going to mind me being up here.'

'She's not back yet, I need to go and get her in a couple of hours. Do you feel up to a sandwich or a cup of tea?'

'Sorry, you've left Pammie there?' I asked tersely.

'Yeah, she doesn't like me going in with her.'

'But you went in with her last time.'

'No, I did the same then, as well,' he said. 'She doesn't want me to see her like that, all wired up and whatever else they do. Silly really, because I'm sure that's when she needs me most, but she's adamant she doesn't want me in there.'

'But . . . last time . . . you told me about the other ladies, how they were all chatting to one another?'

'That's what she told me,' he said, not understanding for a second the implication of what he was saying. 'No doubt to make me feel better about not going in. Apparently, they're all on their own, they don't encourage accompanying visitors because it's only a small room and there's just not enough space.'

'So where does she go when you drop her off?' I asked, my mouth moving too quickly for my brain to keep up. 'Where does she go?'

'To ward 306, or whatever it is.' He laughed. 'I don't know. I just do what she says and take her to the main entrance.'

'So, you don't go with her past that point?'

'What is this, Em?' he asked, still half laughing, but a tension was beginning to seep in.

I needed to sit, be quiet, and think. My brain felt like it was going to explode with all this new information bombarding it from every angle. The inhaler, Rebecca's picture, and the image of Pammie walking straight through the hospital and out the other side, clogged up any sense.

'You really don't look well,' said Adam. 'Why don't you lie back down and I'll go and make a cup of tea.'

'I can't,' I said, feeling suddenly compelled to get out of there. 'I need to go. I need some fresh air.'

'Whoa, hold up,' he said. 'Just take it slowly. Here, take my arm, I'll help you back down the stairs.'

'No, I mean – I can't stay here.'

'What the hell's wrong with you?' he said, his voice a little louder. 'I've got to go back and get Mum in a bit, so just have a cup of tea and calm down.'

'Drop me back to the station when you go. I'll get the train home.'

'That's crazy,' he said. 'You'll have to go all the way into London and back out again to Blackheath. That doesn't make sense.'

I knew it didn't, but nothing made sense anymore. After everything she'd done, I'd given Pammie the benefit of the doubt, and was fully prepared to put everything behind us and get through her treatment together, as a family. But this? This was something entirely different, something that I couldn't even begin to contemplate.

'Come on,' said Adam, beckoning me towards him. 'It's been a tough few weeks and we're all feeling the strain.'

He rubbed my back whilst he held me, blissfully unaware of the knowledge that was slowly poisoning my brain. The realization that not only was Pammie a lying, deceitful schemer who had set out to ruin my life, but a truly abhorrent murderer who had deprived Rebecca of hers.

34

I watched from the car as she hobbled across the car park, hanging onto Adam's arm, and felt physically sick. She'd kept him waiting in the busy hospital reception whilst she finished her 'chemotherapy'. He'd offered me a coffee from the cafeteria, as she stretched it out, no doubt to add authenticity, but I couldn't stomach it. I'd wanted to get dropped off at the station, so I didn't have to face her, so I could no longer be party to her evil lies and deceit. But Adam had refused.

'You look as right as rain now,' he'd insisted, driving straight past the station on his way to the hospital. 'You've got your colour back.'

'I really don't feel well. Can't you just drop me off?' I'd said.

'But Mum will be so disappointed. She'll be upset if you can't, at the very least, have a cup of tea with her.'

If I'd felt stronger, I would have dragged him into the hospital, demanded to be directed to the relevant ward and called her out. Only then would he know what she'd done, what she was capable of. She'd be none the wiser, though, as whilst he furiously searched the list, refusing to believe she wasn't there, she'd be happily pottering around the shops in town, no doubt treating herself to a new blouse. But that's all it would take to make him see. For him to start understanding what she'd put me through, and for both of us to begin to piece together what she'd done to Rebecca.

Once the string was pulled, it would unravel at an alarming rate, but I needed time to work out which thread to pull first. Adam needed to see her for what she was, to believe in the possibility that she could do someone real harm. He'd think I was deranged if I started accusing her of Rebecca's murder with no real evidence, and if he didn't believe me, it would spell the end of us. I wasn't prepared to let that happen, not only because I love him, but because I refuse to let her win.

I wished that the anger I'd been carrying around for so long was still there now, forcing me to stand up and do what was right, whilst I had the chance. But that maddening resentment that had always been so close to bubbling over, had been replaced by fear: not only for the relationship with the man I love, but for me. This woman, who I'd first thought of as nothing more than an annoying, but harmless, over-protective mother, is a jealous psychopath who will stop at nothing to get what she wants.

To think that, looking at her now, is laughable. All hunched over, with her pleated skirt and sensible cardigan buttoned up tightly, shuffling ever so slowly, as if every step pained her. If I wasn't so scared it would be funny.

'Would you mind sitting in the back, dear?' she said as she reached the car. 'It's just that I feel awfully nauseous after that, and I'm better in the front.'

I didn't say a word. Just got out and moved.

'Thanks so much. Honestly, I can't describe what it feels like.'

Go on, try, I wanted to say. Explain to me what it feels like to pretend to have cancer, to wander nonchalantly around the shops whilst your friends and family put their lives on hold and pray for your recovery.

'How was it?' I said instead, my voice level, even though my heart was thumping out of my chest.

'It's not very nice,' she said. 'And they say it's going to get worse. I can't imagine what I'm going to do with myself when that happens.'

'You might be all right,' I said curtly. 'People react very differently to chemotherapy. It's down to the individual. You might be one of the lucky ones.'

'Oh, I doubt that,' she said.

'Doubt what?' asked Adam gently, as he got into the driver's seat.

'Emily thinks I'll sail through this, but I think she might be underestimating it.'

I smiled to myself and shook my head incredulously, just as Adam turned to look at me, his face saying, *what is wrong with you?*

'How did it go, Mum?' he asked. 'You okay?'

She pulled up the sleeve of her cardigan again, as if showing a ball of cotton wool was all that she needed to do to prove she had cancer.

'I feel a bit woozy,' she said. 'I think even the place makes you feel strange. All those stories you hear. They're enough to send you bananas on their own.'

'Why don't you let Adam come in with you next time?' I said. 'He might be able to take your mind off it.'

'Oh no, I don't want him seeing me in there, like that,' she said.

'I'd like to, Mum. If it will help?'

'No, you're a big softy,' she said, reaching over to pat his thigh. 'I can't have you getting all upset. Now, enough of all this doom and gloom, let's get back home and have a nice brew.'

I made the tea while she lay on the sofa, directing Adam as to how to place her pillows so that she was sitting up enough, but not too much.

'Well, isn't this lovely,' she commented, as I carried in the tray with the teas on. 'I just wish I was feeling better.'

'Don't worry, Mum, I'm sure you'll be as good as new in no time. We'll just have to make sure we look after you until then.'

'Well, I was going to say about that,' she said, as she shakily took a cup and saucer from the tray. 'I'm not all that good, as you can see.' She held up a doddering hand as if to prove the point. 'And I had a fall on the day you moved back to be with Emily.'

'Oh no,' he said anxiously. 'Are you okay?'

'Well, I am, and, as you know, I've always been fiercely independent, but . . .' she trailed off.

I turned to look out of the window, waiting for what I knew was about to come.

'But I'm finding it very difficult,' she went on. 'It's hard to admit, but that's the fact of the matter. It would really help if you were around a bit more. I got used to having you here for those couple of weeks – wrong I know, but I can't help it. I feel vulnerable, now that you're gone.'

I forced myself to stay where I was, to concentrate on the sunflowers that were in full bloom at the end of the garden, their brightness at odds with the dark grey clouds looming overhead.

'I can't stay any longer,' said Adam. 'I need to be at home with Emily. But I'll pop in, and James is always around.'

'I know, I know.' She sighed. 'But James isn't quite so reliable these days, now that he's met this new girl.'

I swung round far quicker than I should have.

'New girl?' My stomach turned at the thought of him with someone else, not because I wanted him, but because I didn't want anyone else to have him either.

She looked at me. 'He met her in a bar in town about a month ago. Seems to have knocked him sideways.' I tried to keep my expression neutral, but every muscle in my face was twitching. 'Don't think I've ever seen him like it.'

'Was he going to bring her to the wedding?' I asked nonchalantly.

'No, we chatted about it, but we both felt it was too early. They'd only been together for a couple of weeks, which was far too soon to be throwing her into the lion's den and introducing her to the whole clan.'

'Have you met her?' I asked.

'No, not yet, but I hope to in the next few weeks – whenever James is ready.'

She made herself sound so reasoned, so plausible. I looked at her and wondered what was running through her head. What hell was she planning for this poor girl, if it ever got serious?

'He certainly seems to be smitten, though,' she went on. 'You two will have to be careful – they might well end up beating you down the aisle at this rate.'

'Mum!' Adam laughed, in mock umbrage.

I wondered when the cancellation of our wedding, twenty-four hours before it was supposed to happen, had become something acceptable to joke about, especially by the groom.

'So, the heartbreak diet obviously didn't work for you?' she said, as soon as Adam took himself out of the room.

I smiled and patted my flat stomach. 'Or maybe I'm pregnant from all the amazing make-up sex we've had?'

I raised my eyebrows, and she frowned in distaste.

'Are they not concerned about the effect this treatment might have on your asthma?' I asked boldly.

'Asthma?' she asked, genuinely surprised by the question. 'I haven't got asthma.'

'Oh, I thought I remembered Adam telling me once that you'd had it when he was younger? I'd read somewhere that certain types of chemo can have an adverse effect on asthmatics.' I was fishing, but I needed to know with utmost certainty that the inhaler wasn't hers, though I already knew it wasn't.

'No, never,' she said, whistling and reaching over to touch wood.

'Never what?' asked Adam as he came back into the room.

'Nothing, son.'

'What have I missed?' he asked, smiling. 'It feels like you two have a secret.'

I smiled back and shook my head. 'I was just saying that I'm sure you'd told me that your mum had asthma, when you were younger, but I must have dreamt it.' I caught a glint of his set jaw, and knew I'd pushed my luck, so I laughed to lighten the mood. 'You'd be genuinely terrified if you knew what I dreamt about.'

'So, when are you two lovebirds going to reschedule the wedding?' asked Pammie, clearly desperate to change the subject. 'I guess it will be a while away now, won't it? Be difficult to reorganize everything so quickly, what with getting everyone there again – and that's if the venue even has free dates.'

She was rambling on, answering her own questions with what she'd like to hear. But I'm not one for giving Pammie what she wants. 'No, I think it'll be soon,' I said, knowing full well that the hotel didn't have any vacancies for at least six months. I felt the prickle of hot tears springing to my eyes unexpectedly, and batted them away. I would never allow her the satisfaction of thinking her actions could make me cry. 'I'm hoping that it'll happen in the next month or two.'

I watched her face crumple. 'Oh, that will be such a relief, dear,' she cried, pulling a tissue from a nearby box and dabbing at her eyes. 'That will go some way to assuaging my guilt.'

'I don't know about that, Em,' Adam said, his brow knitted. 'There's a lot to do in that time.' He crouched down beside Pammie. 'And you've got nothing to feel guilty about, Mum. That was my decision.'

He looked up at me. If he was hoping for a smile, a hint of forgiveness, he was mistaken.

I turned it on for Pammie, though, kneeling down beside Adam and taking her hand in mine. 'But obviously we're not going to do it until you're better,' I smiled piteously. 'We need to know you're through the treatment and out the other side.'

'Oh, you're a lovely girl,' she said, patting my hand. My skin crawled at her touch.

'She is,' agreed Adam, pulling me towards him and kissing my cheek. I turned my face so that our lips met, and I parted mine ever so slightly, inviting him to take more. He pulled away, but the act wasn't lost on Pammie, who turned away in disgust.

35

Adam had slept in the spare room for the two nights he'd been back home, as I naively believed that withholding sex would make him understand the severity of what he'd done and the risk he'd taken. But that was childish, and it wasn't what either of us wanted. Yet it wasn't until we came away from Pammie's that I realized I'd been playing right into her hands. She wanted the cancellation of the wedding to ruin us, she was banking on it, so I needed to make sure that what she'd done was never going to have an adverse effect on us as a couple. She had changed me as a person already, had made me see myself differently. She'd stripped away my confidence and had caused hurt that I'd carry with me until the day I died, but I would *not* allow her to take away the one thing she wanted. She would never take Adam away from me. I'd use the only weapon in my artillery that she'd never be able to outgun me with.

The front door hadn't even closed properly before I pushed him up against the back of it, and kissed him, searching furiously for his tongue. He didn't say a word, but I could feel him smiling as he kissed me back, softly at first, then harder. It had been a long time for both of us, and with so many emotions in the space in between, it just felt like a pressure cooker going off. I undid his shirt buttons, ripping at the bottom two in my urgency, and he reached around to unzip the back of my dress, the intensity of our kissing not stopping for even a second. As my dress fell to the floor he swung me round and slammed me hard against the door, pinning my arms up above my head. I was helpless as he kissed my neck, before going down and moving the fabric of my bra aside with his teeth, circling my nipples with his tongue.

I went to pull my arms down, but he held them firm, changing from two hands to one, as he undid his jeans and pushed my legs apart with his feet. It couldn't have lasted more than three minutes but the release was incredible, and the pair of us remained unmoving against the door, our breaths heavy and in unison.

'Well, that was unexpected,' Adam was the first to speak. 'As you could probably tell. Sorry about that.'

I smiled and kissed him. 'We can do it again later, slower if you like.'

He kissed me back. 'God, I love you, Emily Havistock.'

I didn't say I loved him. I don't know why, because I do. Perhaps it's all part of that in-built defence mechanism that women seem to be born with, that bogs us down and keeps us from saying the things we really want to say. Believing that holding back somehow keeps us one step ahead, making us the better, stronger race.

Why then, does pretending to be someone I'm not, leave me feeling weak and bereft?

I waited until we were snuggled up on the sofa together, to broach the subject that was burning a hole in my head.

'Can I ask you something about Rebecca?' I said, careful to keep my voice steady.

'Do you have to?' Adam sighed. 'We're having a lovely time. Let's not ruin it.'

'We won't,' I replied. 'We're just talking.'

He sighed resignedly, but I pushed on.

'Did you get a chance to say goodbye to her? Was she still alive when you found her? Did she ever regain consciousness for long enough to know you were there?'

He shook his head. 'No. She'd already gone. She was . . . cold to the touch, and her lips were blue. I held her and kept calling her name, but there was nothing. No flicker of a pulse, nothing.'

His eyes started welling up. 'Did you have to go through the hell of a post-mortem or inquest?' I asked.

'No, thankfully. She had such a detailed history of asthma, albeit not serious, or so we thought, that it was obviously the cause of death.'

'And your mum was there with you?'

He nodded solemnly. 'She was the one who found her. I can't imagine what it was like for her.'

'Who was the last person to see her? Before she became unwell?'

'What is this,' he said, 'the Spanish Inquisition?'

'I'm sorry, I don't mean to pry, I just . . . I don't know. I just want to feel closer to you, know what goes on in that head of yours. That was a huge part of your life, and I just want to be in that same space, you know, understand how it must feel for you, even now, years later. Does that make sense?'

I wrinkled my nose, and he kissed it.

'Mum had taken up a few boxes earlier in the day, and they'd had a cup of tea, I think, in between unpacking, and she seemed fine.'

'What, absolutely normal?' I asked.

'Yes, but she always was before an attack. It just creeps up on you.'

'So, you'd seen her have an asthma attack before?' I asked.

'A few, yeah. But we both knew what to do whenever she felt it coming on, so it was never an issue, assuming she had her inhaler with her, which she always did. She knew to just stop what she was doing, sit down, and puff away until she was able to regulate her breathing again. It only ever got scary once, after we'd run for a train. It wasn't even that far, but it knocked the stuffing out of her, and I had to get her to lie down on the floor of the carriage, whilst I desperately searched for her pump.'

'But she was okay, though?' I asked.

'Eventually. But you know what you girls' handbags are like.' He tried to smile. 'She had everything in there, as if she was living in it, and I had to turn the whole thing upside down to find it. The first thing she said, once she was able to, was, "If that was my new Chanel lipstick I saw rolling away, I'll kill you!" She was lying on the floor, unable to breathe, and all she was worried about was her bloody lipstick.'

He smiled at the memory. I smiled too. I liked the sound of her.

'If I'd have been there, I could have helped her. I could have found her inhaler and stopped it.' His head bowed and his chest lifted. 'But you just never know when it's going to come. You can be going along just fine, and then bam! You feel the signs, and then if you don't do anything about it, it can take you out, just like that.' He clicked his fingers.

'So, she must have been exerting herself, then?' I said gently. 'Perhaps moving boxes around or something?'

He nodded. 'There was a big box, full of books, up-turned on its side in the hall. It was so heavy, she should never have tried to lift it, but it seemed she did. That kind of work would have put a huge strain on her lungs, plus she would have been running up and down the stairs all day.' His voice cracked. 'I guess she was trying to get it into shape by the time I got home.'

'But you spoke to her that evening, didn't you?' I asked.

'I called her just before I left the office, and she was fine.'

'Was your mum with her then?' I asked. 'What time did she leave?'

'Oh, I don't know,' he said, rubbing his eyes. 'Can we leave it now? Please.'

'I'm sorry, I just don't know how somebody can just die like that,' I said, my voice getting a little higher with each word. He looked at me questioningly.

'It just freaks me out, that's all,' I said.

How could he not see? Surely, he must have asked himself the question. It was so blindingly obvious. Pammie was the last person to see his girlfriend alive, and the first person to find her dead, on the day they were moving in together, on the day he left home. There was no greater motive for her to do something terrible, to stop her worst nightmare from being realized. She would have felt that she was losing Adam, relinquishing control, and she wouldn't have been able to bear that. God knows what hell she'd put Rebecca through in her attempt to get her out of Adam's life. How far had she pushed her? I shuddered at the thought. Poor Rebecca, who once, like me, had so much to look forward to. A life with the man she loved. Her own family. But she'd not backed down. She'd stood up to Pammie and, by doing so, had unwittingly made the ultimate sacrifice.

Was I taking the same risk? Was I signing my own death certificate?

I didn't want to carry this overwhelming sense of foreboding alone. But I had no choice. It was one thing to tell Pippa and Seb about how Pammie made me feel. They had seen for themselves how cruel she could be. But to accuse her of murder? That was something completely different, and, until the time came when I knew for sure, without any shadow of a doubt, that she had something to do with Rebecca's death, I had to keep it to myself.

I smiled up at Adam.

'What are you thinking about?' he asked.

If only you knew.

Over the next few weeks, I threw myself into work, taking on every appointment I could manage. It helped to keep my brain busy, to stop the fear and panic from taking over. I was shattered, both physically and mentally, when I got in from work each night, but Adam would never have known. I did everything in my power to make him want and need me more than ever before.

'What the hell's got into you?' he said, smiling, when he came home from work to find me dressed in a black-lace bra and panties, serving up fillet steak with a homemade peppercorn sauce.

I gave him my best smile. He didn't need to know that I'd have loved nothing more than a snuggle on the sofa, in our pyjamas, watching a box set whilst eating pot noodles. Instead, we had sex on the dining table, before I'd even managed to set the dinner down, and after eating, I listened sympathetically as he moaned about a lazy colleague, whilst I washed up. I am all his

Christmases come at once, so that when the chips are down, when he is forced to make a choice, he will choose me, because he will never be able to give me up.

36

'I've got a big favour to ask,' Adam said, as we sat down for breakfast on Saturday morning.

I looked at him expectantly.

'Are you still off next Wednesday?'

I nodded. 'I'm off every Wednesday, you know that,' I said, as I munched on a piece of wholemeal toast.

He grimaced, and I knew I wasn't going to like what he was about to say. 'I've got a really big client meeting . . .'

I waited. Whatever he was about to ask, I wanted him to work for it, just a little.

'And I was wondering if . . . it's just that Mum has a chemo appointment, and I've already spoken to James, but he's away with his new girlfriend—'

'Is he? Where?' I interrupted.

'Paris, I believe,' he said, shrugging his shoulders. 'Anyways, if you're around, I wondered how you'd feel about taking Mum to the hospital.'

I stared at him blankly. 'Have you asked *her*?'

'No. I'm asking you first. See how you feel about it.'

I smiled inwardly. A good sign.

'It would just be picking her up from the cottage and

running her to the hospital. Perhaps you could go into town for a couple of hours before taking her back home again.' He looked at me hopefully.

I knew this could be my chance. It would give me the opportunity I needed to expose her deceit, to prove beyond any doubt that she'd cruelly hoodwinked everyone around her, including her two beloved sons. But I also knew the risk I was taking, and the potential consequence of my actions. Was it worth it? I couldn't save Rebecca, but I could save myself. As soon as that thought entered my head, my mind was made up.

'Sure,' I said casually, though my heart was beating double-time. 'It'll be nice to spend some time with her. Don't tell her. Let it be a surprise.'

He looked at me sceptically, knowing just as well as I did that I'd like nothing less.

I had it all planned, and I felt confident and in control as I drove down to Sevenoaks, my desire to expose her seemingly far greater than the fear I'd been carrying around for the past couple of weeks. But, as I walked up the path to her cottage, all my resolve disappeared, and I felt like a hand was rummaging around in my stomach, pulling my insides out. I fought through it, refusing to let myself down.

'Pamela!' I exclaimed, as she opened the door.

She looked around me, expecting to see Adam walking up the path.

'Surprise!' I said enthusiastically. 'Bet you weren't expecting to see me.'

'Where's Adam? I thought he was taking me today.' She was still looking past me.

'Nope, he had to work, so you've got me, I'm afraid.'

'Well, there's no need. I can get myself there.'

'Don't be silly,' I sang. 'I'm here now, so let's get going. We don't want to be late for your appointment.'

I watched as she fretted and fussed over the contents of her bag, her mind seemingly distracted by my unexpected arrival. She couldn't find her keys, or remember which book she was reading. I smiled as I listened to her ramblings.

She didn't say another word until we pulled up in the hospital car park and I went to get out.

'What are you doing?' she said. I could hear the panic in her voice. 'Where are you going?'

'I'm just going to take you in. Adam said to make sure you get in okay.'

'I'm perfectly capable of seeing to that myself,' she sneered. 'I know where to go.'

'Yes, but you were very shaky on your feet last time,' I said, loudly and slowly, as if I was talking to someone hard of hearing.

'I'll not be needing your help,' she said huffily. 'I'll take it from here.'

'Are you sure?' I asked. 'I'd feel happier if I took you in.'

I smiled as she nimbly jumped out of the car and made her way across the car park.

'I'll come back for you in a couple of hours, then?' I called out, but she didn't even look back. I watched as she walked through the automatic doors and into the main reception.

I'd downloaded a map of the vast hospital building, and noticed that there were two other exits, both at the rear of the site. I'd estimated that it would take her four or five minutes to navigate her way through the various corridors and departments to either of the other exits. She wouldn't just come straight back out here, that was too risky. She'd go for one of the others – I'd plump for the one nearest the shopping centre. Once she was in there, she could lose herself for hours, hence the reason why I needed to catch her before she got there. I swung the car round and headed out onto the ring road, through the estate, past Sainsbury's, and into the pay-and-display car park for the town centre. I'd done it in less than two minutes.

I parked up so that I could see the hospital exit between the stationary cars, and waited. My mouth was dry, and I was sure I was forgetting to breathe. When I saw a flash of burgundy, the same as her cardigan, my chest caught as I gasped for air.

I slammed the steering wheel. 'Shit,' I said out loud, as if I was surprised to see her, and I suddenly wished that I hadn't. As much as I knew I was right, the revelation that she had lied about having cancer made everything so much more complicated. How was I going to tell Adam? How would he react? Would he believe me? What would I have to do to prove I was right?

I sat there dumbly. I hadn't thought much past this point. She was getting close to the entrance of the precinct and, if I didn't move fast, I was going to lose her.

'Shit,' I said again, as I grabbed the keys from the ignition and pushed the door open. I'd have to take my chances on the pay-and-display. I didn't have time to get a ticket.

I kept a fair distance behind her, shadowing her movements. I didn't know what I was doing, but an impending sense of dread began to engulf me as I realized that I was going to have to confront her. There was no point in doing all this if I didn't. I tried to reason with myself that I could just take the information home with me and deal with it from there, but I knew, even as I was thinking it, that that course of action wouldn't achieve anything. This had to be dealt with here and now.

I followed her for twenty minutes, darting in and out of shops, hiding behind pillars. My chest tightened as I watched her disappear into a Costa Coffee.

'Just sit back and watch it unravel,' I said to myself, as I followed her in five minutes later.

Relief flooded through me as I saw her sitting with her back to the front of the shop, giving me another chance to back out, another ten seconds to change my mind.

'What can I get you?' asked the perky barista.

Too late. 'A cappuccino to go, please.'

I looked over at Pammie, imagining that she must have heard my voice, yet knowing it was nigh on impossible to hear anything over the din of the milk-frother.

I don't take sugar, but I took myself over to the stirring station, so that I came at Pammie head on as I walked out. It needed to look like a happy coincidence.

'P . . . Pamela?' I pretended to stutter, as I drew level with her table.

She looked up, and the colour instantly drained from her face.

'Emily?' she questioned, as if hoping that I'd somehow say 'no'.

'My goodness, what a surprise,' I said, feigning astonishment. 'Finished at the hospital so soon?'

I watched as her head and mouth battled for control, searching for the right thing to say. 'I'm too late,' she said. 'Apparently my appointment was this morning.'

'Oh, really?' I said. 'That's odd.'

'Yes, I'm to come back tomorrow.'

'Did they not let you know in advance that your time had changed?' I asked.

'Apparently, they sent a letter . . . in the post,' she faltered. I was getting a sick satisfaction from her obvious discomfort. I thought she'd be more prepared than this. Ready for this eventuality, should it ever occur.

'Really? How strange that you didn't receive it.'

How long was I going to keep up this charade? I pulled out the chair opposite her and sat down. 'Shall I tell you what's really going on here?'

She looked at me, her eyes like steel, daring me to call it.

I leant across the table. 'What's going on, is that you never had cancer in the first place, did you?'

She looked like she'd been slapped in the face. 'What?' she said. 'What a wicked thing to say.'

I ignored the tears welling up in her eyes. I was used to the waterworks. She could bring them on at will.

'Are you really going to keep going with this?' I asked incredulously.

'I don't know what you're suggesting,' she said. 'I don't know what you're talking about.'

'I think you do,' I said. 'You never even went to the chemotherapy ward, did you?'

'Of course I did,' she said. Her voice was getting higher. 'I'm to go back tomorrow.'

'No, you didn't, and do you know how I know?' I said, calling her bluff. 'Because I've just been up there and they've never heard of you.'

She wiped a tear away and laughed wryly. 'You can believe what you like.'

'Oh, I know what I believe,' I said, feeling slightly

wrong-footed. This wasn't going how I'd imagined. 'I wonder what Adam is going to make of all this?'

Tears fell down her cheeks. 'He doesn't need to know,' she said quietly.

This was more like it. 'You have no idea how long I've waited for this. How long I've waited to expose you for who you really are.'

'You can't tell him,' she said, as she closed her eyes. Her wet lashes stuck together in clumps. 'It'll be the end of—'

'It'll be the end of your lies and deceit. He'll know you for the person you really are, not the perfect mother you pretend to be.'

'You can't tell him,' she repeated.

'Just you watch me,' I said, pushing the chair out from under me and standing up. 'Just you watch.'

I went to walk away, to walk away to a new life without her in it. I dared to imagine my world as it was about to become: free of stress and full of love. I hadn't even got past her when she said, 'And how are *you* going to explain away James?'

I stopped dead in my tracks. 'What?'

She fixed me with her eyes. 'How are you going to explain to your fiancé that you've been seeing his brother behind his back?'

My blood ran cold as my brain back-tracked to James: where we'd met, what we'd said. No one could have seen us, could they? What did she know? I wondered if she'd noticed that every look was just that second too long, or that every time we met, the kiss on the cheek was just that little bit softer. It was nothing, yet everything.

She was double bluffing me, clutching at straws. I looked at her and, despite the white rush of images that were bombarding my vision, I kept my gaze firm.

'Are you honestly suggesting there's something going on between me and James?' I questioned, half laughing.

She nodded. 'Oh, I'm sure of it. And do you know how I know?' she said, turning the tables on me. 'Because I told him to do it.'

37

I was up all night, alternating between crying on the sofa and being sick in the toilet. How had it got to this? I'd finally found a way of destroying her, taking her down once and for all, yet it would be at my own cost. I couldn't win this one, and she knew it.

Aside from the intoxicating rage and sickening revulsion I felt towards Pammie for what she'd done to Rebecca, I was also deeply saddened at the thought of James's ill-fated attempts to seduce me, in an effort to catch me out and appease his psychotic mother. How had she kept him at her beck and call? Why would he have been prepared to do it? It was as if she had some kind of hold over her two sons, one that neither of them was prepared to break.

I felt violated. The very thought of James coming to me under his mother's instruction made me feel dirty and invaded. There was nothing she wouldn't do to dispense me from their lives.

Adam had slept soundly all night and, when he woke up, he came into the living room, took one look at me and said, 'You look like shit.'

I didn't have the energy to answer.

'Do you want a coffee?' he asked.

I shook my head. I couldn't think of anything worse.

'What's up?' he said, filling his cup with hot water. 'Do you think it's flu or something?'

I rubbed at my eyes; yesterday's mascara was still coming off even after all the tears I'd cried. 'I really don't know,' I said. 'I just feel poisoned.'

'What did you eat yesterday? Did you eat anything with Mum?'

I shook my head.

He came and sat down next to me on the sofa, sipping noisily from his mug. The stench of coffee permeated my nostrils and I clamped a hand over my mouth in a futile attempt to catch the vomit that projected across the coffee table.

'Jesus!' shouted Adam, jumping up from the sofa, spilling the offending liquid onto the carpet.

'Oh my God, I'm so sorry,' I said, though even as I was saying it, I wondered why my first thought was to apologize. 'Give me a minute. I'll go to the bathroom and then sort this out.'

My throat was burning from the hot bile spewing up from my intestines, and my eyes streamed as I battled to stop the retching. How had a sixty-three-year-old woman caused my mind and body to fail me like this? I was a strong woman who had never suffered fools gladly, who could carry her own in any situation. How had this happened to me? It defied logic.

I was still hugging the porcelain when it occurred to me that maybe the root cause of my physical state was indeed something more logical. My brain banged against the sides of my skull at the very idea of it.

It had taken all my resolve to drag myself into town, not least because I felt like death warmed up, but because a very real possibility was raging in my head. I bought an exorbitantly priced test at the chemist's in Charing Cross station and spent a further 50p for a toilet cubicle to wee onto a stick in. I'd envisaged walking to work whilst the chemicals did their stuff, but I hadn't even pulled my knickers up when a prominent blue line appeared in the window. My vision blurred as I tried to read the instructions again, begging the question, 'Does a line mean I'm pregnant or not pregnant?' hoping against hope that it was the latter.

I called Pippa as I repeatedly banged into the turnstile to get out of the basement convenience. A girl with blue hair and chewing gum in her mouth watched me gormlessly as I did it four times, my temper fraying with each attempt.

'That's the *in* turnstile.'

'Brilliant,' I said sarcastically.

'What is?' said Pippa's voice from my mobile, as she finally picked up.

'I'm pregnant,' I replied feebly.

'Fuck,' she said, 'and that's brilliant, how?'

'No, that's not brilliant, I was talking to . . . oh, never mind. Shit, Pippa, I'm pregnant.'

'Well, that's something of a surprise,' she offered slowly.

'I mean, what the hell?' My head was unable to compute what was going on.

Pippa remained silent on the other end of the line until I reached the Strand.

'How did that happen? Was it supposed to?' she asked.

'Of course not,' I snapped, though why I was taking it out on her, I don't know.

'I thought you were on the pill,' she said.

'I was. I am. But I forgot to take it for a while, when all the wedding stuff kicked off. I probably missed, I don't know, maybe a week's worth, maybe more. Adam wasn't at home, and I wasn't intending to sleep with him anytime soon, so . . .'

'So, what was it?' she said. 'Immaculate conception?'

'Things just took us a bit by surprise one night, the first night we . . . you know . . .'

I groaned at the memory of telling Pammie how I might be pregnant from all the make-up sex we'd had. Jesus.

'But I thought you wanted to reschedule the wedding for as soon as possible,' she said.

'I do, but I can't now, can I? I'll never be able to reorganize everything before I start showing. I don't want to waddle down the aisle seven months pregnant. Oh God, Pippa, I can't believe this. It's just all too much.' I started to cry, and the delivery driver pulling up outside the post office asked if I was all right. I smiled weakly at him.

'What did Adam say?' she asked.

'He doesn't know. I've just done the test in Charing Cross. Wait. I'll call you back.' I raced to the nearest bin and hurled my head into it. Seeing an upended KFC box with gnawed-at chicken bones made it ten times worse. Commuters were going past me, not knowing whether to rush by, or slow down to gawp, but they all looked disgusted.

'Are you okay?' asked Pippa, as I answered the phone.

I grunted. 'That was just me throwing up into a street bin.'

'Oh, classy,' she joked. 'But seriously, what are you going to do about this?'

'I'll tell Adam tonight and we'll talk it through. Honestly, Pippa, I can't tell you how messed up this all is.'

'It's not messed up, it's a blessing,' she said.

'I mean everything,' I said. 'Everything around me is so screwed up. How can I contemplate having a baby, when Adam and I still have our own issues to deal with? What's he going to think? Oh, God.'

'Calm down,' she said. 'This might be what you both actually need. It'll certainly show *her* that she can't play around with you anymore. This is sticking two fingers right up.' She gave a little snigger.

I understood the sentiment, but knew that the reality of having Pammie's grandchild would mean that we were bound together for evermore. The thought terrified me.

'I honestly can't believe it, Pip,' I said. 'What am I going to do?'

'Right, one step at a time. Talk to Adam tonight and, once we know his reaction, we can work it out from there. Okay?'

I nodded mutely.

'Okay, Em?'

'Yes, I'll try and call you later if I can, otherwise it'll be tomorrow morning.'

'Cool,' she said. 'Ring me when you can.'

I ended the call and realized that I wasn't even walking in the direction of the office. I'd missed Old Compton Street and walked straight on.

I made so many mistakes at work when I finally got there that my boss, Nathan, asked if I'd like to go home early. It struck me then, as he was talking to me, that I hadn't taken any time off since the fall-out from the wedding. I'd had my usual two days a week off, but I'd declined Nathan's offer to take a week's holiday, which should have been the second half of my honeymoon, proclaiming that I was fine and just wanted to get on with it. I busied myself like never before, brushing off the drama of the wedding, and everything else that went with it, as an inconvenient blip. But in that moment, as he looked at me sympathetically, his head tilted to one side, it finally hit me. I needed a break, a rest from the monotony of commuting, from my demanding clients who each thought they were more important than the other thirty I had to deal with, even from the mundane chit-chat with colleagues, and having to keep up the pretence that all was good in my world. It wasn't, and now I had an added problem. A big one.

'We can manage,' said Nathan encouragingly, sensing my hesitation.

I didn't want him to manage. My ego wanted the entire business to fall apart without me there.

'Go,' he ushered. 'Go take some time out.'

I needed to go, but didn't want to. 'You sound like an American life coach,' I said, smiling.

'If I have to pick you up and carry you out, I will.' He laughed. 'Get out of here.'

I gathered up the lip salve, Oyster card, and packet of chocolate digestives from my desk and slung my bag over my shoulder. 'You sure?' I asked him, one last time, as I headed out the door.

'Go!' he yelled after me.

It wasn't yet four o'clock, so I headed over to the City on the Central line, hoping to catch Adam as he was about to leave the office. It somehow felt like it would be easier to tell him about the baby on neutral territory, a busy bar or restaurant, rather than in the solitude of home. I was hoping that the seriousness of the situation would feel less real, less daunting.

'Hey,' he said as he picked up the phone.

'Hey,' I replied hesitantly. 'You leaving work soon?'

'Just tying up one last thing, and then I'll be on my way. Why? What's up?'

'Nothing,' I said. When did I start lying so easily? 'I'm at Bank, just wondered if you fancied meeting up for a drink before we go home.'

'Great, I could do with a bevvy; I've had a shit day.'

I recoiled. Maybe if he'd already had a bad day, I should save my news for another time. For when he was more open-minded, relaxed. I immediately chastised myself for making the decision for him, and vowed to tell him regardless. *I'd* had a shit *month*, but it hadn't stopped anyone heaping it on me, all the more.

'Great,' I said. 'Meet you in the King's Head in ten minutes?'

'Perfect, see you then.'

I got there with six minutes to spare, enough time to have a drink and calm my nerves.

'Can I get a large glass of Sauvignon Blanc, please?' I said to the barman. I watched as he lifted a glass down from the rack above the bar, walked over to the under-counter fridge, and measured out a large vat of amber nectar. It was only when he put it down in front of me, its sweet aroma reaching my nostrils, that I was hit by the thunderous realization that I was carrying a baby.

'Er, can I also get a tomato juice with that, please?' I asked, almost apologetically.

He looked around at the space where I stood, correctly deducing that I was on my own.

'That's an interesting combo,' he said.

I smiled and shook my head. God, was this what the next nine months was going to be like? Walking around with a stomach like a washing machine and a brain full of cotton wool?

'Hi gorgeous,' said Adam, as he came up behind me, and kissed me on the cheek. 'You feeling any better?'

I shook my head, but he was already ordering a drink.

'Pint of Fosters, please, mate.'

I smiled awkwardly while we waited, thankful for a few more minutes before I threw a grenade into Adam's world. I watched him take three long gulps of his beer, as if it was water. He might need another one sooner than he thinks.

'I've got something to tell you,' I started.

Adam took one look at me and grabbed my hands. 'Oh my God, you're not ill, are you?' he asked, panic flashing across his face. 'Because if you are, I really don't think I can cope.'

Funny how the possibility of me being ill was all about him. I hadn't really noticed that before.

I shook my head. 'No, I'm fine, we're fine.'

'Of course we are, aren't we?'

'Not me and you,' I said slowly, as I rubbed my tummy. 'Me and this one.'

'Sorry, I'm not getting you,' he frowned.

'I'm pregnant,' I said quietly, though it felt as if I'd shouted it across the pub.

'What?' he exclaimed.

I watched his expression change from confusion to anger, to joy, and back to confusion again, all in a split second.

'You're pregnant? How?'

'Er . . . do you really need me to explain?' I asked.

'But I thought you were . . . I thought we had this covered.'

'We did, well *I* did, but I missed a fair few days after the wedding, what with everything going on. I just didn't keep on top of it.'

'How many did you miss?' he asked, as if it mattered.

'I don't know . . . maybe ten days, a couple of weeks? I can't remember. But regardless, one way or another, I'm now pregnant.'

'But shouldn't you have thought to be more careful?'

This wasn't going how I'd thought it would. Or maybe it was exactly what I'd expected, deep down.

'So, what are we going to do?' he said, rubbing the bridge of his nose.

I looked at him, unsure of what he was actually

asking. I didn't feel that we had an option. Obviously, he did.

'Nothing,' I said tightly. 'I'm going to have a baby.'

His eyes narrowed, and he was silent for what seemed like an eternity.

'Okay,' he said finally. 'So this is good news, yes?'

'I haven't had a chance to digest it yet, I only found out myself this morning, but it could be good, couldn't it?'

We both stood there, looking dumbfounded, unsure of what to do or say next. He ran a hand through his hair, and I waited for his next move. I honestly wasn't sure if he was going to hug me or walk out.

He did neither. 'So, what are we going to do about the wedding?'

It felt like both of us were walking on eggshells. 'I don't want to get married whilst I'm pregnant, so I suppose it will have to wait.'

'Okay, so that's decided then,' he said half-heartedly, before pulling me into an awkward embrace. 'That's great.'

His face told a different story to his words, but I had to allow him time to come to terms with what this meant for him, and us as a couple. I'd had close to eight hours to get my head around this life-changing news, he'd not yet had eight minutes, so I allowed him time, to give him the benefit of doubt.

'Yes,' I replied hesitantly. 'It is.'

38

'How do I look?' I asked, without taking my eyes off my reflection in the mirror.

Adam came up behind me, put his hands on my burgeoning belly, and kissed my cheek. 'You look really hot.'

'Hot' was not how I felt, but it was obvious that Adam clearly found my changing body appealing, as he hadn't left me alone for the past few weeks. Whilst I wrestled my huge boobs into something resembling a hammock, I'd often find him just sitting on the edge of the bed, watching in amazement, and lust.

It had taken a while for us to get used to the idea of my pregnancy, and we had alternately fought, and then made love, often all in one night.

Just a few weeks before, we'd had a huge row over what I was wearing. 'You're not going out dressed like that,' Adam had said, as he watched me stepping into a new black dress, ready for a night on the town with Pippa and Seb. I'd loved it when I'd seen it in Whistles, as its body-con shape had hugged my slim hips – my bump wasn't yet visible.

'Since when?' I teased. 'You know you love me in a

tight little number, and the beauty of this one is that it's going to grow with me.' I stretched the Lycra material outwards over my tummy, as if to prove the point.

'That was then, but this is now,' he said seriously. 'I don't want you going out like that.'

I turned to face him. 'Are you being serious?'

He nodded and looked away. 'You're carrying my baby now, you need to dress accordingly.'

'And what is "accordingly"?' I laughed. 'Am I supposed to be wearing a tent, even though I'm not showing yet?'

'Just show some respect,' he said. 'For me and the baby.'

'Oh, come on, Adam. You sound like your mother. How I choose to dress or not dress has got nothing to do with you.' I looked down at myself. 'This outfit would have driven you crazy a few months ago. Nothing's changed, I still look the same, but you're honestly telling me I'm being disrespectful?'

He'd come at me then, and grabbed hold of my wrist. 'You're pregnant and you're happy to go out dressed like a hooker, are you? You're going to get the wrong kind of attention, and I'm not having some drunken letch coming on to you when you shouldn't even be out.'

'Oh, I've heard it all now,' I shouted. 'I'm two months pregnant and I'm not supposed to go out ever again? I'm not changing.'

I picked up my bag and headed for the bedroom door.

He'd stood there, his bulk filling the frame.

'Move,' I said, sounding more controlled than I felt.

'You're not going.'

My heart was beating out of my chest, and my throat felt parched. The beginnings of a tension headache banged against my skull.

I looked at him, my eyes imploring him to move, but he stayed fast. It was a battle of wills.

'Move,' I repeated.

'No.'

I banged at his chest with my curled fists. 'Move out the way!' I yelled, tears of frustration streaming down my face. 'I swear to God, if you don't move—'

He caught hold of my wrists, and pushed me back into the wall. I thought he was going to spit more vitriol at me, or worse, raise a hand to me, and I cowered, preparing for the onslaught. But instead he kissed me, his tongue delving deep into my mouth. I didn't want to respond. I wanted to show him that I was still as mad as hell, but I couldn't help myself. He ripped my tights as he tore at them, like a man possessed, and I cried out as he entered me.

'Does that hurt?' he asked.

I shook my head. He'd looked at me then, as if seeing me for the first time.

'I'm sorry,' he said, everything about him suddenly

yielding and docile. 'I don't know what came over me. You just look so amazing, and . . .'

He called out and I felt his legs buckle as his head nuzzled my neck, looking for support. He was panting hard. 'Are you still going out?' he managed between breaths.

'Yes,' I said, smoothing down my dress. I wasn't quite sure what had just happened. Was that normal? How can two people fight and lash out at each other, only to be making love a couple of minutes later?

I'd gone out, but not enjoyed myself. Not drinking when your two mates are getting off their faces does not make for the best of nights. Maybe Adam was right: things *were* different, and they would be different for evermore.

I looked in the mirror now, tucking my blouse in and then pulling it out again. At just over three months, it was becoming more difficult to disguise my protruding tummy, but today it didn't matter. Today, for the first time, I could put it on display, be pregnant and proud, but I just felt fat.

'Nothing fits,' I cried, as I rummaged through my wardrobe, looking for inspiration, yet seeing nothing. I could feel myself getting worked up, and there was a tightness across my chest.

'What you're wearing looks great,' offered Adam again, as he watched me battling with hangers and throwing tops and trousers onto the bed. He could say it until he was blue in the face, but I didn't look great, feel great, or any other great. I just wanted to undo the restrictive buttons on my trousers, lie down on the bed, and cry.

'Do we have to go?' I moaned, sounding like a three-year-old.

'You haven't seen my mother in ages, and we need to tell her our news,' he said, as I groaned inside.

'Can't you just tell her over the phone?' I begged.

'Em, we're going to have a baby, and she's going to be a grandmother for the first time. It's not something you tell someone over the phone. And it won't be so bad, because James is coming with his new girlfriend, so that'll mix up the dynamics a bit.'

I wanted to scream. How the hell was I going to get through this? I hadn't seen Pammie since the whole hospital debacle, and I'd ignored two voicemails. Adam had dropped her at her last 'chemo session' and was thrilled when Pammie called him a week later to say that the doctors were so pleased with her progress that they were going to stop the treatment for the time being. I'd smiled rigidly as he'd relayed the good news to me, all the time tempering down the overwhelming desire to shout, 'She's lying!'

The very thought of seeing her made me shudder. I hadn't felt nauseous for weeks now, but I could feel the familiar wrenching in my gut as it reacted to the idea of being in the same room as her. My nerve endings felt on edge and raw.

I imagined her twisted features as she'd no doubt goad me in front of James, daring me to pull her up, and being ready to pounce with the killer blow that she knew would destroy everything I had with Adam. Or perhaps it would be James who'd turn the screw. I felt light-headed as I wondered, not for the first time, about his motivation for doing what he'd done. Saying what he'd said. What did they have to gain by working together to break me down and split us up? Had James told her the truth? That I'd rebuffed him? Or was he a liar, like his mother, and had told her a different version of events? Either way, it didn't really matter. She could make my life hell and hold me to ransom, but was that what she was planning to do? Surely, she'd realize it wouldn't be wise, knowing what I do about her, but what would it matter by then? Adam and I would be over before I'd even have the chance to tell him how she'd cruelly lied about having cancer.

'I don't feel well enough to go,' I said to Adam. 'I feel sick. Why don't you go along, tell them the news?'

'Come on, Em, pull yourself together. You're pregnant, not ill. It'll be a couple of hours in a nice restaurant and then we'll be out of there. Surely you can manage that?'

I honestly didn't know how I could sit in amongst Pammie, Adam, James, and his girlfriend, forever fearful, waiting for the grenade to explode. Though which one of us was going to pull the pin out first, was yet to be seen.

'I'll look after you,' he said, as if reading my mind. 'It won't be so bad.'

Tears sprang to my eyes, as I realized that the one person I had on my side could be snatched away from me at any time of Pammie's choosing.

39

Unusually, Pammie was already in the restaurant, sitting at the table, laughing loudly with James and his girl-friend, as we walked up to them. It already felt like I was the odd one out, the one they were laughing at.

Pammie stood up to greet us. 'Darling,' she said to Adam, 'it's so lovely to see you.'

I smiled tightly.

'And Emily. Dear Emily, you look . . .' She took a purposeful breath as her eyes travelled up and down my body. 'Ravishing.'

Adam helped me off with my coat.

'Hi, Em, this is Kate,' said James awkwardly. He leant in for a kiss, and it took all my will not to pull away from him. I shook Kate's hand as she loomed into view. She was tall, blonde, and slim, and I felt my heart break a little.

I smiled. 'Lovely to meet you.'

'You too,' she replied, 'I've heard a lot about you.'

I wanted to say, 'How so?' but instead, I gave the standard response. 'All good, I hope?'

No one ever offers an answer to that, yet it's one of

life's few rhetorical questions that everybody wants a response to.

We smiled between ourselves, whilst Adam went off in search of a coat stand. 'So, how's things?' James asked eventually. 'Busy at work?'

I hadn't seen him since our wedding dinner for the wedding that never happened. His hair was a little longer, the front just cutting across the top of one eye, and the sun had lightened it to a dark honey blond. I'd assumed that his deep tan was from spending his days tending to the gardens of England, but I noticed that Kate also had a colour to her cheeks. My chest tightened as I imagined them being away somewhere romantic, a villa or intimate hotel, in Italy or France, perhaps, spending their days lying by a pool, and their nights making love. I tried to banish the thought of it, hating myself for still caring, even after what he'd done.

'Yes, all good,' I replied. 'You? You look like you've been away.'

'We've been to Greece,' said Kate excitedly. 'It was amazing, wasn't it?' She looked to James, who gave her the same look back and took hold of her hand. Did Adam and I look at each other like that?

'Here's the big man,' said James, as Adam came towards us smiling.

They shook hands and I watched as Adam was introduced to Kate, their attempt to kiss each other awkward as he went in for two, whilst she was only expecting one. I could feel a prickle of embarrassment from them both.

She was all eyes and teeth, and I pulled at my dowdy blouse self-consciously, wishing I'd worn the dress that Adam and I had fought over a few weeks ago. At least then I could have begun to compete.

'Isn't she gorgeous?' Pammie whispered, as she stood beside me, watching them. 'She's got it all.'

I didn't react. I just continued to watch the two men fawn over her. This was going to be worse than I had even imagined.

'So, what's new?' James asked, finally bringing me back into the conversation.

'Well, let's just order a bottle of wine and we'll tell you,' said Adam, summoning over the waiter.

'Sounds ominous,' James laughed.

'Not at all,' said Adam. 'We've got some pretty big news, actually.'

I watched Pammie's face, her muscles contracting as she struggled to remain expressionless.

'Oh yes?' she managed. 'Have you set a new date for the wedding?'

'Not exactly,' said Adam. 'Things have moved up a gear or two.' He looked at me and took my hand, and I gave him my best winning smile.

'Ooh, sounds exciting,' piped up Kate.

Adam looked around the table and grinned. 'Well, we're having a baby,' he said.

James's mouth fell open, Kate beamed and clapped her hands together, and Pammie sat there stony-faced, her jowls twitching.

'Wow, guys, that's amazing,' said James. 'That's really cool. Wow.'

'How far gone are you?' asked Kate. 'When are you due? Do you know if it's a boy or a girl?'

I batted the answers back just as fast as she asked the questions.

'Three months. Spring. No.'

James shook Adam's hand again, and he came around the table to kiss my cheek. 'Congratulations,' he whispered, and my body stiffened.

'Mum?' said Adam, still awaiting a reaction.

'Well, it's just a shock,' she said tearfully. 'A good shock, but a shock nonetheless.' She tried to smile through her tears, but it didn't reach her eyes.

'That's wonderful news, son, really.' She wasn't attempting to get up, so Adam went around the table to her. I didn't bother.

She clung onto him, like a limpet.

'Mum, you're supposed to be happy, not crying.' He laughed. 'Nobody's died.'

'I'm all right, son,' she said, sniffing. 'Being a grandma is going to take some getting used to. I'm pleased for you, really I am.'

She extricated herself from Adam's grasp and caught my eye. I almost didn't want to look at her. But I fixed on that smile again, the one that pretends to the world that everything is great, and locked eyes with her. I felt a jolt. The anger and fury I'd expected to see wasn't there. All I could see was fear.

'Talking of good news,' she said, pulling her eyes away from mine. 'James also has something to tell us, haven't you, darling?'

He smiled, as his hand searched out Kate's again. 'Yes, I've asked Kate to marry me, and she said yes.'

A rush of blood flooded my head.

'Isn't that marvellous?' cooed Pammie, as she reached across to take both James and Kate's hands in hers. 'We're going to be great friends, I can tell already.'

I looked at Kate, searching for some kind of recognition, a sign that we were two kindred spirits, battling furiously against the power that was Pammie. But there was nothing but innocent devotion in her eyes, and a warped belief that Pammie was telling the truth.

I didn't know who I pitied the most. Her, for her unsuspecting naivety, blissfully unaware of how this woman, who proclaimed to be her friend, was about to become her arch-enemy, or me, whose life she'd already tried so hard to destroy. I was a shadow of my former self, insecure and paranoid, held together by the love of a man I hoped I could rely on when it all imploded.

I watched Kate as she snuggled into James's embrace, flushed with excitement and passion. Pammie was right. She did have it all, and I wished I were her. I remembered a time, not so long ago, when I was swept along with the thrill of our new relationship, enjoying it for what it was, not thinking for a moment that anyone, least of all Adam's own mother, could cause the pain that she had.

'Let's get a bottle of champagne to celebrate,' gushed Pammie.

Was nobody going to ask what the rush was? How they could be so sure that they wanted to spend the rest of their lives together having only known each other for a few months? Surely Pammie was going to step in, say her piece, as she did with me – but she remained stoical.

I watched as she poured out four glasses of champagne, and handed them out to everyone but me.

'Congratulations!' she said, raising her flute. 'To James and Kate.'

I looked to James. His eyes darted backwards and forwards between his mother and Adam, but didn't rest once on me, in between.

'Mum, can Emily have a glass?' asked Adam.

'Oh, sorry, I didn't think she'd want to,' she said. 'I thought you weren't supposed to drink when you're pregnant. Well, you couldn't in my day, anyway.'

'Times have changed,' I said curtly. 'I'll have a small glass, thanks.'

'Here's to baby Banks!' said James.

I closed my eyes and savoured that first sip, the effervescence popping on my tongue.

'So, have you set a date yet?' asked Pammie excitedly.

'Well, we're thinking springtime next year, if we can get it organized in time,' James said.

'Ah, just in time for the little one to be born,' she said, tilting her head in the direction of my stomach. I smiled to myself, knowing that by then I'd either be the size of a bus, or have a baby latched onto my boob. Neither scenario made me feel very glamorous.

'I've got a scrapbook at home, filled with pictures,' said Kate. 'I've had it ever since I was nine or ten. Some people think I'm a bit deranged.' She gave a little laugh.

Again, I flinched, waiting for Pammie's derisive put-down, but nothing came.

'That's so sweet,' she said, instead. 'I did the very same thing as a young lass. I showed it to my Jim, and he promised me that I could have everything in it.'

Kate smiled at her.

'Well, show us your ring, then,' said Pammie.

'I was so surprised,' said Kate, as she thrust a solitaire diamond in our direction. 'I had no idea.'

'I'm really pleased for you,' Pammie said warmly. 'Welcome to the family.'

Was I missing something here? It felt like I was intruding on a special moment between a mother and her daughter. Had Pammie been like this with me, once upon a time, in the very beginning?

I thought back to our very first meeting, at her cottage, when she left the photo album with Rebecca's picture staring up at me. She meant for me to see it, even then playing mind games with me, daring me to ask the questions that I didn't want to know the answers to. She'd planted a seed and sat back to watch it grow, hoping that, in the meantime, I'd be too weak to deal with the consequences. She thought she could cast me aside, as she'd done with Rebecca, but she hadn't reckoned on my love for Adam. I love him more than life itself, and, as I sit here, with new life growing in my belly, I know that there is nothing she can do to take that away from me.

40

'I promise it won't be over the top,' said Pippa, when I turned my nose up to a baby shower. 'Just friends, a few balloons, and lots of prosecco.'

I rolled my eyes and pointed to my huge stomach.

'Oh, course,' she said, as if suddenly realizing my predicament. 'Just a *few* friends, you *are* the balloon, and *I'll* drink the prosecco!'

Two weeks later, she and Seb turned up at the flat with a tower of pink cupcakes and a six-foot-long 'Mum to be' banner. The 'hen party' posse followed, with the exception of Pammie, who hadn't been invited.

'Don't you think it's mad that the grandmother of your baby isn't coming, yet the woman who slept with your boyfriend is?' Pippa had observed a few days earlier. 'You couldn't make it up.'

I'd had to agree with her; I could never have imagined Charlotte being in my life again, but things are different now. I'm having a baby, and a part of me wants to share it with her.

'Hey, how are you feeling?' she asked as she came through the door, laden down with pink goodies. She pulled me towards her and held me for a long time, as if she never wanted to let me go.

'Fat!' I laughed.

'Fat and gorgeous,' joined in Seb, as he squeezed past us on the landing.

They drank the fizz, whilst Mum and I dunked custard creams into our cups of tea. 'I'll never be drinking again,' she'd said, when Pippa offered her a prosecco. 'Not after the hen weekend.' We'd all laughed at the memory of Mum emerging from the bedroom at 11 a.m. the morning after BJ's, bemoaning why we'd all let her sleep for so long, before asking if we had the provisions to make a bacon butty. 'Oh, what will Gerald make of this?' she'd mumbled, as she'd taken herself off in search of comfort food in an unfamiliar kitchen.

'So, I assume you've not heard anything from Pammie since you told her you were pregnant?' she asked quietly now, whilst the others were playing 'Guess the baby's weight'.

I shook my head. 'She's called a few times and left voicemails asking for me to call her back, but apart from that . . .'

'And you haven't?' she said. 'Called her back, I mean.'

'No. I've got nothing to say to her,' I said.

Mum nodded in agreement. I'd told her everything about the altercation in the coffee shop, bar the part about James. I didn't want her to think badly of me, and I couldn't explain it without running that risk. Seb and

Pippa knew though, yet as much as they tried to convince me I'd done nothing wrong, I still felt a real sense of shame.

We were watching *What to Expect When You're Expecting*, huddled under duvets, when I heard the front door slam, and my heart sank a little as I heard the heavy footsteps coming up the stairs. I could hazard a guess as to how drunk Adam was from those initial steps, and I was rarely wrong.

'Hey, hey, hey! It's the AGM of the WI,' he stated loudly. I caught a glint in his eyes as he surveyed the living room and settled on Seb. I was sure I saw his lips curl in distaste.

'Are you ladies having fun?' he went on, accentuating the word ladies.

Everyone murmured their hellos, quickly followed by musings of, 'Is that the time?' and 'I ought to go.'

I could see Seb bristling, and I shot him a warning look and gave a shake of my head.

'Adam, could I have a word, please?' I said, pulling myself up off the sofa and getting an extra push up from Pippa.

'You okay?' she asked quietly.

I nodded. I walked into our bedroom without saying a word, and Adam duly followed.

'What is wrong with you?' I asked, evenly and calmly.

'What is wrong with *me*?' he said, chortling to himself. 'You're the one who's got The Golden Girls taking up space in our living room. And I see *he*'s here again.'

'Keep your voice down.'

'This is my house, and I'll talk as loudly as I want to.'

'Oh, grow up.'

'And since when did we agree to announce the sex of our baby?' he asked. He obviously wasn't too drunk to have noticed the pink regalia adorning the front room. 'I haven't even told my mother yet, but here you are, shouting it from the rooftops. Though if my mother had been invited to your silly little tea party, I suppose she would have found out along with the rest of them, I guess.' He looked at me with real disdain, and I turned to go.

'I'm not going to play silly games with you, Adam,' I said wearily. 'Your mother's not here because I don't want her here, and the sex of our baby has never been a secret. I suppose if we were having a boy, you'd be happier to share the news.'

I remembered back to our twenty-week scan a couple of months before, and the look of disappointment on Adam's face when the sonographer said she'd put money on it being a girl.

'How often do you get it wrong?' he'd asked, with a little laugh.

'I try very hard not to,' she said.

'But what are the stats?' Adam had pushed.

'If I had to put a figure on it, I'd say about one in every twenty. Something like that.'

He'd looked at me smugly, before she added, 'But in your case, I'm pretty sure you can start knitting those pink bootees.' I'd watched as his shoulders dropped again.

'I just think you should consider me and my feelings a bit in . . . all this,' he said now, gesticulating wildly around the bedroom.

'Oh, for God's sake, Adam, you sound like a baby yourself,' I said, before walking out.

Seb was coming towards me across the landing, his face like thunder. 'If you'll excuse me,' he said, as he went past.

'Seb, please,' I said, going to grab his arm, but instead of walking down the stairs and out of the flat, he walked straight into our bedroom.

'What is your problem?' he said, squaring up to Adam.

'Seb, leave it,' I pleaded, as I watched Adam pull himself up to his full height, his expression disbelieving.

I pulled him back, and Adam smirked. 'Didn't think you had it in you,' he hissed, though which of us he was talking to, I don't know.

'She's too good for you,' said Seb, as I steered him out of the room.

41

There was a constant succession of visitors to the house when I came home from hospital with Poppy. My parents, Pippa, Seb, and even James, popped in with a baby-pink hamper full of goodies. 'Well done,' James said tenderly, as he kissed my forehead, just as Adam had done in the operating theatre when they cut Poppy from my stomach. Our plan for a water birth went out the window after sixteen hours of labour resulted in Poppy getting distressed.

I welcomed them all in a blur; all the time, waiting, dreading Pammie's visit. She'd not wanted to come for the first three days, as she had a cold and didn't want to infect the baby. But I wished she'd just get it over and done with, so I could relax and enjoy my time with Poppy.

'You okay if Mum comes up tomorrow?' asked Adam, just as Pippa went out the door. 'She'll probably stay for the night, and I'll drop her back the next morning.'

I groaned. 'I'm exhausted, can't you take her back tomorrow evening before tea?'

'Come on, Em,' he said. 'This is her first grandchild,

and she's the last to meet her as it is. She might even have her uses.'

That was exactly what I was frightened of. I looked at Poppy's perfect face, her big eyes staring up at me, and felt a shudder run through me. 'I'd really rather she went home,' I said. 'Please.'

'I'll give her a call, see how it goes,' he said. 'I won't offer if she doesn't ask.'

I knew even before he came back into the room that the conversation hadn't gone my way.

'So, I'll go and get her around midday and take her back the next morning.'

'You tried hard,' I said under my breath.

If he heard me, he didn't react. 'I'm going to pop down the pub later, wet the baby's head and all that,' he said. 'You've not got a problem with that, have you?'

Was he asking me, or telling me? Either way, he'd posed it in such a way that it would make me look possessive and controlling if I dared say yes.

'What's the face for?' he said tightly. 'It's just a quick drink, for Christ's sake.'

Funny, I'd not even said anything, but he was happy to start an argument with himself, just so he'd feel vindicated in going.

'When was that arranged, then?' I asked.

He tutted. 'Just in the last day or so. Mike suggested a drink, and all the others have just latched on to it. It's a rite of passage.'

I was well aware of the tradition, so why he was trying to justify it to himself, heaven only knows. I could feel my hackles going up, not because he was going out, but because he was being so defensive about it. He felt guilty, yet he was trying to turn it on me, making me out to be the bad guy.

'Okay, cool,' I said indifferently. 'Try not to be too long though, as I could use some help getting the place ready for your mum.'

When he wasn't home by midnight, I didn't think it was unreasonable to give him a call. Poppy wasn't settling and, in between feeding, rocking and bathing, I was struggling to get anything else done.

'I'll call you back,' I heard him slur, when he answered on the fourth ring. There was a lot of background noise, chattering, clinking of glasses, and loud music.

'Adam?' The line went dead.

Ten minutes later, he still hadn't, so I rang him again.

'Yep,' was all he could offer when he picked up. It sounded quieter now, and I could hear his breath cutting out, as if he was drawing on something and then exhaling.

'Adam?'

'Yes,' he said, sounding impatient, as if he had somewhere he had to be. 'What is it?'

I fought to stay calm, even though Poppy was screaming her head off, and my new mummy brain was struggling to keep everything in perspective. 'Just wondering how much longer you're going to be,' I said.

'Why? Am I missing something?'

I forced myself to breathe deeply. 'No, I just wanted to know whether I should go to bed.'

'Well, are you *tired*?' I could tell from his tone that he was trying to be facetious.

'Yes, I'm shattered.'

'So, what are you waiting for?'

'Forget it,' I said, my patience running out. 'You do what the hell you like.'

'Thank you, I will,' I heard him say before I put the phone down.

I could've ranted and raved, but he was too drunk to care, and it would only have made me upset. He could stay out as long as he liked, if he was just going to be a pain in the arse. He'd only be a hindrance if he was drunk, and I had enough on my plate with worrying about Pammie's impending arrival.

Crazily, my instinct, once I finally got Poppy down, was to run around the flat, making sure everything was just so before she arrived. I didn't want her to have any excuse to goad me, to tell me what I wasn't doing right, and everything I was doing wrong. But the tug on my stitches, as I struggled to get the cover on the duvet for the spare room, had me asking what I was doing it all for. She didn't need a reason to belittle and undermine me. If she didn't have one, she'd just make one up.

Adam got home just after three o'clock in the morning and made such a racket that he woke Poppy up, who then cried solidly until her next feed.

'Thanks a lot,' I spat, as I rocked her back and forth, pacing the bedroom. He belched, grunted, and rolled onto his back.

I didn't see him for another eight hours, when he got up, took two Alka-Seltzers, said, 'I feel like shit,' and went back to bed again. I can't pretend I didn't feel the tiniest sliver of satisfaction as I followed him into the bedroom, threw the curtains open, and said, 'Wakey, wakey. You've got to go and get your mother.' He let out the loudest groan, and just at that moment, I fancied he was dreading her visit even more than I was.

By the time he arrived back with her, the flat was spotless, Poppy was asleep in the nook of my elbow, and there was a fresh pot of coffee on. I felt like a smug superwoman as I sat in the armchair, awaiting my nemesis, with a triangular maternity pillow stuffed under my aching arm.

'Oh, you clever girl,' Pammie said as she came into the front room. 'Didn't you do well?'

She didn't bother to kiss me, preferring instead to fixate on Poppy. 'What a beauty,' she cooed. 'She looks just like you, Adam.'

'You think?' he said proudly, his voice still gravelly.

He took her from me and laid her in Pammie's arms. Every part of me tingled, urging me to snatch her back

361

again. She walked off around the room, her back to me as she looked out of the window and onto the street below. I paced like a lioness, unable to take my eyes off them. Pammie was whispering and bobbing up and down, but I couldn't see Poppy. I knew she was there, of course she was, I just needed to see her, hold her.

'I'll take her now,' I said, going up to them. 'She needs changing.'

'I've only just got her!' Pammie laughed. 'And what's a dirty nappy between a nan and her granddaughter?' She looked down at Poppy, as if she was expecting her to answer. 'I can't even smell anything anyways, and I'm sure I can manage to change her nappy if she needs it.'

I looked to Adam, pleading with my eyes to get my baby back, but he just turned away from me. 'Anyone fancy a cuppa?' he asked.

'I'll have one, son,' said Pammie. 'Are you feeding her yourself?' she asked me.

'Yes,' I replied.

'If you want to express some milk, I'd be more than happy to do the night feed tonight if you like. To give you a break.'

I shook my head. 'That won't be necessary.'

'Well, maybe I can take her out in the pram for a walk? Give you and Adam some time alone? I remember how hard it was for Jim and me once the boys came along. Everything changes, and you have to work twice as hard to make it work.'

I smiled tightly.

'Oh, I bought Poppy a little something, hope you don't mind.'

'Why would I mind?' I asked wearily.

'Well, some mums get a bit precious, don't they? About what they want the baby to wear and how they want the baby to look.'

I shrugged my shoulders.

'But I had to get this when I saw it, because it made me laugh so much.'

She handed me a carrier bag and watched as I pulled out a tiny white sleepsuit. 'That's lovely,' I forced myself to say. 'Thank you.'

'Wait, you haven't seen it yet,' she said. 'Look what it says on the front.'

I turned it over and held it up. *If Mummy says no, I just ask Grandma* was emblazoned across the chest. I flinched. 'Isn't that the cutest thing?' Pammie laughed.

She may as well have bought a dog tag with *Return to Grandma if found.*

'Look at what your mum bought for Poppy,' I said to Adam, holding it up, facing him. 'Isn't it the cutest thing?' I hoped my sarcasm wasn't lost on her.

Adam smiled at me.

'I'll take her while you have your tea,' I said, going towards Pammie.

She laughed. 'I've had two babies myself, don't

forget, and I still managed to drink a cup of tea. I *can* do two things at once, you know.'

Adam laughed along with her, at me. I held my breath as she lifted the cup of hot liquid up to her lips, silently pleading with her not to spill it.

As soon as Poppy started to cry, I was up out of my chair and looming over Pammie, willing her to hand her back to me. Instead, she stuck her finger into Poppy's mouth. 'Goodness me, Emily, you're like a cat on a hot tin roof. She's fine, look, see?'

'I'd prefer it if you didn't do that,' I said, as calmly as I could, whilst my insides bubbled furiously.

'Just because she cries doesn't mean she's hungry,' she said. 'Sometimes she just wants comforting, and if this soothes her, then that can't be a bad thing, can it?'

'I don't want her relying on a comforter,' I said quietly. 'It's also not very hygienic.'

'Honestly, it's madness these days,' she said. 'You're told to buy expensive sterilizing equipment and all these fancy mod cons, but in our day, it was a Milton tablet and some boiled water if you were lucky. If a dummy fell onto the floor, you just picked it up, stuck it in your own mouth, and gave it straight back to the baby. And look at my two boys now. It's not done them any harm, has it?'

'We're new to this game, Mum,' said Adam, finally sticking up for me. 'It's all trial and error to see what works and what doesn't.'

I looked at him gratefully.

'All I'm saying is, don't get too precious. They're hardy little things and don't want for much. If she cries, leave her for a bit. You'll be making a rod for your own back if you go rushing to feed her every time.'

I looked at my watch. Pammie hadn't even been here for fifteen minutes.

Later, after forced conversation, while eating Adam's chicken pasta, I made my excuses and went to bed, taking Poppy with me. The last thing I heard as I shut the door to my sanctuary was Pammie's voice saying, 'She's not eating enough. She needs all her nutrients for the baby.'

Adam still wasn't in bed when Poppy woke up for her midnight feed, but I thought I could hear the TV on in the lounge. I vaguely remembered him coming in later, but I wasn't sure what time it was. I wasn't even sure what day it was, as they all seemed to merge into one. If Poppy slept, then I slept, and all was still quiet when I woke at 6 a.m. My first thought was, *Yes! She's slept for over five hours*. My second was, *Shit, is she still breathing?*

I leant over into her moses basket and saw her pink blanket and muslin square. I listened in the half-light for her snuffles, but the only sound was the early morning tweets of the birds. I tried to adjust my eyes, rubbing at them when the focus was still blurry. I could see the blanket and muslin, but they looked flat, as if they were lying on the mattress, without a baby in between. I sat bolt upright and thrust my hand into the cot, but it was cold and unmoving.

I ran to the light switch by the door, my legs buckling beneath me as adrenaline took hold.

'What the—?' cried Adam, as the room was illuminated.

I gasped as I reached the empty basket. 'The baby. Where's the baby?'

'What?' said Adam, still confused and dazed.

'She's not here. Poppy's not here.' I was sobbing and screaming in equal measure, as we collided into each other in our effort to get out of the bedroom door. 'Pammie! Poppy!'

'Mum?' shouted Adam as he jumped down to the mezzanine and into the spare room. I could see from where I stood at the top of the landing that the curtains had been pulled back and the bed was made and empty.

I sank to the floor. 'She's taken the baby,' I cried.

Adam rushed past me into the living room and kitchen, but I knew she wasn't there. I could sense it.

'She's taken the baby,' I cried again and again.

Adam came to me and pulled me up to my feet, gripping hold of my arms tightly. 'Pull yourself together,' he snapped.

I wished he would just slap me to put me out of my misery. So that I could wake up when the nightmare was over, with Poppy safely back in my arms.

'The bitch,' I screamed. 'I knew she'd do this. This is what she's been planning all along.'

'For God's sake, get a grip,' said Adam.

'I told you. I told you she was a psycho. You wouldn't believe me, but I was right, wasn't I?'

'You need to calm down and watch what you're saying,' he said. 'I'm warning you.'

He called Pammie's phone, but it just rang off.

'Call the police,' I said hoarsely. 'Call the goddamn police right now.'

'Listen to yourself,' he yelled. 'We're not calling the police. Our daughter has gone out with her grand-mother. It's not a crime.'

I sat on the sofa, sobbing hysterically, my breasts seeping milk through my nightie.

'She's going to do something crazy, I know she is. You don't know what she's capable of. I swear to God, if she's hurt Poppy, I'll kill her.'

Every pent-up emotion rose to the surface: the hate, the hurt, but mostly the fear. The fear that I've carried around with me ever since I found out what she'd done to Rebecca. There was no one in the world who I hated more, and no one in the world who I was more scared of.

'You need to find her, Adam, I swear to God.'

'Who are you threatening?' Adam hissed, his face close to mine. 'I'm not even going to listen to your psy-chotic ramblings until you calm down.'

I watched helplessly as he pulled on jeans and a t-shirt. 'Where are you going?' I said.

'Well, she couldn't have gone far, could she? You'll probably find she's taken her for a walk. Wouldn't that be something, eh?'

'She's done this on purpose,' I yelled after him, as he took the stairs two at a time. 'I hope you're happy. You and your fucked-up family.'

I paced the flat as I waited for Adam to call, the longer he was gone, the more I was convinced that she'd done something. All I kept seeing was Pammie cradling Poppy, telling her it was going to be all right, all the time knowing it wasn't. Adam's mobile went straight to voicemail and I threw the phone against the wall, screaming in frustration.

'Where are you?' I howled, falling to my knees. I curled myself up into a ball and lay on the carpet. I couldn't imagine being in greater pain.

I don't know how much time had passed when my mobile rang and I scrambled to reach it, its screen now smashed into smithereens. 'Is she okay? Have you got her?' I asked. I held my breath as I waited for the reply.

'Of course I've got her,' said Pammie, after a long pause.

I sat up, my heart beating twice as fast as it should have been. I'd expected to hear Adam's voice and the air felt like it was being sucked out of me.

'Bring her back,' I said between gritted teeth. 'Bring her back right now.'

Pammie laughed lightly. 'Or what?'

'Or I'll fucking kill you,' I said. 'You've got three minutes to get back here with my baby or I'm calling the police, and you'd better hope that they get to you before I do.'

'Goodness me,' she cooed. 'I don't understand why you're getting so stressed. Did you not get the text I sent you earlier?'

'What text?' I yelled.

'Hold on,' she said. I heard my phone ping. 'That one.'

I looked at the shattered screcn and could just make out the words: Didn't want to wake you. Poppy awake, so I'm going to take her to Greenwich Park. Leave you to have a lie-in. Love Pammie x

'You've only just sent this,' I hissed.

'No dear, I sent it about an hour ago, before I even left the flat. I didn't want you to get all worked up. Perhaps it didn't go through straight away.'

I stared at the phone blankly. I had no words.

'Anyways, we're on our way back now, so should be with you within ten minutes. Am sure she'll be hungry by then.'

The line went dead, and I hugged my knees, rocking back and forth, wondering if I was going mad.

A little while later, I heard Adam thumping up the

stairs. I had no idea whether ten minutes or ten hours had passed. 'There's no sign of them, but I'm sure there's a valid reason.'

He looked at me on the floor, soaked in milk, tears, and insanity. 'They're coming home,' I said quietly.

I watched his shoulders relax, the tension ebb out of him, proving he wasn't as nonchalant as he seemed. 'Where are they?' he asked breathlessly.

'In Greenwich Park. It appears Pammie was doing us a favour.' I gave a soulless laugh. 'Who knew that your mother could be so considerate? To take our baby from beside our bed and disappear.'

'I think you've said enough,' he barked. 'Go and get yourself cleaned up.'

'Take control,' is what I said to myself repeatedly, as I splashed cold water onto my puffy face. But by the time I was dabbing myself dry, I was already crying again. Who was I kidding? I didn't have the control – she did, as she always did. I buried my face in the towel one more time, willing myself to summon the courage I needed. 'Enough, Emily,' I said out loud. 'No more.'

I heard Poppy's cry before I saw her, and rushed down the stairs towards the sound. Pammie was standing there, without a care in the world, with Poppy on her shoulder. 'I think this missy wants feeding,' she said, a hint of a smile on her lips.

'Get out of my house,' I hissed.

'Excuse me?' she said, before immediately dissolving into loud sobs.

Adam came rushing down the stairs. 'What's going on?'

'Oh darling, I'm so sorry,' she said. 'I never meant to upset anyone. I thought I was being helpful . . .'

She looked up at him, her eyes imploring him to believe her, but I already knew he did.

I snatched Poppy from her and went to go back upstairs. 'That bitch better not be here when I come back out,' I said to Adam.

I stormed into the bedroom, slamming the door behind me, got Poppy latched on, and sobbed until I couldn't sob anymore.

42

Adam and I had barely exchanged a word in the two weeks between Pammie's visit and James and Kate's wedding. I'd wanted to talk to him, to tell him everything, but as I went through the catalogue of events in my head, it occurred to me that she'd ensured that I'd look like the evil, paranoid liar every time. There wasn't one occasion when it wasn't my word against hers, and not only would my claims make me look bitter, they'd make me out to be a psychopath myself. I had Poppy to think about now, I couldn't take that risk.

'I'm not going today,' I said, as he was getting his morning suit on.

'Fine,' he said. 'But I'm taking Poppy.'

My legs wobbled. This was what I was most afraid of.

'You won't want her there,' I said softly. 'She'll only tie you down, you should be enjoying yourself today. It's your brother's wedding.'

He shook his head as he did up the top button of his shirt. 'You can do what you like, but I'm taking her.'

There was no way that Poppy was going without me. I slowly went to the wardrobe and picked out my purple-print dress, still in its dry-cleaning wrapper. I'd worn it once before, earlier in my pregnancy, and its pull-in waist gave me enough room for manoeuvre over my post-baby belly without making me look too fat.

'Will this do?' I asked, holding it up against me, knowing that I needed to make an effort. If I was going to have to endure a day with his family, I at least needed him to be talking to me.

He nodded with a hint of a smile, though I'm not sure whether it was self-satisfaction or relief.

We exchanged superficial small talk in the car on the way there, commenting on ridiculous things such as the weather and the price of property. I stood on the pavement as he lifted Poppy out of her car seat, and he took my hand as we turned and walked towards the church. I allowed myself a little smile at the thought of Pammie seeing our united front, even if I didn't believe it myself.

Sure enough, her face twitched as she saw us walking towards her and James, arms already outstretched to embrace her son. We didn't even bother to acknowledge each other.

'James,' I said tightly. He leant over for an awkward peck on the cheek.

'Hey, big man,' he said to Adam, shaking his hand.

'Nervous?' said Adam.

'Terrified.' James laughed.

'How's Kate doing?' Adam asked.

I didn't hear his answer. I thought of the email sitting in my drafts folder.

Dear Kate,

I'm sorry it's taken me so long to write to you, but I've been trying to think of the right words to say.

We hardly know each other, yet we already share so much. You probably know by now that committing yourself to the Banks clan brings about a problem that you should never underestimate.

Your love for James will be called into question time and time again as you encounter the barriers that are put in front of you. No stone will be left unturned in the attempt to get you out of his life. No act too wicked to belittle you, intimidate you, and make you feel worthless.

It's not too late to see the mistake you're making. I'm only thinking of you. Get out now while you still can.

Emily x

I remembered the phone calls I'd made, only to put the phone down when I heard her voice at the other end. I'd wanted to be there for Kate, to tell her that I understood everything she was going through, to put a stop to the hell she was no doubt already experiencing. But I was too weak. I didn't want her life to be ruined, like mine had. I didn't want her character to be changed beyond all recognition. It was too late for me, and it was too late for Rebecca, but I could save Kate, if I could just find the strength.

The vicar's words were swirling around in my head, as if he was talking underwater. Or maybe I was the one drowning.

'If any person present knows of any lawful impediment to this marriage, he or she should declare it now.'

I steadied myself against Adam as my legs threatened to buckle, leaning into his taut frame, trying to pretend that everything was just fine. He felt my weight and turned to look at me with a concerned raise of the eyebrows, but I smiled weakly back. He doesn't know the thoughts whirring frantically in my brain, desperately trying to find a way out, searching for an outlet for the bitterness and betrayal that engulfs me.

The blood rushed to my head, squeezing its way through the maze of capillaries at a rate that caused my neck and face to feel a sudden burning heat.

I prayed that someone, somewhere, would stand up and state their reason as to why this union shouldn't go ahead. But there was nothing but a loud silence.

There was an awkward cough from one of the hundred-strong congregation, no doubt from someone uncomfortable with the enforced hush, and then a small titter followed, but the sound was muffled by the pounding in my head.

I looked down at the Order of Service in my shaking hands. *Kate & James* was scrawled prettily across the top in silver italics, but the picture of them both underneath swam in front of my eyes, their features hazy.

The seconds ticked by like hours as a deafening stillness resounded around the chapel. This was it. This was my only chance. I could stop this before it was too late. The adrenaline surged through my body as I went to step forward. I looked around, at the man by my side, our baby in his arms, and at the friends and family gathered for this momentous occasion, all looking on, dewy-eyed, with proud smiles.

I followed their gaze to Kate, whose eyes were wide in wonderment at the man standing beside her. The realization that she was starring in her very own fairy tale was apparent in her smile. James, with his deep-blue eyes, looked at his bride in awe, and I felt a tug on my heart.

I've had plenty of time to stop this from happening. From letting it get this far. Kate deserved to know the truth. I owed her that much.

But I wasn't brave enough then, and I'm not brave enough now.

The vicar cleared his throat to continue, and Kate looked around coyly, before giving an exaggerated sigh of relief. The guests chuckled, and James's shoulders visibly relaxed. The moment was gone, and with it my last chance.

The soprano sang a rousing rendition of 'Jerusalem', and, as the sun streamed through the stained-glass windows, I felt a hundred hearts sink at the thought of what else they could be doing on this unusually warm and bright April day. For, despite the fixed grins, there is always an underlying bristle of resentment at weddings.

We all rush to support this outpouring of love and commitment, yet scratch the surface, and you'll find we feel more obliged than genuinely willing. There is always something better we could be doing with ourselves on a sunny Saturday afternoon than spending it sitting next to a dull stranger for a long, drawn-out dinner. Especially given that, in order to do so, we've spent money we don't have, on an outfit we'll wear only once, and on the cheapest present we could find on the very expensive John Lewis gift list.

I could quite literally feel the jealousies and insecurities oozing out of the people around me. No doubt there was someone in the pews who was still friends with the groom's ex-girlfriend, and was battling their own conscience as to whether they should really be here. Then there would surely be the woman who had been dating her partner for way longer than she felt warranted a proposal, yet still there had been nothing. There would be the couple who were both looking longingly at the bride, both wanting her body, but for entirely different reasons, and then there would be the rest of the congregation, who'd be remembering the time when this was *their* day, *their* happy-ever-after, and wondering where it had all gone wrong.

But today there was someone who felt all this far more acutely than anyone else. Who suppressed the searing pain in her chest as the vicar pronounced Kate and James husband and wife, and who smiled sweetly as they kissed.

Adam reached for my hand and gave it a squeeze, as I swallowed the tears that were burning the back of my throat. One year ago, this was supposed to be our day, our happy-ever-after, and I knew exactly why it had all gone wrong.

I watched Pammie, a smile fixed on her face, as she played the perfect mother of the groom in her raspberry-pink satin dress and matching short-sleeved jacket. I wanted to see her pain, to know that watching her younger son get married was killing her, but the mask was rigid.

I wished I could disguise my own feelings, but they were too close to the surface, too raw. I cried as James and Kate walked back down the aisle together, jealous that their union was sealed, and scared for our futures.

If Kate had any concerns, she didn't show them as she embraced Pammie warmly outside the church. 'That was beautiful,' Pammie cried. '*You're* beautiful,' she added, touching Kate's cheek.

Kate smiled and hugged her again. 'Let me introduce you to everyone,' she said, taking Pammie by the hand and heading off in the direction of the biggest group there.

In that instant, I'd gone from seeing Kate as a kindred spirit, the only other person that could relate to me, to someone on the other side, *her* side, and I suddenly felt so desperately alone.

Adam spent the rest of the day smiling at me at all the right times, but whenever he could, he'd be as far away as possible. I clung onto Poppy, my social barrier, and used her to bat off any uncomfortable situations. Adam's aunts and cousins came over to coo at her, and to ask if we'd set a new date for our wedding.

'No, not yet,' I said, on repeat. 'Hopefully soon, but we've got our hands full at the moment.'

'Aye, haven't you just,' replied lovely Linda, Pammie's sister. 'But fingers crossed that by then, we'll know that Pammie's in the clear. We'll really have something to celebrate then.'

'She was given the all clear months ago,' I said, confused.

Linda grimaced, as if berating herself. 'Sorry, I assumed you knew . . .'

'Knew what?'

'That it had come back again. I shouldn't have said anything . . .'

'You've got to be kidding me.' I laughed. So, she'd

tried her luck and pulled off the same stunt to try and stop James and Kate's wedding? I felt a warped sense of satisfaction that it wasn't personal, but then I had to laugh at myself. How could anything she'd done *not* be personal?

I had to take my hat off to Kate, and even more so to James, for not allowing his mother to ruin their special day with her cruel lies. I felt touched, and, if I was honest with myself, a little envious, that James had stood up for Kate and ignored Pammie's wicked attempt to derail their happiness. He'd made a stand against her; he'd done what Adam should have done months ago.

'So, what's she got this time?' I asked Linda.

She looked a little taken aback. 'It's in her lungs.'

'How long have they given her, then?' I couldn't stop myself.

'They haven't,' she said tightly. 'She's having treatment, and we'll have to see where we get to. If you'll excuse me . . .'

'Of course,' I said, as I watched her walk away. Maybe it *was* me. Maybe Pammie wasn't the problem. What if it was me? Or even worse, what if Pammie had made me believe that it was me?

I made my way over to Kate, who was being the consummate professional bride, making sure she got round everyone, thanking them all for their good wishes. I thought how funny it was that, as a guest, you don't want to take up too much of the bride's time, you feel that you're keeping them from something or someone far more important. Yet she must feel constantly rebuffed, as she moves from one person to another, each of them telling her that they don't want to hold her up. I tapped her on the shoulder, and she swung round, a big smile on her face.

'You look stunning,' I said, acutely aware that she'd probably heard it a thousand times already today, and it was beginning to wear thin.

'Thanks,' she said, flashing those perfect white teeth. 'Is this little Poppy? Oh, she's beautiful.'

Now that she was finally in front of me, I didn't know what to say to her. How to articulate everything I needed her to know. Wasn't it too late now, anyway?

'Kate . . . I'm sorry I've not been in touch these past few months. I could have done a better job at welcoming you into the formidable Banks family.'

She laughed. 'Don't be silly, you've had more than enough on your plate and, besides, Pammie's been great. I can't tell you what a help she's been, especially with my own folks being over in Ireland.'

I wasn't aware that I was pulling a strange face but I must have been, as she said, 'What? What's up?'

'Sorry, are we talking about the same woman?' I laughed.

'Um, yeah, I think so,' she said, confused.

'Pammie's been great, has she?' I asked. I could feel that I'd put her on guard.

'Yeah, she has. I don't know what I would have done without her, to be honest.'

Was this a joke? I'd imagined us arranging to meet up once she came back from honeymoon, to discuss what we were going to do about Pammie, how we were going to deal with her, together, as a team, but Kate was making it sound as if Pammie might as well be going with them.

'What, she's helped you, without incident?' I asked. I couldn't quite get my head around this.

'Incident?' she said. 'I'm not sure I understand what you mean.'

'Pammie's helped you, genuinely helped you? Like, without judgement or comment? Without making you feel as if you were going mad?'

'Oh, I know what you're talking about!' She laughed, as if she'd finally got it.

I felt myself breathe out. Thank God.

'I honestly thought I was losing it,' she said. 'When I went to pick up my dress . . .'

I nodded encouragingly, spurring her on. 'Yes?'

'I offered my credit card, but the shop said it had already been paid for. I was like, "Er, no, I definitely need to pay", but they wouldn't have it. I felt like some kind of scammer when I left there with a £1,500 dress over my arm. I couldn't work it out, but then when I called Pammie that afternoon, she told me it was a present from her. I honestly couldn't believe it.'

Nor could I. I stood there open-mouthed as she went on.

'We try and meet up every other Saturday morning, just for a coffee and a bit of brekkie. Why don't you come along, if you have time? We know how busy you are.'

We? I couldn't ever imagine using the word 'we' in a sentence about Pammie.

'Does she ever say anything? About me, I mean?'

Kate looked perplexed. 'In what way?'

'Just anything. Do you talk about me? What does she say?'

'Only that you're doing so well with the baby. She loves Poppy.'

I nodded. 'Great, well, give me a call once you're back, and we can put something in the diary.'

'Cool,' she said, before picking up the bottom of her train and gliding off.

I looked around for Adam. It was getting late and I needed to get Poppy to bed. We'd booked a room in the hotel, just across the courtyard, but we'd barely managed to live together in the flat for the past fortnight, so I didn't imagine that sharing a room was going to be much fun.

'You looking for Adam?' asked James, coming over to me.

'Yes,' I said bluntly.

'The last time I saw him, he was heading outside,' he said. 'Probably to have a cigarette.'

I stopped in my tracks and looked at him as if he was stupid. 'Funny, I didn't know he smoked.'

'There's a lot you don't know about him,' he said, under his breath.

Ignoring him, I walked to the patio doors, towards the garden, but could feel him still behind me. It was dark outside and I pulled Poppy's blanket tighter around her. The days were warm for April, but the evenings were still chilly.

There was a gaggle of revellers smoking to the left, the grounds beyond them gently lit, but Adam wasn't there. I turned to go right, past the gargoyles at the top of the steps, and headed towards the darkness, when James pulled at my arm. 'Why don't you come back in? It's cold out here.'

I shrugged him off and blindly carried on walking. I needed to create as much space between me and him as I could. I saw the entrance to the hedged maze which earlier had seen visitors pay a small fortune to enter. I didn't know where I was going much beyond that. I could feel tears welling up, and I hugged Poppy closer in the vain hope that she'd hide them.

'Will you just wait a minute?' he called after me.

I turned to face him. 'Please, James—'

I think he heard the laughter coming from within the box-hedge walls of the maze before me.

'Look, Em, why don't we go back inside,' he said quietly. 'It's too cold out here for Poppy.'

I looked at her sleeping soundly in my arms and knew he was probably right, but I couldn't tear myself away from the sound.

'Ssh!' squealed a female voice. 'I've lost a shoe.'

There was more laughing.

'Got it, got it,' she said drunkenly.

'Make sure you look decent,' said a man's voice. 'Can't have you going back out there with your knickers round your ankles.'

Everything seemed to go in slow motion. I felt myself falling and instinctively curled myself over Poppy to protect her. I could see flashes of colour and light as I sank further into what felt like a turning kaleidoscope. I squeezed my eyes tightly shut and imagined a cover over my ears, stopping me from hearing what I knew I'd just heard. I willed my brain to scramble the words so I was unable to decipher them, change the voice to one I didn't know. I was still falling, bracing myself for the bottom, but it never came. I opened my eyes and saw James peering down at me, his arms enveloping me and Poppy.

'Let's get you back inside,' he said.

'No,' I said breathlessly. 'I want to wait here. See his face.'

'Please, Em,' he went on. 'You don't need to do this. Please come back inside.'

'Don't you dare tell me what I do and don't need,' I

cried. He went to put his arm around me, but I shrugged it off.

It may have been the darkness or his drunken state, but it took a while for Adam to register that it was me when he emerged from the maze. I felt numb as I watched his brain work it out.

'Em?' he slurred. He turned to look at his dishevelled companion, her hair on end, and her bra straps hanging halfway down her arms. I recognized her as one of the congregation from earlier in the day. But then her mink satin dress and fancy up-do had looked classy. Now, the material was ruched up around her hips, and her lipstick was smeared all over her face.

'What are you doing out here? Poppy will catch her death of cold.'

If I hadn't been holding her in my arms, I would have swung for him. 'How sweet,' I said, icily. 'So considerate.'

'Hi,' said the woman beside him, lurching forward with an outward hand. 'I'm—'

'Knock it off,' spat Adam at her.

'No, it's okay,' I said. 'Why don't you introduce me to your friend?'

'Leave it, Em,' said Adam.

'Introduce me to your fucking friend,' I hissed.

'Er . . . this is . . . this is . . .'

'Oh, don't tell me . . .' she slurred. 'This is your wife and kid.' She laughed to herself. 'Wouldn't that be something, eh?'

I remained silent.

'Oh, Christ, really?' she said, the obvious suddenly dawning on her.

'I'm afraid so,' I said tightly.

'Sorry,' she managed before stumbling away. I watched numbly as she headed back to the hotel, zig-zagging across the lawn.

'Do all your women need to be in that state?' I asked coldly.

'Em, let's get you back inside,' said James, holding onto my elbow and trying to steer me away. I held firm.

'Believe it or not, some sober women do actually want to fuck me as well. Unlike my fiancée.' He put the last word in inverted commas with his fingers.

'Okay, that's enough, Adam,' interjected James. 'Emily, let's go.'

I shrugged him off. 'So, there's more than one?'

Adam laughed. 'What did you think was going to happen? You haven't let me near you for months. What do you think I am, a monk?'

'Go fuck yourself,' I cried.

'Gladly,' he called out, as I turned my back to him.

'I'm so sorry you had to see that,' said James.

'Would you mind calling me a cab, please?' I said numbly. 'I'd like to take Poppy home.'

43

Pippa was my rock for the next five days, whilst I processed what Adam had done and what it meant. I used to scorn women who'd found out their partners were cheating and said things like, 'I just didn't see it coming. It was so out of character.'

I'd pitied them for not seeing what was clearly in front of their eyes. Yet here I am, thinking the very same thing. I couldn't even begin to compute it. We'd had a tough time recently, what with Pammie and the baby, but I didn't think we'd reached the stage where he'd happily risk throwing everything away.

'What are you going to do?' Pippa asked for the umpteenth time. 'What do you *want* to do?'

'What I *want* to do and what I *should* do are two entirely different things,' I said.

She knew what I meant. We'd had enough 'what would you do if your boyfriend strayed?' conversations to last us a lifetime. Except, when you thought he wouldn't, it was a whole lot easier to take the moral high ground, and declare that if he ever did, that would be it; you'd be out of there. Yet now, in the mire of it all, having loved that person and believing I was going to spend the rest of my life with him, suddenly things aren't quite so clear-cut.

'It wasn't what he did, it was how he did it,' I said.

'Does it make a difference?' Pippa asked. 'A cheat's a cheat.'

'It was the way he spoke to me, the way he alluded to there being more. Lots more. Why would he feel the need to hurt me like that?'

'Er, because he's a first-class tosser?'

'How could this have happened to me again?' I cried. 'What a fool I've been.'

Pippa put a reassuring hand on my back. 'It's not you who's the fool,' she said. 'If he can't see what he stands to lose . . .'

'So where do I go from here?' I asked.

'Do you love him?'

'Of course I do, but I'm not prepared to take this lying down. If he's coming back, it's going to be on my terms.'

'You can't take him back,' she cried. 'You just can't.'

'But I've got Poppy to think about,' I said. 'It's not just me I need to think about anymore. She needs a dad.'

'Em, I think if we're being honest with ourselves, he's probably been doing this for a long time,' she said.

I nodded knowingly. I knew she was right, but I didn't want to believe it. I thought about all his 'Thursday nights out' with the boys in the City.

'It's a given,' he'd said, not long after we met. 'Thursday nights are the holy grail. They can't be moved for life, love or death.'

I'd laughed and thought little of it. I knew that was how the City worked, but had he been sleeping with other women all that time? Was there someone special that he went to on a Thursday, the pair of them happily ensconced, knowing that they had one night a week to be together? He'd often not come in until three o'clock in the morning, but at worst, I'd imagined him spending his heavenly money in a lap-dancing club, not in the arms of someone he cared about. But if that was the case, why hadn't he just left me? He could have easily walked away before the wedding, before Poppy.

'What? And not have his cake and eat it?' Pippa exclaimed, as she patiently listened to me ponder the question. 'I'm not saying he doesn't love you, of course he does – why else would he have asked you to marry him? And have Poppy?'

'Yes, but Poppy wasn't exactly a life choice, for either of us,' I said, feeling instantly guilty as the words tumbled out.

'Sure,' she acknowledged. 'But you knew the chances you were taking, and you did have choices – whether or not you took them was up to you.'

I peered over into the moses basket where Poppy slept soundly, her little arms laid casually above her head. I couldn't imagine ever making the choice not to have her.

'But what we're forgetting in all of this,' I said, 'is that we're assuming he wants to come back. What I want might not even come into it.'

'Oh, believe me, after a few days back out there, he'll see that the grass isn't just "not greener", but it's covered in moss, weeds, and bald patches too!'

I had to laugh. I was bored of crying. When I thought about it, I'd spent the best part of a year being miserable and sobbing over something or another: the wedding being cancelled, Pammie's abhorrent behaviour, feeling hormonal with Poppy. 'Thanks Pip,' I said, hugging her to me as she left.

'Love you,' she whispered in my ear. 'Don't let him walk all over you.'

Adam turned up on the doorstep later that night. I could have sworn, slapped him, and slammed the door in his face, but instead, I just stepped aside and let him in. What was the point in all the dramatics? We were parents now, supposedly responsible adults, so it was time to start acting like it.

'You look like shit,' I mused. His eyes were sunken into grey-coloured skin, a five o'clock shadow peppered his chin and cheeks.

I sat down opposite him at the dining table. 'Can I see Poppy?' he asked.

'No, she's sleeping. What do you want?'

'I want to come home.'

I sat back in the chair and folded my arms. 'What, that's it? You're honestly expecting to turn up here and tell me you want to come back?'

He nodded.

'So, are we just going to skirt over the tiny issue of you sleeping with someone else?' I asked. I was aware my voice was rising, and I made an effort to lower it. I didn't want to wake Poppy.

'It wasn't what it looked like,' he said.

I laughed. 'Tell me what it looked like, then.'

'We were just fooling around,' he said earnestly. 'We had a kiss, that's all.'

'That's all?' I exploded.

'I know, I know it doesn't make it right, but that's all that happened. I promise you.'

He must think I'm stupid. 'And you think that's okay, do you? You think it's acceptable to be touching up another woman at your brother's wedding, within three feet of your fiancée and child? You think that's *acceptable*?'

I could hear myself getting louder and louder with every syllable, like a stereo system reverberating in my head, yet there was a faint sound coming from the rear speakers, a word of warning. *People in glass houses shouldn't throw stones.*

'How many others have there been?' I asked. He dropped his head, and stared at the floor.

'Well?' I asked, when he didn't answer.

He looked at me. 'She's the only one. I swear to you. I don't know what I was thinking. It's been so difficult . . .'

I held my hand up to stop him.

'No, listen,' he said indignantly. 'It's been so difficult for me. I don't know what's been going on with us. Things haven't been right, have they? You know they haven't.'

I glared at him, daring him to say the next sentence.

'You've not been yourself for quite a while, and it's made me feel really low. You've been pregnant and had a difficult time having Poppy, and then the whole thing with my mum. I don't know where I am from one day to the next. I don't seem to figure in your list of priorities anymore.'

I allowed myself a wry smile. 'Poor you,' I said snidely. 'Poor Adam for having a pregnant girlfriend, who then has to nurse and look after a new baby, and deal with your psychotic mother.'

'Don't start, Emily,' he warned.

'Yet despite all that, it's not about me, is it?' I went on, ignoring him. 'You've somehow made it about you. How *you're* hard done by. How *you're* missing out.'

He looked down at his feet.

'So, what do you do about it? You go out and screw whoever you can, to make you feel like a man again, to validate yourself as a red-blooded male. Because that's what it's all about, isn't it? Proving to yourself that you've still got it.'

'I felt rejected, like you didn't find me attractive anymore.'

I laughed. 'Isn't that supposed to be my line? Yet instead of giving me time, or talking about it, you decided the way to solve it was to sleep with somebody else.'

'You don't know how you made me feel.'

'For Christ's sake, Adam, listen to yourself. What about me? What about my needs? Imagine how I feel, how difficult it is for me. Everything's changed in my world: my body, my daily life, my priorities . . . everything. What's changed for you? A little less sex, and a cute baby to come home to, play with for an hour, and then go to bed.'

He went to speak, but I cut him off.

'But do you see me trawling the streets at night, desperate for a shag? Am I sloping off at a wedding to have a seedy encounter with a man whose name I don't even know?'

'It won't happen again,' he offered, as if I was supposed to be grateful for the sentiment. 'I was drunk, I was lonely, and it was a mistake.'

'Is that it?' I asked. 'Are you honestly expecting to just move back in, and then everything will be rosy again?'

'I never meant to hurt you . . . I promise I'll never hurt you again.'

His words echoed in my head, but it was as if some-one else was saying them. I closed my eyes as a memory of James flashed before me: of him standing in front of me, saying the very same thing. 'I promise I'll never hurt you,' he'd said. I felt sick at the sudden realization that his words were never about him making the promise *not* to hurt me. It was him warning me that Adam *would*.

'What would you do if you were me right now?' I asked Adam. 'If you found out that I'd been with some-one else?'

His face contorted, and a muscle spasm twitched along his jawline. 'I'd kill him,' he said.

44

Adam moved back in two weeks after James and Kate's wedding. His pleas for me to take him back grew louder the closer it got to them returning from honeymoon, when no doubt he'd be kicked out of their flat.

'You can always go and stay with your mum,' I mused.

'Are you joking? She's bloody mad,' he said.

We were getting somewhere. We were finally getting there.

Pammie was at the top of my list when it came to setting down a few ground rules when he came home. She could see Poppy whenever he chose to take her down there, but she was never to be left alone with her, unsupervised.

'But what about when—?' he went to say.

'Under *no* circumstances,' I said authoritatively.

He nodded solemnly.

There were to be no more Thursday nights out with the lads, and he could play rugby at the weekend, but after a quick drink, I expected him back home, not to still be getting drunk four hours later.

He stayed in the spare room for a few nights, but if

we were going to make it work, there was nothing to be gained from sleeping in separate beds. I didn't feel ready to be close to him, emotionally or physically, but I felt like I was sitting on a ticking time bomb, wondering how many hours and minutes would pass before he felt he was justified in getting it somewhere else. I hated that he made me feel that way.

'What do you want to do about the wedding?' he asked one night, as we were having dinner. He'd just returned from Pammie's. He and James were alternating taking her for her 'second round of chemo'. I was surprised that she was still keeping up the charade, since Kate and James were married now. She'd failed in her attempt to stop them, so I wondered what the point was in her continuing to lie.

'I don't feel it's something we should do anytime soon,' I said. 'But I would like to get Poppy christened though.'

He nodded in agreement. 'How do you want to go about that?'

'I was thinking just a simple ceremony in church, and then have some food and drink somewhere.'

'I'd like to do that sooner rather than later,' he said. 'I want Mum there.'

I ignored the comment. 'Well, I'll look at it when I get time,' I said.

'I don't think time is on our side,' he said, his voice breaking. 'I don't know how much longer she's got.'

'Oh, I'm sure she's going to be fine,' I said matter-of-factly.

He shook his head. 'It's really taking its toll this time round. They think it's spreading. I don't know if she's strong enough to get through this—' He choked on the last sentence.

I half-heartedly reached over and put my hand on his. I couldn't offer him sympathy I didn't have.

I looked at Poppy in her bouncer at my feet, her trusting eyes smiling up at me, and wondered how a mother could possibly put their child through this hell. How cruel would you have to be?

'What will I do?' Adam began to sob. 'What will I do when she's gone?' His shoulders shook, and I begrudgingly got up and went to him. 'She doesn't deserve this. She's been through enough.'

I kissed his head as I rocked him back and forth in my arms. 'She's a tough cookie,' was all I could offer.

'She makes out she is, but she's not. Not really,' he said. 'She's had to toughen up, because of what he did to her, but inside she's just as frightened as she's always been.'

I held him away from me so I could see his face.

'What *who* did to her?' I asked.

He shook his head, and went to lean into me again, but I held him firm. 'What are you talking about?'

He wiped his nose with the back of a shaky hand.

'Will you please tell me what you're going on about?' I said impatiently.

'Jim,' he sneered. 'Or Dad, if we're going to pretend he ever was one.'

'What's your dad got to do with anything?'

'He was a bastard,' he spat.

'What? Why?' My mouth was moving faster than my brain.

'He destroyed her. He beat everything out of her.'

I felt like I'd been slapped round the face. I dropped onto the sofa.

'What are you talking about? She loved him. He loved her. What are you saying?'

His head fell into his hands again.

'What did he do?' I pressed.

'He would come home and beat the shit out of her, that's what he'd do. Night after night, it was like watching a beautiful flower die a little bit more every time.'

'She told you this?' I asked, flabbergasted.

'She didn't need to,' he said. 'I saw it with my own eyes. We both did, James and I. He'd go to the pub after work, and she'd have his dinner ready on the table for when he came home. But almost every night, he'd tell her she'd done it wrong, throw it against the wall and slap her.'

I sat unmoving. 'I'd see his hand moving through the air, as if in slow motion, before it hit her. She'd make this small yelping sound, but held anything more in, so as not to wake us, but we'd be sitting at the top of the stairs, watching everything through the banisters, praying for it to stop.'

'Are you sure? I mean, are you sure you saw what you think you saw? You were young. Maybe it wasn't what it looked like.' I was scrabbling around for reason, when all around me was insanity.

'I saw things no one should ever have to see, let alone children as young as us. We were too little to understand why our dad was hitting our mum and making her cry, but we knew it was wrong. We'd hatch secret plans for the three of us to run away to the seaside, back to Whitstable, where we'd been on holiday the summer before Dad died. He hadn't come with us, we'd gone with Auntie Linda, Fraser and Ewan. Mum had seemed so happy there, away from him.'

'How did he die?' I asked gently.

Adam looked to the floor, as if lost in thought. 'He had a heart attack late one night after he'd come home from the pub. He just collapsed in the kitchen and that was it. Mum let me and James have the next day off school, and put us in shirts and ties, whilst the house buzzed with police and funeral directors.' He smiled ruefully. 'I remember how scratchy those shirts were, the collar irritating my neck. I remember worrying more about that than my dad being dead, and I thought there must be something wrong with me. I didn't feel anything. I was just numb.'

'Did he ever hit you?' I asked.

'No, he never touched James or me. He played the perfect dad and husband whenever we were around, but I knew. I knew what he'd do later. Mum knew too, she had a fear in her eyes, but she tried so hard not to let it show.'

'Did you ever tell her what you'd seen?'

He shook his head. 'It would break her to know that I knew. She's gone to such great lengths to pretend that he was the best husband and the best dad. Even back then, all their friends thought he was the catch and she was the lucky one. But none of them really knew him. They didn't know what he was like behind closed doors. How could they? She protected him then, and she still protects him now.'

I thought back to all the photos I'd seen of a couple so in love. Their friends seemingly jealous of what they had.

'I'm so sorry,' I said, going to him and cradling his head to my chest. 'No child should ever have to see that.'

None of this made any sense. How could this be? I willed myself to find a way to exonerate Pammie from everything she'd done. Surely, there must be a reason in all this, an explanation as to why she was like she was, but as much as I tried, I couldn't find it. The more I rolled it all over in my head, the more difficult it was to understand her actions. If she'd been treated so badly in the past, why would she set out to intentionally inflict harm on someone else?

45

By the time the christening came around, I'd worked myself up into a frenzy about seeing Pammie, James, and for some reason or other, Kate. In my mind's eye, she'd gone from being an ally, the only person that could possibly relate to me, to Pammie's partner in crime. It gave Pammie more power to goad me with, and I found the prospect of seeing them together intimidating.

I'd bought a new dress for the occasion, something to give me confidence, I'd reasoned to myself, to ease the guilt when handing my credit card over.

'Blimey, that's a bit bright, isn't it?' commented Adam. 'I'll need sunglasses.'

'Too much?' I asked, looking down at the canary-yellow chiffon. I felt good in it. The asymmetrical cut gave me my pre-baby shape back – no one needed to know I was bound up with Spanx underneath.

'No, I like it,' said Adam. 'I'm just glad the daffodil season is over, as otherwise we'd have the devil's own job to find you.'

He laughed as I hit him with my clutch bag.

Poppy was looking on from the middle of our bed, happily gurgling away as her parents bickered.

'Good job I put a bib on you, missy,' I said, scooping her up in a ball of ivory taffeta. 'We can't have you dribbling down your dress, can we?'

'Are you sure she wouldn't be more comfortable in a Gap all-in-one?' Adam asked, as he struggled to get her and her oversized gown into the car seat.

I tutted and pushed his fumbling hand out of the way. 'There it is,' I laughed as I burrowed deep into the fabric to retrieve a strap. 'Now, where's the other one?'

'We should have got her a Cinderella carriage,' he joked. 'She'd look right at home in that.'

I didn't want to jinx it, but it finally felt like we were getting our old rapport back, on the way to becoming the couple we had once been. I couldn't wait to get to the church to show the doubters that we'd made it. Show them that, despite everything they'd tried to throw at us, we'd still survived. I don't know why I think of it as *them* when in reality it's only *her*, but sometimes it just feels like the whole world's against me, and I struggle to keep things in perspective. But not today, because I've got what she wants. I've won.

We greeted our guests as they filed through the church gate, me happily batting away Adam's rugby mates' jibes about my resemblance to a bumble bee. I saw James and Kate get out of their car, just up the lane, and busied myself with over-exaggerated hellos. I fussed over my cousin Fran's young boy, and bent down, with Poppy in my arms, to introduce her to another baby in a buggy. Anything to take my mind off the impending arrival of the Banks clan. Without even realizing, I'd turned my back, but I could hear people behind me saying hello and asking Pammie how she was feeling.

I coughed to clear the lump in my throat and started counting down from ten in my head, to give me time to put my face on before I turned around. *Just pretend everything's normal*, I said to myself. *You can do this.*

'Good to see you, Pamela,' I said, spinning round, already on full offensive. 'You look—'

I sucked the word 'well' back in. What I was greeted with stopped me in my tracks, rendering me speechless. Pammie was completely bald, her eyebrows were missing, and her face was bloated. I was paralysed with shock. I needed to say something, anything, as the three of them stood there waiting, but I just couldn't put the words together.

'Hi, Em,' said James, leaning in to kiss me. 'It's been a while. You okay?' It wasn't a question that warranted answering.

'Em,' Kate cried. 'You look gorgeous, and Poppy – wow!'

I stuttered a response. Pammie and I stood there for a split second, sizing each other up, neither of us sure how to react. We somehow met in the middle, our limbs colliding awkwardly. She pulled me towards her and held me. 'It's lovely to see you,' she whispered hoarsely. 'You look beautiful.'

My breath caught in my throat and tears welled up in my eyes. I don't know what it was. I was just struck by her words, not what she said, but the way she said it. For the first time, I could almost hear a sincerity in her voice, as if she really meant it. But perhaps I was allowing her appearance to play with my mind. I fixed a smile on and searched desperately for Adam. I needed him with me.

'If you'll excuse me,' I said, extricating myself and Poppy. I headed in Adam's direction, but Mum caught my hand as I passed by.

'Is that Pammie?' she asked, confused.

I nodded numbly.

'But how . . .'

I shook my head. 'I really don't know,' was the best I could offer. 'Can you just take Poppy for a minute?'

'Of course,' she said, her concerned face instantly breaking into a wide grin as her granddaughter gurgled happily at her.

I caught Pippa's eye as I reached Adam. She looked as shocked as I felt. I could do nothing but shrug my shoulders at her.

I willed my brain to focus, but the wires literally felt like they were crossing over and sparking off as they made the wrong connections. I needed to see Pammie again, just to make sure, but I daren't turn around, as I was sure I could feel three pairs of eyes on my back. Would she really have gone that far to convince people she was telling the truth? I pictured her face, with its puffy cheeks and sunken eyes. Was that even possible?

I needed to think of the right words before I reached Adam, knowing that the wrong ones would set us back for months. 'You didn't tell me your mum was . . .' I didn't know how to finish the sentence.

'Ill?' he said.

I nodded.

'You didn't ask,' he said tightly. 'Because you didn't care.'

I thought back to the times he'd tried to talk to me, and every time I'd shut him down. I felt a wave of nauseous guilt wash over me.

Every time I looked over at Pammie, she was watching me. Every time I sensed her coming towards me, I invented a reason to move. I don't know if I was more frightened to talk to her in case she told me she was really ill, or because of the very real possibility that she'd gone to such lengths to keep up the pretence. I didn't know how to respond in either case.

James caught me just as I was heading towards the ladies'.

'That was a lovely service, Em. I've not had a chance to thank you for asking Kate and I to be Poppy's god-parents.'

'It wasn't my choice,' I replied without stopping.

'How are things?' he asked.

I turned to look at him, searching his eyes for recognition of what he'd done to me and why. But they were the same as they'd always been. Warm and kind.

'Fine,' I said tartly.

'Are you okay?' he asked. 'After the wedding and everything?'

'We're working on it,' I said abruptly.

'What have I done to upset you?'

'Your mother told me everything,' I said. 'I thought you were on my side. I naively believed that what we had was—'

'It was,' he said, cutting across me.

I gave a hollow laugh.

'I *am* on your side . . .' he said. 'And I'll always be, but you made your feelings quite clear, remember?'

I narrowed my eyes at him. 'So, whilst I'm confiding in you, you're running straight back to Pammie and telling her everything?'

'What? No,' he said sharply. 'I never repeated anything that you said, apart from when you told me that nothing could come of us.'

'So, she didn't tell you to come on to me? You weren't doing it under orders?'

'What?' he said, screwing his face up, as if he was unable to comprehend what I was saying. 'No. What do you take me for? I'd never do that. I told her I had feelings for you, and how guilty I felt about it . . . I confided in her because she's my mother.'

I rolled my eyes and shook my head.

'You have to believe me,' he said.

'Hey, little brother,' called out Adam as he sidled up to him. 'What's she got to believe?'

James's face coloured. 'Nothing. It was nothing.'

'No, come on, I'm all ears,' went on Adam, his speech a little slurred. 'Why is my lovely lady here calling you a liar?'

'We were just joking around,' offered James unconvincingly.

'Nah, I'm not having that, fella,' said Adam. Both James and I knew him well enough to know that he was getting bolshie, fuelled by alcohol and paranoia.

I put my hands on his chest and looked up at him, trying to engage him.

'We're just having a joke,' I said. 'James is trying to wind me up. And he's doing a good job of it too.' I gave him a playful slap on the arm.

I tried to guide Adam away, but he wouldn't let it drop. 'So, what didn't you believe?' he asked again.

I gave a big sigh. 'For God's sake, we were just fooling around. It was nothing.'

'It didn't look like nothing,' he said petulantly.

I stopped him in his tracks and put my arms around his waist as he turned to face me. 'I love you,' I said, reaching up and kissing him on the lips. 'Now go be with your mates. Enjoy yourself, and I'll see you later.'

He kissed me back. 'I love you too.'

As I walked back in, Pammie was at the doorway,

practically ready to pounce. 'Emily?' she said, almost in surprise, even though she'd clearly been standing there waiting for me. I ignored her, but when she called out a second time, loud enough for others to hear, I had to acknowledge her for fear of causing a scene.

She stood in front of me, as if waiting, and I honestly didn't know what to say. There was so much rage bubbling up within me, but as I looked at her, really looked at her, the anger gave way to confusion. The whites of her eyes were yellowed and her swollen skin, smooth and shiny, was pulled tight over her cheekbones. There was nothing I wouldn't put past her, but this?

'Pamela,' was all I could muster.

'Please don't call me that,' she said quietly. 'You know I don't much care for it.'

'Look, if you're going to start, I'm really not—'

'I'm not. There's just something I need to say to you.'

'Whatever it is, I'm not remotely interested. There is nothing that you can say or do that will surprise me anymore. You are here because you have to be, as Adam's mother, but don't for a second think that there's anything more to it than that. You can see Poppy whenever Adam sees fit to bring her down, but honestly, that's where you and I end.'

She ran a hand over her hairless scalp and offered a small smile. 'I'm sorry,' she said. 'Truly sorry.'

I don't know what I was expecting her to say, but 'sorry' wasn't on the list, especially given that there was no one else in earshot. She looked down, as if ashamed, but I'd seen that a thousand times before. She'd used it whenever she was backed into a corner and was on the verge of being found out. I'd been hoodwinked into falling for the Little Miss Naive act myself, but that was a long time ago. She was never going to fool me again.

'I really don't have time for this,' I said. 'This is my daughter's christening and I have a room full of people, more deserving than you, whom I'd like to talk to and be with. I'm not going to stand here and waste my time on you.'

I tried not to look at her as I said it because her appearance was throwing me off track, making me feel guilty.

'I understand that,' she said. 'And I don't blame you, but I just want you to know that I'm truly sorry. I never meant to do what I did to you, and I know that you'll never forgive me, but I haven't got much longer, and I wanted to at least try and make amends before it's too late. Please.'

She reached a hand out to me, and I backed away, but she kept coming forward, falling towards me.

There was a split-second hush all around us, and then a sudden rush to catch her before she fell to the floor. If anyone had caught it on a slow-motion camera, they would have seen me, walking backwards, with my arms up in the air. I was the only one who could possibly have cushioned the blow, yet whilst everyone was moving forward in vain, I was moving away.

There was a collective gasp as she hit the unforgiving wooden floor.

'Mum!' called out James. 'Pammie!' cried everyone else.

'What the . . .' shouted Adam, as he ran forwards and fell to his knees. 'What the hell happened?' He turned to look at me for an answer, but I just shrugged. 'Why would I think to ask you?'

I could hear a sharp intake of breath from the crowd that had now gathered.

'That's enough,' said James. 'Mum . . .'

'I'm okay,' she managed, as she was helped up to a sitting position. 'I just lost my footing. I'm okay.'

She'd done it again.

I weaved away through the throng, trying to find Poppy, who I'd last seen with Mum. 'I want to go,' I said as I reached her.

'What on earth's going on?' she asked. 'She couldn't fake this, surely?'

I shook my head. I didn't know what to think anymore.

'Can you and Dad take me home?' I asked.

Dad looked at his watch. 'It's getting late anyway,' he said, as if he needed an excuse. 'I'll bring the car round.'

I gathered up the presents that had been brought for Poppy, and said discreet goodbyes to Pippa and my

Auntie Bet. They were the only people still there whom I cared about; the rest consisted of Adam's rugby crowd and a few of his work colleagues. None of whom would even be aware that I'd been there, let alone gone.

'You okay?' said Pippa, as I hurriedly rounded things up. 'Do you want me to come with you?'

I shook my head. 'I just want to go home and put my pyjamas on,' I said honestly.

She smiled. 'I know the feeling. I'll give you a call in the morning.'

I gave her a kiss and ducked out the door.

Mum insisted on coming into the flat with me, to get me settled. 'I'm twenty-seven,' I half laughed.

'You're never too old for your mum to care about you,' she said. 'You sure you're going to be okay?'

I nodded. 'I can't see Adam being much longer. The bar will be shut in an hour or so.'

'Whatever's going on, please don't let it get to you,' she said, kissing me on the forehead. 'You're doing a great job, and we're very proud of you.' I had tears in my eyes as I gave her a hug and begrudgingly waved them off.

46

I must have fallen asleep on the sofa, as the next thing I remember was the banging on the front door. For a moment, I was totally disorientated and thought I was still dreaming. I could hear the distant ping of a text on my phone, but I had no concept of time or even what day it was. I didn't know what I should respond to first, but then I remembered Poppy. Was it time to get her up? Had I even fed her before putting her down?

I stood up too quickly and instantly fell back down again, light-headed and dizzy. I put both hands against the sides of my head, willing it to put the jigsaw pieces together quicker than it seemed to be doing. The banging from downstairs was still going, the text messages still demanding to be read. I peered into Poppy's room and saw that she was sleeping soundly. Tick. It was just after midnight. Tick. Adam wasn't home yet. Tick . . . where the hell was he? I'd left him three hours ago. I fumbled for my phone under the cushions of the settee and struggled to focus on the missives that filled the screen. I scrolled down the missed calls, voicemails, and texts. Pammie, Adam, James, Pammie, Adam, James.

'Jesus,' I said aloud, wondering what the hell had happened.

Confused, with phone in hand, I headed for the door. I'd just reached the bottom step when it rang again, displaying Pammie's name across the screen. I was going to ignore it, but then I thought it might be somebody else using her phone. There was obviously something amiss. I just prayed nothing had happened to Adam.

'Yes,' I snapped.

'Emily. It's me, Pammie. Adam's on his way to you. Don't let him in.'

'What?' I gasped.

'Don't let him in. He's really mad. He knows, Emily. I'm so sorry. Don't let him in.'

'What the hell are you talking about?'

'He knows about James,' she choked.

The blood rushed to my ears as she kept talking, and I couldn't hear anything she said.

'What?' I cried, my breath catching in my throat.

'They've had a fight,' she said breathlessly. 'I'm so sorry.'

My head was too full of panic to think straight.

I moved closer towards the door, my hands shaking as they grappled with the latch, unable to get a grip. I jumped back as a fist struck the other side, the low-grade wood barely withstanding the pounding.

'Adam?' I called out shakily.

'Open the door,' he yelled, so close now I could hear his breath.

'No,' I answered. 'Not until you calm down.'

'I swear to God, Emily, open this fucking door right now.'

'Don't let him in,' warned Pammie again.

'What *have* you done?' I hissed down the phone, before throwing it onto the floor. I wouldn't allow her lies to consume me. Us. I *had* to talk some sense into Adam.

'You're scaring me,' I called through to him. 'You'll scare the baby.'

I heard him inhale and exhale slowly, deliberately.

'Emily,' he said, his tone suddenly measured. 'Will you please open the door?'

I put the chain across. 'Do you promise you'll stay calm?'

'Yes, I promise.'

As soon as I twisted the latch, the door took flight, the sheer force snapping the chain off its hinge. I fell to the floor as it swung towards me, my arms flailing helplessly against the power of Adam on the other side. He was looming over me and I knew then the terrible mistake I had made. I willed myself to get up, but my legs wouldn't work. I stumbled, half crawling up the stairs, scrambling for the top, yet knowing that by doing so, I was blocking off any means of getting out. But I had to be what stood between Adam and Poppy. I couldn't let him anywhere near her.

I made a grab for the top step, still on all fours, when he yanked my ankle, pulling me back down. My scalp felt like it was lifting off my skull as he picked me up by my hair. I had one arm up in the air, trying to unfurl his fist that was twisted deep into my hair, and the other reaching down to get some leverage on the stairs. My hip took the brunt, as it slammed against each unforgiving step as Adam dragged me up. I wanted to cry out, but I needed to stay quiet for Poppy. I didn't know what Adam was capable of.

He hauled me along the landing. I tried to get to my feet but he was too strong, and the more I struggled, the more force he used.

'Please,' I cried out. 'Please stop.'

He threw me into the living room and looked down on me. It was the first time I'd seen his face, his eyes bulging with fury, his features distorted by rage.

'Please, will you just listen to me,' I pleaded.

'You whore,' he spat, his breath reeking of alcohol. 'Do you think you can make a fool out of me?' Spittle was hanging from his mouth.

'No, never. I never would.'

His hand flew down and struck me across the face, catching my browbone. My skin stung and I could feel a lump instantly form.

He paced up and down, clenching and unclenching his fists as I cowered in front of him.

'It's not what you think,' I said. 'Please, you have to believe me.'

'I know exactly what it is. You're fucking my brother.' He threw his head back and gave an exaggerated laugh. 'My fiancée, mother of my child, has been sneaking around, behind my back, to fuck my brother.'

'I haven't,' I implored. 'You're being ridiculous.'

He stopped stock-still and stared straight at me with wild eyes. 'Is she even my daughter?' he bellowed. 'Is Poppy even mine?'

I knelt at his feet. 'Of course she is. You know she is. I've never been unfaithful to you. Please, you must know that.'

He crouched down beside me and clamped hold of my face. 'So why is he so caught up with you then?'

'I don't know what you're talking about,' I managed.

'He's just dragged me away from the girl I was with, and punched me in the face, because, apparently, I was disrespecting you.'

The tiny part of my heart that wasn't already broken smashed into a million pieces. 'You were with another girl?' I asked, determined to keep my voice calm. 'At our daughter's christening?'

'Yeah, and we were having a good time, a really good time.'

'You bastard,' I spat.

He looked at me and laughed. 'Oh, you bought all that shit the last time?'

I didn't say a word, just watched him as he kept laughing at me.

'You did, didn't you? Oh, that is fucking brilliant. But here, I'll let you into a little secret . . .' He leant in close, his breath hot on my cheek. 'I've never been faithful to you. How could I? There's nothing you do that turns me on. You leave me cold.' He shuddered for effect. 'Yet you're so pathetically grateful every time I come near you.'

I spat at him, a big globule landing on his cheek.

His hand came from nowhere, hitting the side of my head, sending me sprawling backwards. It felt like my teeth were spilling out of my mouth one by one, like they do in my dreams, and I clamped my mouth shut in an effort to stop them.

He pushed me onto my back and sat astride me, pinning me to the ground. 'But that's okay, because now I know you've been screwing around too.'

He'd reminded himself why he was so mad, and he bore down on me, putting his hands around my throat.

My eyes searched his, trying to find a way back from this madness, looking for a sliver of light to make this all stop. But they were as black as night, his pupils so dilated that they almost filled the colour around them. I tried to get my fingers between his and the skin on my neck, but his grip was too tight. He wasn't squeezing yet, he was just enjoying the fear it provoked.

'I didn't, we've never . . .' His grip around my throat

was getting tighter with every word I uttered. I felt like I was going to another place, somewhere other than here, but in the distance, I could hear a cry, faint at first, then growing louder. I snapped my eyes open at the realization that it was Poppy, and Adam, stopped by the same sound, started to lift himself off me.

'No!' I screamed, making a grab for him, pulling on his hair, his shirt collar, anything I could get traction on. He hit my hand away, but as he went to stand up, I launched myself at him with all my strength. I couldn't let him near Poppy. I hung onto his back, clawing and scratching at any part of him. I reached around to his face, my thumbs blindly searching for his eyes, all the time his bulk was trying to shake me free, but I clung on. I would not let him near my little girl.

He reared up and smashed me into the architrave of the living-room door as he went towards Poppy's room. 'No!' I wailed again. I pulled him back with all my might and he lost his footing, stumbling on the landing, with me underneath him. He got to his feet as I manacled myself around his leg, trying to hold onto him, but I lost my grip. Poppy's cry was getting ever louder or we were getting ever nearer, sending my senses into overdrive. I could hear her tears, could hear my screams, but there was something else, another noise I couldn't decipher.

Blinded by blood and tears, I waited for Poppy's cries to stop as her daddy picked her up. She wasn't to know that the man comforting her was as far away from a father as anyone could possibly be.

'It's over,' said a voice. A woman's voice.

My brain banged against my skull, as I willed myself to make sense of what was going on. I looked up, through the slit of an eye that was fast closing up, and saw a figure standing in the doorway of Poppy's room. I dragged myself up to a sitting position and forced myself to focus. I saw my baby first, nestled in the arms of this unknown entity, her little body being gently rocked back and forth. A fear that was almost tangible shot through me as I took in the face of the person holding her. Pammie.

I couldn't make sense of it. Were they in this together? Is this what they had been plotting all along?

'Give me my baby!' I scrabbled to get up, but Adam, standing between us, pushed me back down.

'It's over,' Pammie repeated, her voice shaking.

'Give her to me,' I cried out again, desperate to feel her in my arms. My mind fast-forwarded to see Pammie running down the stairs and out into the street with my baby. To where, I didn't know. My heart felt like it had stopped beating – a dead weight in my chest.

'Please,' I begged, holding my hands out towards her.

'Mum,' said Adam, his tone suddenly calm. 'Give her to me.'

'I know what you did,' she said. 'I saw you.'

'Mum, don't be stupid,' he said, as if warning her. 'Give Poppy to me.'

The front door banged again. 'Mum, Emily . . . the police are on their way,' called out James, breathlessly, as he came up the stairs to the landing. He took one look at me through the banisters and said, 'Jesus.'

The four of us just froze, as if holding our positions, weighing each other up. Pammie was the first to speak, but when she did, it was the last thing I expected to hear.

'Emily, come and take Poppy,' she said. I looked from her to James, and then up at Adam, who still loomed above me. I crawled on my hands and knees towards Pammie and, once I was sitting up against the wall beside her, she gently handed my baby to me. I held her to me and breathed her in.

'I saw you, Adam,' Pammie said. 'And you saw me. It's over.'

'What the hell is going on?' said James.

'I was at the house that night,' she said to Adam. 'When Rebecca died.'

Pammie's shoulders shook as she gave in to her tears. 'I heard you goad her as she struggled for breath . . . I watched you deny her the inhaler.'

I gasped, as James uttered, 'What?'

'I don't know what you're talking about,' said Adam defiantly. His shoulders back and jaw set.

'Adam, I was there. She begged you to help her, and you could have. You had her life in your hands. All you had to do was give her the inhaler. But you just stood over her, watching her die. How could you do that?'

'You're crazy,' Adam sneered, although I saw there was a panic in his eyes.

'And when you disappeared and took yourself back to the train station to start your walk home again, I was left there, desperately trying to save her life.' Her voice broke as she sobbed. 'I will never forgive myself for not being able to.'

'What are you going on about?' barked Adam. 'I was at work. *You* called *me*, remember? You were the first one there. You were also the last one to see Rebecca alive. Some would think that's one coincidence too many, don't you think?'

'Don't you dare,' spat Pammie. 'I will carry the responsibility for my part in this for the rest of my days, for the way you've turned out, and for the callous things you've done. But I did everything I could to help that poor girl, just like I've done for Emily.'

She turned to look at me, her eyes pleading with me to believe her. 'I'm so sorry it had to get to this before I made you see what he's capable of.'

I could hear her words, but they weren't making any sense.

'What are you saying?' I asked.

'I tried to help you,' she said through her tears. 'I did everything I could to warn you off, but it was never enough. You kept coming back at me for more. Why couldn't you see what I was trying to do?'

'But you hate me,' I said, the words tumbling from my mouth, faster than my brain could control. 'You did the most wicked things.'

'I had to, can't you see?' she sobbed. 'I had to get you away from him and I thought it was the only way. But that's not me. That's not who I am. Ask anyone . . . You may think you know Adam, but you have no idea.'

'This is crazy,' he said, rubbing his hand furiously back and forth through his hair, as he paced up and down the landing like a caged animal.

As I looked at him, every conversation that we'd ever had ran through my head, his words in stereo sound-bites. *You're being disrespectful. You're not going out dressed like that. Why is Seb going? I'm calling the wedding off. What do you think I am, a monk?* The force of his blows still stung, but it was the memory of his vicious words that cut the deepest, the realization of the control he'd had over me causing the most pain.

'I'm sorry for hurting you, I truly am,' Pammie continued, 'but I couldn't think of any other way. I thought I was doing the right thing. I knew it was eventually going to come to this, if you stayed.'

'But why . . . why didn't you just tell me?' I stuttered, turning to Pammie. 'If you knew what he'd done to Rebecca?'

She shook her head and wouldn't meet my eyes.

'Babe, she doesn't know what she's talking about,' said Adam, looking at me imploringly. He was clearly hedging his bets, trying to work out which of the women in front of him had his back. 'She's crazy, insane. You've got to believe me.'

'I thought you loved me . . .' I started.

I flinched as he crouched down in front of me, on tenterhooks as to what he might do next. 'I do, you know I do,' he said. His hands were shaking and he had a twitch in his jaw, a tell-tale sign of the adrenaline that was rushing through him.

'But now it all makes so much sense,' I went on quietly. 'You never loved me, you just wanted to control me.' I pulled Poppy closer to me as she let out a sleepy cry.

I went to stand up, in the vain hope that it would make me feel stronger, but was reminded of the pain in my hip. My legs buckled. James rushed forward to support me and I fell into his arms.

Adam lunged at the pair of us. 'Get your filthy hands off her,' he yelled. 'She belongs to me.'

James moved to shield me, and pressed me back against the wall, out of harm's way, as he grappled with Adam in the tight space.

'You've always wanted what I had,' sneered Adam to his brother. 'Even when we were little. But you'll always be second best – you'll always be the poor relation.'

As I slid back down the wall, with an ever-protective

arm around Poppy, my mind flashed to a bizarre image of two young boys racing crabs along a beach. I could hear the crack of its shell and James's tears. I wondered how far back Adam's murderous tendencies ran.

'Enough,' screamed Pammie, putting her slight frame between the pair of them. 'I can't deal with this anymore. I can't go on pretending everything is okay. Nothing has been okay since your father died. You've held me to ransom ever since, with your threatening comments and cruel notes. All designed to let me know that you know. I gave you every last penny that I had, whatever I could afford, but it still wasn't enough to make you stop. I'm sorry for what I did, and I'm sorry that it made you the way you are, but enough now.'

James took hold of his mother's hand. 'Ssh, Mum, it's okay.'

She collapsed into his arms. 'I can't go on, son. I'm too weak.'

Adam's face crumpled at the sight of two policemen rushing up the stairs towards us. 'It doesn't have to be like this,' he said, looking at me pleadingly. 'We've got Poppy to think about. She needs the both of us. We can be a family, a proper family.'

'Adam Banks?' enquired the police officer.

He looked at me again and reached for my hand. 'Please,' he begged, with tears in his eyes. 'Don't do this.'

The policeman held Adam's arms behind his back and handcuffed him. 'Adam Banks, you do not have to say anything. But it may harm your defence if you do not mention when questioned something which you later rely on in court. Anything you do say may be given in evidence.'

'You've just made the biggest mistake of your life,' Adam spat at me as he was led away down the stairs.

As the door closed behind them, the three of us remained where we were, unmoving and paralysed with shock. James was the first to speak.

'If you knew all this, why didn't you go to the police back then, when it happened?' he said to Pammie. 'Why did you put Emily at risk?'

'And the inhaler was in your house,' I said, in a trance-like state, still trying to piece together events and remembering out loud. 'I saw it. You hid Rebecca's inhaler in your house.'

'I couldn't tell the police,' she cried. 'And I had to take the inhaler, otherwise why wouldn't she have used it? He left it right there beside her. Like all the other attacks she'd had, a few puffs would have got her round the right way. People would have known that, her parents would have known that, and would have started asking questions. I had to keep Adam out of the picture.'

'But why?' asked James, seemingly as confused as I was.

'Because he saw me,' she said quietly.

We both looked at each other as Pammie bowed her head, her whole body shaking. James went to her, and put an arm around her, but she shrugged it off. 'Don't,' she said. 'It will only make things worse.'

'How much worse can it get?' asked James.

'I'm so sorry,' she cried. 'I never meant for it to happen.'

'Tell me. What is it?' he asked, terror in his voice.

'Your father,' she sobbed. 'He wasn't the man you thought he was . . . he abused me.'

'Mum . . . I know,' said James quietly.

She looked up in shock. 'But how . . . ?'

'We both knew. Adam and I used to sit at the top of the stairs, trying to think of ways to make it stop, but we were too scared.'

She reached out for his hand. 'One night, he came towards me and . . .' The words caught in her throat. 'It was an accident. You have to believe me. He was drunk, and he was coming for me. I was so scared. I backed away, but he had me cornered. He raised his arm, and I pushed him. So lightly, but it was enough to knock him off balance. He lost his footing and fell backwards, hitting his head on the hearth as he went down.'

James bit down on his lip and tears sprang to his eyes.

'He was so quiet as he lay there,' Pammie went on, 'and I didn't know what to do. I knew he'd kill me when he came round, so I had to get away. I had to get us all away. I ran out of the kitchen, but there he was.'

Her eyes glazed over.

'Who?' I asked.

'Adam,' she cried. 'Sitting at the top of the stairs, watching through the banisters. He was there one minute, and then he was gone. In a blind panic, I ran up the stairs, but he was back in his bed, pretending to be asleep. I reached out to touch him, but he shook me off and turned to face the wall.'

'It was an accident, Mum,' said James, pulling her in to him. 'It wasn't your fault.'

She allowed herself a small smile. 'You've always been such a good boy,' she said to him. 'Even that night, when I came in to check on you, you woke and said, "*I love you, Mum*." I'll never know what I've done to deserve you.'

'It wasn't your fault,' he said again softly.

'It is!' She was sobbing now. 'I've turned him into the monster he is. He's never said a word, but he knows what I did. It's why he did what he did to Rebecca. It's why I feared he was going to do the same to Emily. I had to get her away from him.'

I sat there, numb and open-mouthed as the realization of what she was saying sank in.

'I need to tell the police,' she said, shaking herself down. 'I have to tell them what I've done before Adam does. He was so young, he won't remember events clearly. He'll just say that I killed his father. I need to be there to give myself a fighting chance.'

James took hold of her shoulders and forced her to look at him. 'Adam won't say anything.'

She tried to pull away from him. 'I have to go,' she said impatiently. There was a sudden urgency about her, a need to get her story across.

'Adam won't say anything,' James repeated.

'He will, I know he will,' she said, panicking.

'He won't, because it was me,' he said.

A sob caught in her throat as she looked at him, confused.

'It was me, not Adam, sitting at the top of the stairs.'

'But . . . but it couldn't have been,' she stuttered.

'I saw what happened, and it wasn't your fault.'

'No . . . it was Adam. It had to be, because you told me you loved me.'

'I still do,' said James, and Pammie fell into his open arms.

EPILOGUE

The daffodils are in bloom and Poppy is crawling in amongst them, much to the chagrin of her mother. She catches my eye as she scoops her up, and we laugh at her muddied knees. Poppy giggles as Emily hoists her into the air and blows a raspberry on her tummy. She looks like her mother when she smiles, she has the same kind eyes and button nose.

'You've got all this to come,' I say, as I pat Kate's hand, who instinctively rubs her rounded tummy and smiles.

'I, for one, cannot wait,' says James, as Emily puts Poppy back down on the grass and she immediately heads to the beckoning land of yellow again. We laugh as James crawls after her, making a roaring noise, and she doubles her speed.

'He'll make a wonderful dad,' I say after him.

I think of all those letters from a dad that Poppy will never know. I don't know what they say because I've never opened them, but he must know what he's missing. She'll be a teenager before he's out, and by then, Emily will have moved on, will be living the life that she deserves.

I hope she meets someone who will love her and Poppy the way I do.

Who will care for her in the same way she cares for me.

Not a day has passed without her coming to see me, not even when the court case was on and I was too weak to go.

'You okay?' she asks as she puts her hand gently on my shoulder.

I smile and reach up to hold it.

Yes. I am okay.

I'm free of the fear I've lived with for so long.

I just wish I had longer to live.

ACKNOWLEDGEMENTS

A huge thank you to my agent Tanera Simons, who had to endure me hyperventilating when she told me I had a publishing deal. She has also had to convince me (several times since) that it wasn't a wind-up. Thank you Tanera and everyone at Darley Anderson – I feel very lucky to have found you.

My incredible editors, Vicki Mellor at Pan Macmillan and Catherine Richards at Minotaur Books, who both 'got' *The Other Woman* from the word go. It has been a pleasure to work alongside you to make the book the best that it can be.

To the fabulous Sam, who was my soundboard and kept pushing for more pages, before I'd even written them. And to my very special friends who will all, no doubt, find something of themselves in *The Other Woman* – be it a shared memory, a familiar character trait or a hidden meaning. Thank you for the inspiration, support and encouragement.

To my much-missed mother-in-law who couldn't have been further from Pammie if she tried. And to my own mum – well, you'll have to ask my husband!

To my wonderful husband and children, who had no

Acknowledgements

idea that I was even writing a book – thank you for just letting me get on with whatever you thought I was getting on with! This is what I was doing!

And finally to everyone who has read *The Other Woman* – thank you from the bottom of my heart. I hope you enjoyed it.

extracts reading groups
competitions books new
discounts extracts extracts
competitions events
books new extracts
events books discounts
extracts new reading groups
new reading groups
interviews events
discounts events books
new books events interviews
events new events
discounts extracts discounts
www.panmacmillan.com
extracts events reading groups
competitions books extracts new